PRAISE FOR A GOOD KILLING

A "Best of the Best Summer Books" pick
by O, *the Oprah Magazine*

"Dark secrets, a small town, and one supercharged trial . . . [Leotta]
scores big."

—*Kirkus Reviews*

"Former prosecutor Leotta, who clearly knows her way around a
courtroom, explores the bonds between women in this suspenseful
tale with surprising twists and an ultimately satisfying conclusion."

—*Booklist*

"Leotta is one of the very best crime writers today. If you haven't
read her powerful series yet, start here. Great storytelling."

—Linda Fairstein

"[Leotta is] a writer exceptionally well-informed about crimes
against women. These are smart, tough-minded tales, well worth
a look."

—Patrick Anderson, *The Washington Post*

"A perfect 10 . . . It's too good to miss."

—*Romance Reviews Today*

"Leotta spins a delicious tale of suspense that will have readers
hurrying to find out what happens but at the same time wanting
to savor each page. This highly entertaining thriller shouldn't be
missed."

—*Library Journal* (starred review)

"*Speak of the Devil* is not your garden-variety escapist fiction. It's intelligent, probing and clear-eyed about the evil among us and how easily that evil can permeate a society when people are afraid to confront it. Part morality tale, part riveting drama, *Speak of the Devil* is very, very good."

—*Washington Independent Review of Books*

"Entertaining."

—*Minneapolis Star Tribune*

"Anna is a strong protagonist and Leotta's weaving together of the prosecutor's professional and personal life is seamless. . . . A surprise twist midway through the book will make you turn the pages even faster. . . . It's almost impossible to put this book down before its satisfying, and unexpected, conclusion."

—*Mystery Scene Magazine*

"Her characters are richly detailed and seem like they could be real largely because the situations are drawn from actual cases."

—*Detroit Free Press*

"*Speak of the Devil* is another well-written, tense novel to enthrall readers."

—*Romance Reviews Today*

"Leotta, a former federal sex-crimes prosecutor, has the background to make *Speak of the Devil* seem authentic. She also keeps the story line moving without delving too much into the minutia of how the office runs on a daily basis. And with the focus on the characters rather than on courtroom proceedings, the novel works quite well."

—*Associated Press*

"This is a true thriller, and this author—who was once a prosecutor—shows her immense judicial savvy when it comes to everything from the descriptions of the back rooms of power and the inner workings of the Federal Witness Protection Program, to the gang rituals that speak only of evil. An excellent story, fans will certainly hope that this is not the last installment in the life of Anna Curtis!"

—*Suspense Magazine*

"Leotta is on fire in the literary world."

—*Deadline Detroit*

"Her confident and mature style complements her impressive grasp of plotting and pacing. She is as skilled in ratcheting up tensions as she is in describing delicate moments of contemplation. . . . Leotta leavens the intensity with humor . . . and deftly weaves the story between Curtis's private and work lives, reminding us that personal crises can be as fraught with consequence as the most terrifying professional quandary. Doubt and surprise creep in on both fronts, inspired by Leotta's trademark whipsawing plot twists. Terrifically entertaining."

—JoAnn Baca, *The Federal Lawyer*

PRAISE FOR DISCRETION

Named One of the Top Ten Best Books of the Year
by *Strand Magazine*

Named Best Suspense Novel of the Year
by *Romance Reviews Today*

"Leotta, a former federal prosecutor, writes with authority and authenticity. Imagine one of the best episodes of the TV series *Law and Order: SVU*, but set in Washington, D.C., instead of New York City. Besides the realistic feel of the courtroom machinations, Leotta also takes readers on a journey inside the elite of Washington and the world of escort services."

—Associated Press

"A first-rate thriller. Leotta nails the trifecta of fiction: plot, pace, and character. Ranks right up there with the wonderful Linda Fairstein."

—David Baldacci

"Allison Leotta scores big again with *Discretion*, her top-notch follow-up to *Law of Attraction*. Smart and sexy, *Discretion* showcases Leotta's rock-solid plotting as well as another star turn for her protagonist, Assistant U.S. Attorney Anna Curtis. If you liked *Law of Attraction*—and who didn't?—you'll love this one!"

—John Lescroart

"The best legal thriller I've read this year, beautifully crafted and frighteningly real. Leotta knows her stuff cold and will bring you into a world of big money, corruption, high-end prostitution, and murder. If you're a fan of Grisham or Richard North Patterson, you simply have to buy this novel."

—Douglas Preston

"Fresh, fast, and addictive, and Allison Leotta's experience as a federal sex-crimes prosecutor shines through on every page. The result is a realistic legal thriller that's as fun to read as it is fascinating."

—Lisa Scottoline

"Allison Leotta is quickly making her place at the table of D.C.'s finest crime and legal thriller novelists. She's an assured and authentic voice, and a highly entertaining storyteller. *Discretion* is another winner from this talented writer."

—George Pelecanos

"A terrific read. Slick, sexy, and very smart. Allison Leotta is a master at creating tension and then mercilessly tightening it. This is the kind of book I love to read, crafted by a wonderfully imaginative writer, who really knows what she is talking about. Allison Leotta is headed to the top of the heap."

—Michael Palmer

"*Discretion* is full of treachery and betrayal, but it's the characters who rule these pages. Allison Leotta expertly ratchets up the suspense and brings to life a fictional world that is cutting-edge current."

—Steve Berry

"Fantastic! Smart, gritty, and fast-paced—*Discretion* is everything a great thriller should be. I'm a Leotta fan for life."

—Allison Brennan

PRAISE FOR LAW OF ATTRACTION

Named One of the Best Legal Thrillers of the Year
by *Suspense Magazine*

"With this riveting debut legal thriller, Leotta, a federal sex crimes prosecutor in Washington, D.C., joins the big leagues with pros like Lisa Scottoline and Linda Fairstein. A vulnerable, tenacious heroine, surprising twists and turns, and equal parts romance and danger are a recipe for success. Readers will feverishly hope for a second book."

—*Library Journal* (starred review)

"The balance between romance and suspense can be difficult to sustain in a mystery. In this debut novel, Leotta smoothly blends both into an engaging legal thriller that's far better than anything I've read from Grisham or the like."

—*Minneapolis Star Tribune*

"[A] racy legal thriller . . . tackling a still-taboo subject."

—*The Washington Post*

"A winning legal thriller . . . creating a buzz with critics."

—*Detroit Free Press*

"Sharing an insider look into the intricate dynamics of the criminal justice system blended with the powerful draw of intense and realistic characters, Leotta has created more than your typical thriller. This is an author to keep your eye on. [Leotta is] an up-and-coming literary giant."

—*Suspense Magazine*

"This is a major debut, and Leotta is a female John Grisham."

—*Providence Journal*

"A beautifully written and suspenseful debut, offering not only an inside look at crime and the courts in D.C., but an exploration of the family dynamics that affect so much of who we are and what we do. A fabulous book!"

—Barbara Delinsky, author of *Not My Daughter*

"A stunning debut."

—Robert Dugoni

"Domestic violence is front and center in this brilliantly written debut. . . . This gripping novel is the work of a former federal prosecutor who knows firsthand the problem of domestic violence. Her gritty, harrowing novel has the ring of truth."

—*Tucson Citizen*

"One of the most notable new faces to debut in 2010 is Allison Leotta. By day, she's a federal prosecutor specializing in sex crimes and domestic violence. By night, she turns her experiences into visceral prose."

—*Washington City Paper*

A GOOD KILLING

ALLISON LEOTTA

TOUCHSTONE
New York London Toronto Sydney New Delhi

Touchstone
An Imprint of Simon & Schuster, Inc.
1230 Avenue of the Americas
New York, NY 10020

First Touchstone trade paperback edition June 2016

TOUCHSTONE and colophon are registered trademarks of Simon & Schuster, Inc.

For information about special discounts for bulk purchases, please contact Simon & Schuster Special Sales at 1-866-506-1949 or business@simonandschuster.com.

The Simon & Schuster Speakers Bureau can bring authors to your live event. For more information or to book an event, contact the Simon & Schuster Speakers Bureau at 1-866-248-3049 or visit our website at www.simonspeakers.com.

Manufactured in the United States of America

10 9 8 7 6 5 4 3 2 1

The Library of Congress has cataloged the hardcover edition as follows:

Leotta, Allison.
  A good killing : a novel / Allison Leotta.—First Touchstone hardcover edition.
      pages ; cm.—(Anna Curtis series)
1. Public prosecutors—Washington (D.C.)—Fiction. 2. Traffic accident victims—Michigan—Fiction. 3. Murder—Investigation—Fiction. I. Title.
  PS3612.E59G66 2015
  813'.6—dc23
                                                2014047320

ISBN 978-1-4767-6099-5
ISBN 978-1-4767-6102-2 (pbk)
ISBN 978-1-4767-6103-9 (ebook)

For my sisters, Kerry and Tracey,
my best friends and most biased witnesses

Since the house is on fire, let us warm ourselves.

—ITALIAN PROVERB

1

When I was fifteen, my favorite place in the world was the high-jump setup at the school track. The bar provided a simple obstacle with a certain solution. You either cleared it or you didn't. In a world of tangled problems with knotty answers, that was bliss.

I guess it all started out on that field, the summer before my sophomore year. That's when I fell in love with Owen Fowler. I never could hide how much I wanted that man.

That's why everyone immediately thought I murdered him. Watch any TV crime show, and the person who says "I couldn't have killed him—I loved him!" is the one who did it. Nothing fuels hate like love gone wrong. So when the coach went up in flames, people naturally looked to see if I was holding the match. But I swear: I didn't kill him.

You don't believe me, Annie, I can see it in your eyes. But I'll tell you everything, exactly how it went down. You probably won't agree with what I did. You definitely would've done things differently. But by the end, I hope you'll at least understand.

So—ten years ago. The athletic field was the most beautiful place in Holly Grove. A girl could feel like she was part of something good on that rectangle of perfect grass, surrounded by bleachers shining silver in the sun. Come fall, the football players would own the field, and the stands would hold ten thousand screaming fans. But in July, the stadium was empty, and the kids who went to Coach Fowler's sports camp got to use the spongy red track that circled the field. The air smelled of fresh-cut grass, the clean sweat of a good workout, and the occasional whiff of Icy Hot. To this day, I still love the smell of Icy Hot.

And I loved the feel of the high jump itself. That moment at the peak, as my back sailed over the bar and I looked straight up at the sky—suspended above the earth, touching nothing but air. Like I could detach from the physical world with all its problems. For a second, at least. I was free. It was my little piece of heaven.

You know what I mean, right? You were a pretty good sprinter yourself. What'd you place in the two hundred meter? Eighth in the state? But track didn't mean the same to you. You'd found another way out. By the time I turned fifteen, you'd already accepted that scholarship to U of M. That summer, you were just killing time before college, hanging out at the track a lot. You told Mom you went to watch me, but you were really there to flirt with Rob. Don't fuss, you know it's true. He was a hottie. And not just because he'd been starting quarterback that year—king of the town! He was objectively hot. Guess he peaked early.

You know why he suddenly got interested your senior year, right? After all those years of not knowing your name? No offense, but. You finally grew some boobs. My own chest didn't show signs of catching up any time soon. The high jump was the one place where my resemblance to a wall was still an advantage.

I was aiming to break your school record for high jumping. Six feet, one inch. I thought if I broke it, people would finally start calling me "Jody" instead of "Anna Curtis's little sister." I remember the day I first believed I could do it: July 15, 2004.

I was trying to figure out why my jump had stalled. I was doing everything right, but it just wasn't taking. I tried again: stood at my starting place and sprinted toward the bar. I hit my mark and rounded the turn toward the mat: five strides, pivot, jump! I flew backward, arched my spine, and kicked my feet up. But something was off, I knew it even before my butt knocked down the pole. As my back hit the mat, I heard the bar clatter to the ground and Rob laughing in the distance.

I said, "Fuck."

"Watch your language, young lady."

Coach Fowler stood next to the mat, which was a surprise. He was the head of the whole camp and mostly stayed with the football team, leaving the lesser athletes to the lesser coaches. The thrill of him noticing me was canceled by the fact that it was when I'd messed up.

"Sorry, Coach!"

I jumped off the mat and fetched the pole. We set it on the risers together. He was tan and tall, with an athletic build and that aura of authority. The sun threw golden glints off his blond hair. He must've been forty at that point, but he was way cuter than the teenage boys he coached.

"You're a good jumper," Coach said. "You could be great—but you have to really want it. Do you really want it?"

I looked over where you and Rob were sitting. Rob was tugging on the tie of your hoodie. The coach followed my gaze.

"Your sister's a good runner. Fast, determined, scrappy," he said. "Jody—you're better."

I blinked with surprise. He knew my name. And . . . not many people thought I was better than you at anything. He reached over and pulled my hand away from my cheek. I hadn't even realized I was touching my scar.

"It's barely noticeable," he said. He cleared his throat and pointed to my pink chalk mark on the ground. "The problem is your approach. Your mark is too close. You shot up this spring, so your stride is longer. You need room to stretch out those long legs."

I tried not to blush at the implication that he'd noticed my legs. Coach took a piece of blue chalk out of his pocket and drew a line on the ground, about three feet behind my pink mark. He also moved back my starting mark. "Try that."

I trotted to the new starting place, feeling the blue nylon of my team shorts brushing against my glamorously long legs. I looked at the coach's marks and wasn't sure I could do it. I glanced at him, and he nodded. You and Rob stopped talking to watch me. I took a deep breath, squinted at the high-jump bar, and sprinted toward it. I reached the coach's mark and counted off my curve, demanding my legs cover as much ground as they could with each stride: one, two, three, four, five. Pivot. Go!

I jumped. And I flew.

I knew it was perfect the moment I took off. I felt it in my legs, my hips, my spine. I soared back over the pole with inches to spare. Suspended in the air, I looked at the bright blue sky and the soft white clouds and felt a moment of perfection.

I landed on my shoulder blades and let myself somersault backward. A few runners broke out into applause. You yelled, "Go, Jody!"

I jumped on the mat. "Yes!"

"There it is!" Coach yelled. "Good girl! Do that at a meet, and we'll be putting your name up in the gym."

I bounced to the edge of the mat, and Coach met me with a high five. Then he held out his hand to help me down. I took it, feeling honored, shy, and electrically happy. His grip was steady and strong. Dad had never held my hand like that. Coach's fingers tightened around mine as I stepped down, then opened to release me. But I didn't want to break the connection. I kept holding on to his hand for a few seconds after he let go.

2

Anna felt a gentle nudge on her shoulder but kept her eyes closed. Another nudge followed, more insistently. She smelled fresh-brewed coffee and heard morning birds chattering, but all she wanted was to stay curled in warm oblivion. She closed her eyes tighter, determined to hold on to her sleep. It was like trying to hold on to water; the harder she squeezed, the faster it slipped away. She cracked an eye.

The unfamiliar bedroom was bright and lovely, decorated in expensive neutrals. Her black pantsuit was draped neatly over an ivory chair. She glanced down and saw that she was wearing only her bra and panties from the night before. She became aware of a dull headache, throbbing with each beat of her heart. Blinking, she pulled the blanket to her chest, sat up, and tried to remember how she'd gotten here.

A pair of warm brown hands handed her a steaming mug of coffee. Anna looked up at the hands' owner. Her friend Grace smiled down at her.

"You look like your hair got caught in a blender," Grace said.

"I feel like it was my whole head."

At least she understood where she was: Grace's guest room. The night before came back in a series of images that grew blurrier toward the end: placing her engagement ring on the table at the Tabard Inn; walking through Dupont Circle with tears streaming down her face; meeting Grace, Samantha, and the detectives at Sergio's restaurant to toast the jury's verdict in the MS-13 case. And wine. Endless glasses of wine, which, despite Anna's wholehearted efforts, had succeeded in blotting everything out for only a few short hours.

And left her with a massive hangover. She groaned and rubbed her temples. Grace handed her two Advil, which she gratefully swallowed down with coffee. It was sweet and milky, which coaxed a smile through the blur. Her life was a mess, but at least she had a good friend who knew how she took her coffee.

Anna spotted her cell phone on the nightstand. She had two "unknown" calls from a Michigan area code, and a string of worried texts and calls from her fiancé. Correction: her ex-fiancé. She let the phone thump back down.

"I would've let you sleep longer," Grace said, "but you have a phone call."

"Jack?"

"Who else?"

Anna shook her head, which was a mistake. She wondered how long it would take for the caffeine and ibuprofen to kick in. "We're done."

"He tracked you down here," Grace said. "That's doesn't sound 'done.' That sounds kind of romantic."

"He's the Homicide chief. If he can't locate his ex-fiancé, he should resign."

"I didn't want to hit you with this, but . . . he's distraught. And you know he's not the distraught type."

Anna plucked unhappily at the blanket. She wanted to talk to him—she wanted it like a dieter wants cupcakes. But there was nothing left to say. She knew Jack loved her. He loved another woman, too.

"Please tell him I'm fine, and I'm sorry, and I can't talk to him now."

"Okay, sweetie."

Grace handed her a box of Kleenex and left. Anna banished a rogue tear, as her phone buzzed from the nightstand. It was the "unknown" caller from Michigan again, the same 313 area code as her sister. She blew her nose and picked up.

"Hello."

"Hi, Anna? It's Kathy Mack. From Holly Grove High School?"

That was another world, and Anna needed a moment to get there. She stared at the ceiling until her memory caught up with the conversation: Kathy was an old friend of her sister's. Anna saw her occasionally, when she went home to visit Jody in Michigan. They'd never traded phone calls.

"Kathy—hi! Is everything okay?"

"Actually . . . no. There's a lot going on here. I don't know where to start. I guess I should start with this: Coach Fowler died. He— Some people are saying he was killed."

"Oh—that's terrible."

Anna sat back against the pillows. Since she was a kid, Coach Fowler had been a major figure in her hometown, leading Holly Grove's football team to the state championship several times. He was the most successful member of their community, and one who gave back. His recommendation helped Anna get a college scholarship and out of their small, rusting town.

"It is terrible," Kathy said, "but that's not exactly why I'm calling. See, the police want to question Jody."

"What? Why?" The coach had mentored Jody in high school, but that was ten years ago. As far as Anna knew, they hadn't been in touch since then.

"I have no idea," Kathy said. "And no one can find her. The police went to her house, but she's not answering her door. I've tried her number; she's not picking up."

"Thanks for calling me," Anna said. "I'll try her now."

They hung up and Anna dialed her sister's number. She got an automated message she'd never heard on Jody's phone before: "The person you're trying to reach is no longer available." It didn't let her leave a voice mail.

Anna chest tightened. She was always vaguely worried about her little sister. For the last few months, they hadn't spoken as often as usual. If Jody were in trouble, Anna might not even know.

She welcomed a reason to get out of town for a while. Get away from Jack, D.C. Superior Court, and the inevitable sympathy from everyone she'd have to uninvite from her wedding. She could take a couple days off. Prosecutors often did after a big trial.

She swiped through her phone, tapped the Expedia app, and clicked on a last-minute deal to Detroit. Then she called Kathy back. "Thanks for calling, Kathy. I'm flying to Michigan this afternoon."

3

As soon as the airplane screeched to a halt on the runway of Detroit Metro Airport, Anna powered up her phone and tried to call her sister again. No luck. Her headache was receding, but the worry in her stomach grew.

She got off the plane and hurried past a wine bar, golf shop, and day spa—besides the casinos, the airport housed the most sophisticated commerce in Detroit—and took the escalators down to baggage claim, where she looked for Cooper Bolden. Kathy had arranged for Cooper to pick Anna up. He'd been a friend in high school, a sunny, bookish kid whose family owned a farm on the outskirts of the county. She hadn't spoken to him in ages. Last she heard, he'd become an Army Ranger and gone to Afghanistan. She scanned the area for him now, looking for a tall, skinny boy with knobby knees and flapping elbows.

Standing against a pillar, scrolling through his phone, was a man with a chest like a Ford 350. He wasn't wearing glasses, and his black hair was shorter, but under a couple days' worth of stubble was a familiar lopsided grin.

"Cooper?"

He looked up and she could see his eyes: light blue rimmed with indigo. She rushed forward to hug him. He stumbled, laughed, and hugged her back.

"Anna. Hi! Easy."

"Easy? You're three times as big as you were in high school."

Cooper laughed. "Maybe only twice as big." He pulled up the jeans on his left leg, lifting the hem. Below was a silver prosthetic limb. "Compliments of the Taliban."

"Oh, Coop. I'm sorry."

"It's okay. They didn't get the best part of me."

"Your spleen?"

"No. My enormous"—he held his hands two feet apart—"intellect."

"Of course."

"You look great," Cooper said. "Just like I remember you. Except more . . ."

"Weary?"

"No. Grown-up."

Anna grabbed her suitcase off the conveyor belt. When she packed it two days earlier, she thought she'd spend a few nights at Grace's house, in the process of moving out of Jack's. Now she had the dizzying sensation of being a nomad, with no true home anywhere on earth. For the last year, she'd lived with Jack and his six-year-old daughter in their pretty yellow Victorian. After their engagement, Anna started calling it "our house." At Jack's urging, she'd begun to make it her own: rearranging where the mugs were kept, registering for silverware. But now she'd have to find her own apartment. She had to go to that pretty yellow Victorian and pack everything up, deciding which things to take and which to leave forever. She'd see all Olivia's toys and first-grade artwork and know that she had no claim to them. Because, much as she wanted to be—as often as she'd gone to parent-teacher conferences, braided the girl's hair, pored over parenting books trying to figure out the right answer to every six-year-old question—she wasn't Olivia's mother. Without Jack, she was nothing to Olivia. She was just a woman with a suitcase and a hangover.

Cooper took the bag from her hands. "I got it," he said.

She came back to the present and glanced at his leg. "But—"

"Can't stop me from being chivalrous."

She'd had a hard breakup, but he'd lost a limb for his country. It put things in perspective. Normally, she'd insist on carrying her own luggage, but now she just said, "Thanks."

As they walked toward the parking lot, she saw that Cooper's gait had changed too. It used to be a long, loping bounce, like a frisky colt finding his balance. Now his stride was shorter, more deliberate, and with a little hitch that could be interpreted as a swagger if you didn't know better.

"Have you heard from Jody?" Anna asked. "I still can't get ahold of her."

He shook his head. "All I know is the police want to interview her."

"I wish she'd called me. I'm a lawyer."

"I expect she knows that," Cooper said with a smile. "And she doesn't need a lawyer. She'll be glad to see her sister, though."

"I hope so. Can we go right to her house?"

"Sure."

In the parking garage, she followed him to a handicapped parking space and reached for the door to a gray sedan. He shook his head. "That's not mine." He walked to the other side of the sedan, where a huge black Harley-Davidson sat in a motorcycle spot. She glanced at the bike and then at Cooper's prosthetic leg.

"Don't worry. There's a double amputee riding across America." He strapped her bag to a luggage rack and handed her a helmet. "He was fine when he started, but he lost both legs in a motorcycle accident."

She laughed, weighing the risk to her life versus the risk of hurting his feelings. She'd never ridden a motorcycle before and was mildly terrified. She reached for the helmet. Cooper opened a saddlebag and pulled out a black leather jacket, similar to the one he was wearing, and held it out to her. But it was mid-June, warm and balmy.

"No thanks," she said.

"It's to protect your skin if we have a crash."

"Oh, that's reassuring."

She put on the leather jacket. It smelled of cedar, cherries, and the faint hint of another woman's perfume. Cooper straddled the front seat. She climbed onto the seat behind him and grabbed the metal handles on the sides, leaving a wide berth between their bodies.

Cooper glanced back. "Don't be shy. Scooch up nice and close and hold on to my waist."

She hesitated, suddenly wary. Who picks someone up from the airport on a motorcycle? What if she'd had more luggage? She met his clear blue eyes and found only earnestness there. She slid forward and put her arms around him.

He started the engine and pulled forward. As the motorcycle drove past the parked cars, her heartbeat quickened. She was very aware that she had a large man between her legs, her breasts pressed against his back, and a giant engine humming beneath her. She could feel Cooper's lean muscles beneath his leather jacket. She wasn't cheating on Jack, she reasoned. First: she was just getting a ride. Second: she and Jack were done. Third: she hoped she didn't die.

Anna tried to pay for parking, but Cooper beat her to it. He pulled out of the parking structure and onto the service road. Anna could reach out and touch the car in the next lane—which would take her arm off. As he pulled onto the highway's on-ramp, Cooper yelled, "Ready?"

"Yeah," she lied.

The bike roared up to Michigan's 70 mph speed limit. She held tight to Cooper's waist. The motor filled her ears and the pavement flew under her feet. She wondered how it would feel if her body hit it. The bike angled low into a curve, and Cooper swung between her thighs. Her adrenaline surged. She was scared and thrilled and very aware of being alive.

Halfway between Detroit and Flint, Cooper slowed the bike and took the exit ramp marked "Holly Grove." Anna's grip relaxed, but her chest tightened. She'd been relieved when she left this town, and she never liked coming back. The only thing she really loved here was her sister.

Cooper passed through the historic downtown. It must have been charming once, but it wasn't used for much these days. The courthouse and city hall still looked respectable enough, but the storefronts in between were mostly vacant and dilapidated. With each auto factory that closed, the town took a hit. And the commerce that still remained in Holly Grove was in the suburbs. Cooper continued out there, passing subdivisions anchored with strip malls, big-box stores, and massive parking lots. He turned onto a smaller cross street, leaving the commercial strip behind.

As they came up to the curve before Holly Grove High School, Anna noticed an acrid smell, growing stronger. The football stadium came into sight, and she stared at it in shock.

A burned-out car was smashed into the center of a blackened circle at the bottom of the stadium's cement wall. The ground beneath it was an oily scab of scorched earth. The top of the stadium appeared unscathed, with the word *BULLDOGS* still gleaming in blue and silver. Yellow crime-scene tape surrounded the area. A few police officers lingered around the perimeter.

Cooper pulled the bike to the shoulder, put down the kickstand, and took off his helmet. The roar of the engine was replaced with the chirping of insects. She took off her helmet too, smelling fresh-cut grass, ashes, and gasoline.

"What happened?" she asked.

"This is where Coach Fowler died," Cooper said.

"How?"

"He came around this turn. Guess his car was going pretty fast. Crashed right into the stadium. His car went up in flames. He didn't make it out."

She climbed off the bike and walked to the edge of the yellow tape. A cop on the other side glanced over but didn't shoo her away. She guessed the crime-scene work was done and they were just waiting for a tow. Cooper stood next to her.

The car was a classic Corvette. A few spots of blue paint were still visible, but most of the outside was burned black. The hood was smashed in so far, the car looked like a pug. A circular web cracked the windshield in front of the driver's seat.

Anna looked at the ground between the road and the stadium. There was a dirt shoulder, a section of grass, and then a cement apron abutting the concrete wall. There were no skid marks.

"You know what's weird?" Cooper said.

"Other than Coach Fowler crashing right into his stadium, without making any apparent attempt to stop?"

"Cars don't generally explode on impact. I mean, it happens sometimes, but it's not like the movies. It's rare. And when cars do catch fire from a crash, there's usually a more heavily burned area where the fire started, like around the battery or gas tank, and then some less burned parts. But the coach's car is blackened all around. To me, cars look like this when someone has taken serious steps to make it happen."

"How do you know so much about burning cars?"

"I saw a lot of them in Afghanistan." Cooper ran a hand through his short black hair. "I was in one."

Anna glanced up at his face. He was looking at the stadium, but seeing something else. Before she could respond, a police officer came up to them. "Help you?"

"Actually, yes, sir." Cooper straightened and put a hand on Anna's shoulder. "We're looking for my friend's sister, Jody Curtis. I understand you are, too. Do you know if she's been located?"

"She's at the station now."

"Is she okay?" Anna said.

"Seems so."

"Thank God." She was flooded with relief. "What's she doing at the station?"

"Being interrogated," the officer said. "In connection with Coach Fowler's death."

That made Anna pause. *Questioned* was one thing. *Interrogated* sounded a lot more adversarial.

"Thanks, Officer." She turned to Cooper. "Can we head to the station?"

"Let's go."

4

Mom always told us not to use the word *hate*. "Hate is a very strong word," she said. "Save it for the very worst things." We could say we "disliked" something, or we "didn't care for" it. But let me tell you: I hated Wendy Weiscowicz. Not like cleaning the toilet or global warming, which I merely disliked. I *hated* her.

We'd never been friendly—she was a princess and I was a jock—but Wendy and I really started beefing at the Homecoming game of 2004. That game was always a big deal at Holly Grove High, and it was seriously big that year. The team was undefeated, and everyone hoped we'd take back the state title. In a town where everything was turning to rust, football was our last shining thing. That night, I was also excited to be out hanging with friends. After you left for college, the house felt empty. Mom was working two jobs, and the dinner table was a lonely place. Football games meant a place to go, excitement and crowds, tailgating and after-parties.

It was ten years ago, but I remember that night as perfectly as if it were recorded on video. Funny, things from last week are stored in my brain with less clarity. There's something about being fifteen that makes everything that happens stay clear and bright.

I stood with my friends, our cheers making cloudy puffs in the cold night air. The wave came around and we shouted and raised our hands toward the bright lights. Down below, Coach Fowler stalked the sidelines, shouting commands at his players. The cheerleaders were in frenzied dance mode, flashing their silver-and-blue pom-poms.

Wendy Weiscowicz stood on the sidelines near the cheer squad. She'd been the head cheerleader the year before but graduated last spring and enrolled in Holly Grove Community College. In her spare time, she helped train the current crop of cheerleaders. She called that "community service," but actually it was her way to keep hanging out at the high school. In the real world, she was just another college freshman. Back at the Holly Grove stadium, she was still queen bee.

One of the cheerleaders grabbed Wendy from the sidelines and pulled her out with the cheering squad. Wendy made a momentary show of resisting. Then she smiled and threw off her jacket. Beneath it, she wore a blue top and black leggings—the closest thing to the cheerleading uniform a civilian could get away with. She grabbed a pair of shimmery pom-poms and seamlessly joined the routine. She knew the moves better than some of the actual cheerleaders did. It was pathetic how much she missed high school. But the crowd cheered for her. At least, the adults loved her. Me and my friends rolled our eyes.

A few minutes before halftime, someone in the stands called to Wendy, and she made her way up there. She was chatting and animated, her cheeks flushed pink. She was kind of a celebrity in the stadium. And she was beautiful, with that amazing head of red-blond hair and those big green eyes. A crowd was soon gathered around her. But when the clock reached zero, she excused herself and went to the rail overlooking the tunnel where the players ran to the locker room. That happened to be right in front of where I was standing. She leaned over the rail and called to the coach as he passed.

"Owen! Yoo-hoo!"

He looked up at her and stopped. The players jogged past him.

"Good game!" she called. "You're looking good out there!"

Which was true—the Bulldogs were up by seven—but I couldn't believe she was taking precious seconds out of his halftime to personally give him platitudes the rest of the crowd was yelling.

"Idiot," I muttered.

She glanced at me, and the coach took that opportunity to move on. Wendy was furious.

"What's your problem?" she asked me.

"Can't you see he's got coaching to do? He doesn't need an old cheerleader interrupting his halftime." Ah, for the days when eighteen seemed old.

"He's a big boy. He can make his own decisions. I certainly don't see how that's any of your business," she said. "Frankenstein."

I was used to kids making fun of the scar on my cheek. It was a cheap shot, and usually I could shrug it off, but I was pissed, and, yeah, I'd had a few beers in the parking lot before the game. We exchanged some words, none of which were kind. Some f-bombs were dropped, and insults concerning our relative chastity. There was snatching at clothes and grabbing of hair. I pushed Wendy, hard, and she stumbled down two risers, into the arms of some spectators. She bounced right back and clawed me in the face. We started trying to hurt each other in earnest. Kids chanted, "Catfight! Catfight!"

I know, it was stupid, right? What can I say? The teenage brain isn't fully formed. And my method of resolving conflict has always been more likely to involve physical force than yours. It wasn't my first fight. Or my last.

Some adults eventually pulled us apart. When I got home later that night, I saw that I had four red fingernail scratches going across my forehead. I got a month's detention for that. Wendy got nothing, since she wasn't actually a student anymore.

The whole town saw it. Seriously. Holly Grove had, like, fourteen thousand residents, and the stadium had ten thousand seats. Everyone showed up for games. Wendy and I were the unofficial halftime show that night.

The silver lining was, after that, people stopped calling me "Anna Curtis's little sister" and started calling me "the chick who got in a catfight with Wendy Weiscowicz."

After the coach died, everyone remembered that fight. From what I hear, hundreds of people claim to have held back me or Wendy. There's an ongoing dispute about which one of us won. But everyone agrees on one thing: "Those two girls always did have it out for each other."

5

The police station was a low-slung brick building across the street from the Meijer superstore. Anna hopped off the motorcycle and strode through the front doors before Cooper finished strapping the helmets to his bike. A young officer with a Bulldog amulet and a cleft chin sat at the front desk, tapping at a computer. His name tag read F. Ehrling.

"Hi," she said. "I'm here to see my sister, Jody Curtis."

His eyes flicked up. "Ms. Curtis is being questioned right now."

"I'd like to be there with her for that."

"Sorry, you can't go back there."

"I'm a prosecutor, from D.C."

"Then I'm sure you know everyone is interviewed *alone*."

His eyes went back to the screen. Anna felt the full sting of being an outsider. She was law enforcement; she was used to being one of the guys. Not here. She made a quick decision. Blood might be thick, but in a police station a J.D. carried more water.

"I'm also Ms. Curtis's lawyer," she said.

The kid glanced up but didn't seem impressed. "You just said you're a prosecutor."

"A prosecutor can represent a family member in matters outside of her own jurisdiction." Anna said, with more certainty than she felt. That was the written rule, but she probably needed a supervisor's permission to do this. She hadn't asked for, much less received, that permission. "If you don't take me to my client right now, I'll make sure that anything my sister says from this point forward—the point at which her lawyer was denied to her—will be suppressed. And you can spend the rest of your life explaining to your drinking buddies how you were the rookie who screwed up Coach Fowler's investigation."

Ehrling's hands hovered over the keyboard. "Bullshit?"

Anna took out her phone and flicked to video recording mode. She handed it to Cooper. "Film this?"

He took the phone and pointed it at her. She turned back to the rookie.

"It is 2:17 P.M. on June 4, 2014, and I'm here at the Holly Grove police station requesting to see my client, Jody Curtis, who is apparently being interrogated somewhere inside. She has invoked her right to counsel, through me. Officer Ehrling?"

The officer stood and looked nervously at the cell phone. There was nothing like videotape to spook a cop.

"Turn that off," he said.

"I'll turn it off when you take me to my sister. If you don't, I'll post it to YouTube."

The officer stood, opened his mouth and closed it. "Fine," he said. "But just you. Not the big guy. Follow me."

"Nicely done," Cooper said quietly. He handed back the phone. "Just holler if you need me."

Ehrling led Anna through the bowels of the station, then gestured to a closed door. She grabbed the handle and pushed in.

It was a run-of-the-mill interrogation room, small and windowless, with scuffed white walls and a video camera mounted in one corner. At one end of a faux-wood table sat a police officer with a badge hanging around his neck. Facing him sat Jody, wearing jeans, a pink T-shirt, and a stoic expression. Her blond hair was pulled back into a ponytail, and her eyes were red and puffy.

Both of them looked up. In unison, they said, "Anna!"

Anna did a double take. The officer was Rob Gargaron, her high school boyfriend. Ten years ago, he'd been a lean, mean, borderline-gorgeous quarterback. Now he wore a mustache, a short-sleeve shirt and tie, and thirty extra pounds. The cocky kid who used to sneak beer into parties had been transformed into a staid authority figure. Their relationship in high school had been short and intense, and ended badly. He was not the person Anna wanted interrogating her sister.

Jody appeared surprised but not overjoyed to see Anna there. She didn't stand up. Anna looked from her scowling sister to her smirking ex-boyfriend.

"I didn't know you were in town," Rob said. "I'd love to catch up, but your sister and I are in the middle of something."

"I see that. What's going on?"

"It's nothing," Jody said. "It's under control. I'll meet you outside."

"Are you in some kind of trouble?"

"No," Jody said. "Rob asked to talk to me, so of course I came down here. Did you hear about Owen? It's awful. I want to do everything I can to help."

"I'm all in favor of cooperating with the police," Anna said. "Can you tell me what we're cooperating in?"

Rob said, "We're trying to determine the circumstances of Coach Fowler's death."

"What does that have to do with Jody?"

"She was the last person to see him alive," Rob said.

"So she's a suspect," Ehrling added, from behind Anna.

"Dammit, Fred!" Rob glared at his colleague.

"Do you hear that, Jody?" Anna said. "You're a *suspect*."

"I'm sure once I talk to Rob, he'll realize he has nothing to suspect me of."

"Doesn't always work that way," Anna said. "As your *lawyer*, I advise that you consult with me before you say anything else to Detective Gargaron."

"My lawyer." Jody looked at Anna for a long moment. "I like that. Do I get to boss you around?"

"The opposite. I get to boss you around. Seriously, Jo. Can we talk?"

Jody flashed the officer an apologetic smile and stood. "Sorry, Rob. My sister flew all the way in from Washington, D.C. I guess I should go catch up with her. We can talk more later."

Rob stayed in his seat. "This is your chance, Jody. If you don't talk to me now, I can't help you."

"Help her with what?" Anna asked. He shrugged. "Let me take your card. I'll talk with Jody and then call you. Let's go, sis."

Anna put an arm around her sister's shoulders and ushered her out of the room, through the hallway, and into the lobby.

"Jody!" Cooper stood and gave her a sideways hug. "Good to see ya. It takes a lot to get your sister out here for a visit, huh?"

They walked out of the police station. The natural sunlight and warm summer air were a relief after the air-conditioned fluorescence of the police station.

"Where the hell have you been?" Anna asked, as soon as the door swung shut behind them. "Why haven't you returned my calls?"

She studied her sister, parsing her appearance for any signs of what was going on in her life. Jody looked the same as always, which was to say, a lot like Anna. Jody was two years younger, but people always asked if they were twins. They both had standard midwestern blue eyes, blond hair, and easy smiles. In recent years, their different lifestyles had started to carve their bodies in different ways: Anna was thinner, from the stress of being a prosecutor and the habit of walking everywhere in D.C., while Jody was stronger, more muscular, as a result of years of installing panels on the GM assembly line. The most notable difference in their appearance was still the scar on Jody's cheek. Today, Jody looked exhausted and pale.

"Sorry," Jody said. "My cell phone fell in the toilet. I haven't been getting any calls or messages. But it's great to see you, Annie."

"You too." Anna pulled her into a tight hug, relieved to have her sister out of the police station and in her arms.

"Ouch," Jody stepped backward, out of her embrace.

"What?"

Jody whispered, "I hurt my wrist. Can you drive my truck?"

Anna glanced around the police parking lot to see if anyone had noticed Jody flinch. Thankfully, it seemed to be empty.

Anna drove Jody's GMC Yukon while Cooper followed on the motorcycle. She steered the big SUV past the trailer park where their family lived, years ago, when their father lost his job on the assembly line.

"What's going on, Jo?"

"I should ask you the same thing. What are you doing here? I thought you were in the middle of a trial?"

"It finished up."

"How'd you do?"

"The bad guys went to jail."

"They always do when you're on the case. Congrats. How's Jack? Just a few weeks till your wedding! You must be stressed."

"Not in the way you think," Anna said. "I called it off last night."

"Oh, Annie." Jody looked almost as hurt as Anna. She knew the reasons behind the breakup. Anna's relationship with Jack had changed forever as a result of her prosecution of the MS-13 gang case and the secrets it revealed. Jack had been the victim of a terrible tragedy, the full extent of which even he hadn't known. Olivia's mother had come back into his life. Now, he had to see if he could make things work with her. Anna had to give him the space he needed to do it. Jody reached over and squeezed her arm. "I'm sorry. I'm sure it's for the best."

"Yeah," Anna said unconvincingly. "What is going on with Coach Fowler? Why were the police questioning you?"

"I—well, I don't want to disappoint you."

"The police called you in for questioning about a man's death. Disappointing me is the last thing you have to worry about."

Jody took a deep breath. "I was hanging out with him last night. Before his car crash."

"Define 'hanging out.'"

"I brought him home with me, okay? From Screecher's bar. We were—how would you say it in D.C.? Intimate."

"Isn't he married?"

"I didn't say he was a saint. Neither am I. We were adults involved in an adult relationship." Jody glanced at Anna's face. "See, I knew you'd be mad."

"Not mad," Anna said, although she was disappointed. Why did Jody always have to get involved with the least appropriate guy in any ten-mile radius? "When did he leave your house?"

"Around two, maybe two thirty, this morning."

"Were you guys drinking?"

"Now you sound like Rob. Yeah, we were drinking. I told the police that. Can I get in trouble for letting him drive drunk?"

"Maybe."

"Shit."

"Was this a onetime thing, or something more?"

"We've been . . . er . . . friendly, for a few weeks. We ran into each other at a Lions game and reconnected. We met the next day for an innocent little coffee, and things took off from there. I wonder how many affairs have started at Starbucks."

Anna turned the truck into Jody's subdivision, a neat grid of ramblers, each a slightly different take on white aluminum siding. Anna could just make out Cooper's Harley in the rearview mirror, behind a blue sedan.

"What happened to your wrist?" Anna asked.

"I fell in the shower."

"I've handled enough domestic violence cases to know a cover story when I hear one."

"You've gotten so cynical, Annie. To a hammer, everything looks like a nail, huh? I'm not a domestic violence victim. I'm not Mom. I took a shower after Owen left, while I was probably too tipsy to be taking showers."

"Is that when you just happened to drop your cell phone into the toilet?"

"Actually, yeah."

"I came to help you, Jo. Kathy thought you needed help. But I can't help if you don't tell me what's going on."

"I appreciate that, Annie. But I didn't ask Kathy to call you. I didn't want you to come here today. And I don't need your help."

Anna turned the car into Jody's driveway but had to brake quickly. The drive was already filled with other cars, many of them flashing red and blue lights. Three police cruisers, a white van, and two unmarked sedans were parked in Jody's driveway and at the curb. Men with badges walked in and out of the house like ants from an anthill, carrying boxes instead of crumbs.

The blue sedan pulled up behind her, followed by Cooper's Harley. The car door opened and Rob got out. He waved at Anna, then walked right into Jody's house, calling hello to another officer he passed.

Anna stared at the activity. She recognized the execution of a search warrant when she saw it. She turned to her sister. "Still think you don't need my help?"

Jody met Anna's eyes. For the first time, Anna saw fear there.

6

As prosecutor, Anna was accustomed to search warrants—but being on the government side of them. She liked sifting through the seized items looking for evidence, like combing through pebbles and fragments on a beach, looking for that one perfect shell. This was the first time she'd been on the other side. This wasn't evidence; the police were carrying out boxes of her sister's private possessions.

"Stay in the car," Anna told her sister. "Do not say *anything* to *anyone*."

For once, Jody just nodded. The sight of the officers at her house seemed to have knocked the air out of her. Anna jumped out of the Yukon and strode up to an officer who was toting a box out of Jody's home.

"I assume you have a warrant," Anna said. "I'd like to see the paperwork."

"Detective Gargaron's in charge." The officer nodded at Rob and kept walking. Cursing under her breath, Anna went up to Rob. He stood on the front steps with another officer, going over papers on a clipboard.

"Detective Gargaron," Anna said. "You seem to be everywhere."

"Ms. Curtis." He looked up. "It's not personal. Your sister's case came up on my watch."

"What are the chances?"

"I know half the people who live in Holly Grove. Chances were pretty good."

Cooper walked up and greeted Rob with a vigorous jock handshake.

"'Sup, Gargaron?"

"'Sup, Bolden?"

Cooper put a hand on Anna's shoulder. Only then did she realize she was shaking.

"You guys take your car accidents seriously here in Holly Grove," Cooper said. "In Detroit, the police don't even show up for gunfire."

Rob said, "How's that working out for Detroit?"

"May I see the warrant, please?" Anna said.

Rob was required to give her a copy, and he knew it. He pulled a folded sheaf of papers from his back pocket and handed it to Anna. She skimmed the first page: judge's signature, clerk's stamp, proper address. The technicalities were in order. She looked to the dotted line where the suspected crime would be named. Her heart hitched as she read the words: *MURDER IN THE FIRST DEGREE.* She forced herself to read on to the next page, which listed the items the police could take out of the house:

BEDSHEETS; BLANKETS; REASONABLE SWATHES FROM ANY CARPETING, UPHOLSTERY, WALLS, OR OTHER SURFACES WHICH APPEAR TO CONTAIN OR TEST POSITIVE FOR THE PRESENCE OF HUMAN SECRETIONS; SPONGES, RAGS, MOPS, CLEANING PRODUCTS; WASHING MACHINE; ALL SINKS, TOILETS, SHOWERS, AND PIPES ATTACHED THERETO; ANY OBJECT THAT COULD BE USED TO INFLICT BLUNT FORCE TRAUMA TO THE SKULL.

Anna looked up, stunned. "What are you looking for? There was a car crash at the stadium. A one-car drunk-driving accident. What's that got to do with Jody's toilet?"

Rob shrugged. "It's too soon to tell."

"Can I get the affidavit?"

The affidavit would have all the details explaining why the police thought there was probable cause to search Jody's house, and it would tell Anna a lot about the investigation they'd conducted so far.

"No," Rob replied. "It's sealed."

Anna had reached the end of the information he was obligated to give her, and now she wanted to strangle him. But the most effective attorneys weren't the ones who berated cops, but befriended them.

"Can I talk to you alone for a sec?" she asked, glancing at Cooper and the other officer.

Rob seemed pleased. They walked to the end of the driveway, away from the crowd. Anna met his eyes and kept the anger out of her voice. "You obviously know your stuff, Rob, and you're doing a thorough job. You don't have to tell me anything else, and I don't want to put you on the spot. But I would really appreciate if you could clue me in on what the police theory is."

Rob looked at her for a long moment, then grinned. "What made you come home anyhow, Anna? You miss me?"

She forced herself to return his smile. But she couldn't banter—not with this man, not while her sister's house was being searched. So she went with the truth. "I missed Jody," she said. "I haven't been here for her much since I left for college. And I certainly haven't been around for her enough the past few months. I can see that she's really in trouble. I'm a prosecutor, Rob. I want to do the right thing here. What's going on?"

Rob ran his thumb across his brushy straw-colored mustache. "I'll tell you something off the record. If you go to the press with it, though, I swear I'll never tell you anything again."

"I won't go to the press with it."

"The coroner says Coach Fowler didn't die in the car crash. He was dead before the car hit the wall. The side of his skull was bashed in, and not from the windshield. From blunt force trauma that occurred before the accident."

Anna blew out a breath. She realized why the police were taking Jody's pipes. They were looking for blood, evidence that Jody had washed up a crime scene. They thought she'd killed Coach Fowler in her home, then cleaned up afterward. That was ridiculous.

"How is my tiny sister going to kill that big man? And drag his body to a car? And get the car to crash into a stadium?"

"Your sister is just as smart as you," Rob said. "If she put her mind to something, she'd get it done."

7

hoped you would come home for the Homecoming dance, but you were off on some important college thing, a debate tournament or something. Mom took a hundred pictures of me wearing a frilly hot-pink dress. My date, Ben Ohebshalom, wore a not-quite-as-hot-pink cummerbund, which kind of clashed with my dress, but which Mom still thought was adorably thoughtful. I used concealer to try to cover up the scratches on my forehead, but it didn't really work. On the bright side, Wendy's fresh fingernail marks drew attention away from the old scar on my cheek. For once, there was something more dramatic for people to try not to stare at.

Ben was a nice guy—cute, smart, and funny, but not too full of himself. He had those dreamy hazel eyes that made all the other girls go gaga for him. He liked me, and I knew it. But I didn't feel the same way. Maybe it was *because* he was so nice and smart. I always did fall for the worst possible guy in any ten-mile radius, right? Or maybe it's just impossible for a fifteen-year-old boy to compete with a fully grown man. I was already smitten with the big crush of my teenage life, and no cummerbund, however thoughtfully chosen, could change that.

The school gym was done up as best as it could be, though it was still obviously a gym. But the fluorescents were off, little white Christmas lights and paper flowers hung from the walls, and we had a DJ, so at least it had the proper sense of occasion.

Wendy was at the dance too, obviously. She came with one of the seniors, "as friends." He got the status of bringing last year's Homecoming queen, and she got to bask in her fading glory one more time.

I was talking to Ben and some other sophomores, when Wendy

came up. She looked me up and down and said, "Where did you get that dress?"

"The Gap," I said, blanking on anything higher end.

"That's a lie," she said, and she was right. I got it at the consignment shop on Main Street for forty-three dollars. "The Gap doesn't sell prom dresses. I know where you got that dress. It was mine. I wore it two years ago."

This was true, I confirmed, too late. The next day, I looked in the yearbook, and there was Wendy at the 2002 Homecoming dance, all resplendent in the frilly horror. Only it was new then.

I could feel everyone looking, silent and embarrassed for me. I wanted to crawl out of that dress and leave it on the floor. But I wouldn't give Wendy the satisfaction of seeing me squirm. I raised my chin and said, "Oh, I'm sorry, Wendy. Did you want to wear it again? I didn't realize adults were allowed to come to kids' dances."

My friends laughed, and I flounced off while I still had the last word. Also, before anyone could see the tears in my eyes. I walked over to the DJ and pretended to look at the list of songs. That's when Coach came up to me. He was chaperoning the dance. He wore a dark suit and light blue tie that matched his eyes. For a minute, I was stunned by how good he looked.

He handed me a tissue and said, "Don't worry about Wendy. She's just jealous. You look better in that dress than she ever did."

"Thanks." I turned so no one could see me dabbing my eyes. I hoped my blue eyeliner wouldn't run.

"I don't know what's worse," he said. "Being a chaperone at these dances, or being a kid at them."

"That's easy. All *you* have to do is stand there, looking all . . . nice . . . in your suit."

"Ah, so it must seem. But in fact it's a tricky job. Look over there." He cocked his head at a bunch of boys—football players— standing in a darkened corner, passing something around.

"Booze?" I asked.

"I expect so."

"Are you going to bust them?"

"That's the million-dollar question."

"You're the chaperone. Seems like a pretty easy call," I said, even though I didn't want those kids to get in trouble.

"Yeah? Say I bust them for alcohol. What then? They get suspended or expelled, in their senior year. Arrested, even. Not good for their careers. And then how do I field a team? We'd never make it to state finals."

I laughed.

"Maybe you can just talk to them?" I said. "Tell them to pour it out?"

"That might be just the answer." He smiled at me, like I'd come up with a wise and insightful solution. Then his face got serious. "But listen, Jody. There's going to be a lot of drinking tonight. Things can get out of hand at these parties. Take care of yourself."

"Okay." I shrugged. I certainly hoped things would get out of hand. What was the fun otherwise? He handed me a piece of paper. It had his phone number written on it.

"Call me if you ever need help. I'll pick you up and take you home, no questions asked. And I won't tell your mom if you don't want me to."

I held that little piece of paper like it was the Hope Diamond. I didn't have many adults I could count on in my life.

"Thank you," I said. I folded it into a neat square and put it in my purse.

"I want to show you something." He steered me to the other side of the gym and pointed up at the board that listed the school records. It was black with faded yellow lettering. But bright white letters spelled out one new entry:

GIRLS' HIGH JUMP: JODY CURTIS, 6'2", 10/12/04

I'd set the school record at a track meet a couple weeks earlier. I got a big golden trophy, which sat in the middle of my bedroom dresser. But this was even better. They'd taken your name down from the gym and put up mine. Sorry, sis. But it was the first time I was better than you in anything. And the coach made sure the record was up on the board in time for the dance.

He said, "I'm really proud of you, Jody."

I'd never heard Dad say that. Tears welled up again, but for a different reason. I turned and hugged him. He stiffened, and I knew that I shouldn't have done that. He was an adult and couldn't be seen hugging a student at a dance. I dropped my arms and just looked up at him. "Thank you."

"Don't thank me. You're the one who did it."

"You taught me how."

We smiled at each other, because it was an accomplishment that we'd achieved together: his coaching and my jumping. It was one of the best moments of my life. That, of course, was the moment Wendy chose to come over and tap me on the shoulder.

"Sorry to bother you," she said, "but Ben is looking for you. He said he *really* needs to talk to you."

"Guess I should go." I said reluctantly. "Bye, Coach."

"Bye, Jody. Have a good night. Be careful out there."

When I got to Ben, he was standing in a group of guys, joking and laughing. Ben's face lit up when I walked over—but he hadn't been looking for me. I turned back and saw that Wendy was now talking to the coach. Her hip was cocked to one side, and she was twirling a long strand of red-blond hair around her finger in the unmistakable gesture of the Flirting American Woman. I'd been had. She glanced at me, smiled, and then turned back to Coach. She reached out slowly and straightened his tie. It was a gesture of intimacy, and it stung in exactly the way she'd hoped.

I was comforted by one thing. Coach said I looked better in that pink dress.

8

Anna glanced back at Jody, who was still sitting in the passenger seat of the Yukon. Jody met Anna's eyes with a question in hers. Anna held up a finger: hang on another minute. She turned back to Rob, standing on Jody's driveway with his arms folded on his chest.

He was right that Jody was smart. In many ways, Anna knew, Jody was the smarter sister. Anna had more credentials—but it was only because she had more to prove. Because of their turbulent childhood, and her impotence in the middle of it, Anna needed a job helping the world, trying to find the justice that had eluded her. Jody, on the other hand, had always been the tougher and more proactive sister, and now had nothing to prove to anyone.

Rob was right: Jody could do anything she wanted. But killing someone was not something Jody would want. She was a kind, gentle soul: giving a dollar to anyone on the street who held out a hand, volunteering to walk dogs at the animal shelter. Anna remembered the time Jody splinted a stray cat's leg before taking him to the Humane Society. Anna couldn't imagine her sister beating anyone over the head with a heavy object. Something was going on—Anna thought of Jody's injured wrist and drowned cell phone—but it wasn't her sister killing the most respected man in town.

Anna said, "Can Jody get some stuff out of her house?"

"What do you think, counselor?" Rob said. "Would you advise your D.C. police officers to let the suspect enter her home during the execution of a search warrant?"

"Fine. We'll wait till you're finished."

"It's gonna take a while. And you might want to get a place to stay for the night. After we're finished, Jody's not gonna have a pot to piss in. Literally."

They walked back to the front porch, where Cooper was taking cell-phone pictures of the officers going in and out. Good idea, Anna thought. "Cooper, can Jody and I stay at your house tonight?"

"Sure." Cooper turned to Rob. "Gargaron, go easy on the house."

"Like a virgin," Rob said.

Anna shook her head with disgust and got back into her sister's Yukon.

"What's the story?" Jody asked.

"Essentially, the police are gutting your house." Anna met her sister's eyes. "What are they looking for, Jo?"

"Honestly, I have no idea."

Anna didn't like when people used the word *honestly* like that. It suggested that everything else they'd said had been dishonest, and they were just making an exception now.

"They think the coach was murdered," Anna said. "They think they'll find evidence of that in your house. Any idea why that might be?"

"Oh my God. No. I guess it's just because I told them we were together."

"Did anything else happen last night, Jody? Anything you haven't told me yet?"

"I did eat some Doritos. I brushed and flossed and gargled. Is that what you mean?"

Anna sighed. They watched a police officer come out of Jody's home carrying a box full of her sports trophies.

"So what are the police doing?" Jody asked.

"Taking out your pipes, sinks, and toilets. Cutting out sections of your walls and carpeting. Taking anything that looks like you could club a man to death with it."

"Christ." Jody sat back in her seat. Four officers carried her washing machine through the front door and put it into a white police van. "This is what you do for a living? Destroy innocent people's homes?"

"We don't think they're innocent," Anna said.

"You think I did something to Owen?" Jody's voice was hurt.

"No. The police do. I'm well aware that the police can get things wrong."

"Will they replace my stuff?"

"No. You might get some of it back, months from now."

"This is awful! It's a total invasion. I don't have money to buy new carpeting and drywall and a washing machine. What happened to innocent until proven guilty? How can you do this as a career?"

Now it was Anna's turn to feel hurt. As a prosecutor, she thought of herself as the good guy. She earned a fraction of what her law-firm colleagues did but loved having a job where her goal every day was to do the right thing. That was a luxury most lawyers didn't have.

"When I apply for a search warrant," Anna said, "I'm not thinking about the cost of the drywall. I'm thinking about how to get a predator off the street. I'm trying to catch a bad guy."

"And I'm the bad guy here." Jody shook her head.

They sat in silence. Eventually, Anna called Kathy and told her what was going on. "I found Jody," she said. "She's fine, although the police are searching her house."

"Oh my God," Kathy said. "Can I talk to her?"

Anna handed the phone to Jody, who updated Kathy on her morning and thanked her for calling Anna. As she hung up, two police officers were carrying Jody's toilet out.

Jody said, "We're gonna need to pee at some point."

"Cooper says we can stay at his place."

"Oh, man." Jody slumped back into her seat. "That's nice of him, but, if there's one place worse than Holly Grove, it's Detroit."

9

After the Homecoming dance, Wendy stopped showing up at school functions. *Finally!* I thought. The woman realized she had to get a life of her own. Maybe she was aiming for some grown-up dignity?

Nope.

The rumors started swirling around school one chilly day in November. I was dissecting a frog when my lab partner whispered that Wendy Weiscowicz was getting married. Well, that was fine. That proved that the world was unfolding exactly as it should. Community college had clearly been a holding pattern for Wendy until she got her MRS degree. I said something to that effect and went back to unraveling an amphibious intestine. My main thought was, hopefully she'd be so preoccupied with married life that she'd stop hanging out at school and pretending she was still a student.

When I got to my locker, more details filtered in. Ben told me that Wendy was marrying an older man. *Okay*, I thought. *She's into wrinkles and Viagra, good luck with that.* But then Ben added: she was marrying a *rich* older man. That was more annoying, because that meant *she* was going to be rich, and back then, I still thought that "rich" automatically meant "happy." I didn't think she deserved to be happy.

But, all in all, it didn't affect me. I could take my classes and moon over the coach and dream of getting a college scholarship, and she could look after her geezer and his moneybags, and we'd never have to deal with each other again. Then I heard the next—and totally unbelievable—twist to this rumor.

I was sitting at my usual spot at the lunchroom, at the table in the back corner so my left cheek was next to the wall, hiding my scar. My friends were sitting in their usual spots, when Susan Mindell rushed over holding a lunch tray. Her eyes gleamed with the bright urgency of a girl bearing news.

"Did you guys hear?" she said, sitting down.

"Wendy's getting married," Jenny said with a yawn. I nodded and took a nonchalant bite of my baloney sandwich, to telegraph that this was old news to me, too.

But Susan shook her head. "She's marrying Coach Fowler. This Friday."

The bread became cement in my mouth. "No."

Susan leaned forward excitedly. "My mom is a clerk at the courthouse. They scheduled a civil ceremony."

I swallowed the bite with effort. "There must be some mistake. He's probably just helping the family—he mentors a lot of kids—and his name got put in the reservation."

"He's listed as 'groom' in the paperwork."

I stared at Susan's lunch tray, but barely saw the cafeteria's gray meatloaf and soggy fruit cup. What I saw was Wendy reaching out to straighten Coach's tie at the Homecoming dance.

Was that the sort of girl he liked? Someone dumb and shallow, whose only redeeming quality was her dimples? Was he that superficial? I hated him for choosing her. I hated her even more for being chosen.

The engagement was all that kids could talk about the rest of the day. Everyone kept saying I looked pale and asking me if I felt all right. I didn't.

That afternoon, I was in a line filing out the side door to get on the school bus, when I saw Wendy driving into the school parking lot. She was at the wheel of the coach's 1967 Corvette. Everyone knew that car; it was painted the Bulldogs' signature robin's-egg blue. The fact that she was driving it meant the rumors were true. She bounced out, flipped her strawberry-blond hair over her shoulder, and sashayed toward the school.

She saw me waiting on line for the bus and waved. "Hi, Jody!" The keys to the Corvette jangled triumphantly in her hands. I wanted to stuff them down her throat.

10

Anna steered the Yukon through Detroit's desolate streets, past abandoned skyscrapers with plywood windows, burned-out shells of houses, and a vast patchwork of vacant lots filled with biohazardous trash. The late-afternoon sun painted the empty asphalt gold and gray, the shadows creeping longer every minute. The streets were spookily empty; she didn't see a single person. There weren't even pigeons—she supposed urban pigeons needed people, leaving trash and crumbs, in order to survive.

"When filmmakers need a postapocalyptic scene, they come to Detroit," Jody said. "The city's ugliness is its biggest asset."

Anna nodded. Once home to 1.7 million, Detroit's most recent census put the population at 700,000. But it was larger in square miles than Manhattan, San Francisco, and Boston combined. The vacant land alone could hold the entire city of Paris. With so much land and so few people living in it, many of the lots had gone back to nature. As Anna pulled onto Alfred Street, a wild pheasant flew out of a weedy lot, and she had to swerve to avoid hitting it.

"What the . . . ?" she muttered.

"Welcome to America's last frontier," Jody said.

Cooper pulled his motorcycle onto a street that had only two buildings: a burned-out house on one side, and, a bit farther along, a shabby but still functional mansion on the other. If other houses once existed on the surrounding lots, they were long gone. Anna followed his bike onto the circular driveway of the mansion. She stared at the structure. It was a crumbling redbrick frivolity with an arched stone entranceway, multiple turrets, and a slate roof. She looked at the surrounding yards. Instead of the tall

grass and trash that filled most of the vacant land, the lots around
Cooper's house were planted with neat rows of cherry and apple
trees, dotted with red fruit. It was surreal: a leafy green oasis in
the middle of a shattered cement desert. The orchard ended at an
abandoned warehouse whose windows were as broken and empty
as if it had survived a bombing. Beyond the warehouse, Anna
could make out the shimmering silhouette of the Renaissance Center's skyscrapers—Detroit's failed attempt at revitalization in the
1970s—less than a mile away.

The two sisters got out of the car and met Cooper on the driveway. Anna said, "What is this?"

"My farm," Cooper said, taking off his helmet. "The house was
built by a lumber baron in 1892. Now it's what you'd call a bit of
a fixer-upper."

She'd been out to his family's farm countless times when she
was in high school. That was five hundred acres in a rural corner
of Holly Grove County, where the most threatening creatures were
the deer that might carry Lyme disease. This was a new kind of
farm.

Cooper climbed the front steps—surprisingly agile on his prosthetic leg—and opened the door. He threw his leather jacket and
helmet inside. Underneath he wore a faded black THE NATIONAL
T-shirt and jeans. A giant white dog came out onto the porch, sat in
front of Cooper, and grinned up at him, a happy pink tongue loll-
ing out of its mouth. Cooper scratched under its chin. "Come on,
Sparky," he said. "Let's show the ladies around."

Sparky trotted down the steps, sniffed Jody's hand, and licked
it. He did the same to Anna. She scratched under his chin, like Cooper had, and the dog sat on her feet.

"He looks like a big German shepherd, except all white," she
said.

"That's what he is," Cooper said. "A white shepherd. He likes
you. He only sits on the feet of the people he likes."

"I'm honored."

Cooper led them to the back of the house. The backyard was

a square of grass surrounded by the rows of cherry trees. A few free-range chickens pecked around the dirt, ignoring Sparky, who did the same to them. A dirt patio off the back of the house had a makeshift stone fire pit flanked by a few plastic chairs. A pile of firewood was neatly stacked against the house's brick wall, near a tree stump with an ax in it. A small pond, maybe three feet wide, was dug to one side, lined with a black tarp and more stones. It was filled with monstrously large goldfish.

"I always wondered, as a kid—and it's true," Cooper said, pointing to the fish. "They do grow as big as their bowl."

On a back corner of the orchard stood a big red shed with white trim. It was the perkiest building for miles. Cooper pointed at it.

"That's where I keep my equipment and store the fruit. I also dry some of the fruit and make my own granola. I'm branching into cider, too. That way I'll have stuff to sell at the farmers' markets all year long." They walked toward the barn, Sparky trotting by Cooper's side.

Anna asked, "Why urban farming, Cooper? Why not just take over your family farm? You're so far away from where you grew up."

"So are you," he said with a smile. "My brother's taking care of the family farm. You know what I liked about Afghanistan? Not the fighting. I liked helping people. Digging wells, bringing water to a village, that sort of thing. Once I lost my leg, that was over. But there are a lot of people here that need stuff as badly as they need it in Afghanistan or Iraq."

"What do your mom and dad think? Are they worried about you, out here all by yourself?"

"Sure. But my mom was worried before I moved out here. After I came home from Afghanistan, she was always hovering, doing everything for me, trying to help me around. I had to get out and show I could take care of myself."

"If you can make it here, you can make it anywhere," Jody said.

He smiled. "People like to use this city as a punchline. But Detroit today is home to one of the greatest urban experiments in the world. After everything is lost, there's freedom, a space to try new things. Today we've got musicians and artists, hipsters and farmers, city planners and community activists, all sorts of creative thinkers figuring out how to find beauty and meaning in the ruins."

"That's a very optimistic way to think of a city that's declared bankruptcy and can't reliably pick up the trash," Jody said.

At the edge of the orchard, Cooper stopped talking and stood strangely still. His eyes narrowed as they scanned the orchard, and his hand went to his waist. As he pulled up his shirt, Anna saw that he had a gun holstered there.

A moment later, two kids emerged from the trees. They looked to be about sixteen, both wearing black skullcaps and baggy pants that displayed several inches of underwear. The bigger one had a menacing silver grille covering his front teeth. Anna tensed up.

"Yo, Coop!" said the kid with the grille.

"De'Andre, Lamar, hey!" Cooper took his hand off his gun. "I wasn't expecting you guys so early."

"It's six o'clock. We're right on time."

Cooper glanced at his watch. "So you are. It's been a busy day."

"I see," said the kid, grinning appreciatively at Anna and Jody. "You gonna introduce us to these lovely ladies?"

Cooper did. The kid with the grille was De'Andre; the shyer one was Lamar. Lamar smiled at Anna, then studied her shoes. Cooper explained that they were students at Cass Tech, a nearby high school, and were working on his farm for minimum wage and internship credits. They were here to pick up some produce for a farmers' market the next day. They went into the shed, where crates of fruits and vegetables were stacked. Anna helped the guys load the crates onto an old red Ford pickup truck. The doors sported a circular logo: a cartoon cherry tree in front of a cartoon Renaissance Center. "Bolden Farms" was written in cherries on the tree.

When it was all loaded up, De'Andre got behind the wheel of the pickup and Lamar sat in the passenger seat. De'Andre called out the window, "Ladies, if he don't treat you right, call me!"

Cooper smiled and shook his head as they drove off.

Anna said, "You let teenagers drive your pickup?"

"They're good kids. Plus I can't drive it anyway."

Because of his prosthetic leg? Anna remembered skinny thirteen-year-old Cooper driving his dad's huge John Deere tractor around the fields. Driving at a young age was a farm thing. She had a hard time picturing Detroit as one big farm, despite all the empty land.

He was several steps ahead, opening the back door to his house. Inside, the place was a testament to glorious architecture fallen on hard times. Tall ceilings were spotted with water stains. Beautiful woodwork abutted peeling wallpaper and crumbling plaster. Stained-glass windows remained where bars covered them; anything else of value on the exterior, Anna guessed, had been stolen. A majestic curving staircase dominated the foyer, dangerously missing its iron handrail, which had probably been taken for scrap. The foyer floor was covered in a white tarp, on which stood a stepladder, tools, and paint cans.

"Sorry for the mess," Cooper said. "I'm renovating. Slowly."

"You've been here, like, five years," Jody said.

"You should've seen it five years ago."

Jody was holding her wrist.

"Does it still hurt?" Anna asked. Jody nodded. "Let's go to a doctor and get it looked at."

"No, it's fine. Just needs a little ice."

Cooper led them to a kitchen, which looked like it hadn't been updated since the days of Ozzie and Harriet. He loaded ice into a Ziploc bag and handed it to Jody, who put it on her wrist.

"Let me look at it," Cooper said.

Jody held out her arm, and Cooper examined it gently. "You've got a sprain," he said. "What happened?"

"No," Anna said. "I don't want Jody saying anything that you could be forced to repeat in court, Cooper."

"You're such a lawyer." Jody rolled her eyes. "I slipped in the shower."

"Uh-huh," Cooper and Anna said at the same time.

Cooper got out a first-aid kit and wrapped Jody's wrist in an Ace bandage. His calloused hands moved with gentle expertise. Anna guessed he'd learned some first aid in the army.

"Try to keep it still." He finished wrapping Jody's wrist. "You'll be fine."

He went to the fridge and pulled out three beers, then led the women to the living room. It was a cavernous, wood-trimmed space that dwarfed the mismatched furniture. A marble fireplace, taller than Anna, dominated the far wall. A stack of apple crates against the side wall served as bookshelves, filled with hundreds of novels and agricultural textbooks. Anna went over and looked at the books. She knew Cooper had majored in agriculture at Michigan State, which had one of the best programs in the country. Looking at the textbooks—about biotech, veterinary medicine, ecology, and the environment—Anna appreciated that modern farming was about much more than sticking seeds in dirt.

Cooper handed each sister a bottle of beer. Anna twisted off the top and looked at the label: *Detroit Doppelbock*. She took a sip of the brown ale, which was malty and smooth. "This is good," she said.

"Remind me to take you to the Detroit Brewing Company," Cooper said. "They rehabbed this great old building downtown and have a restaurant and microbrewery there now."

Jody twisted open her beer and drained the whole thing. She set the bottle on the coffee table, which was a giant tree stump that had been sanded and polished so the growth rings shone. Her bandaged hand covered her mouth as she belched. "Excuse me."

"Impressive," Cooper said, handing Jody the third beer. "I'm gonna make dinner. Stay here, relax. You've both had long days."

After he left, Anna and her sister sat looking at each other, sizing each other up. Anna spoke first.

"I think you need to hire a lawyer."

Jody shook her head. "Hire a lawyer and everyone automatically thinks you're guilty."

"The police are searching your house. They already think you committed a crime."

"Well, they're not going to find anything there. The only criminal activity in my house last night was a criminal lack of foreplay—but I wasn't planning on pressing charges."

Her sister grinned, waiting for the laugh. Anna was too upset to give it. Jody's affect was all wrong. "Coach Fowler is dead, Jo. Aren't you upset?"

"Of course I'm upset. Don't get me wrong. You know I've always laughed when I'm nervous. It's terrible. I was just with him, and now he's gone."

Anna looked at her sister, trying to figure out what was going on in Jody's head. Anna decided to stick around until this was sorted out. If Jody wouldn't hire a lawyer, she would need someone who could give her legal advice.

For dinner, Cooper made pasta tossed with fluffy white chunks of mozzarella and fresh tomatoes and arugula from his garden. Afterward, they played euchre, betting their spare change on the card game. Jody soon amassed a pile of coins. She also drank three more beers, which Anna noticed but didn't comment on. Their father had been an alcoholic. Jody had received the scar on her cheek during the final, and most cataclysmic, of his whiskey-fueled rages.

The sky outside became blacker than any sky in D.C. Anna went to the foyer and looked out the front windows. Only one of the ten streetlights on Cooper's block worked.

"You need some lighting out there."

Cooper came and stood next to her. "Yeah. The cool thing is: it's one of the few cities in America where you can see the stars. I got a telescope last summer—"

A shot rang out, and Anna was thrown to the floor. Cooper lay on top of her, his hands covering her head. Her cheek pressed into the white tarp. She could feel the length of Cooper's body covering hers. For a moment, they both were perfectly still. Silence followed, then the sound of Jody and Sparky running over.

"What the hell?" Jody said.

The dog began poking his snout persistently into Cooper's thigh. Cooper glanced at the dog, and then down at Anna, and

seemed to shake himself out of some kind of trance. He sat up looking embarrassed.

Anna pushed herself up to sitting and looked around for whatever was attacking them. "What was that? A gunshot?"

Cooper took a deep breath. "Maybe. Or maybe a car backfir-
ing. Hard to say in Detroit. But you probably didn't need to hit the
deck. I'm sorry."

He stood, held out a hand, and helped Anna to her feet. As she
stood, Anna met his eyes. She was reminded of a few cops she'd
worked with, guys who'd joined the police force after serving in
the military.

"Is it PTSD?" she asked.

Cooper nodded. They went back to the living room, where he
pulled out a bag of dog treats and threw one to Sparky. The dog
caught it in his mouth. "Good boy." Cooper sank onto the couch
and ran a hand through his dark hair. Anna sat next to him, while
Jody went to the fridge. Sparky sat at his feet, and Cooper stroked
the dog's thick white fur.

"What does it do to you?" Anna asked. "Posttraumatic stress
disorder?"

"Mine isn't debilitating, like I've seen in some of my friends.
But I'm constantly on alert, looking for something to jump out of
the corners. I go into code red really quickly. My fight-or-flight instinct is on a hair trigger."

"That's probably the only way to live in Detroit," Jody said. She
handed him a fresh bottle of Doppelbock. He smiled and took a swig.

"What was Sparky doing?" Anna asked. The dog tilted his head
up at the mention of his name. "I've never seen a dog poking someone like that before."

"He's a PTSD dog," Cooper said. "Specially trained to sense
when I'm having an episode. There are times when he can tell even
before I do. He alerts and lets me know. Sometimes, just realizing
that it's happening is enough for me to be able to take steps to stop
it. The group I got him from also says that petting a dog helps al-
leviate stress."

Jody rubbed the dog behind his ears. "Good puppy."

"What happened," Anna asked softly, "to your leg?"

He looked toward the fireplace, and she regretted asking about something he might not want to talk about. But he turned back to her and spoke in the calm way of someone who has told a story many times and doesn't mind.

"We were going to set up a checkpoint outside Kandahar. I was riding in a light armored vehicle. I'd just swapped places with a buddy. I was in the sentry position in back, so the top part of my body was sticking out.

"The dirt road was quiet. I remember thinking how peaceful the countryside looked; if you didn't know there was a war, we could've just been a bunch of guys off-roading. A second later, there was an explosion. We rolled over an IED. I got ejected, though I don't really remember that part.

"When I came to, I was lying in the dust, trying to figure out how I got there. I saw my boot by my head, but I didn't realize what that meant. The LAV was on fire. I tried to get up and go help the guys inside, and that's when I realized my leg was gone. Everyone else inside died. I'm the lucky one, I guess."

"Coop, I'm so sorry." Anna touched his arm.

"It's okay. I'm glad you asked. It's better when people ask. And you should know why I might throw you down to the ground at a moment's notice."

"I thought you were just getting kinky with her," Jody said. "I was like: Go, Cooper!"

"Nah, when I make a move, it's even less graceful than that."

Anna suddenly understood his motorcycle. "Is that why you drive a Harley instead of a car?"

He nodded. "I have nightmares about what it was like to die in there. My friends. Trapped. Burning. I have a hard time being in cars now."

"This is a bad city for that." Michigan had very little public transportation. Not surprisingly, it was a state where you needed a car to get around.

"I do okay on my bike," Cooper said.

"What about winter?"

"When it gets too cold, I just stay in. I have an epic soup collection. It's a good excuse to catch up on my reading."

Anna shook her head. She pictured him alone here for days at a time, during the darkest, coldest stretches of the year. It was a remarkable life he'd chosen for himself. It took serious fortitude to pull it off—and some serious problems to inspire it. She felt equal measures of admiration and sympathy.

It also reminded her of the old saying "Be kind, for everyone you meet is fighting some hard battle." Anyone who'd seen Cooper in the airport this afternoon would think he was a shockingly handsome man in the prime of his life. But he bore deep scars, inside and out, and was trying to heal them by helping a city that was even more badly wounded than he was. She leaned over and gave him a hug. He let her, and she was glad.

That night, Cooper insisted on sleeping on the couch. The sisters shared his king-size bed, which was the only real piece of furniture in his massive bedroom. His house had five bedrooms, each with a fireplace and almost no furniture.

Lying next to her sister, Anna felt like a kid again. After their parents split up, they had moved with their mother into their great-aunt's house and shared a bed. She and Jody used to sleep like twins in a womb, curled into each other. Their physical closeness had been the most comforting thing in their lives, back then. Anna had an urge to put her arm around her sister now—but couldn't imagine what the reaction would be. Everything had been so prickly since she arrived.

"Anna?" Jody said softly.

"Yeah?" She could barely make out her sister's face in the darkness.

"Thanks for coming."

"Of course, Jo. I'm here for you."

Anna tentatively reached out and pushed a strand of Jody's hair out of her eyes. Jody sighed and closed her eyes. Anna kept stroking her hair until her sister's breathing came slow and steady. She'd learned from Jack's daughter that a little patting could go a long way in soothing someone to sleep. Or maybe Jody was just exhausted.

Once her sister was asleep, Anna rolled onto her back and stared up at the ceiling. She wondered what Jack was doing. Probably sleeping, too, in his pretty yellow house. Maybe packing her things into boxes. She wanted to call him and tell him everything that happened today. She wanted to ask his advice, legal and emotional. Mostly, she wanted to cuddle into him and let his steady heartbeat lull her to sleep.

She wondered how long it would take to get used to sleeping without him. She wondered how much trouble her kid sister was in. Sleep did not come easily. She stared up at the ceiling and listened to the strange silence of a ghost town.

11

Anna woke up before Jody did. The sky was bright, but the city was quiet. She slid out from under the covers, unplugged her cell phone from its charger, and tiptoed down the stairs so her sister could keep sleeping.

Anna knew that the first forty-eight hours of an investigation were crucial: rounding up the evidence, finding witnesses, collecting specimens for DNA testing. If a case wasn't solved in the first two days, its chances of ever being solved plummeted, so this was always a time of intense police work. Rob Gargaron and his squad would be out there, talking to witnesses and looking for evidence. Anna could just sit back and wait, hoping they never put a case together. But sitting back and waiting wasn't in her nature.

She hoped there would never be a case against Jody. But the search warrant at Jody's home suggested otherwise. She had to be prepared. She had to scramble if she was going to keep up with the police.

Anna had never been on the defense side of a case, and she didn't really know where to start. If she were the prosecutor, the first thing she'd do was look up the criminal history of everyone involved. Here, she was at a disadvantage. She couldn't use her DOJ databases to do defense work for her sister, and she didn't have access to any of the local databases. She needed local help.

She sat on the bottom step of Cooper's big staircase and called the Holly Grove Public Defender's service. A harried-sounding receptionist answered. Anna explained her situation and asked if she could consult with a lawyer there or borrow their computers to investigate her sister's case.

"There's no actual case, though, right?" said the receptionist.

"No one's been charged. Yet. But my sister's house was searched by the police yesterday."

"And you say you're a *prosecutor*?"

"Yes, but not for this case. I'm the defense attorney on this case."

"But there is no case yet." The secretary's skepticism was clear. Another phone was ringing in the background. "I'll run this past a lawyer. If you don't hear back from anyone, call again next week."

Anna hung up, knowing she wouldn't get much help from them. No one in Detroit had much to spare. The public defenders' resources were stretched thin just taking care of their own cases.

Her phone buzzed with an incoming call. She looked down. It was Jack. She wanted to talk to him. She would probably start crying if she did. She hesitated, then sent the call to voice mail.

She followed the scent of coffee to the kitchen. Cooper stood at the stove making scrambled eggs, while coffee brewed in a French press. He wore green running shorts and a white undershirt, which hugged his torso in a way the concert T-shirt yesterday hadn't. His shoulders were broad, with muscles forged from labor rather than a gym. With his back to her, Anna allowed her gaze to travel down to his leg. It ended just under the knee and was tucked into a rubber sleeve inserted into a silver-and-black prosthesis. The artificial leg looked high-tech, like it could be the underskeleton of the Terminator. The prosthetic foot was encased in a running shoe. Cooper's other leg was long and muscular, and his other foot was bare. Standing in his kitchen, he looked both very strong and very vulnerable. Anna understood his mother's instinct to protect and coddle him. She understood his need to refuse coddling.

"Morning," she said.

"Hey." He looked over and smiled. "How'd you sleep?"

"Meh. I have a hard time sleeping when I'm worried. But your bed is comfy, so thanks for the few hours of shut-eye that I got. Sorry you had to sleep on the couch."

"Don't apologize—you did me a favor. It's more comfortable than my bed. I might switch to the couch permanently."

She looked at sofa, which sagged in the middle like an old swayback horse. She smiled at him. "That's chivalry. Can I steal some of your coffee while you're at it?"

"'Course. Milk? Sugar?"

"All of the above."

He pulled out the fixings, then pressed down the plunger on the press. She fixed herself a cup. The first sip was so delicious it made her groan.

"This is great coffee," she said.

"Roasted right here in Detroit," Cooper said. "Great Lakes Coffee Roasting Company, on Woodward Avenue. You should check it out sometime; it's a great space. Nice food and wine, too. Small batch, locally sourced. They buy me out of kale every season."

"I didn't know Detroit had such a good local food scene." Anna took another sip. "But what I really need is a local criminal lawyer for Jody. Do you happen to know a good one?"

"Seriously? Didn't you go to Harvard Law School? You're a federal prosecutor. And you love Jody. Who could give her better legal advice?"

"I've never *defended* a case. It's a different animal. I have no idea what I'm doing on the defense side."

"You're one of the smartest people I've ever met. I can't imagine anyone who'd do better than you."

"Thanks for the vote of confidence. But she needs someone who knows the lay of the land here."

"I know the lay of the land. Plus I make a mean scrambled egg."

He set a plate in front of her. Anna took a bite. "Wow. What's the secret?"

"The eggs were laid this morning."

She smiled. "We'd have to have a contract. You'd officially be my 'investigator,' then anything we talk about would be protected by attorney-client confidentiality."

"Pay me a dollar to make it official. The rest you can work off in farm chores."

"Let's try it today, see how it goes." They shook hands with mock formality.

After breakfast, Anna called her boss, Carla Martinez, the chief of the Sex Crimes unit at the U.S. Attorney's Office. She asked to take a weeklong vacation. "Sure," Carla said. "You've been working too hard, with the MS-13 trial and everything else. You deserve a break. Go somewhere beautiful."

Anna looked out Cooper's back window, at the shattered warehouse behind rows of cherry trees. She wasn't sure this qualified.

When she went upstairs to shower, Jody was still sleeping. Anna tried to be quiet, but as she shuffled around, Jody sat up, sleepy and disheveled. "Hey, Annie."

"Hey, Jo. Welcome to the world. How's your wrist feeling?"

Jody looked at her bandaged arm. "Okay. But I don't think I can work today." Her job on the GM assembly line involved physical labor and repetitive motions.

"Call in a sick day?"

"Yeah. Want to help me buy a new phone?" Jody asked. "I need to go back to my house and check out the mess the police made. I have a plumber coming at four."

"Actually, first I want to go out and investigate," Anna said. "Talk to witnesses and stuff. The first few days are important."

"Ugh. Fine. I'll get dressed and come with."

"No. You need to keep a low profile, talk to as few people as possible. The fewer statements you make in the next few days, the better."

"Annie, it's not a good idea for you to be going around Holly Grove all by yourself."

Anna was touched by Jody's worry. If anyone were at risk here, it was Jody.

"Cooper's coming in case I need a gunslinger. Let's do this: You go buy your phone. I'll do my lawyer stuff. We'll meet at your house at four. Maybe you can call Kathy for company?"

"Nah. She's always working double shifts, then going to visit her mom at the nursing home. What can I do to help you?"

"Go online and print out your cell-phone log. All your outgoing and incoming calls over the last six months. Do the same for your credit card bills. Any prosecutor worth her salt will get those eventually. I'd like to see your text messages, but those died when your phone fell in the toilet. Print out any e-mails between you and the coach. Don't delete anything. That'll give me a head start on what the prosecutor might subpoena. And read all the local papers, front to back. Cut out any story about the coach's death. I want to read them tonight."

Jody nodded, seeming glad to have something to do.

"Right now, draw me a map of the houses around yours, with the names of all your neighbors," Anna said. "I'll do some door knocking. You don't by chance have any video cameras mounted outside your house? Anything that would show people coming and going?"

"What do I look like, a Chuck E. Cheese?"

"You were always good at skeeball. How about your neighbors?"

"It's not that kind of neighborhood."

nna knew what Jody meant. As Cooper drove his motorcycle into Jody's subdivision, she held tight to his waist and looked at the neat rows of houses. Homes were ranchers on quarter-acre plots. Tidy landscaping spoke of pride of ownership without frills. This was not one of the gated communities of wealthy Bloomfield Hills, which installed video cameras for the same reason they had swimming pools: so they could advertise an amenity that was rarely used. Nor was it inner-city Detroit, where no shop would be wise to open without a video camera. These were blue-collar workers who mowed their own lawns on Saturdays and knew one another's names. This was the middle of the middle class, at least what was left of it. Over the last few decades, as one auto plant shut down after another, crops of foreclosure signs sprouted on these green lawns.

Cooper parked at the curb across the street from Jody's house. Anna took off her helmet and leather jacket and stowed them on the bike. She glanced at the map Jody had drawn and went up to the house next door. A pretty, tired-looking young mother opened the door.

"Oh, hi! Jody's sister! Anna."

"Hey, Tammy," Anna said. "Nice t'see ya."

She found her midwestern accent coming out. She introduced Cooper to Tammy.

"Come on in," Tammy said, giving him an appreciative once-over.

Inside, a toddler played in the living room. He waved a sticky hand at her. "Hi, Jo Jo!"

Tammy laughed. "Billy thinks you're Jody. You do look alike. He loves her. She's great with him."

Tammy lifted the child and handed him to Anna, who had no idea how to hold him. Billy didn't seem to mind as she shifted him about, figuring out how to perch him on her hip. The toddler patted her cheeks with sticky hands.

Tammy said, "I'm dying to hear what's going on at Jody's house."

"Funny, I was hoping you could help me figure it out."

"Absolutely. Want a cup of coffee?"

"Sure."

"Jo Jo! Jo Jo!" Billy yelled.

They went into the little kitchen. Cooper held out the chair so Anna could sit at the table. She set the little boy on her lap while Tammy poured coffee.

"Thanks." Anna said. "So were you home two nights ago?"

"Yep."

Billy stuck a tiny finger into Anna's ear. She let out a ticklish yelp, which made the boy giggle. Cooper smiled too and took Billy from her arms. He put the little boy on his shoulders and galloped around the house like a horse. The boy held on to Cooper's black hair and squealed with delight.

"Did you notice any activity around Jody's house that night?"

"I did see her leave around eight. She was dressed to kill." Tammy clapped a hand over her mouth. She'd obviously heard the rumors. "I didn't mean that. She just looked—nice. Hair all curled into pretty waves, and high heels. Ready for a night on the town."

Anna blinked. That didn't sound like her sister. "Did you notice when she came home?"

"I'm early to bed and early to rise these days. I'm sure I was in bed long before she got home." A note of longing tinged Tammy's voice. "But I did notice something strange."

"What was it?"

"Look, I feel weird about this. I don't want to get anyone in trouble. I love Jody. But I don't want to lie. I heard Jody yelling in the middle of the night."

Anna's stomach clenched.

"What was she yelling?"

"I couldn't tell. I'm not even sure it was her. Maybe it wasn't! But it sounded like it was coming from her house." She looked down. "It sounded like her."

"Definitely a woman?"

"Yeah."

"Was there a man's voice too?"

"I didn't hear one. But I was groggy. Billy had a cold and he was fussy. The yelling next door only went on for a few minutes, and I heard it in between my own cranky kid."

"What did it sound like? Someone in distress? Calling for help?"

Tammy sighed and looked uncomfortable. "It sounded like a fight."

"What time was it?"

"I'm not sure. Probably somewhere between two and four in the morning. That's when Billy gets up for his feeding."

"Did you happen to see a blue classic Corvette in the neighborhood at any point?"

"Coach Fowler's car? Nope."

Anna asked a few more questions, then thanked Tammy and wrapped up. Outside the house, Anna turned to Cooper. "Shit."

"Yeah. But you know there's a reasonable explanation."

Anna nodded. But any theory that would explain everything was becoming less reasonable.

Cooper pulled a green bandanna from his pocket. "Billy got some sweet potato on you." He wiped Anna's cheek. His touch was gentle and surprisingly comforting.

They knocked on the next door, which opened with another warm greeting and invitation for coffee. This was a different experience than a knock-and-talk in D.C., where more doors were slammed in her face than opened. Here, she wasn't an authority figure—she was just the sister of a neighbor. Folks invited her in, offered her danishes, wanted to chat. The challenge wasn't getting in, but getting out.

By one o'clock, they had covered all of Jody's neighbors. Many gushed about how much they loved Jody. An older couple described how she shoveled their driveway whenever it snowed. A single mom said that Jody bought ten boxes of Girl Scout cookies from her daughter every year, then gave them away to coworkers in her lunchroom. Many people asked how they could help. No one had seen the coach coming or going. No one besides Tammy had seen or heard anything strange two nights earlier.

Their next stop was the bar. Screecher's was Holly Grove's favorite watering hole. On the outside, it was unremarkable, just a big section of a strip mall. Inside, it was a shrine to what the town was most proud of: its football team. The walls were covered with pennants, signed jerseys, and pictures of the teams over the years. Coach Fowler smiled from many of the pictures. He was a handsome man: golden haired, athletic, notably good looking even in middle age.

At two in the afternoon, the place was almost empty. A few men sat drinking at the dark wood bar. In the dining room, a couple ate cheese fries and watched a Tigers game on the big screen. Most of the tables were empty.

Behind the counter, a bartender ran a cloth over the polished surface. Anna immediately pegged him as Jody's type. He was tall and ripped. Tattoos covered his arms. His nose had been broken, a few times. He looked like a great party that ended with a night in prison.

"Hey, Grady," Cooper said.

"Hey, Coop." The bartender's eyes went to Anna with interest.

"I'm Anna Curtis." She reached over the bar. "Jody's sister."

"I coulda guessed that." He wiped his hand on a clean cloth and shook hers. "Grady Figler. Where's your sister today?"

"Just hanging out."

"Tell her I said 'hey.'"

"I will."

Grady went back to wiping out glasses. "What can I get you?"

"A Coke, please." He filled up a glass and handed it to her, popping a maraschino cherry on top. She set a five on the bar. "Thanks. Actually, I was hoping to ask you some questions. About two nights ago."

"Police beat you to it."

Cooper glanced at the men nursing their drinks and said, "Can we have a minute with you in private?"

Grady turned to a waitress in the dining room. "Lakisha! Can you cover the bar?"

"Again?" The waitress rolled her eyes but set down a tray and came into the bar area. Grady led them to a back table.

"How do you know my sister?" Anna asked.

"I've seen her around. She's hard to miss."

"What do you mean?"

"When she comes here, she comes to be noticed. Tight, tight jeans or itty-bitty skirts. That long blond hair all curled up like she spent the day at the hairdresser. Stilettos as tall as a beer bottle. Every man in this bar saw her."

He had to be describing someone else. Jody was a tomboy. When Jody went out with Anna, she usually wore the same clothes she'd had on all day: well-loved Levi's and hiking boots. In the winter, she wore the same puffy red ski jacket she'd had for years. Her hair was long and blond, yes, but always tied back in a ponytail. Jody fell for bad boys but was pretty much one of the boys herself. But Anna remembered that Tammy had described her sister's outfit the same way. Anna pulled a photo out of her purse: she and Jody hiking the Sleeping Bear Dunes last summer. She showed it to Grady.

"This woman?" she asked.

"Yeah. With a lot more eye shadow. And a Jim Beam in her hand."

Her sister drank whiskey? Anna digested his words. Okay, so Jody partied. She was a single, twenty-five-year-old woman. She was allowed to get dressed up and go flirt in bars. Just because Anna had never seen it didn't mean there was anything wrong with it. She wondered if Jody hid that side of herself because she didn't want her big sister to disapprove. The idea made her sad.

"So what happened two nights ago?" Anna asked.

"What happened every time she came in. She flirted with Coach Fowler."

"How do you mean, flirted?"

Grady pushed his chair next to Anna's and let his knee brush hers. He put his arm around the back of her chair and gazed meaningfully into her eyes. His thumb brushed her shoulder as he said in an exaggerated singsong, "You're funny when you ask so many questions."

"Okay." Cooper's eyes narrowed. "We get it."

Grady smiled, removed his hand, and pushed his chair back.

"Look, I don't blame her. The coach was the closest thing we had to a celebrity. He used to come in two, three nights a week. Most every woman who stepped into my bar took a swing at him at least once."

"How did he respond?" Anna asked.

"Everyone struck out—until Jody. That man has gotta be the most faithful husband in Michigan. Or something."

"What do you mean, until Jody?"

"They hung out a couple times over the last few weeks. And Thursday night was completely different."

"How so?"

"He got wasted. Sloppy drunk, like I've never seen him. Most nights, he could drink all night and still walk straighter than me."

"Do you know how many drinks he had? Is there a tab?"

"No. We always comped the coach. As long as he was in here, so was everybody else."

"Do you remember what he was drinking?"

"What he always did. Jim Beam, neat. Four, five, six in a night."

"And you'd let him drive home after all those drinks?"

"Tsk, tsk, tsk." He wagged his finger. "Don't look at me. He made it home all those nights. Only night he didn't was the night your sister drove him."

"So what happened that night?"

"He was stumbling drunk. Could barely keep his head up. I

helped her get him to the car. That was a little after ten o'clock. She drove his Corvette."

"Did they fight or argue about anything?"

"No. They seemed *very* happy with each other."

"Where were they going?"

Grady gave her a grim smile. "When a young lady and a married man leave together, I don't ask 'em where they're going. Let's just say I doubt she was taking him home to his wife."

"Did you see or hear from either of them after that?"

"Next I heard was the news that Coach's car crashed later that night."

"When did the police come talk to you?"

"That afternoon—yesterday."

"Did they ask you anything I haven't asked yet?"

"They asked if I'm willing to testify about this in court."

"Are you?"

"Of course. I'm just a simple, law-abiding bartender." He stood. "Gotta get back to work. Tell your sister to stop by sometime. Next round's on me."

■ ■ ■

At four o'clock, Anna was relieved to see Jody sitting in her Yukon parked in front of her house. Anna had been uncomfortable leaving her sister alone for the day. But what additional trouble could Jody get herself into at this point? As Cooper pulled up behind the truck, Jody got out and met them on the driveway.

"How's it going, Sherlock?" Jody asked, as Anna climbed off Cooper's motorcycle.

"Okay." Anna took off her helmet and shook a hand through her hair. She looked at Jody's face, trying to find the woman who dressed in stilettos and got into screaming fights at three A.M. She just saw her sister. "Got a new phone?"

Jody pulled a black iPhone out of her pocket and made an exaggerated Vanna White–displaying gesture.

"Nice," Anna said.

"What'd you do with the old one?" Cooper asked.

"I just threw it out. The people at the store said it wasn't useful after it got wet."

"Too bad," he said. "I know a guy who could rehab it."

"I know you love rehabbing broken stuff," Jody said. "But some things just need to be thrown away."

Anna wanted to ask Jody about everything she'd heard today—when they were alone. While Cooper was with them, they could check out the house.

Taped to the front door of Jody's house was a white envelope. It held a police inventory of all the things that had been taken from the house. Anna unfolded the paper and skimmed it:

> *Kitchen sink (and attached pipes), toilets (2) (and attached pipes), washing machine (1) (and attached pipes), shower pan (1) (and attached pipes), pots (3), pans (2), hammer (1), shovel (1), sledgehammer (1), sports trophies (23), sheets (2), pillowcases (2), blanket (1), tool box (1) w/assorted tools (18), baseball bat (aluminum) (1), metal fish statue (1), wooden butcher's block (1), wooden carving board (1), blender (1), white sock (1), bottle of 409 (1), bottle of Clorox bleach (1), Greenworks spray (1), box of S.O.S. scrub (1), box of Borax (1).*

"You have a camera?" Anna asked. Cooper nodded and pulled his cell phone out of his pocket. Jody unlocked the door. Anna stepped into the foyer and looked around.

"Christ," she said.

13

Once upon a time, Holly Grove's Main Street must have served the purpose of the proverbial "Main Street" that all American small towns are supposed to have. It had stopped being "main" in any sense of the word, long before we were born. By the time I was in high school, most of the buildings in the old downtown were empty and scabbed, dilapidated storefronts whose best windows were soaped over and whose worst were covered with spray-painted plywood. There was that one consignment shop, and a XXX video store. Most of the commerce was fueled by the courthouse: lawyers' offices, bail bond shops, and stores specializing in nail files, ha ha.

Everyone's parents talked about the Good Old Days. Back when everyone had a nine-to-five job at the auto plant and could afford a house, a lake cottage, and a little boat on that salary. It's hard to imagine now, isn't it? A few surviving vestiges of Main Street seemed like archaeological clues to that time: a peeling Coca-Cola mural on the side of a shuttered soda fountain, a blank theater marquee with flaking gold trim. I bet it was nice, back in the day. By 2004, Main Street had become what it still is: pre-rubble.

We never went to Main Street. We went to Meijer.

Meijer wasn't just *a* store—it was *every* store. You could get groceries and guinea pigs, lawnmowers and live plants, chainsaws, rifles, bulk candy and eye shadow. It stretched forever, one boxy story sprawling so far they advertised it as "Meijer's Thrifty Acres!" Meijer was Holly Grove's Main Street, the place where everyone met and swapped stories about the crazy snowstorm or latest round of jobs that went overseas. You drove there knowing you'd see your neighbors. You put on a little lipgloss before you got out of the car.

One day, about a month after Homecoming, I was hanging out there with Jenny, Kathy, and Kathy's two-year-old girl, Hayley. We were looking for hair paint to streak our hair blue for the Friday night football game. Outside, it was a cold November afternoon, grayed by a low winter sun and seasoned with coarse salt on the ground. Inside, it was bright and warm and full of distractions made in China.

To pass the time, we were trying on hats, not the kind we would actually buy, but the kind that made each other laugh. Kathy put on a huge straw one with plastic fruit all over the brim and became the Queen of England. She waved the cupped-hand royal greeting at passing shoppers. "Ma-ma," said Hayley. "Gapes. Nummy." The baby tried to grab the plastic grapes from the hat, smacking her little lips with anticipation. God, she was a cute kid. Like a miniature Snow White: jet-black hair, green eyes, and roses in her cheeks.

Kathy herself didn't look so great. She put all her energy into that little girl, and not much was left for herself. Her dark hair was listless and frayed, and she hadn't lost all the baby weight. She looked thirty, though she was only seventeen. She'd lived a lot in those last two years, and the living wasn't easy.

Kathy and that worthless husband of hers rented in the trailer park, always a few weeks behind in their payments. Her husband cemented driveways, but not often enough. She'd gone through a few menial jobs by then and tried to study for her GED when Hayley was sleeping. She was exhausted to a degree I'd never seen in any other teenager. But she doted on that little girl. Said it was all worth it because she got her.

She patted her daughter's head and said we'd go to the grocery section to buy her some real grapes. Kathy kept the hat on and continued to be the Queen as we pushed the cart down the toilet paper aisle, using a snooty voice to describe the absorbency necessary for royal arses. We were laughing until we turned a corner.

Wendy Weiscowicz was there with her mother, beaming a scanning gun at an infant car seat. When they saw us, Wendy's mother had the good sense to look embarrassed, but Wendy smiled broadly. She was barely showing then—she must've been about three or four months along—but she already wore a maternity shirt. When she saw me, she smoothed down the front, so I could see the little round bump on her previously concave stomach.

Only Wendy could be proud to be registering for baby items a week after getting married. Seeing her gut hit me in mine. A baby is way more permanent than a marriage.

At least I understood why Coach married her. I imagined she'd tricked him into it, claiming to be on some sort of birth control that she wasn't. I felt sorry for him. Wendy was so manipulative and selfish; his life was going to be pure misery. Of course, I didn't say that.

I said, "Hi, Mrs. Weiscowicz."

Wendy's mom was a nice lady. After Dad left, Mrs. Weiscowicz was one of the women who brought Mom casseroles. Mrs. Weiscowicz's tuna noodle was the best in town—she didn't skimp on the potato chips on top. I felt a pang of guilt. For what it's worth, I had no idea Wendy was pregnant when we got into it at the Homecoming game.

Mrs. Weiscowicz smiled and launched into nice-midwestern-mom small talk, asking after our families and cooing over little Hayley. When there was a pause, Kathy looked pointedly at Wendy's stomach.

"So how are *you*, Wendy?"

"I couldn't be better," Wendy trilled. "Married life suits me."

She held out her hand and waved her diamond ring under our noses. The other girls said *ooh!* and *wow!* and *congratulations!* It struck me that I didn't know a single person who'd been invited to the wedding—and that was the sort of thing you'd hear about in Holly Grove.

"Was it a big wedding?" I asked sweetly. "Did everyone throw rice?"

Wendy's smile dimmed. She probably started planning the color of her bridesmaids' dresses around the time she entered kindergarten. Instead, she got a quickie shotgun wedding at the courthouse. But she had a talent for putting on a good face. She turned her smile back up to its full wattage so quickly, most people might have missed the flicker. "Oh no." Wendy flashed her ring casually in the air. "Owen and I didn't need a big silly deal. We're just so in love, we couldn't wait for our lives together to get started."

I had never heard anyone call Coach Fowler by his first name. I'm not sure I even *knew* his first name before that moment.

"Looks like you got started right quick," I said, nodding at the infant car seat.

She refused to be shamed. "Yes. A big family was always part of our long-term plan. We are blessed. Owen is so excited. He's home right now, painting the baby's room." She looked right at me. "Have you ever been to his house, Jody?"

I had to admit that I hadn't. She looked happy.

"Well, you'll have to come over some time," she said, sweet as apple pie laced with arsenic. "It's just gorgeous. I'm having a hard time getting used to so much space."

Thankfully, Hayley started fussing for grapes again. We said our good-byes and escaped to the produce section.

We held our tongues until we finished shopping and were in the privacy of Kathy's old Dodge Ram in the parking lot. Jenny called shotgun, so I sat in the back, where Hayley was bundled into the car seat. The little girl's face was the only part of her visible under her puffy purple jacket and hood. I popped grapes into her rosebud mouth while the car warmed up.

Kathy looked back at me, grinning mischievously. "Should we go see the house? Wendy said we really *must* swing by."

Kathy didn't get out much those days. But then again, neither did I. There was nothing else to do that night. I giggled and pulled out my cell phone. None of us had GPS back then, but 411 did the trick. We found out the address, looked at a map, and headed there.

It was a corner of the county I hadn't seen before, not too far out of the town proper, but far enough to be away from riffraff like us. We turned onto a long smooth road lined with big new houses. The sky was black by then, but many of the houses had spotlights pointed at their façades, making them shine like palaces. Coach's house was at the end of a cul-de-sac. It was three stories tall and made of light pink brick with black shutters. It looked like what I imaged a French château would look like, if they built châteaus in the 1990s. It took my breath away.

By that point, Mom had moved us out of Great-Aunt Bessie's house and into the apartment. It seemed like such a luxury just having our own place: a bathroom where we didn't have to compete for counter space with Bessie's Preparation H. Our own fridge, which didn't smell like onions. Control over the remote!

But this was a different world. Even for Wendy Weiscowicz, whose parents were doing pretty well, this was a big step up. To me, it seemed impossible.

Wendy had it all—the mansion, the coach, a cherished baby on the way, parents who were still together and had time to shop with her. I felt nauseous. Envy can be worse than the flu.

"Look at that." Kathy pointed at two deer statues on Coach's lawn. "Shall we?"

I smiled, Jenny laughed, and we all opened our doors.

"Ma-ma!" Hayley squeaked from her car seat.

"Shhh, it's okay," Kathy said softly. She reached back and handed the girl a couple grapes. "Be right back, baby doll."

We crept through the chill night air onto the lawn, the sod squishing under our shoes. The deer were surprisingly heavy. It took all three of us using all our strength to push one over. It fell with a quiet thump on the lawn. Then we pushed the other. It tipped and clunked onto its buddy. We muffled our laughs and waited for something to happen. But the neighborhood was still. No one came to a door to yell at us. No more lights went on in Coach's house. We stood there, breathing clouds into the night. We piled back into the car, quiet with the anticlimax.

"Dee go boom!" Hayley said, pointing a chubby finger at the fallen statues. At least that made us laugh.

"You're right, lovey, the deer fell down and went boom," Kathy said, patting the girl's leg. "Don't worry, they're just taking a little nap."

She turned on the ignition and flipped the radio to 95.5, where Sheryl Crow informed us that the first cut is the deepest. As we pulled off, Kathy lit a cigarette, cracked her window, and blew the smoke out into the black world. Our eyes met in the rearview mirror.

"Wanna buy some lottery tickets?"

"Sure."

We stopped by the 7-Eleven and got some scratch-offs and a couple Powerballs. No one won.

14

Anna remembered when Jody bought her house, three years ago—she'd been so proud. Jody worked on the line at GM for years, scrimping and saving for a down payment. The white rancher was the first big thing that was truly Jody's. She took ownership of it in every sense, not just buying it, but using creativity and elbow grease to make it hers. Jody hand-painted the walls of every room a different color. She bought a pretty tile backsplash that she installed—herself—in the kitchen. She pored over furniture sales and decorated every room to be cheerful, modern, and bright. And she spent hours at Home Depot's weekend classes, learning how to do home improvement and minor repairs. Jody's home was the ultimate expression of her independence, creativity, and competence. She kept it beautifully.

After the search warrant, Jody's house was chaos.

Anna, Jody, and Cooper walked from room to room surveying the damage. Large patches had been razored out of the carpet and couch. Bits of fluff poked out from the sofa cushions and drifted up from the carpet as Anna walked through. Chunks of drywall had been cut out from walls. Papers were piled on the floor, and utensils and dishes sat on the kitchen table. Jody's collection of mystery novels was piled against a wall. In the kitchen, there was a hole where the sink used to be. The pipes beneath it were gone, too. In the bathrooms, only porcelain footprints remained where the toilet seats once lived. The entire bottom portion of Jody's shower was gone, as were the pipes under it.

The house was also dirtier than Anna had ever seen it. Unlike dinner guests, the police did not ask Jody whether they should take off their shoes. Soil was tracked all over the beige carpeting. Black fingerprint dust covered the counters, walls, and appliances. Tears welled up in Jody's eyes as she walked around.

Jody and Cooper walked around the house, taking pictures and noting what was gone. Anna checked the missing items against the police list. They matched up. While the place was a mess, the police hadn't done anything illegal. Rob Gargaron and his officers had simply done their jobs.

Anna followed Jody into her spare bedroom, where Jody was relieved to find her computer still sitting on the collapsible card table. It was a bulky desktop computer, which she'd had forever. Jody turned it on; it was still working.

"I need a cigarette," Jody said.

"I thought you were trying to quit," Anna said. "Again."

"Sometimes I just have one if I'm stressed out. I think this qualifies."

Jody walked out to her back porch. Anna sat next to her for company. Jody lit up and inhaled deeply, then turned to blow the smoke away from Anna.

"Jack called me today," Jody said. "He wanted to make sure you were okay."

"Oh." Anna's heart hitched. "Did he say anything else?"

Jody ashed into a plastic cup half filled with soil. Not owning an ashtray was Jody's way of pretending she wasn't really a smoker.

"I'm supposed to tell you he loves you."

Anna nodded. She knew he loved her. It didn't change things. Jody reached over and ruffled her hair. Anna tried to give her a smile.

The plumber arrived at 4:15 and looked around. He whistled when he saw all the missing fixtures. "What'd you have, a police raid here?" he joked.

"Yeah," Jody said.

He told her that she could buy the sink, toilets, and shower pan herself, or he could sell them to her, but going through him would be more expensive. She said she'd buy the stuff herself, and the plumber arranged to come back in two days. When he left, Jody turned to Cooper.

"Can I borrow your pickup truck?" she said. "I guess I need a trip to Home Depot. A big one."

"I don't know. Can you drive as well as De'Andre and Lamar?" Jody laughed. "Yes. Thanks."

"And can we stay at your house a few more nights?" Anna asked.

"Of course."

They were all hungry and tired. There was no usable food left in Jody's fridge. They decided to clean up tomorrow. Anna climbed into the passenger seat of Jody's Yukon. They drove back to Cooper's house.

On the console sat a pile of Internet printouts from the local library and cut-out newspaper clippings. Jody had done what Anna asked this morning, cutting out today's articles about the coach. Anna looked at the first clipping. The headline from the *Detroit Free Press* announced, "Owen Fowler Dead at Age 50." Anna read as Jody drove.

> A legend in Michigan football, Coach Owen Fowler died early Wednesday morning in a single-car accident. Police are investigating the circumstances of the crash.
>
> Fowler was one of the most successful high school football coaches in the state of Michigan. He led the Holly Grove football team to six state titles in twenty-five years. Several of his players went on to earn college scholarships, with dozens eventually playing in the NFL. In 2008, Fowler famously turned down a job offer to coach at the University of Michigan, noting "My place is here in Holly Grove."
>
> Fowler is survived by his wife, Wendy, and their ten-year-old daughter, Isabel. A public memorial service will be held Sunday at 2:00 P.M. at the family's residence in

Sanilac County. In lieu of flowers, the family asks that do-
nations be made to the Owen P. Fowler Athletic Scholarship Fund.

"There's going to be a memorial service," Anna said. "Open to
the public. We should go."

"No," Jody said. "We shouldn't."

"There could be a lot of good information there."

"Anna. I was having an affair with him. Anyone who didn't
know before certainly knows by now. I can't go to his memorial
service and give condolences to his grieving widow."

"But I can."

Jody sighed. "Okay. But don't call me if she punches me in the
face. So who'd you talk to today?"

Anna told her about the day. Jody was particularly interested
when Anna mentioned the bartender at Screecher's.

"What did Grady say?" Jody asked.

"He said you've been hanging out, flirting with the coach."

"Did he seem mad when he said that?"

"He seemed like a smart-ass who wouldn't let anyone know if
he was mad. Why would he be mad anyway?"

"We once had a little flirtation ourselves."

Of course. She'd pegged him as Jody's type.

"Are you seeing him?"

"No."

"Jo, when did you start hanging out at Screecher's? In stilettos
and tiny skirts?"

"There's not that much to do here."

"There's never been much to do here."

Jody shrugged. Anna couldn't tell much from her sister's profile.

"I also talked to your neighbors," Anna said. "Tammy said she
heard you screaming in the middle of the night."

Jody turned, her eyes wide. The pickup truck in front of her
stopped for a red light, and they nearly drove into it. "Jo!" Anna
cried. Jody braked sharply, sending Anna and the newspaper clip-

pings flying forward. The brakes screeched as they skidded to a halt, inches from the truck in front of them.

"Jody, what the hell is going on?"

Jody stared at the road. The light turned green, and she kept driving, keeping her eyes ahead.

"Tammy's wrong," Jody said to the windshield. "I wasn't yelling. Maybe she just heard the TV. I watched *Game of Thrones* after Owen left."

"Really?" Anna said. "I can probably access your HBO GO account and find out. So can the prosecutor."

"Hm. I'm not sure."

"Did you get in a fight with him, Jo? Did he touch you? If he hit you and you did something to fend him off, we'd have a self-defense claim."

"Jesus, Anna. Who do you think I am? What do you think I'm capable of?"

Anna stared at her sister. She wasn't sure.

15

The night that changed everything came a couple weeks before the 2004 football state finals. The regular season was over, and the Bulldogs had won the playoffs and were gearing up for the Division I championship game, which would take place in Ford Field on December eighteenth. It was all anyone could talk about. Holly Grove High banners hung on every house. People tied blue ribbons around their trees and decorated their cars in blue and white washable paint. The cheerleaders toilet-papered all the football players' houses. The town was football obsessed in any year, but it went nuts when a state title was in play.

December was always big party season, too. With the regular football games over, and the weather turning cold, there wasn't much to do on Friday nights except go to keggers when someone's folks were out of town.

You were never a big partier, but I liked to hang out. I wasn't so much into the binge-drinking, but I'd have a couple beers to make everything softer. That night was different.

I think I drank so much that night because of Wendy. I was bummed about seeing her fabulous life with the man I loved. I was also frustrated with my own life. I missed you. Mom was barely ever home, working two jobs. I was lonely. Being drunk-stupid-crazy with everyone else who was drunk-stupid-crazy brought a sense of togetherness. It pushed the loneliness down, at least for a few hours. Also, there were Jell-O shots.

The party was at Devin Hughes's house. You remember, his folks had a place out on Route 9, a few miles past Cooper's farm. They grew something—soybeans, maybe?—in the field before the woods. Devin was a starting lineman that year, a little full of himself, but generally a nice guy. It was cold outside, and everyone was crammed into Devin's house. There were so many bodies that the windows fogged up completely, which was just as well, since we were a bunch of minors drinking.

It was the usual scene. A couple kegs of Natty Light, a few cheap bottles of the hard stuff, and lots of pop for mixers. Everything sloshing in red plastic cups. The jocks held the girls upside down to do keg stands. Yeah, I did a few. A bunch of us played Tippy Cup on the kitchen table. The drinking game, I think, was what got me the most hammered. It also got beer all over my shirt. I stood up to go clean myself and almost fell down. My friends laughed and so did I.

I stumbled to the bathroom to clean myself up. When I came out, Rob—before he was Detective Gargaron—was standing there, looking glazed and forlorn. He pulled me into a corner of the den and started asking about you. *Why doesn't Anna call? Does she talk about me? Is she seeing someone else at college? Doesn't she know how much I love her?*

He slunk down the wall and sort of collapsed into sitting on the floor. I knew you were trying to wind things down with Rob—cute, dumb Rob, who couldn't possibly hold your attention once you saw a world of other options. But at the moment, I felt sorry for him. He was really broken up.

I knelt down on the brown carpet and tried to comfort him. *You're a special guy. If Anna needs space, let her have it—some other girl will snatch you right up.* That sort of thing.

"You're so smart, Jody," he said, which was not something I heard from football players often. Not that I wasn't smart. Just that it wasn't a quality football players scoured the earth for. "And you look a lot like Anna."

He pulled my head to him and kissed me. I was so surprised, I didn't react for a second. He smelled more beery than the keg, but he was a pretty good kisser—you must know that. Then his hand was on my boob—or at least where a boob would've been if I'd had any when I was fifteen—and another was going down my pants, and that was *definitely* not going to happen. I pushed his chest, hard, and his head knocked back against the wall.

"Sorry," he slurred, closing his eyes. He was almost as drunk as me.

"You don't deserve my sister," I said.

"Fuck your sister."

"That's seeming less and less likely for you, Rob."

I went to stand up, but he grabbed my wrist. He had quick reflexes for how drunk he was. I tried to pull away but he was stronger. He opened his bloodshot eyes and met mine.

"You look like her except for the scar, Frankenstein. You should have enjoyed me when you had the chance. No man will touch you sober."

I tried to shake him off, but he held tight to my wrist. I started yelling at him while trying to flail out of his grasp, but he laughed and pulled me closer, and for a second we were a loud, thrashing mess.

Then Cooper was there. He pulled me away from Rob. "Chill out, Gargaron," he said. Rob opened his mouth, then reconsidered whatever he was going to say, nodded, and closed his eyes again. He probably fell asleep right there against the wall.

Cooper ushered me into the kitchen, where the drinking game had changed to Quarter Bounce and had gotten much sloppier. No one was able to bounce their quarter into the red plastic cup. This fact was hilarious to everyone at the table.

"Are you okay?" Cooper asked. My arm was pink where Rob had held it. But it was Rob's words that stung.

"I'm fine. Guy's an asshole."

"Agreed. You want some water, or pop, or something?"

"No, I'm just gonna go outside and get some fresh air." I turned to the back door.

"I'll come with you." Cooper fell into step next to me.

"No." I stopped walking, making him stop too. "Go," I said, shooing him back toward the crowd. "I'm fine. I just want a second alone. Seriously."

He paused. "Okay."

I stepped out into the backyard, muffling the sound of the party as I closed the door behind me. It was freezing outside, but I didn't care. I stood on the hard dirt and gazed out at the bare brown field and the forest behind it. Now that I was alone, I let the tears come. Even if Rob was a jerk, at least he was a jerk who wanted you. I was just a scarred, second-best substitute. I wondered if anyone would ever want me.

A blast went off, and I ducked. It was unmistakably the sound of a shotgun. A second shot followed, then male laughter. I squinted to the side yard and saw a group of three guys standing together. I recognized a loud male hiccup.

"Ben Ohebshalom, is that you?"

"Guilty as charged."

"What the hell are you doing?"

"Target practice."

I wiped my tears on my shirtsleeve and walked over. The guys were standing twenty yards away from a tall stack of hay bales that had a big picture of Osama bin Laden tacked to it. The terrorist was unscathed.

"You're drunk," I said. "Gimme that."

Ben handed me the shotgun. I cracked the barrel, let the empty casings fall to the ground, and held out my hand. Devin fished two more rounds out of a box of ammo, but I just took one.

"I don't need two," I said as I loaded the single shell into the chamber. This was one of Kathy's brother's favorite pastimes, and I'd gotten pretty good while hanging out at her mom's house.

I lifted the shotgun to my shoulder and peered through the sights until it covered bin Laden's nose—but not for long. The barrel swayed back and forth, pointing to the left of his turban, then the right, then to the black field behind the hay wall. I tried to blink my way to sobriety. It did occur to me that I shouldn't be firing a gun in that state. But the confidence of the drunken brain is so much more powerful than its sense of caution. I stepped one foot back to steady myself, cradled my cheek into the handle, and fired.

Only then did I realize I hadn't put in any earplugs. The sound was insane. I couldn't hear out of my right ear for days. The recoil was also surprisingly strong. I stumbled back several steps. When the smoke cleared, I saw that Osama no longer had a face. Ben clapped me on the back and hiccuped. "Nice shot."

I grinned at the guys and felt better. Then I heard the sound of engines gunning from the field behind the hay. In the near distance, two ATVs rumbled by. A wailing female scream came from one of them.

My heart stopped. *Dear God*, I thought. *I shot someone. Kids were riding ATVs in the field behind the target, the shot went through the bales of hay, and I killed one of the riders.* I dropped the gun and put my hands to my mouth.

"Oh my God," I whispered. "Oh my God. Oh my God."

I pictured the corpse bleeding on the field; Mom collapsing when the police told her I'd been arrested; me ordering my last supper in prison the night before my execution. Who had I killed? How could I ever face their parents again?

"Chill," Devin said.

I looked, trembling, at him. He waved for me to follow him to the edge of the hay wall. I could see the field better from there, and I saw that the ATVs were still going, roaring over the dirt, with two perfectly healthy riders on each one.

"It's Susan Mindell," he said. "She's been hooting it up all night. I can't tell if she likes the speed or just the chance to hold on to Michael Blum."

I took a deep breath. The scare had terrified me a couple inches closer to sobriety, which was still not terribly sober, but close enough to see the lunacy of this party game.

"Christ," I said. "I could have killed someone."

The guys laughed and walked back to their starting line. They reloaded the gun and aimed it at the remains of the terrorist. "Hey!" I said. "You gotta stop. There are people out there." Ben probably would've come in, if it was just him, but the other two guys were crazy stubborn.

"I'm not gonna shoot anyone," Devin said. He turned his back on me and fired at the target. An upper corner of the hay wall exploded into a shower of straws.

I tried to flag down Susan, but the ATV riders didn't notice me. I called her cell, hoping she had her phone on her. She didn't answer. I'm not sure if she ever did get my message. The ATVs kept rumbling around in the field as the blasts kept coming from the shotgun.

Coach Fowler had said I could call him if things ever got out of hand at a party and I needed help. I thought this qualified. Even if it didn't, I admit I was excited to have a reason to call him. I scrolled to his number.

Coach answered on the first ring. His voice was steady and calming, even as the shotgun fired in the background. He said he'd come right over. When we hung up, I slid my phone into my pocket and smiled up at the night sky.

16

The morning of the coach's memorial service, Jody was still sleeping when Anna got up. She threw on jeans and a sweatshirt and tiptoed downstairs. The kitchen was empty, but the French press sat on the counter, full of coffee. As Anna poured a steaming cup, she heard loud rhythmic thunking coming from outside. She looked out the back window. Cooper was placing a section of log onto the large tree stump. He lifted an ax above his head and swung it down in a wide arc. The log split neatly in two. He tossed the pieces onto the firewood pile and reached for another log. His muscles moved smoothly under his skin, which glistened with sweat. Anna stood watching him chop wood for longer than she would've liked to admit.

She opened the back door and stepped outside. The dawn scattered ribbons of pink across the gray sky. The yard smelled of grass and sweet fruit. Sparky sniffed around the orchard, intent on something only he could detect.

Cooper turned to her with a smile. "Morning."

"Morning," she said. "Looks like hard work."

He wiped his forehead on his sleeve. "Abraham Lincoln said, 'Chop your own wood and it'll warm you twice.'"

Anna smiled and set her coffee mug on the table. "Can I try?"

He handed her the ax, which was heavier than she expected. She held it over her head and brought it down. She missed the stump entirely, and the blade sunk into the grass next to it.

"Don't cut off your foot," Cooper said. "We need all of those we can get."

"That's so much harder than it looks. I'll stick with collecting eggs."

She handed back the ax, grabbed a metal bucket, and went to the chicken coop, where the chickens curled into their nests at night. She reached under one and took the egg, feeling like a thief. The chicken shared this view and pecked her hand. "Ouch." She looked at the triangular red mark on her knuckle. She moved a lot quicker with the next chicken.

As the sky brightened, De'Andre, Lamar, and a few other teenagers came over. They worked for a couple hours in the morning before going to school. The kids goofed around a lot and teased Cooper about his pretty blond houseguests, but they also got a surprising amount of chores done.

On the empty lot across the street, Cooper ran a community garden, where anyone could plant rows of vegetables or flowers. A posh riding club in Grosse Pointe donated manure for fertilizer. Anna delivered a wheelbarrow of the stinky stuff and met some of the neighbors who were tending their beds: a retired autoworker, a minister running a storefront church, a local teacher—all of whom professed their ardent love for Cooper. She was glad he had some neighbors who cared for him here.

When Anna finished the morning chores and returned to the bedroom, Jody sat up in bed and rubbed her eyes. She wore no makeup, and the morning sun lit up her hair in an angelic glow. She looked like the cheerful little girl Anna had always known, not someone who could kill a man. Certainly, she could not have killed a man. Right?

"Morning, sleeping beauty," Anna said. Jody waved a sleepy hello. Anna took a shower, then put on a navy sundress and tan espadrilles. She started down the stairs, then changed her mind and returned to the bathroom. Jody was standing at the sink, squeezing toothpaste on a toothbrush. "Sorry, I'll just be a sec," Anna said. They shared the mirror as Anna put on mascara and then lipgloss. She put her hair up in a ponytail but decided that looked too harsh.

She tried it halfway up. Jody brushed her teeth and watched Anna with amusement.

"What?" Anna said.

"You don't wear makeup that often," Jody spoke around the toothbrush. "Or fiddle with your hair."

"So?"

"So"—Jody spit the minty foam—"Cooper would make an excellent rebound for you."

"Stop. We've been friends forever."

"Exactly." Jody pointed her toothbrush toward the ceiling like an exclamation point.

"I don't want to use him. He's been through enough."

"I'm pretty sure he wouldn't mind being 'used' that way."

"My wedding would've been in four weeks."

"But it's not. You're a free woman." Jody rinsed her toothbrush. "Wear your hair down. You look really pretty like that."

Anna took out the hair band, and let her hair fall to her shoulders.

"That's what I'm talking about," Jody said. "Rrowr."

Laughing, Anna decided she was done with her primping.

At the top of the steps, she looked down and saw Cooper standing on the white tarp in the foyer. He wore a dark suit and narrow black tie. His dark hair was damp and neatly combed, and his cheeks were shaved. He stood before a mirror, struggling with his tie.

"You want help with that?" she asked, coming down the staircase.

"Sure." He turned with a sheepish smile. "It's generally black-tie-only at the farmers' market, but I use a clip-on."

She undid the tangle and started over. With both of them dressed up and meeting in the foyer, it almost felt like they were going on a date. She was very aware of how close he was. He smelled of soap and pine trees. Under her hands, she could feel Cooper's chest rising and falling with his breath. She had to remind herself that they were only going out for more investigating. She finished knotting the tie and smoothed it down on his shirt.

"You clean up real nice, Bolden." She tilted her face up to smile at him.

"Thanks. You too."

He met her eyes, and she felt a frisson of electricity that hadn't existed in high school. There was a knock at the door. "You expecting anyone?" he asked. She shook her head. Cooper glanced out the window, then opened the door.

The woman standing on the porch looked familiar in a frightening way, like the corpse of someone Anna used to know. It was the face of Kathy Mack, on the body of an emaciated famine victim. The bones of her shoulders and chest strained against her pale white skin. Kathy had constellations of stars scattered across her arms and neck, hinting at more tattoos below her gray tank dress and army boots. Her black hair was tied back in a fraying ponytail.

"Kathy?" Anna said.

"Anna. Thanks for coming to Michigan."

"Thanks for calling. I'm glad I'm here."

Anna stepped forward and gave Kathy a careful hug. The woman's shoulders were painfully thin; she felt fragile. Poor Kathy had lived a whole lifetime during the time Anna had mostly been a student. Kathy had a baby at fifteen and dropped out of school to care for her. Her mother had helped at first but was now in a nursing home. Last Anna had heard, Kathy had split up with her husband, and he'd moved out of state. She was a single mom, raising Hayley entirely by herself. The girl must be twelve or thirteen now.

"How are you?" Anna asked. "How's Hayley?"

"She died," Kathy said. "Two months ago."

"Oh my God." Anna hadn't heard. She'd been so wrapped up in her own drama and tragedy over the last few months, she hadn't asked Jody what was happening to old friends. Anna reeled from the terrible news and the guilt of only hearing it now. "I'm so sorry, Kathy."

"Thank you. It's been hard." Tears rose in her eyes.

Anna stepped forward and put her arms around Kathy again. Kathy held tight to her. The woman adored her little girl; Hayley had been her life. How could she go on without her?

When they pulled back, tears streaked Kathy's face. Anna pulled a Kleenex from her purse and handed it to her. She needed one for herself, too.

"Thank you." Kathy dried her eyes. "Please, let's talk about something else. How's life in D.C.?"

Anna cleared her throat and tried to make small talk. But the whole time she was thinking about Kathy's beautiful, raven-haired daughter. Kathy probably was too.

"Are you still working at the casino?" Anna asked.

"Yeah. The commute is a pain, but the tips are good."

Jody came downstairs. "Kathy!"

The two women gave each other a tight hug. Anna was glad her sister would have company while she and Cooper were out. They all said good-bye and Anna headed out to the driveway with Cooper. She took a deep cleansing breath of the summer air. After Cooper shut the door behind them, she asked, "What happened to Hayley?"

"She committed suicide," Cooper said softly. "Slit her wrists in the bathtub."

"Oh God. Did Kathy find her?"

Cooper nodded. Anna winced at the image. It was almost unbearable, the idea of Kathy—kind, hardworking, cosmically unlucky Kathy—finding her only child in a tub of blood. Anna didn't know how she was still walking around and functioning.

"I think that's why she's lost so much weight," Cooper said, as he fastened his helmet. "I don't think she's eaten a decent meal since."

"Why did Hayley do it?"

"I'm not sure. I hear there was some bullying, online crap, from other kids."

Cooper made Anna put on leather chaps under the dress and a leather jacket over it. He turned away while she pulled on the pants.

Anna held on to Cooper as he drove to the northeastern side of Michigan's thumb. She was no longer scared riding with him. She felt a little woozy from Kathy's news and was glad to have something solid to hang on to. Every time the bike turned, they leaned together.

The service was at the coach's summer cottage on Lake Huron. After Port Huron, Route 25 headed north, skimming along the great lake. Industrial Michigan receded into the rearview mirror as farms and forests gently took over the landscape. To the right, the water went as far as the eye could see. The lakeside was dotted with trees, white-sand beaches, and the occasional cottage or motel, but this wasn't a tourist hub. Vacationers went to the taffy-filled resort towns of Charlevoix, Traverse City, or Mackinac Island instead.

Anna wondered why the coach's family was holding the memorial service in his second home, so far from Holly Grove. If it was to keep the crowds away, that hadn't worked. The coach's driveway and the road leading up to it were packed with cars glimmering under the mid-June sun. Guests had to park far down the road and walk back to the house. Cooper rolled his motorcycle into a slim space between two cars on the shoulder. Anna stood behind the cars to take off her leather outerwear.

They walked to the coach's house, which wasn't visible from the road. It was surrounded by a high iron fence, the gates standing open. The driveway wound through a thick stand of trees. They came around a turn and Anna finally got a glimpse of the coach's "cottage." It was enormous, in the rough-hewn, stone-and-log, rugged-man-of-nature way that can only be produced by a professional architect with a large budget. A swath of land around it was covered in perfect sod. On either side of the clearing, thick trees surrounded the house as far as Anna could see. If the coach had neighbors, their homes were not visible. Behind the coach's house, she could see the steel-gray waters of Lake Huron. She calculated the value of the land and the house. Even in this remote corner of Michigan, it must have cost more than a million dollars.

"How could he afford this?" she said softly to Cooper.

"Advertising," Cooper said "Every waterbed warehouse and used-car dealer in mid-Michigan had him in an ad at some point. And swag. He got a cut of all the Bulldog merchandise. Every man, woman, and child in the county owns at least two of those sweatshirts."

Inside, the foyer opened to a giant living room with cathedral ceilings and three-story glass windows overlooking the lake. The walls were made of massive logs and stacked stones. People in dark clothes packed the large space. The crowd was mostly men: generations of former athletes looking uncomfortable in their best suits.

The coach's widow stood by a massive table covered in gorgeously catered food. Wendy Fowler, née Weiscowicz, looked even better today than she had in high school. She'd always been the local beauty, renowned for her fiery hair. But as an adult, she had acquired the grace that only years, confidence, and money could produce. Her black sheath dress, pearls, and patent leather pumps were the perfect widow's outfit: expensive, understated, beautiful. She'd also acquired excellent posture since high school. Anna supposed that years of being the queen of their small town had given her the regal bearing.

Although they'd graduated in the same class, Anna and Wendy had never been friends. Wendy had made it clear that Anna was beneath her. While that stung, Anna had never tried to win Wendy's favor; anyone who basked in being a snob and an airhead wasn't worth her time.

There was a break in the line of people waiting to talk to Wendy, and the widow looked up—right at Anna. Wendy's eyes got big, then narrowed. She walked over.

"Anna Curtis, right?"

Anna nodded, as a shot of adrenaline pulsed through her. She'd hoped to mingle and observe without talking directly to Wendy. Despite her reassurances to Jody, Anna thought there was a chance the widow would confront her about Jody's relationship with the coach. She took a deep breath and braced herself.

"Hi, Wendy," Anna said. "I'm so sorry to hear about your husband."

"Thank you." Wendy leaned forward and turned her head, presenting Anna with her cheek. Anna glanced at Cooper, then kissed it. Wendy's skin was incredibly smooth and smelled of Chanel No. 5. Cooper gave Wendy a hug, too.

"Hope you're hanging in there," he said.

"Thank you." Wendy turned to Anna. "I understand you're a prosecutor, now? And living in D.C.?"

Anna nodded. "It's a great city. We don't have views like this, though. Your house is beautiful."

"Thank you. How is your little sister? Jody, right?"

"She's fine, thanks."

"Is she coming today?" Wendy's tone was like an undertow: a calm surface hiding strong and possibly dangerous currents below.

"Oh, I don't think so."

A little girl with the same red-gold hair as Wendy came up and tugged her hand. The girl looked about ten years old, and Anna guessed she was Wendy's daughter.

"Isabel," Wendy said. "Say hello to Mr. Cooper and Miss Anna. They're old friends of mine."

"Old friends" was not the way Anna would have described their relationship. She wondered if Wendy was mocking her.

"Hello," Isabel said dully. Her eyes flicked to Anna, then flicked away again. The girl tugged on her mother's hand again, pulling her down. Wendy leaned over till her ear was level with Isabel's mouth. The girl whispered something.

"Yes, you can go upstairs, honey." Isabel floated away. "She adored her father," Wendy said, watching her daughter climb the stairs. "This has all been very hard on her."

Anna recalled when her own mother died. Anna had been in law school. She'd gotten the call from Jody: their mother was killed in a car accident, plowed into by a drunk driver. It had been devastating. Their father had left town years before; their mother's death effectively orphaned them. The two sisters were all the family they had left.

"At least she has you," Anna said. She pictured her own mother's sad, beautiful smile. "A mother is so important to a little girl."

"Yes," Wendy eyed her coolly. "But so is a father."

17

A herd of enormous teenage boys came over to the widow. They were the only people not wearing black: instead, they wore blue football jerseys. Anna assumed they were members of the current Holly Grove football team. A bear of a kid with a blond mohawk seemed to be the leader.

He said, "Mrs. Fowler, we, uh, wanted to offer our condolences."

"Thank you, Hans." Wendy looked at Anna and Cooper. "Excuse me. Please do get something to eat and drink. There's an open bar on the boat outside. Owen loved that boat. He would want people to toast to him there."

Wendy turned back to the football team. As they walked away from the cluster, Cooper leaned down and whispered, "See the kid talking to Wendy now?"

Anna glanced back. The one with the blond mohawk had the name BAKER on the back of his jersey. "Mr. Baker?"

"Yeah. I hear he was one of the boys who was part of the bullying of Hayley Mack."

Anna knew Cooper had his ear to the ground. He kept up with Holly Grove athletics, spoke to people at his community garden, and still had family in Holly Grove.

Anna nodded. "Let's go outside. I need some air."

They walked out of the sliding glass doors and onto the back deck. It was beautiful summer day, the blue sky dotted with cotton candy clouds. Pine trees swayed in the breeze, which rippled the silver water of Lake Huron. They walked down to the large lawn. At the bottom was a flagstone patio, set up for the service with hundreds of white chairs facing a podium.

Anna and Cooper followed a stone path to the edge of the yard, which ended at a sandy cliff encircling a cove. Stairs went one way down the cliff side, while a wooden ramp went the other. They took the ramp.

At the bottom, Anna's shoes sank into the soft white sand. She couldn't see the house from here, only the sandy cliff, trees, and miles of water. It was a beautiful, secluded spot.

A long wooden dock went out into the water, with a large pontoon boat tied at the end. A bar was set up on the boat, with a bartender handing out generous drinks. People stood on it drinking and chatting, while more guests gathered on the end of the wide dock. Anna had to admire Wendy's skills as a hostess. Putting the bar there made the guests see the entire impressive property and also dispersed some of the crowd from the house.

Anna saw the familiar faces of people she'd known from high school. Cooper leaned down and whispered, "You want to stay together, or split up and cover more ground?"

"Let's split up." He nodded and headed to a cluster of guys on the dock. Anna stepped onto the boat. She saw a woman she recognized from high school. "Jenny?"

"Anna! Hey!" Jenny said. "You're in from D.C. That's awesome. Everyone here is so proud of you."

"Aw, thanks." Anna was touched, especially because the feeling she actually got was that she was an outsider whom no one quite understood or trusted anymore. Including her own sister.

She chatted with Jenny, who'd married and had two little girls. Her husband was an auto exec, and, it turned out, they lived down the street from the coach's house in Holly Grove.

"What was the coach like, as a neighbor?" Anna asked, casually.

"Oh, such a nice guy. Always friendly, kept his yard real nice. And very sweet to our little girls. Paid them lots of attention. Though we didn't see him much this summer."

"What do you mean?"

"I got the impression he was staying here the last few months.

We saw Wendy and Isabel around, but never the coach. I haven't seen him at the Holly Grove house since early this spring."

Anna noted this with interest. The crowd swirled and she mingled, until a man in a dark suit asked everyone to go back up to the lawn; the service was about to start. Cooper was waiting for her on the dock; he held out his hand to help Anna step off the boat.

They took seats at the back of the audience. Soon, every seat was filled. More guests stood in the back. A minister took the podium and thanked everyone for making the trip to Lake Huron.

"Owen Fowler was a pillar of the community, a sports champion, and a role model. He left behind a legacy of charitable work with underprivileged children, and an athletic camp that will persist long after he's gone. In his football championships, he gave Holly Grove honor and a cause in which everyone could take pride. And he was a devoted husband and loving father. He will be missed by many."

Wendy and Isabel sat in the front row. Isabel leaned into her mother, who kept an arm around the girl. The minister gave a sermon about the importance of public service, and how that was fulfilled by the coach. Then Wendy walked to the podium. The breeze ruffled her hair as she gazed out on the audience. The crowd grew so quiet, Anna could hear the seagulls cawing from the water.

"Thank you, Father Dirksen," Wendy said. "And thank you to everyone who came here today. I know many of you traveled a great distance. Owen would have appreciated it, truly.

"Most of you knew Owen as the coach of the Holly Grove football team. That is certainly what he'll be remembered for. It was his life. He loved bringing along young men: finding raw talent and helping to shape it into something hard and good. I know he touched many of your lives. His athletes were so important to him."

She smiled into the audience. "Ron Surocka, he helped you get your job at the tire factory after you graduated. Ben Ohebshalom, he advocated until you got a football scholarship at Penn State. Devin Hughes, I do believe he bailed you out of jail a couple times."

The crowd laughed. Anna remembered that Coach Fowler had

written her a letter that helped her get a college scholarship. Without that, who knows, she might not be where she was today. She saw several mothers nodding in the audience. Women were always asking the coach to write recommendation letters for their sons. Perhaps even more than the fathers, the mothers of Holly Grove adored Owen Fowler.

"But you already know how much he contributed to our community. What I want to talk about today is something much more personal.

"I fell in love with Owen when I was young. I had a terrific crush on him, the sort of puppy love for a local hero that usually goes unrequited. But I was lucky. He loved me back. We courted, and it was like a dream come true. Then one day he invited me on a drive. We went to Hell, Michigan. That's where he proposed—because he'd always said it would be a cold day in hell when he got engaged."

Everyone laughed.

"That's how he was. Funny, surprising. He loved beautiful things: cars, clothes, women. And they loved him back. When he proposed, I was over the moon. He had so many choices and—"

She paused, her attention drawn to something to the side. Anna followed where she was looking. A dark cloud floated toward them from the trees. Anna blinked and the cloud came into focus: it was a flock of butterflies. The crowd let out a collective "Ah!" A bunch of monarchs, orange spotted with black, flitted around one another. They flew right over the gathered audience and, for an instant, the air was filled with the butterflies. Anna felt the soft touch of wings on her cheek. They circled Wendy and kept going toward the beach. When they reached the cliff, they floated down and disappeared from view.

"Well, that was lovely," Wendy said. "We get those here sometimes, but I'd like to think that today it's a sign from the angels. God is celebrating—celebrating Owen's life along with us." She cleared her throat, looked down, and seemed to gather her thoughts. "As I was saying, Owen had so many choices—and he chose me. He wanted to build a life with me, for me to be his partner.

"Owen Fowler gave me many things. But the greatest gift he ever gave me was Isabel. You can win all the football games in the world. There's nothing like a beautiful, smart little girl to change your world. I thank God for her every day, that I have the privilege of being her mother." She looked down at her daughter. "Isabel, honey, I know this is a tough time for you. But we're going to make it. We have each other. And look around you. All these people are here for your father. They're also here for you. You have a lot of people supporting you."

The little girl wiped a tear away with the back of her sleeve. Wendy opened her mouth to say more but choked up. She excused herself, left the podium, and sat next to her girl. Isabel cried into her mother's chest. Wendy held her and rocked her. Anna had to pull out her own Kleenex. She saw several other people doing the same thing.

Whatever faults Wendy had, it was clear that she loved her daughter. And her elegance and fortitude were unexpected. Clearly, Wendy had grown up quite a bit since high school. As the crowd was herded back into the house, Anna mused: Maybe she had been wrong about Wendy. Maybe there were some redeeming qualities in the former Homecoming queen after all.

When the service was over, they walked back to Cooper's motorcycle. "Did you find out anything?" Anna asked quietly.

He looked around and saw that they were alone. He leaned over and whispered in her ear. "My friend is a receptionist at a family law firm. Today, he had a few too many trips to the open bar and told some tales. He said that Wendy visited the firm about a month ago and consulted with one of the lawyers. She wanted a divorce."

18

t was close to one A.M. when the coach's 1967 Corvette came growling up the Hugheses' dirt driveway, kicking up a cloud of dust. The coach sprang out and strode over to the front porch, where I was sitting on the steps. He was wearing jeans and a blue pullover, and his blond hair had the rumpled look of someone who'd been called out of bed. He held out a hand, which I took, and helped me to my feet. I tried to stand steady, because I didn't want him to know how much I'd been drinking. I was not successful. I stumbled, and he had to grab my elbow to steady me.

"Are you okay?" he asked.

It was the second time that night someone asked me that, but this time it made my heartbeat quicken.

"Yeah, I'm okay," I said. "Maybe just a little tipsy. Sorry."

"Your hands are freezing." He pressed them between his, which were warm and big. "Where's Devin?"

I pointed toward the side yard. He let go of my hands and strode in that direction. I followed. As we turned the corner, another blast echoed out into the night.

"Devin Hughes!" Coach roared. "You are in a world of hurt!"

I stopped walking and stepped into the shadow of an elm tree. It was a chickenshit move. I didn't want the boys to know I'd snitched on them. I tucked my hands under my armpits, leaned against the trunk, and watched from the darkness.

The boys looked like dogs who'd been caught eating slippers. They hung their heads and stared at their coach with sad, guilty eyes. Coach marched over to Devin and snatched the gun out of his hand.

"Are you crazy, Hughes? Do you want to kill someone?"

"No."

"No, what?" Coach popped open the shotgun and ejected a shell.

"No, sir."

"Aren't you supposed to be staying at Ben's house while your parents are in Milwaukee?"

The coach knew everything about his players.

"Yes, sir."

"Here's what's happening now. You're going to march into that house and tell everyone the party's over. Clear it out. I'll give you the dignity of doing it yourself, which is more than you deserve. If I have to do it, it will not be pretty."

"I understand. Sir."

"We're going to have a long talk about this on Monday, Hughes."

"Yes, sir." Devin hung his head lower.

Coach pointed at the house. "Go! Now."

The three boys fairly ran into the house. It struck me that they were boys—but Coach was a man. He wasn't just older. He had this presence, an aura of leadership and authority, that made kids do what he said. I wondered if he was born with it, or if he'd earned it through years of coaching.

"Idiots," he muttered as he walked back to the car. He waved me out of the shadow of the elm. "Come on, Jody."

I trotted next to him, weaving a bit. I was still very drunk. "I'm . . . um . . . I'm not sure everyone in there is sober enough to drive home."

"I'm not a taxi service. They found their way here, they can find their way home again." Coach glanced at me. "But I'll give you a ride."

He opened the Corvette's trunk, tossed the shotgun in, and slammed it shut. Then he went around and opened the passenger door for me. No Holly Grove boy would have done that. I felt like I was in a fairy tale, or a soap opera. I'd often seen Coach driving his famous car and dreamed of being inside it. Now I got to slide in. The car smelled of polished leather and men's cologne. The dash was rich, shiny wood, curving around the instrument panels so sensually it looked like a woman's body. Coach slid in the other side.

The seat was a long bench seat, covered in supple black leather.

I learned some years later that Corvettes normally come with two bucket seats, separated by a console. The coach had his car specially fitted with this single, long seat. I only understood how horrible that was afterward.

"This is a beautiful car," I said.

"Thanks. It's my baby."

He turned on the ignition, and the tires purred against the gravel of the driveway. I thought of his other baby, the real one, growing inside his wife.

"How's Wendy?" I asked.

"She's sleeping."

"Yeah, it is pretty late."

"She sleeps a lot these days." He turned onto Route 9. We were the only car on the road.

"I hear that being pregnant can do that."

He nodded and turned on the radio to an oldies station. John Cougar Mellencamp sang about how it hurts so good.

"Wendy woke up when my phone rang," Coach said, looking straight ahead at the road. "I told her it was an emergency. I didn't tell her it was you."

"Why not?"

"She can feel it."

"What?" My breath came fast and shallow.

"The attraction between us."

I nodded and swallowed. We passed farms, stands of trees, and small houses. I stared at the road's dotted yellow lines, hoping their steady passage could sober me up. They didn't.

He turned onto a dirt road. It's funny what we wish for, isn't it? For months, I wanted to be alone with Owen Fowler. I knew this wasn't the way home, but I didn't say anything. Because I desperately wanted to find out: What was at the end of that road? Now, of course, I know the answer. It was a monster.

19

After they got home from the memorial service, Cooper built a fire in his backyard pit. He, Anna, and Jody sat in the plastic chairs around it, drinking beer as the sun went down. The chickens scratched around the grass by their feet, and the goldfish floated to the surface of their pond. Cooper threw some food in and the fish devoured it with big round gulps. Sparky sat at the edge of the water and watched them, his head tilted quizzically. The chirping of insects was loud and steady, and the warm air was scented with earth. If she didn't look at the shattered warehouse or the sunset reflecting off the curved glass of the Renaissance Center, Anna could imagine she was sitting in the countryside.

"How was the service?" Jody asked.

"A flock of butterflies flew right through the speeches," Cooper said.

"Ha," Jody said. "I bet Wendy bought them and had them released at just the right moment. She's always been a drama queen. I'm sure she was enjoying her role as Grieving Widow."

"She did play it well," Anna said. "Although I'm sure she'd also be good at Aggrieved Divorcée."

"How do you mean?" Jody asked.

Cooper described what he'd learned at the memorial service. Anna added, "I checked the court system, and *Fowler versus Fowler* hadn't been filed. Yet. But it makes sense. A neighbor said they seemed to be living in separate houses."

"Wow," Jody said. She took a sip of beer. "You are good, Annie. Bust into town and find out everyone's deepest secrets in less than seventy-two hours. Impressive. But . . . so what?"

"So it's a motive," Anna said, with satisfaction. "From the person most likely to kill the coach to begin with."

"How do you figure?"

"When someone's murdered, unless the person is a drug dealer, it's usually by a lover or spouse. And with a separation, there's even more motive. Wendy and Coach Fowler were about to get into the messiest thing two people can get into. Custody battles, splitting the assets, dragging each other's reputations through the mud. Considerable assets, considerable motive to kill. If they got divorced, Wendy would get half of everything—if she was lucky—minus lawyer's fees. Now, she has everything. Murder is a lot cheaper than divorce."

Anna was thrilled to suspect someone besides her sister. The ongoing stomachache she'd had since coming to Michigan had abated at the news that Wendy was contemplating divorce immediately before her husband was killed.

Jody said, "Do the police know about this?"

"If they did, they'd be searching *her* house." Anna looked at her sister. "Did you know they were separating? Was he leaving her for you?"

"I'm not sure," Jody murmured, looking into the fire. "I had certain hopes and dreams about the situation. I was stupid."

Jody went inside and returned a moment later with three more beers. She gave one to each of them. They sat in silence, watching the fire dance and pop. Sparky rested his head on Cooper's knee.

"Today was hard," he said, petting the dog. "All the tears and grief. How do you do it for a living, Anna? Every day, seeing people go through the hardest time of their life? Immersing yourself in the most terrible things people do to each other?"

"It can be tough." She stretched her legs out toward the fire, enjoying the warmth on her feet. "But I really believe being a prosecutor is the most rewarding job I could have. There's nothing like putting a predator in jail. Knowing that my efforts every day are to keep my community safe. What about you, Coop? You weren't exactly seeing lollipops and roses in Afghanistan."

"No, though there were quite a few poppy fields. Which are beautiful, really. These huge pink flowers, going for acres. You know what they're for, right?"

"Heroin," Jody said.

"Yep. We burned those fields. Had to be careful, because if you inhale that smoke, you can get sick." He looked into the fire. "I hated that part. I grew up on a farm. Can't imagine how much I'd despise anyone who came by and burned our fields."

"Your family grows wheat and corn," Anna said. "Your fields are legal."

"Still. We made a lot of enemies." He poked the fire with a stick, sending sparks dancing up. "Eventually, the army changed the policy, after the farmers turned to the Taliban for protection. Then we were in charge of protecting the poppy fields."

"The world is complicated." Jody said. "Sometimes right and wrong aren't so clear."

"And sometimes people just change their minds," Cooper said. "Like Michelle."

Anna remembered Michelle Zamarin, a pretty brown-haired soccer star. She and Cooper had dated in high school.

"Whatever happened with her?" Anna asked.

"We got engaged before I went on my tour. When the IED went off, I thought I was dying, and all I wanted was to get a message to her. I kept telling the guys who put me on the helicopter: 'Tell Michelle I love her.'

"A medic told me I could tell her myself, and he was right. Eventually, they got me to Germany, where I had a couple operations. And then I spent a year at Walter Reed hospital, getting rehab, learning how to walk with this." He knocked on his metal prosthesis. "You and I missed each other in D.C. by a couple of years. But Michelle came to visit. Brought me a basket of bagels. Spent a couple days holding my hand. And then told me she was very sorry, but she'd fallen in love with an accountant."

"Oh." Anna was pained on his behalf. "Speaking of terrible things people do to each other."

"Nah. She didn't want to hurt me. And it wasn't because of the leg—I don't think. I'd been away for a long time, and she'd just moved on. Still, I can't help but hate bagels now. And accountants."

Anna felt fierce anger at the woman who'd hurt Cooper when he was already wounded. "I think that's pretty rotten."

"You know what's rotten?" Jody said. Her words bled together at the edges, like a kid's watercolor painting. Anna wondered how many beers she'd had. "You know a terrible thing one person can do to another? What they did to Hayley Mack."

"What happened to Hayley?" Anna asked.

Jody looked at her. She shook her head. "I don't want to talk about it."

But she pulled out her phone. Something about a campfire made everyone want to talk. Jody scrolled to a picture, then handed it over. Anna looked at the screen.

It was a picture of thirteen-year-old Hayley, asleep on a couch. Or, more accurately, passed out on a couch. The girl's eyes were closed; her mouth hung open with a thin line of saliva hanging from it. Her shiny black hair spilled down the couch like a waterfall. Her shirt had been pulled up, revealing a taut patch of her stomach between her rib cage and her jeans. Someone had written all over her belly with thick black marker. *I'M A SLUT. FUCK ME. I LIKE IT HOT AND WET.* On Hayley's cheek was a crude drawing of a penis, with liquid erupting from it toward her mouth. The boy with the blond mohawk stood by the couch, laughing. Anna inhaled sharply.

"They posted this online," Jody said. "It's been deleted, but I saved it in the iCloud before they took it down. In case the police ever wanted it. Which they didn't."

Jody swiped to another picture. Now Hayley was on a bed. The mohawked kid held a teddy bear's crotch to her mouth, simulating oral sex.

"This was posted too?" Anna asked. Jody nodded. "Did the police look into whether she was sexually assaulted? These boys could have done anything while she was passed out. You can see what was on their minds."

"Those are football players. You think the Holly Grove police are gonna do anything that'll hurt the team?"

"There was no investigation?"

Jody shook her head.

"Did the school do anything?"

"To their darlings? Of course not. Hayley was teased by the kids for a couple weeks. They were merciless. She was slut-shamed and mocked and cast out. These pictures were all over Twitter, Instagram, and Facebook. The sites eventually made the kids take them down. But the adults in Holly Grove, the ones she trusted to help her, did nothing but hurt her even more. Even the moms—they were all saying that Hayley shouldn't have been drinking so much, that anything that happened was her own fault. And then she killed herself."

Sparky sat up suddenly and looked at Cooper. The dog poked his nose persistently into Cooper's legs. Anna realized Cooper was having a pre-PTSD reaction. Hearing about Hayley made him almost as upset as it made her.

"It's okay, boy," Cooper ran his hands through the dog's fur. "It's okay. It's okay. Everything's okay."

They all knew it wasn't.

20

The next morning, Anna sat at the kitchen table sorting eggs into cartons to be sold at a farmers' market, while Cooper stood at the stove, making breakfast. Sparky lay on her feet. Jody came down the stairs, her hair disheveled from sleep, still wearing pajamas. She looked pale and exhausted.

"Hey, Jo," Anna said.

"Come have some breakfast," Cooper said.

Jody shuffled over to the table and sat next to Anna. She leaned over to read the headlines of the *Detroit News*, which, thankfully, did not have a story about the coach on the front page today. Cooper gave Jody a plate heaped with bacon and scrambled eggs, sprinkled with fresh cilantro. Jody took one look at the plate and bolted from her chair. Anna heard her in the bathroom, retching, and followed her there. She held Jody's hair back while Jody heaved into the toilet. When she was finished, Anna gave her a wet washcloth to wipe her face.

"Thanks," Jody moaned. She flushed, put the lid down, and buried her head in the washcloth. "Ugh. I feel awful."

"I didn't realize you had that much to drink last night," Anna said.

"I didn't either."

Anna looked at her sister. "When was the last time you had your period?"

"I dunno." Jody's eyes got wide. "Oh God."

One trip to the pharmacy later, the women were back in the same bathroom, looking at the pregnancy test stick that Jody had peed on. The line in the little window became an unmistakable blue, darkening at approximately the same speed that Jody's face drained of color.

"You're pregnant," Anna said. "Congratulations?"

■ ■ ■

The first thing Anna wanted to know was, "Who's the father?"

Jody just shook her head. "Nobody."

"It's a miracle!"

Jody didn't laugh. Anna pushed a plate of dry toast closer to Jody. They sat at the kitchen table. Cooper was outside with Sparky, working in the orchard.

"Eat. It'll make you feel better."

Jody took a bite, chewed, and looked repulsed.

"Seriously?" Anna couldn't hide the hurt in her voice. "You're not going to tell me who the father is?"

"Maybe *I* don't know who the father is," Jody said.

Anna looked at her sister, trying to figure out if she was kidding.

"Never mind." Jody pushed the toast away and went upstairs. Anna could hear the shower going. She sighed and cleaned up the dishes. When Jody came down again, her hair was damp and she'd changed into jeans and a yellow T-shirt. She said, "I want to go home."

"You don't even have a toilet yet," Anna said.

"I'll get one. I need to go home."

Anna went outside to tell Cooper.

"You don't have to leave," Cooper said. "It's great having you guys here."

"I need to be in my own house now," Jody said, standing on the dirt patio. "Maybe I'm nesting. But I really appreciate your hospitality."

Anna met Cooper's eyes and nodded. She went inside, changed the sheets on Cooper's bed, and packed up her few things. Down in the foyer, she realized she was wearing his T-shirt and promised to return it soon.

"Keep it," he said. "I like the idea of you wrapped in my shirt."

Cooper helped them load their few belongings into Jody's truck. Sparky sat on Cooper's foot as he waved good-bye to them. Both dog and master tilted their heads to the left, looking mournful as they pulled out.

Anna steered through the empty streets of Detroit. An overpass a few blocks from Cooper's house was covered in graffiti. *#NOHIPSTERS* stood out in puffy red letters. They passed the old Packer auto factory, which was now an abandoned shell, similarly covered in graffiti. *EPIC DECAY* was sprayed across the top in electric blue.

"Do you want to keep the baby?" Anna asked.

"I don't know." Jody leaned her head against the seat and closed her eyes.

"Do you want me to schedule an appointment with your ob-gyn? Or Planned Parenthood?"

"Eventually."

"Do you want to talk about it?"

"Mm. Yes. But . . . not right now."

Jody kept her eyes closed. They drove the rest of the way in silence. Jody might have been sleeping, or she might have kept her eyes closed to shut down any more attempts at conversation. Anna drove, but hardly noticed the traffic on the street. She tried to picture her fiercely independent little sister as a mother. She couldn't do it.

At Jody's house, they began to clean up the chaos the police had left behind. Anna had never been on this side of a search warrant—trying to put the pieces back together again. She wasn't sure where to start. She began putting pots and pans away. Jody tried to push the kitchen table back into place.

"Hey, not in your delicate condition," Anna said.

"I've been drinking all week," Jody said. "And I have to keep working on the line. This kid is gonna have to be hardy."

Together, they moved the table back to its spot. Anna cleaned the kitchen while Jody tackled the spare bedroom. In a stack of papers on the floor, Anna found her own wedding invitation. She held the creamy white cardstock.

It is with great happiness that
Jack Bailey and Anna Curtis
invite you to celebrate the beginning of their life together
at their marriage ceremony.

The Blown-Away Inn, Shenandoah, Virginia
July 5, 2014, at 5:00 P.M.
Dinner, dancing, and merriment to follow.

Three weeks and five days from today. She ran her fingers over the embossed text. Drops splashed onto the cardstock. She leaned back against the wall and let the tears come. She hadn't allowed herself to cry since the night she'd broken up with Jack. Jody's problems had distracted her. But now she couldn't help but compare where she was to where she thought she was going to be today. She loved this man. She loved his daughter. She thought she would spend the rest of her life with them—and this made her life finally make sense. She was going to be a wife, and a mother, and live in a beautiful yellow Victorian. The invitation in her hands led to a perfect life, surrounded by love and security. And it was nothing but scrap paper now.

She was adrift from everything that had tethered her for the last few years. And the one thing she'd always counted on in her life—Jody—seemed like a kite whose string had snapped and was flying away from her. Anna felt like she didn't even know her sister anymore.

She tried to muffle the sound of her crying. How ridiculous to be crying about her wedding when her sister was being investigated for murder.

She tucked the wedding invitation into her purse. She took several deep breaths and wiped her eyes. She went back to cleaning the kitchen. The only way to get through grief was to keep moving forward, hour by hour, tackling one small job at a time until, one day, enough space and time would exist between her heart and the reason for its ache, and she wouldn't feel it so much.

They worked all day putting things back into place. Jody ordered Chinese for lunch. The plumber came and installed the sink, toilets, and washing machine. By the time the sun was setting, most of the stuff was back in place. They still needed to wash off the black dust that had been left from the police fingerprinting, and the grime from all the police walking through, but at least it felt like a home again.

Jody sank down at the kitchen table, looking exhausted but more comfortable now that she was back in her own home. "God, I want a cigarette," she said. Anna raised her eyebrows and glanced at her sister's stomach. Jody sighed and stayed in her seat.

Anna went to the fridge and peered into the take-out containers, wondering whether there was enough lo mein left to provide dinner for two. For three, really. Jody had to eat for two. She scooped some noodles onto a plate and stuck it in the microwave. When it beeped, she put most of it on a plate for Jody, and a small portion on a plate for herself. If there was any left over from Jody, she'd eat it.

She set the plates down, and Jody dug in. "Thanks, Annie."

While they were eating, the doorbell rang. Anna looked at Jody, who shrugged. Anna went to the door and peered out the peephole. On the porch stood a uniformed police officer and Detective Rob Gargaron, who wore a shirt and tie and a badge on a metal chain around his neck. This was not a social call. Anna opened the door and glared at him.

"I thought you were going to go easy on the house," she said. "Like a virgin."

She was surprised by how angry she was. She knew the police were just doing their job. She'd been part of it plenty of times herself.

"I'm sorry," Rob said. He met her eyes and seemed, for a brief moment, actually sorry. "Is your sister home?"

Jody came to the foyer. "You could have at least left me a toilet."

"I couldn't, actually. I was required to search your house and seize anything described in the warrant. A warrant is a court order.

So is this." Rob reached into his pocket and pulled out a paper. He handed it to Anna. She opened it and saw the title across the top: ARREST WARRANT. The charge was first-degree homicide.

"You have the right to remain silent," Rob said, as he pulled out a pair of handcuffs.

21

There were no streetlights on the dirt road, and the night was as dark as night can be. The Corvette's headlights cut a small slice of visibility, only lighting up the brush directly in front of the car. My senses were so heightened, it seemed like I could feel every pebble the car went over. Coach put a hand on my thigh and squeezed gently. The world seemed to tilt.

"I love your legs," he said. "You have the most beautiful, strong sprinter's legs."

My breathing came fast and shallow. He slowed the car and pulled onto a patch of grass that was blocked on three sides by trees. He looked at me, then turned off the headlights. The world went black.

After a minute, my eyes adjusted enough that I could see his face ever so faintly, just the vaguest impression of his features. He leaned in and kissed me. His lips were dry and insistent. I was dizzy—partly from everything I'd had to drink, but also because the situation felt so surreal.

I shook my head, trying to clear it. This was everything I'd ever dreamed of. And it was so wrong.

"Coach," I said. "I'm not sure I want to do this."

"Shh," he whispered. He unzipped my winter jacket and squeezed my breast through my shirt. "Be a good girl, now."

"Stop," I said. "Please. Let me think."

He murmured, "You want this too."

I thought of his pregnant wife. I thought of Mrs. Weiscowicz bringing Mom a casserole. I thought of how I felt at the peak of the high jump. This felt like the opposite.

"It's not right," I said.

"No one will ever know."

"I'll know," I said. "I don't want to do this. Please, Coach. Please take me home."

I scooched as far from him as I could, till my back was pressed against the passenger door. He was breathing hard as he looked at me. Then he grabbed my legs and pulled me down flat on the leather seat. He angled himself on top of me.

"You called me out of my house in the middle of the night. You made me drive halfway across the county. We're not going anywhere till we finish what we came here to do."

He pulled my jeans and panties down. Then he fumbled with his own zipper.

"No," I said, panicking. "No!" I pushed his chest, trying to get him off. But he was so much bigger than me. It was like pushing a brick wall.

"Shut your mouth." It was the same voice he used at sports camp when giving an order: *Give me twenty push-ups* or *Take two laps around the track*. It was the same voice he used with Devin back at the house. But now it didn't make me think how much of a man he was; now it just made me fear him. "You know this is what you want," he said. "You've been begging for it all year. It's why you called me tonight. Now lie back and enjoy it."

I started to cry. He freed himself from his pants and pressed into my thighs, fumbling to get it in. "No, no, no, no." I pushed at his chest and hit him in the face. He grunted with pain and pinned my arms above my head. I couldn't move.

"Please, Coach," I sobbed. "Please. I don't want to do this."

"You trashy little dicktease." His hands tightened around my wrists. "I'm not going to say this again. Shut up and take it."

I couldn't stop crying, so he kept my wrists pinned with one hand and covered my face with the other. He had big hands that covered my mouth, nose, and eyes. I couldn't yell anymore. I couldn't see, or breathe, or talk. And then he tore inside of me.

I was stunned by the pain. Before that night, I hadn't gone past second base. I stilled from the shock of how much it hurt.

He liked that I stopped moving. "There's a good girl," he said. He took his hand off my face and went back to just pinning my wrists. I sucked in a rasp of air as he started to pump. He kept going for a long time. My head banged rhythmically against the car door. Tears streamed down my temples, soaking my hair and the leather seat beneath. I looked at the stars through the windshield. Then the glass fogged up, and all I could see was blurry black nothing. I closed my eyes and waited for it to end. Finally, he shuddered and collapsed on top of me. I don't know how long he lay there. It seemed like forever.

When he sat up, I expect the world was pretty much the same for him as it had always been, only he'd just gotten laid. For me, I sat up into a whole different world, a world where I wasn't in control of my own body, a world where a person I trusted had hurt and violated me. My whole body shook as I pulled up my pants and zipped up my winter coat. I sat there, looking at the fogged windshield and trying to get used to the dizzying feeling of existing on a different planet.

"I'm sorry it got a little rough there at the end," Coach said, re-fastening his own pants. "Next time, don't make it so hard. This can be a beautiful thing."

Next time? Beautiful? These were words that had a real meaning in the English language, but in this context, I couldn't process them in any logical way. He might as well have been speaking Chinese.

He started the car, three-pointed it around, and drove. I couldn't stop shaking. We didn't talk. When we got to my apartment building, he pulled to the curb.

He patted my leg, all friendly, like he hadn't just raped me. "Have a good night," he said. "Come to my office after school next week, and we'll work on your high jump."

I fled from the car and stumbled into the building. I could hear the Corvette zipping away. I ran up the two flights to our apartment, which was dark and empty. Mom was working the graveyard shift at the hospital. I turned on the TV, a rerun of *The Simpsons,* just so there'd be some noise to compete with the screams echoing through my head. I stripped off my clothes and left them in a pile on the bedroom floor. I looked at your empty bed and imagined telling you what had happened, and I started crying again.

I went to the shower and turned on the water as hot as I could stand. The mirror fogged up, like the windows at the house party, like the windshield of Coach's car. I stepped under the steaming stream of water and stood there even though the water scalded my skin pink. I must have been in there for a while. The water turned lukewarm, and then cold, and even then, I still stood there, shivering.

22

The uniformed officer handcuffed Jody's wrists behind her as Rob recited her rights. Jody looked terrified. Rob wore the steely expression of a man who believed in the righteousness of his actions.

Anna felt dizzy. She had seen this scene dozens of times before. It usually brought relief and the satisfaction that a bad guy was being taken off the street. Now it was all wrong. This was her sister. This was a good guy. She had to stop this.

"Wait," Anna said. "It was Wendy. They were splitting up. She has to be the one who killed him."

"Thanks for the info, but that's not going to work for you," Rob said. "Cell-phone records and hotel receipts show that Wendy Fowler was a hundred miles away, with family in Ohio, when the coach was killed."

The officers led Jody out of the house. Anna ran after them. "Rob, does she really need to be handcuffed?"

"Procedure, sorry." He opened the squad car door and put his hand on Jody's head to guide her to sitting in the backseat.

"Jody, don't say anything, to anyone!" Anna's voice was an octave higher than usual. She recognized the tone as panic. "Not to the police, not to your cellmates, nobody. Do you understand?"

Jody nodded. Her eyes were wide with fear.

"As her lawyer, I am invoking her right to remain silent and to be represented by an attorney," Anna told Rob. "No one is to ask her questions without me present."

"You know you're not her lawyer." He got into the car. "She can talk to us if she wants to."

She opened her mouth to tell him that Jody was pregnant. They might treat her better in lockup if they knew her medical condition. Then she paused. She didn't know who the father of the baby was. What if it was the coach? Someone might wonder if Jody fought with the coach *because* she was pregnant. Anna had wondered it herself. She closed her mouth.

The cruiser backed out of the driveway. Her sister looked out the window at her. Anna held up her hand, not so much to wave, but as if she had some magical powers she could conjure to stop this from happening.

Anna watched the car drive off. She'd known this might be coming, but actually seeing her sister behind the cage of a police car was shocking. Whatever Jody had done, she was the only family Anna had.

She shook herself, strode back into the house, and grabbed her cell phone. She had to punch in the passcode three times before she got it right. She forced herself to stop and take a deep breath. She was no good to Jody if she was a shaky mess. She had to organize her thoughts.

First, if she was actually going to represent her sister in open court, she needed to get permission from the Department of Justice. She hadn't filed anything with DOJ so far, because she didn't want her bosses to know about this unless it was absolutely necessary. There was no avoiding it now. She pulled up an e-mail from her Drafts folder and hit Send.

This wasn't the sort of request where she could wait for a return e-mail. It was 6:35 P.M. so there was a chance that some supervisors would still be in the office. She dialed her phone. Carla didn't answer, and neither did the ethics adviser. But the U.S. Attorney himself picked up. "Marty Zinn," he answered. Anna was surprised to have gotten straight through.

Marty was the head of the entire office of 350 prosecutors. He was a mild-mannered guy, whom she didn't know well. The office was so big that the boss had very little contact on anything but the most high-profile cases. Plus, Marty came from the civil side of the office, and mostly deferred to Jack Bailey, his Homicide chief, on criminal issues.

After a minute of small talk, she told Marty why she was calling. "I have to ask a big favor. My sister has been charged with a violent crime in Michigan—by the State of Michigan, so the prosecutor is a separate sovereign, not our office. It's a terrible mistake, and I'd like to represent her. The Code of Federal Regulations says this is doable, but I understand I need your permission first. I'm calling to ask for your permission."

"I see. Well, in situations like this, there's a memo for you to fill out . . ."

"I sent it to you a couple minutes ago."

"Ah." She heard his keyboard clicking. "Indeed you did. First-degree homicide. That *is* a violent crime."

"She didn't do it." Anna's voice sounded so certain, she almost convinced herself. "And she needs a good lawyer."

"But how will you continue to do your own work at the office, while representing your sister in Michigan?"

"I was hoping to transfer to the Appellate section for the duration of my sister's case. You'll still have my full dedication and effort, but I could research and write the briefs from here in Michigan. I understand that a few prosecutors have telecommuted this way before, for example, while their spouse took a job in Europe or on a military base out of state."

Marty paused. She could feel his discomfort radiating through the cell phone. The spouses she spoke of hadn't been accused of murder.

"Anna, I don't know. It could be very awkward to have one of my prosecutors arguing to keep someone *out* of jail. And it would be a burden on both the Sex Offense section, to lose you, and the Appellate section, to take on a long-distance employee."

"I know," she said. "I'm very sorry to put you in this position. But my sister needs me. After this detail, I'd be willing to go anywhere the office needs me, however I can help out."

"And if I say no?"

"I can't abandon her. I'd have to quit." As she said it, she felt like her lungs were being squeezed inside a vise. She didn't want to quit. She loved her job. And she had no financial cushion. But she would do what she had to do.

The U.S. Attorney sighed. She could picture him at his desk, staring out the window and running a hand over his bald head. He said, "I'll look at your memo and make my decision in due course. But I have to warn you: I'm leaning toward no."

"I understand. Please let me know as soon as possible. My sister will probably be arraigned tomorrow."

"In the meantime, you may want to look at the information on our website about separating from the government. I don't want to sound dire, but you'll want to have some health-care coverage lined up before you resign."

"I see. Okay."

They hung up. Health-care coverage. Oh God. She was not in any way prepared for what resigning entailed.

Anna looked around the house, which was eerily quiet. It felt spooky to be here alone. But it wasn't spookier than where Jody was: in the central cell block being fingerprinted and having her mug shot taken. Then she would spend the night in a holding cell with a bunch of women who'd been arrested for street crimes over the last twenty-four hours. They would not be easygoing women. A current of fear buzzed steadily through Anna's body. Her stomach hurt more than ever.

As the sky grew black, she walked through the house turning on all the lights and TVs. Soon every room was filled with canned laughter and bright light. But the darkness she was trying to chase away wasn't amenable to electricity.

23

The Lawrence P. Upperthwaite Courthouse was one of the few living buildings in Holly Grove's old downtown. It was a stately old structure, with marble pillars, a gold dome, and big arched windows. Across the street was a square park, planted with grass and trees. That's where the pretty part ended. Around the square, the old storefronts ranged between shabby and vacant. They'd been built when many more people worked in the nearby auto plants. As the car companies left town, so did the rest of the commerce.

Anna arrived at the courthouse promptly at 8:00 A.M., the time the website said the doors opened. She wore her standard black pantsuit. Her purse was overstuffed with legal pads, a *Local Rules Book* for Holly Grove County, and Clif bars. She wasn't sure how long she'd be here today.

The courthouse was as beautiful inside as out, built in an age when the county had money for public projects. The walls alternated between peach marble veined with ivory and a green marble veined with gold. Gold trim laced every door, window, and painting. Oil portraits of old men covered the hallways.

Anna was directed to a large courtroom. The contrast between the courthouse and its current clientele was startling. People waiting for their arraignments sat in the jury box. They wore jeans and dirty T-shirts; they had the bloodshot eyes and stubbled chins of people who woke up in a cell. Several had the brown teeth of meth addicts. Anna didn't see her sister among them. Worry twisted through her chest. What had happened to Jody?

A man in a shiny gray suit sat at the defense table, sorting through a large stack of files. He had to be the public defender. Anna walked up to him.

"Excuse me, sir, I'm wondering if you know where my sister is. Jody Curtis?"

He looked up at her, then through a stack of files. There had to be at least twenty of them on the table. He flipped through them until he came to one in the middle. He picked it up and read the label. "Here we go, Julie Curtis. First-degree murder."

"Jody Curtis."

"What?"

"Her name is Jody, not Julie."

"Okay." He scratched a note on the file. "The violent criminals are kept in restraints in the holding cell in the back."

Anna winced at the image of her little sister cuffed and in leg irons. The defense lawyer stuffed the papers back into the folder, crumpling several in the process. Anna watched in horror. This was her sister's case. It was precious. Seeing him crumple the papers was like seeing her engagement ring thrown in the dishwasher for a cleaning.

She introduced herself and said, "I'd like to help."

"Are you going to represent her?"

"I'm working on it."

"Sorry, miss," he said. "Either you represent her and I don't, or I represent her and you don't. We're woefully understaffed here. If she's got a lawyer, she can't also be represented at taxpayer expense."

"I'm waiting to hear back from my boss."

"Let me know when you've either got DOJ permission to do this or you've officially resigned from your position at the U.S. Attorney's Office. Until then, I'm representing Julie."

"Jody."

"Right."

Anna sat in the second row and checked her e-mail. Marty Zinn had still not written or called to tell her whether DOJ would permit her to do this. She felt a hand on her arm and looked up to find a pair of friendly blue eyes. Cooper sat next to her. "Hi," he said. "You okay?"

"How did you know Jody was arrested?" Anna asked.

"I'm smart that way. Also, everyone knows."

She nodded. She should've guessed word would travel quickly in their small town. "Thank you for coming."

At 8:59, a woman entered the courtroom towing a giant boxy briefcase on wheels. Anna had wheeled the same cumbersome litigation bag countless times. The woman was young, African American, and wearing a black pantsuit similar to Anna's. She set up her files on the other table, wearing the focused expression of a competent person in the process of being overworked. Anna recognized enough of herself in this woman to know that this was the prosecutor. She stood to talk to her, but at precisely nine o'clock, the judge walked in through a side door.

Both lawyers at the front stood, as did Anna; the rest of the crowd needed a little prodding from the court personnel. "All rise!"

Judge Lawrence P. Upperthwaite looked like he'd been plucked from a Norman Rockwell painting: he was old and white, with a patrician nose and an impressive head of silver hair. Anna had seen his face numerous times in campaign posters around town. Unlike federal judges and prosecutors, who were appointed, local judges in Holly Grove were elected. Upperthwaite had been the county DA throughout Anna's childhood. Five years ago, he'd been elected to a position on the bench. It was a mark of how respected and influential he was that the courthouse was named after him while he was still alive. Usually, that honor was reserved for a long-serving jurist after he passed away.

His law clerk, a young man with a nervous smile, stood at the table to the side. "Hear ye, hear ye," the clerk said. "All rise and come to order. Court is now in session, the Honorable Lawrence P. Upperthwaite presiding." The clerk looked nervously to the judge, who nodded back with a reassuring smile. It was clear that the young man was not used to speaking in court. This was probably his first job out of law school.

The judge said, "Please be seated."

"Calling the case of *Michigan versus Jody Curtis*," said the clerk.

"Harold Elliott for the defendant."

"Desiree Miller for the State."

Anna sat up straighter. She was glad for a chance to see her sister, but she'd hoped to hear from DOJ before the case was called. An officer led Jody out from a side door. She still wore her jeans and the yellow T-shirt. Her hands were cuffed behind her back and her hair needed brushing. Anna raised her hand so Jody could see her. Jody met her eyes and nodded. She looked tired but unbroken. She stood next to the public defender.

"The defendant is charged with one count of first-degree homicide," the judge read from a paper. "How do you plead?"

The defense attorney said, "She pleads not guilty, Your Honor."

"What is the government asking in terms of release?"

The prosecutor replied, "We ask that the defendant be held pending trial. She is charged with a crime that carries a life sentence. She has every reason to flee."

A trial would be months away. If Jody was held pending trial, she would serve her pregnancy in jail. She might have her baby in jail.

"Defense?" said the judge.

"Julie Curtis is not a flight risk. She owns her own home, located at . . ." Elliott looked down at the file, trying to find the information. He flipped through the paperwork. "I'm sorry, court's indulgence."

He kept skimming the papers, apparently unable to find the address. He leaned over and whispered to Jody. Anna couldn't take it. She stood. "Your Honor, may I please be heard?"

Heads swiveled. Judge Upperthwaite looked over his reading glasses at Anna. "Come forward, young lady," he said. "Please identify yourself for the record."

Anna walked through the little gate and stood next to her sister. "May it please the court, my name is Anna Curtis. I'm Jody Curtis's older sister. I live in Washington, D.C., where I'm an Assistant U.S. Attorney."

"I take it you're not here in your role as a prosecutor," said the judge.

"No, Your Honor. Pursuant to the Code of Federal Regulations, a federal prosecutor may defend a family member if the Department of Justice approves it. I have asked for DOJ's permission to represent my sister. I am awaiting word from them. But in the meantime, I would ask to be heard on the detention issue."

"You may be heard."

"Thank you, Your Honor. My sister—*Jody* Curtis—grew up in Holly Grove and now lives in neighboring Swartz Creek. She works full-time at the GM plant and has for nine years. She owns her own home and has never missed a mortgage payment. She has lifelong ties to the community and no criminal record. We would ask that she be released on her own recognizance, or that bail be set at a reasonable amount. We don't have many assets, my sister and I, but between her house and my retirement fund, you could be assured that she will have plenty of incentive to appear for trial."

Jody whispered, "I don't want you to risk your retirement fund."

"It's only a risk if you flee the jurisdiction," Anna whispered back. "Don't go to Brazil."

"And what will happen if the Department of Justice doesn't approve your request to represent your sister?" the judge asked.

"I'm prepared to resign from the office and continue to represent her. "

Jody stared at her. "Annie," she whispered. "No."

"Shh."

"I will put the defendant on GPS monitoring and set bail at four hundred thousand dollars. Can you and your sister meet that, Ms. Curtis?"

They only had to come up with 10 percent of that, as collateral. Anna had almost $20,000 in her TSP retirement account. Jody had almost as much in her IRA. The other 90 percent they would get loaned from a bail bondsman, who would attach Jody's house and Anna's future earnings as collateral.

"We can do that, Your Honor. Thank you."

"I take it you are licensed to practice law in Michigan?" the judge asked.

"Yes, sir, I took the Michigan bar when I graduated from law school, then waived into D.C., where I practice. I'm current on all my Michigan CLE and pro bono hours."

"Very well. You have the court's permission to represent your sister. Good luck with DOJ's. Please file the necessary paperwork if and when you get it. Make sure you read the local rules. I expect every lawyer in my courtroom to abide by them, even if you are from a federal practice in D.C."

"Yes, sir."

"Welcome home, Ms. Curtis. It is heartening to see one local girl who has made good."

"Thank you."

Anna turned to Jody, but the officer tugged her away and led her back to the holding cell. Jody wouldn't be released until Anna secured the bail bond. It was a sharp reminder that, even though Anna had won her temporary release, Jody's life was controlled by the system now and would be until the case was over, even in the best possible scenario. In the worst scenario . . . Anna didn't want to think about that. She watched the heavy door close behind her sister.

The judge called the next case. Anna and Cooper walked out into the hallway. As they did, her phone buzzed. It was someone from the U.S. Attorney's Office, the caller ID showing the office's main number.

She answered. "Hello?"

"Sweetheart, hi."

Her heart lurched. His voice was warm and familiar—in many ways, more familiar than her own hometown. She felt homesick.

"Hi, Jack."

24

The morning after the coach attacked me, Mom could tell something was wrong. Over Cheerios, she asked me if I was okay. I said: *I'm fine*, in that voice teenagers use to communicate: *Nothing is fine, the world is crap, but I'm not telling you about it.* In fact, I was sore all over. But the physical pain was nothing compared to what was going on in my head. It was Sunday, so we went to church, where I was too numb to pray. When we got home, I locked myself in my room. Mom had worked the midnight shift at the hospital the night before and needed sleep. But she knocked on my door.

"What do you want?" I mumbled.

"What's wrong, Jody?"

"Nothing."

"Whatever's bothering you, you'll feel better if you talk about it."

"I *said*, nothing's wrong, Mom."

She let out the long sigh of a single mother working two jobs who isn't sure she has the energy also to handle her moody teen. "Fine."

Her footsteps faded away from my door. She went to sleep. When the house was still, I lay on my bed and stared up at my ceiling. I did that all day long, wondering how things would be different if I'd just said yes.

Would I still be in love with Coach Fowler? How long would it take for me to realize he was a monster? Is that what happened to Wendy? Did she know what she'd married?

I was still in bed that afternoon when Mom woke up. I heard her padding around the house, jiggling my door, then giving up. I got some small satisfaction out of locking her out of my room. At least I had *that* power.

After some shuffling, the house became quiet again. I got out of bed, stepped around the clothes still piled on my floor, and peeked out of my bedroom. Our tiny living room was empty. The Cheerio bowls were washed and sitting in the drying rack. Mom must've gone to work.

The next wave of despair hit me. I didn't want to be all alone again. I wished I'd let Mom in when she tried.

I saw a movement on the porch. She was sitting out there in one of those white plastic chairs, bundled in her winter jacket, smoking. She blew a stream of white-gray smoke into the white-gray sky. She was always trying to quit smoking but had to have "just one" whenever something particularly stressful went down. Which could be several times a day. I put on my coat over my pajamas and went out there.

She turned when she heard the door sliding along its track but didn't say anything, which was good. I sat in the other white plastic chair. There was just enough room for us and a plastic cup filled with soil and cigarette butts. Not owning an ashtray was Mom's way of pretending she wasn't really a smoker.

We also pretended that I didn't smoke, although she must've smelled it on me and known that I did what a lot of kids did: smoking at parties and occasionally on the south side of the school, where teachers couldn't see from the classrooms. Not a habit, not yet anyway, but often enough that I had a taste for it. Especially when something particularly stressful went down.

I didn't feel like pretending that day. I reached out for Mom's cigarette. She looked at me for a few seconds, then handed it over. I took a long drag and let the bittersweet smoke burn down to my lungs. I looked out past our balcony at the parking lot, a culvert, a skinny stand of trees, and the highway beyond. Everything was gray. I blew out the smoke and handed the cigarette back to Mom.

Then I laid my head on her shoulder and cried. She put her arm around my back and patted me softly, the way she used to when we were kids and she was trying to get us to sleep. I cried, and cried, and cried. I cried so much, I wondered if there was a limit to how many tears your eye ducts could produce, and when I would max out. She just stayed quiet and patted my back, and although I'd intended to never tell anyone, eventually it was all pouring out of me, between sobbing and hiccuping and wiping my nose. She listened quietly, until the whole story was out there. And then her first question was: "Why didn't you call *me* to the party at Devin's house?"

"Um. Well. I guess because I didn't have a crush on you."

We both laughed through our tears. But it was the truth, and because of that, I felt it was my fault. I had been jealous of Wendy and lusted after her husband. I had *dreamed* of him kissing me. I called him because I wanted him to rescue me, like I was some beautiful fucking princess and he was some handsome fucking knight. I was a dicktease.

"Jody, this is not your fault." Mom stabbed her cigarette into the soil-filled cup, where it crumpled among its fellow butts. "You're fifteen, he's forty. Lots of girls have a crush on their teacher—but a teacher can't do this. No matter what. But especially when you said no."

She shepherded me inside, where she nuked a mug of water for hot cocoa, then sat me on the couch while she made some phone calls. We ended up driving to the hospital where she worked.

I learned some new phrases that day, stuff that must be familiar to you. I met a "sexual assault nurse examiner." I learned that "stirrups" didn't just relate to horses. I added the terms "rape kit" and "vaginal swab" to my vocabulary. The nurse asked me a lot of questions, most of which were embarrassing to answer. But she seemed to be evaluating things from a technical, rather than a moral, standpoint. She was disappointed that I had taken a shower, because that washed away a lot of evidence. But she said that since Coach hadn't used a condom, his semen might still be found inside of me. She said it can stay inside a woman's body for up to seventy-two hours.

She told Mom not to touch my clothes from the night before, that the police would come to our house to collect them. She gave me some white pills to prevent diseases and a yellow pill to prevent pregnancy. The whole process took a couple hours. They let Mom stay with me. She held my hand the whole time. It wasn't a day in the park, that hospital visit, but it wasn't so terrible, either.

It wasn't until Mom drove me to the Holly Grove police station that I had the experience so many rape survivors talk about: the feeling that I was raped all over again.

25

t's so good to hear your voice," Jack said.

"Yours, too," Anna said, although she wasn't ready to talk to him. Her reaction right now was why. Because now that she heard his voice, she wanted to drive straight to the airport and book the next flight back to D.C.

She looked at Cooper, who was still standing next to her in the courthouse hallway. There was no reason to feel strange, talking to Jack in front of Cooper. But she did. Cooper seemed to understand; he gave her a little wave and walked to the men's room. She sat on a bench.

"Marty sent me your e-mail this morning," Jack said. "We had a long talk, the result of which is: he's going to give you the green light. You can represent your sister while keeping your job here, and you can work remotely from the Appellate section in the meantime. The approval is being written up now."

She knew Jack had convinced Marty. The U.S. Attorney never would have allowed this without Jack's prodding. Anna had spent an hour last night filling out forms to get temporary health insurance to cover her when she quit today. She started crying from relief.

"Shh, baby," Jack said. "It'll be okay. Do you want me to come out to Michigan and be there for you? I can take some time off work."

"No, no. Don't do that." Anna fumbled around her purse looking for a tissue. "How's Olivia?"

"She's good. She misses you. Almost as much as I do."

"I miss her, too," Anna said. "And you."

"Do you want to come home, spend a few nights, and pack whatever you need to tide you over for the next few weeks? It seems like you're going to be in Michigan for a while."

Home. That sounded so good. She wanted Jack to hold her. She wanted to open her own arms, have Olivia fly into them, and bury her head in the sweet smell of the little girl's hair.

She asked, "Has anything changed with your . . . situation?"

"Mm." Jack cleared his throat and paused. "Not really. You were wiser than me. I did need time to sort things out. I'm sorting."

She imagined the "sorting" and felt a little sick. She pictured him kissing another woman. She imagined him looking into the other woman's eyes as he laid her back in his bed. Anna's chest tightened painfully.

She said, "I better stay here in Michigan. If I e-mail you a list of things, would you mind sending them to Jody's house?"

"Of course. Let me know if there's anything else I can do."

"Thanks. Well. Good luck with everything."

"You too."

"Bye, Jack." She hung up before an accidental "I love you" slipped out. She sat back and closed her eyes.

"You okay?" Cooper asked a few minutes later.

She opened her eyes, stood up, and straightened her spine. "I got the DOJ approval. That's the important thing."

Out on the courthouse steps, three local reporters came up to her. One guy held a video camera.

"Did she do it?" asked a journalist.

Anna stopped walking and looked at the camera.

"My sister is completely innocent. She is a gentle soul, a good person, and one of the kindest women I've ever known. She wouldn't hurt a fly. I don't know how the police could have come to the conclusion that she would hurt Coach Fowler, but with all due respect to them, that is completely wrong. I know there is a tendency to assume the worst when someone is charged with a crime like this, but I would ask the people of Holly Grove to reserve judgment."

"Was she romantically involved with the coach?"

"Where was she on the night of his death?"

"Is it true that she works at GM? So she has expert knowledge of cars?"

Anna wasn't getting into specifics now. If she only said a few sentences, that would be the sound bite the TV stations would play tonight. She could control the message by saying only what she wanted heard. She ignored the rest of the questions and walked down the steps. But she knew that she'd have to answer all of them soon.

26

That night, Anna waited in the parking lot outside the central cell block for Jody to be released. Cooper waited with her, and she was grateful. Several prisoners had come out over the last few hours, but there was no sign of Jody. The warm summer air smelled of asphalt and broken people. She and Cooper sat on a bench facing the tall chain-link fence, watching the sun set behind the monolithic brick building. Cooper put an arm around her shoulders. She tensed, then relaxed and rested her head against his shoulder. She was grateful to find anything solid in Holly Grove.

The sky was dark when the chain-link gates finally slid apart and the facility's large metal door creaked open. Jody looked worn and pale as she walked out the gate.

Anna stood and wrapped her sister in a hug. Jody laid her head on Anna's shoulder and cried. Anna's own chest tightened. She was the only thing standing between her sister and thousands of nights behind a fence like this one. They said good-bye to Cooper and drove home in the darkness.

"Did you get hurt in lockup?" Anna asked.

"No," Jody said. "But I desperately need a shower. Can the ankle bracelet get wet?"

Anna didn't know. The question didn't come up on the prosecution side of things. "It must be able to get wet," she concluded. "You're supposed to have it on all the time. If it breaks, it's not your fault."

"I'm not so much worried about it breaking as it electrocuting me."

When they got to Jody's house, Anna watched her sister's first few moments of showering, to make sure she didn't get fried. The bracelet's red light blinked continually and Jody didn't get shocked. Anna left a towel on the cabinet and gave her sister some privacy.

Afterward, Jody wanted to go right to bed, but Anna forced her to eat some soup first. "You have to take care of yourself," she said. And that baby, she thought.

After the soup, Jody stood. "I can't wait to sleep in my own bed."

Anna wanted to ask her a hundred questions, but she knew they could wait. "Good night, Jody."

Anna watched her walk down the hall. She was too keyed up herself to sleep, which was fine. Now that her sister had been charged, she would be able to get a lot of the information the police had. As a suspect, Jody wasn't entitled to anything. As a defendant, she was.

Anna made some tea and turned on Jody's computer. She wrote a letter to the prosecutor, requesting every item to which she was entitled under Michigan's discovery rules, and more. All the police paperwork on the case, the criminal history of the defendant and victim, DNA testing results, expert reports, witness statements, grand jury transcripts, the video of Rob interrogating Jody. She requested the opportunity to look at all the items the police had taken from Jody's house during the search warrant. She asked for a recording of any 911 calls made from the coach's houses over the last ten years. She asked for the name of every police officer on the case, and for their disciplinary records. She named Rob Gargaron in particular.

When she tried to print the letter, Jody's printer jammed. Anna's attempts to fix it only made it groan and release a burnt-rubber scent. The machine looked to be ten years old and was covered in dust. Jody manufactured cars for a living. Her garage was full of wrenches and drills, but she didn't use much ink. Anna worked with words. She didn't own a drill but couldn't go a week without a printer.

Anna went to Meijer, which was open twenty-four hours, and

wandered through the deserted aisles, picking out a new printer, ink cartridges, reams of paper, and legal pads. If she was going to represent Jody, she needed to be able to run her own little legal shop out of Jody's spare bedroom. She also grabbed an extralarge bag of Starbucks Italian Roast.

Back at the house, she set up the guest bedroom until it resembled an office. When there was nothing else she could do—at around two A.M.—she finally changed into pajamas and lay down on the air mattress. She lay awake for a long time.

She awoke the next morning to the roar of a vacuum cleaner. She moaned, shuffled out of her bedroom, and found Jody, bright eyed and dressed, vacuuming the hallway.

"Why?" Anna asked groggily. "Couldn't you have waited a few more hours?"

"It's disgusting from all the police in here. They left crap all over. I want to erase every trace of those thugs invading my home."

Anna closed her eyes and nodded. "Did you make coffee?"

"In the kitchen."

The house smelled of artificial lemon and Pine-Sol. The living room carpet was scored with neat rows from a fresh vacuuming. A rag and a bottle of Fantastik sat on top of a counter. Jody was scrubbing the police off the house, while wearing an ankle bracelet. The actual dirt might be gone, but they had a long way to go to clear the mud from her name.

Later that morning, as Anna cleaned out the coffeepot, Jody sat at the shining kitchen table, called her ob-gyn, and made an appointment. When she hung up, she turned to Anna.

"I'm not sure what I'm gonna do with this baby," Jody said. "But I want to explore my options. I've heard good things about open adoption."

Anna nodded. "Can I come with you to your doctor's appointment?"

"That would be great, Annie."

"Do you want to contact the father and let him know?"

"I told you. There is no father."

Jody pursed her lips and left the kitchen. Anna swallowed a wave of anger. She'd been willing to quit her job to protect Jody—and Jody wouldn't even tell her who the father of her child was. Anna set the carafe down on the counter so hard it cracked. The web of fissures in the glass reminded her of the Corvette's windshield.

■ ■ ■

Over the next few days, they settled into a routine. Jody's wrist healed enough that she went back to work at the GM plant. Anna started working on appellate briefs that the U.S. Attorney's Office sent. Her work was all research and writing: recapping the trials and arguing why the convictions should stand. While Jody was at the plant, the house was totally silent. Anna could go all day without using her voice.

Her first three appellate cases involved three sex-offense convictions: a priest who assaulted his altar boys, an ice-cream man who molested local kids, and an uncle who raped his niece. When Anna was in college, she and her friends had worried about a stranger jumping out of the bushes to rape them. Now that she was a prosecutor, she knew that predators were far more likely to be someone the victim knew and trusted. They used that trust to gain access. These days, Anna worried less about someone breaking in through a window, and more about who she allowed through her front door.

She enjoyed crafting the appellate briefs, knowing her work would help keep these predators off the streets. She missed the buzz and collegiality of her office—but there was a certain relief to being far away. If she were in the office, she'd be dealing with the gossip and sympathy from her wedding being called off. She'd have to see Jack in the hallways. This felt like a different world, and Anna didn't mind being in a different world for now. She wondered if Cooper felt that way, too.

In the evenings, after Jody came home, the sisters ate dinner, talked, and watched old movies. As long as they didn't talk about the case or Jody's pregnancy, their time together felt a bit like a vacation. Anna tried to savor it. If Jody went to jail, it would be a long time before they got to hang out again.

The first time the doorbell rang in the middle of the afternoon, Anna's heartbeat sped up; the last doorbell ended with her sister's arrest. But now it was a FedEx package arriving for her signature. It was from the Holly Grove DA's office. She signed and ripped it open while the delivery guy was still walking back to his truck.

As she read it, the fear crept back in. It was the autopsy report. She parsed through the technical language, extracting a few key points. As Rob had confided, the coroner concluded that Owen Fowler's cause of death was not the car accident, but blunt force trauma to the head that occurred prior to the crash. Anna looked at the pictures and diagrams and saw why. The coach's skull had two areas of fracture. One was his forehead, in the area you would expect would hit the windshield. But the other was the left side of his skull. And that area was more badly fractured. Anna looked at the attached pictures. It showed long, straight indentations in the side of the coach's charred skull. A few of the indentations appeared to have been made by something with a square corner. The coroner estimated that Owen Fowler had been struck at least six times with something that was not part of the car.

The coroner was unable to tell what time the coach died. By the time the fire was put out, his body had been completely exsanguinated—his blood burned away. His flesh was mostly gone, leaving a charred black skeleton. However, his eyeballs had remained intact. Protected inside his skull, they survived the heat of the blaze. The coroner was able to extract some liquid from them and determine that there was the presence of both alcohol and metabolites for the drug gamma-hydroxybutyrate, also known as GHB.

Alcohol was expected, although the coroner couldn't determine how much the coach had been drinking. Fluid in the eye didn't provide a blood alcohol level like blood did. Nor could the coroner determine how much GHB the coach had in his system or when he'd ingested it. Fluid in the eyeball held on to chemicals for longer than blood did, and for an uncertain time.

Anna was familiar with GHB. In her experience, she saw it used for two purposes. One was as a date-rape drug, which if taken in sufficient quantity, could make a person black out. The other was as a steroid substitute for athletes, who used it to build muscle. Both purposes were illegal—it was a controlled substance with no legal use. The coroner didn't speculate on how or when the GHB got into the coach's system.

Anna's cell phone rang from her pocket. She looked up. She was still standing in her sister's front vestibule; she had read the whole document right there. She answered her phone.

"Hello?"

"May I speak to Anna Curtis?"

"This is."

"Hello, Ms. Curtis, this is Desiree Williams, from the Holly Grove DA's Office."

"Oh, hi. I just got your package. You can call me Anna."

"Call me Desiree. I understand you're a prosecutor in D.C.?"

"Yes."

They talked about their backgrounds. Desiree had graduated from the University of Michigan Law School a few years before Anna had graduated from Harvard Law. They both had been debaters in college and knew a few of the same people.

"Small world," Anna said. In slightly different circumstances, they would have been colleagues, friends. Now, this woman was trying to put her sister in jail. "I'm glad you called. The autopsy report noted the presence of GHB in the coach's system. I wondered if the government has a theory on that?"

"Yes," Desiree said. "It seems that he used the substance to build muscle. His wife says he was always diligent about staying in shape, and in recent years he started to try . . . alternative methods."

"Thanks," Anna said. The prosecutor had no obligation to tell her that.

"You're welcome. But the reason I'm calling is to discuss your discovery requests. I'll obviously give you everything required under the rules. But some of these requests—I don't see a basis for them. For example, the 911 calls from the coach's house."

"So there *are* some?"

"Nothing that involves your sister."

"They involve his wife?"

"I'm not getting into that. I've listened to them and they're not relevant."

"If they involve his wife, they are relevant. My theory is that his wife killed him. Anything that would give her a motive to do so is *Brady* material and should be turned over to me."

"You're going to put the poor family through this?"

"I'm thinking about my own poor family," Anna said.

"There's absolutely no evidence that Wendy Fowler hurt her husband."

"The jury can decide that."

Anna didn't have much to support her theory, yet. But the *Brady* case required prosecutors to turn over any material exculpatory evidence. Even if the prosecutor didn't think it was exculpatory, she risked having her conviction overturned on appeal if she didn't turn over evidence that could support a defense theory that someone else did it. By staking out this position early on, Anna was trying to expand the information the prosecution would have to give her.

It worked. Late one afternoon the following week, the doorbell rang again. This time the FedEx envelope was marked with the words: *FRAGILE, DO NOT BEND*. Anna opened the package and pulled out a letter from Desiree Williams and an attached silver disk marked *Holly Grove Police Communications*. It was a recording of all the 911 calls from the coach's house.

Anna tried not to get too excited. The calls could be nothing: a cat caught in a tree or a downed power line. But she'd found, amid the ocean of lies she had to navigate in every case, 911 calls could be tiny islands of truth.

She slid the CD into Jody's computer.

27

After the sex-assault exam at the hospital, the nurse told Mom to take me to the Holly Grove police station to file a report. The nurse said she'd notified the police that we were coming. No one seemed to be expecting us at the station, though. Mom and I sat in those plastic chairs in the lobby for a couple hours. I remember it was decorated for Christmas, and the cardboard Santas were the only ones who smiled at us.

Eventually a young officer led us back through the cubicles to an actual office with a door. The laminated wood name tag announced the office of Sergeant Herb Gargaron, your boyfriend Rob's father.

He was eating a massive roast beef sandwich from Arby's and surfing the Net. I stood in the doorway, staring at him. I did *not* want to talk to him. I didn't want to tell Rob's dad about the sloppy fight Rob and I had the night before. More important, I didn't want everyone in town to know what happened between me and the coach. Once Rob knew, I was afraid he'd tell all the other kids.

"Is . . . is there a different policeman I can talk to?"

"Sorry, missy, you don't get to pick your officer," Sergeant Gargaron said with a forced chuckle. He looked like an older, fatter, more highly decorated version of his son. He wrapped his half sandwich in the foil and gestured for me to take a seat. The office smelled like sweat and curly fries. I realized I hadn't eaten anything since breakfast, and it was dark outside now. I felt hungry and sick at the same time.

Today, I would know how to handle myself in that situation. I would have politely refused to talk to Sergeant Gargaron, saying the reasons were personal. I might have joked about not wanting to interrupt his dinner. I might say I was more comfortable with a female detective. I would definitely hold my ground. But that night, I was a kid.

I sat. So did Mom.

Sergeant Gargaron folded his hands together on the desk. "How can I help you?"

I had no idea. It was not a question with a clear answer. This wasn't McDonald's, where you could order a number 3 with Sprite.

I looked around the office. A big trout was mounted on one wall, near a picture of the sergeant standing proudly with Rob, two rifles, and a dead twelve-point buck. On the other wall hung a Holly Grove football pennant and four framed pictures of the team, one for each year Rob had played.

"We need to make a report," Mom said.

"Go ahead, then." He had a blue Holly Grove football ribbon pinned on his chest, just above his badge and over his heart. Mom patted my arm, signaling for me to talk, but I shook my head. I couldn't make the words come out.

So Mom told my story, piece by piece, occasionally turning to me to confirm that she was getting a detail right. Sergeant Gargaron did not move his hands from their folded position on his desk. I hadn't told Mom the part about Rob, and so she did not tell his father. After she finished, he opened a notebook.

"So let me get this right," he said. "Your daughter is the one who called Coach Fowler, correct?"

"Yes," Mom said.

He took the cap off a ballpoint pen, touched the tip to his meaty tongue, and finally jotted something in his notebook.

"Your daughter didn't call you?"

"I was at work."

"You do have a cell phone."

"Yes."

"Mm hm. Coach Fowler allegedly went to this party at your daughter's request."

"Yes."

"He drove her home at her request too."

"I . . . suppose you could say that."

"Although no one saw her leave with him."

"I'm not sure." She looked at me. I shrugged and shook my head. Another jot in the notebook.

"When she came home, she didn't tell anyone what allegedly happened?"

"No one was home. I told you, I was working."

"Mm hm." Another mark in the notebook. "In fact, she showered and went to bed?"

"Yes."

"And then had breakfast in the morning? Without telling you anything?"

"Yes, and then we went to church." Mom started to sound annoyed.

"Where she didn't mention the alleged incident to anyone. Not even to your minister? Or her Sunday school teacher?"

"She doesn't go to Sunday school anymore. She's fifteen."

"Just the facts, ma'am."

"That is a fact."

He frowned and wrote the longest entry yet in his notebook, as if my waning religious education or Mom's snark were the most important pieces of information in the case.

"And you say she was a virgin."

I wanted the chair to swallow me up.

"Yes. But I don't see how that matters."

He turned and picked up a faxed sheaf of papers. "This is the report from the sexual-assault nurse." He handed it over to Mom. I glanced over her shoulder and saw from the time stamp that he had received it more than two hours earlier. I wondered if he'd deliberately made us wait those last two hours. He said, "Page five." Mom flipped to page five. I gaped at the picture. It was a huge diagram of a vagina.

"You'll see that the nurse noted there was no vaginal tearing, no intact hymen, and no indication that Jody's hymen was recently punctured."

"What are you saying?"

"There's no evidence that Jody was a virgin who was deflowered last night."

Deflowered? What was I, a daisy? If so, I was the most mortified daisy in this garden. My petals would have all fallen off the moment I had to start discussing my vagina with Herb Gargaron.

Mom cleared her throat. "It's my understanding that a girl can lose her hymen before having sex."

"Maybe so. It can also indicate that your daughter was not being entirely truthful. You know, she might not want to tell you if she'd had sex before."

I sunk in my chair. This was a nightmare.

"Now you listen here, sir," Mom's hands were clenched so tight, the papers crumpled. "This is not about my daughter's chastity or choices she might have made with boys her own age. This is about what Coach Fowler did to her last night."

"No offense intended, ma'am," Sergeant Gargaron said, with condescending calm. "I'm just pointing out the evidence in the case. In a he-said-she-said like this, the victim's credibility becomes very important. Any evidence that she lied about, well, anything, could be very damaging. I'm not trying to tell you what to do. But you should know: questions will be asked. You might not like the answers. You should consider how your daughter's name will be tarnished if she decides to pursue this claim."

He sucked on the straw in the Arby's cup, pulling up the last inch of pop with a long, strangled slurp. He gestured for her to give him back the papers. She obeyed. Her hands were shaking; her voice, too. "I assume she'll get a victim's advocate? Someone who can counsel her besides you?"

"Ah, a victim's advocate." Sergeant Gargaron smiled. His eyes were as small and mean as Rob's. "I almost forgot. You know the system quite well, don't you, Mrs. Curtis? As I recall, you were a frequent flier in our domestic violence program for a while."

I hadn't thought about it, but Mom probably came to this very station a few years before, after Dad was arrested for the Big One. Plus, there were all the times she'd called 911 on Dad for hitting her before that. She probably knew many of the officers in the station, but not in the way she knew people in the hospital. There, she was a respected colleague, the med tech who could draw blood from patients with even the tiniest veins. Here, she was just a "victim."

We tend to rise or sink toward others' expectations of us. It takes a lot of conscious will not to. Although she'd gotten stronger since Dad left, Mom seemed to grow smaller in her chair.

"It's one thing to go making accusations about your husband," Sergeant Gargaron said. "But it's another thing to accuse a respected man. A pillar of this town. You might find there are more drawbacks than benefits to yourself this time."

"I am not making this up," I said. "And neither is my mom."

His eyes slid toward me. "*I* would never say you made it up. I'm just telling you: other people might."

"What he did was wrong." Mom's voice was quiet. "We want to press charges."

"I'll note that in the file." He sighed loudly. "But I just take the reports. The DA makes the final decision on cases like this. We'll let you know."

Sergeant Gargaron stood up. The meeting was over. As we showed ourselves out, he sat down with a grunt and started unwrapping the remains of his Arby's sandwich.

The police didn't come to our apartment to collect my clothes that night.

28

Windows Media Player showed four different tracks, which meant that there were four different 911 recordings from the coach's house. Anna clicked on the first one. An audio recording began.

"911 Emergency," said a male operator. "Do you need police, fire, or ambulance?"

"Police," a woman sobbed. A baby cried near the phone, too. "Maybe an ambulance."

The operator got her address. Several words had to be repeated because of all the crying. Then he asked her name.

"This is Wendy Fowler."

"What's going on, ma'am?"

Her words were obscured by the sound of banging and a male voice yelling. Wendy screamed louder. "He hit me. My husband punched me in the face, and he pushed me down, and I'm scared that he's going to hurt me more. He's very, very drunk."

"Where is he, ma'am?"

"He's outside the door!" More banging. "I'm locked in the bathroom with my baby daughter!"

"Does your husband have any weapons, ma'am?"

"No. I mean, yes, he owns a couple guns, but I don't think he's got them now."

The banging continued and the yelling got louder. The baby squealed again.

"Please hurry," Wendy cried.

"Yes, ma'am, stay calm, a unit has been dispatched and should be there any minute."

He stayed on the line with her for another three minutes, during which Coach Fowler yelled and Wendy sobbed. His slurred words were mostly indecipherable, with the occasional "bitch," "whore,' and "fuck you up" loud enough to be heard. Then there were two more male voices.

"Sir, sir, calm down. We're here to help you and your wife."

"Back away from the door, sir."

The recording ended. Anna felt a sick sense of familiarity. In her job, she had heard countless phone calls like this one. Growing up she had, too.

She clicked on the next recording, then the next. They were all similar, Wendy calling the police because her husband was beating her and she was afraid he'd get more violent. As the dates of the recordings progressed, the baby changed into a little girl, who expressed her fear in words instead of baby cries. Anna stopped at one part and played it again. "Please come before Daddy kills Mommy!"

Anna shuddered. She looked at the attached paperwork, which listed the dates and times of the calls. Wendy had dialed 911 from her house four times over the course of her ten-year marriage.

Anna looked up and saw Jody standing in the doorway. Anna had been so engrossed in the tapes she hadn't heard her sister returning home from work.

"Is that Wendy and the coach?" Jody asked.

"Yeah," Anna said.

"God, that's horrible."

"Did you know he abused her?"

"No one knew."

"Did he ever do this to you?"

"No." Jody shook her head. "He was a perfect gentleman."

Anna suspected there were even more violent incidents, but Wendy only called when she needed someone to physically restrain her husband from *continuing* an assault. If he just hit her and walked away, she didn't call the police. This was someone who wanted to keep things private.

Most likely, Wendy forgave him afterward. That's how it worked in most cases. In 80 percent of domestic assaults, the victim didn't want to press charges. It wasn't like a mugging: the victim often was in love with her assailant. She might blame herself for "causing" the assault. And in Wendy's situation, where all the money and power in the relationship was held by the coach, she would have even more incentive not to take him to court.

But in the end, Wendy *had* consulted a divorce lawyer. Anna took the CD out of the computer and held it up. "We just found your defense."

"Ugh. I don't want that, Annie."

"Why not? Let the blame go where the blame goes."

"I want you to defend me. But I don't want to drag someone else into this. I wouldn't wish this on my worst enemy."

"She *is* your worst enemy."

"She's more similar to us than different. She's just a woman trying to live her life." Jody pointed to the CD. "How can you want to hurt her after hearing that? Don't you feel sorry for her? And her daughter?"

"I do. But I also think Wendy might have killed him. Don't you?"

"I don't know, but I don't want to put Wendy or her kid through any more than I already have."

"We're not putting her through anything. We're not charging her with a crime. We're just saying someone else had a motive to kill the man."

"We don't need to destroy her to win. I didn't kill the coach. They won't be able to prove I killed him. There won't be any evidence, because I didn't do it."

"The system doesn't always reach the right result," Anna said softly. And, she thought, *I'm not even sure what the right result is.*

"But I've got you on my side," Jody said. "So this time it will."

29

On a warm Tuesday afternoon a few days after Jody's arrest, Anna got a call from Rob.

"Hello?" she answered.

"You're asking for my disciplinary record?"

"And anything else I can cross-examine you on."

"Anna, you have to realize, this is not about me. This is about Jody."

"Sure. She's the one facing life in prison—because of you."

"No, because she killed Coach Fowler. You act like she's some innocent little dove."

"She's not a dove. She is innocent."

"Meet me today," Rob said. "I'll show you something. Then tell me if you still think she's innocent."

Anna paused. Her gut clenched at the thought of meeting him. She was always telling women to trust their instincts. She thought of the many times she had said, *Trust that feeling in the pit of your stomach. If your body is telling you not to meet with a guy, don't do it.* But she needed whatever information she could get.

"Okay," she said.

He told her where and when. The pit in her stomach deepened. She called Jody but didn't get through. Anna left a voice mail telling her sister where she was going.

She followed Google Maps' directions to the address Rob gave her: a building in downtown Detroit. There was no problem finding parking on Washington Street. Tall buildings rose up around her, most of them unoccupied. She pulled to the curb right in front of the address, turned off the car, and looked around in amazement.

The Metropolitan Building was a fifteen-story neo-Gothic tower that had obviously been abandoned years ago. Its windows were either glassless and open to the air or boarded over in plywood. Multiple layers of graffiti covered the bottom. Anna got out of the car. Instead of city sounds, she heard only insects and a faraway siren.

The glass doors to the lobby were all boarded up. She was only slightly surprised to find one of them propped open. She walked into an entrance hall that had been completely gutted. Shattered bits of plaster and glass covered the floor, and the wind whistled through holes that used to be windows. Wires hung from the ceiling. Rob stood in the middle of the lobby, looking at her quietly. She suppressed a shudder and walked up to him.

"Hey, Rob. You always knew how to show a girl a good time," she said. "This is . . . extraordinary."

"I can't be seen talking to you like this. Here, there's solitude."

She walked over to a glassless window and looked out. She could see the Detroit River flowing a few blocks away. On the other side of the river was Windsor, Canada. It was a pretty view, gray and green, surreal to see from an abandoned skyscraper.

"You want to go up?" Rob said. "The view is worth the hike."

She looked at him. She saw no malice in his face. And she did want to see this.

"Yeah," she said.

Rob smiled. "There's the Anna I knew."

She followed him up a stairwell. Anna had no problem going up fifteen stories—she ran miles every day at home—although Rob was winded by the end. But he must have done this before, because he knew exactly where to go. He led her through a grim, graffiti-covered hallway to another set of stairs, and up to a deck marked ROOFTOP.

He pushed through the door, and Anna found herself on the top of the tall building. She could see a 360-degree view of Detroit from up here. It was incredible. The river shimmered to the east, with flat Windsor sprawling as far as the eye could see beyond it. The Renaissance Center was a few blocks away, tall, gleaming, only half occupied. And she could see the rest of the buildings of Detroit, dozens of which were abandoned. It was like looking at archaeological ruins, standing before Machu Picchu or the Roman Forum.

"Wow," Anna said. She walked to the edge and looked down. There was no one down there. Several blocks away, inland, she saw a rectangular patch of green, with trees planted in neat, symmetrical rows. She realized she was looking at Cooper's farm. It was one of the small patches of life in an otherwise decimated landscape.

She could feel Rob coming up behind her. His meaty hand was on her shoulder. She tensed, realizing how alone they were, how little effort it would take to push her over the ledge.

"I'm sorry things ended badly, ten years ago," he said. "I always felt bad about that."

She turned slowly and met his eyes. She couldn't gauge his intentions. She stepped back, away from him and the ledge.

"It's okay," she said. "It's just one of those things. Growing up."

He turned to face her and rested his rear on the ledge. "Yeah. But I didn't behave very well as it was happening. I shouldn't have called you those names. I'm sorry about that."

He wasn't going to push her. She half thought he wanted to kiss her.

"I'm sorry too," she said.

He ran his thumb over his mustache. "But I want you to know: this isn't because of us. I hate to be in this position. But your sister is not the saint you think she is."

"You keep saying that. Do you have anything to back it up?"

He reached into his pocket, pulled out a folded piece of paper, and handed it to her. She was starting to dread every time Rob showed her a piece of paper. She looked at him as she unfolded it. Someone had put an evidence bag on a Xerox machine and made a color copy. The bag was clear and Anna could see that inside it was a single white athletic sock. On the sock were several rust-colored stains, ranging in size from pinprick to lima bean.

Anna recognized bloodstains. Most of these were long and teardrop shaped. The pattern indicated that the blood had landed on the sock after the liquid flew through the air, launched at fairly high speed. It was the sort of pattern that happened during stabbings or beatings, where blood flew off the victim onto the assailant. The pit in Anna's stomach became a sinkhole.

"What's this from?" she asked, although she could guess.

"That was found in your sister's home," Rob said. "Behind the washing machine. No other clothes had blood on them. We think she washed everything else, but overlooked this one."

Anna started to make arguments about all the reasons there might be a few bloodstains on a sock in Jody's house. But she wouldn't be standing here if it were Jody's blood.

"You tested it?"

"The blood is Coach Fowler's. You'll get the full DNA results from the prosecutor in a few weeks. But I wanted to tell you now. For old times' sake. And because you deserve to know what you're defending."

He was looking at Anna with pity, which was far worse than anger. She liked the world better when Rob was a bad guy from whom she had to defend her sister. If her sister was the bad guy, and Rob was just a beleaguered public servant trying to do his job . . . she didn't know where she fit in that world. She stepped next to Rob, put her hands on the ledge, and threw up over the side.

30

B y the time she got back to Jody's house, Anna had already come up with multiple scenarios where Coach Fowler's blood got on Jody's sock in a perfectly innocent way. One thing Anna had learned as a sex-crimes prosecutor was: fluids are exchanged in romantic relationships. One speck of blood does not a murder case make.

The coach had probably been to Jody's house many times. He could have cut himself while slicing an apple, for example, and if Jody had been standing near him, his blood easily could have dripped onto her sock. He might have slipped while clipping his toenails, and . . . Jody had been sitting next to him, their feet touching. Maybe he had a nosebleed . . . right onto Jody's sock. Each theory grew less plausible, but Anna kept spinning them out, rolling her mind over each scenario like a penitent rolling her fingers over rosary beads, for comfort and with a little prayer.

Her prayers weren't answered. Later that afternoon, as she sat at her computer trying to concentrate on an appellate brief, Desiree Williams called.

"I'm calling about some more discovery issues," the prosecutor said. "You requested every case involving the decedent or the defendant. There are six cases involving Coach Fowler, but they've all been filed under seal. And there's no reason to unseal them now, except for one."

"Why is that?"

"It involves both the defendant and the decedent."

"Jody and Coach Fowler?"

"Yes. Ten years ago, your sister accused him of sexually assaulting her."

"What?"

That couldn't be true. Anna would know about it if it were true. She calculated back; ten years ago, Anna had been in her freshman year at college. Jody would have been a sophomore at Holly Grove High School. It was possible that something happened to Jody that Anna wasn't present for. But Anna couldn't believe Jody wouldn't tell her.

"I take it you didn't know about that?" Desiree asked.

Anna didn't want to answer and make herself a witness in her sister's case. "Were charges brought?" she replied.

"The case was declined."

"What was the basis for the declination?"

"Complainant did not wish to press charges."

"Why not?"

"You'll have to ask her that. I'll e-mail you the file and you'll have everything I have."

A few minutes after they hung up, Anna had a PDF of the police report on her computer. It was a witness statement form dated December 4, 2004. The complainant was listed as Jody Curtis; the suspect was Owen Fowler. Their DOBs were listed, showing Jody was fifteen at the time and the coach was forty. The text of the report was two sentences long.

> **CW reports that S-1 had vaginal intercourse with her while in S-1's car. The event took place at approximately 23:30 hours on 12/3/04.**

CW was shorthand for "complaining witness"—Jody—while S-1 stood for "Subject #1"—the coach. A line had been drawn diagonally across the entire report, above which was an illegible signature and the handwritten words CW *not cooperative, doesn't want to press charges.*

Anna had seen similar reports hundreds of times. Whenever someone told the police about a crime, the police were supposed to write it up and present the paperwork to a prosecutor, who would decide whether to bring charges, decline charges, or investigate further. A common reason for declining a sex-assault case was because the victim didn't wish to press charges or wouldn't cooperate.

But in the case of a sexual assault of a *child*, more work should have been done, even if the child wasn't cooperative. Here, the prosecutor might have been able to make the case if Jody had gone to the hospital and had a sex kit done, and they found the coach's semen. Just the presence of his semen and their two birth certificates would be enough—even if Jody had "consented"—because consent was not a defense to statutory rape. But there was no indication that any other work had been done.

Anna printed the report and stared at it for a while. Each time she learned another fact about the coach's death, Anna had the sensation of being a boat with a deep keel. Each bit of evidence against Jody knocked her to the side, almost capsizing her. But her deep belief in her sister eventually righted her, as she found a way to fit the information into a narrative where her sister was innocent. But what Anna learned today swamped her.

A monstrous theory began to form in her mind. She tried to push the idea away, but the more she fought it, the bigger it grew.

■ ■ ■

When Jody came home that night, Anna was sitting at the kitchen table waiting for her. The evening was still light; Michigan is on the western edge of the Eastern time zone, and the sky doesn't get dark until after ten P.M. in the summer. Jody wore jeans, a T-shirt, and hiking boots, her usual work attire.

"Hey, sis." Jody took the last sip of a yogurt smoothie and threw the plastic bottle into the recycling bin. "I got your voice mail. Glad to see you made it back from your date with Rob. Did he try to kiss you at the end?"

Anna shook her head and didn't smile.

"Uh-oh." Jody said. "What's wrong?"

Anna had two pieces of paper lined up in front of her. She slid the first across the table. It was the 2004 police report of Coach Fowler's assault. Jody sat down next to Anna and looked at the report. She read the handwriting aloud: "'CW not cooperative, doesn't want to press charges.'" She made a sound halfway between a laugh and a sob.

"What happened, Jo?" Anna asked.

Jody looked out the window. "We had sex. Mom found out. She made me go to the police. It was considered an assault because I was fifteen. But I didn't want to press charges, I guess. So they dropped it."

"Why didn't you want to press charges?"

Jody looked out the window. "Because I loved him."

"Why didn't you tell me ten years ago? Or any time since? For example, when I moved to Michigan to represent you because you were charged with his murder?"

"Oh, Annie," Jody met her eyes, looking pained. "You were always the golden girl. The smart one, the one who was going to make it out of here. Ten years ago, you were doing so well at college. You'd come home with these stories about parties, and clubs, and the debate team, and I thought you were living the most glamorous life. I didn't want any more evidence that I was the fuckup sister. The bad one. I didn't want your sympathy or pity. I still don't."

Anna felt like she had the wind knocked out of her.

"Have you been seeing him since you were fifteen?"

"No. We lost touch after he got married. We just reconnected the last month or so."

"Was he angry about this?" Anna touched the report.

"No. He knew it was a stupid thing Mom made me do. He didn't blame me. He never got in trouble for it anyway."

Anna had met plenty of underage statutory rape victims who didn't consider themselves "victims" at all, but simply the "girlfriend" of their adult assailant. But she had a hard time believing Jody was one of them.

She leaned forward. "Jody, I need you to tell me everything. Now. If I'm going to defend you, I need to know everything about your relationship with the coach. There can't be any more surprises."

"Okay, Annie. I'm sorry. There isn't anything else, honestly."

Honestly again. Anna shook her head, her anger growing. She slid the second paper across to Jody. It was the picture of the bloody sock. Jody looked at it calmly. Anna had to hand it to her: Jody had a good poker face.

"What's this?" Jody asked.

"The police found this sock behind your washing machine. It's covered in specks of Coach Fowler's blood."

"Huh!" Jody said, in the way that someone responds to an interesting but minor tidbit, like: *Did you know that girl is double-jointed? Huh!*

Anna stayed silent for several minutes. Most people felt the need to fill gaps in a conversation and would rush in with words. Police could often get good answers simply by waiting for them. Anna hated the fact that she was using interrogation techniques with her sister. Worse—her sister didn't fall for them. It was pissing Anna off. She shouldn't have to dig through a haystack of lies to find the needle of truth.

Anna finally broke the silence. "Any idea how his blood might have gotten on your sock?"

Jody shrugged. "Maybe he cut himself while he was at my house."

"Well, did he cut himself or didn't he? You were the one with him." Anna's voice was too loud. "I don't need a theory here. To defend you, I need to know what actually happened between the two of you. It can't come as a surprise from the government. Tell me what we're up against."

Jody looked back down at the paper and studied it for a long time. Finally, she looked up at Anna. "He cut himself. Definitely."

"How?" Anna fought the urge to cross her arms on her chest.

"Opening a can."

"A can of what?"

"Beer."

"Do you still have that can?"

"Yeah, I saved it right next to my little blue dress with the President's jizz on it."

"You're gonna laugh yourself right into prison."

"Look, I probably recycled it weeks ago, okay?"

"Don't lie to me!"

"Don't judge me! I'm always going to come up short of you. You're the smart one."

"Gimme a break. You're just as smart as me. You just have no ambition. You have a job you're way too smart for. You're only attracted to losers and jerks. You've stayed in this sad, rusting town because you're too scared to leave. You're acting just like Mom. Cut it out."

Jody sucked in her breath. Anna did too. That was the nuclear option, and she hadn't even planned to deploy it. She and Jody had both led lives deliberately to avoid ending up like their mother.

"You think you're better than Mom." Jody's words were slow and dangerous. "Just because you moved to D.C. and got a job prosecuting domestic violence. But you're more like her than I am, aren't you? Deep down inside, you can't trust anyone. Sure, you moved out of Holly Grove. Congratulations. You're completely alone in the world."

Anna felt like she'd been punched in the gut. It was true. Over the last few weeks especially. She'd never felt so alone in her life.

"I am trying to be here for *you* now," Anna said. "I'm not sure I can do it, though, if you just keep lying to my face."

"What is that: a threat? Well, guess what? I don't *want* you here. I didn't ask you to come. This is *my* business and I can take care of it. Go back to helping strangers in D.C. and leave me the fuck alone!"

Jody stormed to her bedroom and slammed her door.

Anna stood there, shaking with fury. Eventually, she went to the fridge and grabbed a can of Bud Light. She cracked it open, noting how easy it was to avoid cutting herself in the process, and took a sip. Then she pulled out her phone and swiped to the Expedia app. She searched for flights back to D.C.

31

The next day, Anna waited on the sidewalk in front of Reagan National Airport, until a gleaming white BMW came around the bend. She waved at the car, and Grace pulled it to the curb. Her friend hopped out and embraced her.

"Thanks so much for coming," Anna said.

"Of course." Grace glanced at her. "You need a haircut and a manicure."

"And a bottle of tequila and a month of therapy."

Anna loaded her suitcase into the trunk and got in. Grace pulled out of the airport and onto the GW Parkway. The Potomac River flowed calmly next to the road. Monuments gleamed in the distance. The city looked so civilized.

"You want to talk about it?" Grace asked.

"I don't know where to start," Anna said.

"You got in a fight with your sister. Which is not at all surprising, given the stress that you're both under. But what did you ladies actually argue about?"

"Everything and nothing. What happened yesterday and what's been simmering for years. We both said the meanest things possible. Hit each other in our weakest places."

"Ah, sisters." Grace had two sisters herself. "There's no one a woman can be meaner to than her own sister. No one else knows where your bruises are and how to press on them. And family is forever, which liberates you to be extra cruel."

"I was there to help her. I moved to Michigan and put my job on the line to defend her. And she lied to me, over and over."

"What you did was amazing," Grace glanced at her. "Did Jody ask you to come to Michigan?"

"Actually, no. Her friend Kathy did, because she was worried that Jody is in trouble. Which she definitely is."

"Hm. Your little sister has lived her whole life in your shadow a bit, hasn't she?"

"She wants to prove herself by making her own way in her first-degree homicide trial?"

"Maybe you could *ask* her what she wants."

Anna stared out the window. She just assumed Jody would want her there. Obviously she was wrong.

"Or not," Grace said. "I, for one, am very happy to have you back in D.C. I'll make an appointment at Red Door for us."

They turned onto North Capitol Street, passing Union Station. Anna stared at the lovely landscaping. The federal part of D.C. was neat, symmetrical, and showy. Marble pillars abounded; golden statues gleamed atop pedestals. Mounds of flowers lined every building. The expensive beauty was jarring after Holly Grove.

Anna had lived in D.C. for over two years. But driving through today, it didn't feel like home. Holly Grove didn't either. Wherever she was, she had a feeling that "home" was somewhere else. She wasn't sure where she belonged anymore.

Soon they were in the sylvan neighborhood of Takoma Park. A post-hippie mecca of crunchiness, the downtown was lined with coffee shops, bead stores, and even a pet shop featuring organic, free-trade wares. Grace turned onto a residential street where giant trees towered over colorful bungalows and cottages. She pulled in front of a yellow Victorian. Anna stared at Jack's house.

"Want me to come in?" Grace asked.

Anna shook her head. "I just need a couple hours. I don't want to ruin your whole day."

"Okay, I have some chores to run. I'll pick you up at four."

"Thanks."

Grace drove off, and Anna stood on the sidewalk in front of

the house. It looked even prettier than she remembered. She walked up the steps, smelling the mint and basil in the garden. She fished the key out of her purse and slipped it into the doorknob. It still worked. She stepped into the foyer, dizzy with nostalgia and a sense of displacement.

A streak of orange flew across the floor and hurled itself at her feet. Her cat, Raffles, rubbed enthusiastically against her legs. She picked him up and buried her nose in his glossy fur. He butted his head under her chin and purred so loudly he sounded like a motorboat. She rubbed his neck and carried him with her.

The living room was as she remembered it. Jack's reading glasses were folded on top of some papers by the dragonfly lamp. Olivia's favorite *Princess and the Frog* backpack sat on floor, a pink bathing suit poking out of the top. But on the coffee table was something different: a thick white photo album that had not lived there before. Anna set Raffles down and flipped to the front page. It was the wedding album of Jack's marriage to his first wife, Olivia's mother. Her chest tightened painfully. She closed the book.

In the cheerful kitchen, things had been rearranged. The blue vase she and Jack registered for had been replaced with a red one. The mugs had been moved from the cabinet by the sink—the location Anna had chosen—to their old space above the microwave. That spot made no sense for mugs, which was why Anna had moved them in the first place. She fought an urge to transfer the mugs back into the cabinet by the sink.

She went upstairs. The door to Olivia's room was open, and Anna stood in the threshold, looking at the purple bedspread and shelves full of books and toys. The nightlight she'd bought Olivia was still plugged into the wall. How many nights had Anna perched on that bed, patting the girl to sleep and trying to dispel her nightmares? How many times had she sat on that stool, braiding her hair? In this room, she had been a mother.

She kept going, to her own bedroom. Correction: Jack's bedroom. She had no claim to it anymore. She walked into the room with its red walls and colorful quilt. She had never slept better than on that bed. She had done delicious things with the man she loved on that bed. In this room, she had been a wife. Well, almost.

She went into the walk-in closet. At least her clothes were still hanging where she left them. Not for long. She took out two large suitcases and began to fold the clothes into them. She hadn't had a chance to pack after their breakup, because she'd gone immediately to Michigan. But now that she was reestablishing herself in D.C., and would no longer be telecommuting, she'd need her work clothes.

She was finishing the second suitcase when she heard the front door open. She stopped and listened. Footsteps walked purposefully around the first floor of the house, then came up the steps. She stood and tried to prepare herself.

Jack walked into the bedroom. Seeing him was a visceral experience. She wanted to both run into his arms and run out of the house. She felt all the love she had for him, and all the pain. He stared at her like he was seeing a ghost, which was ironic, since he was the one who haunted her.

Jack was a tall African American man with caramel skin and light green eyes, so handsome he often drew double takes. He wore his hair cleanly shaved and his clothes neatly pressed. Today, he wore a dark suit and red tie. He had come from work. But it was three in the afternoon.

"Why are you home?" Anna asked. Her maternal instinct kicked in. "Is everything okay with Olivia?"

"It's nice to see you too." Jack smiled. "Everything's fine. Olivia's at her summer camp. I came home because I thought you might be here."

"Did Grace tell you?"

"No." He put his hands in his pockets and looked down at his polished leather shoes. "Your cell phone is still on my account. Sometimes I log in to see where you are. I've been following your little green dot around Holly Grove and Detroit for the last few weeks. It makes me feel better to see you, somewhere in the world.

And today I saw that you were here. I couldn't believe it. I thought I might be dreaming. I dream about you a lot."

Her heart pulsed in the base of her throat. "Me too."

They stepped toward each other at the same time, and she was in his arms, resting her cheek against his chest. He stroked her hair and kissed her temple. He smelled of mint and soap. He felt like home. This, she realized, was the one place in the world where she felt like she belonged.

When she opened her eyes, she saw a red negligee draped on a chair. It wasn't hers. She stepped out of his arms. He followed her gaze, then shook his head.

"I'm sorry."

"No need to apologize," she said briskly. "It's why I'm packing up."

She forced herself to turn away from him and pick up a suitcase. She had to give him the time and space he needed to figure out his heart. The distance was for her own benefit too. A protective measure. She could no longer trust that this man, whom she loved, and whom she knew loved her, was going to be with her forever.

"You can stay here tonight," he said.

"I don't think that'd be a good idea."

Jack nodded and lifted the other suitcase. They went down to the foyer and set the luggage by the door. Raffles performed ecstatic figure eights around her ankles.

"How long will you be in town?" Jack asked.

"I'll stay with Grace until I find my own place to rent."

"In D.C.?" His brow wrinkled in confusion.

"Yeah."

"What about your sister's case?"

Tears filled her eyes. She tried to fight them back, and when she couldn't, she looked down so he wouldn't see. Jack's hand cupped her chin, gently tipping her head up until she met his eyes.

"Tell me," he said quietly. "Maybe I can help."

"I can't do it, Jack."

He took her hand and led her to the living room couch. They

sat down next to each other. Raffles jumped up and made himself a ball on her lap. And then she was telling Jack everything she could. She wanted his legal advice; he was the best lawyer she knew. She wanted his emotional support. She wanted to curl into his arms. She wanted to tell him the whole story, but she couldn't. The statements Jody made to her were attorney-client privileged. She couldn't reveal it to anyone outside the defense camp. But she could sketch out many of the broad outlines.

"Hypothetically," Anna said, "what if Jody is lying to me? What if she's been lying to me since I got there?"

"Welcome to the defense side of a case," Jack said wryly. "The first thing any good defense lawyer learns is: Don't trust anything your client tells you. There are a lot of ways you can figure out what really happened, but asking your client is often the least reliable."

"I know. But she's not just my client. She's my sister. I thought we told each other everything. I went to defend her thinking she was innocent. I believed her when she said she was. But what if she's not?"

"Sounds like the world might be a better place with the coach gone from it."

Anna stared, shocked to hear that sentiment come from the mouth of the chief homicide prosecutor. He smiled.

"Don't look so surprised, Anna. I don't believe in vigilante justice. But I've handled enough cases where the community believes that a murder victim got what he deserved, that their children were safer with him gone. Over and over, I've argued that we need a system where citizens don't take justice into their own hands. Over and over, I've heard the response, 'That man needed a good killing.' Believe me, those cases are harder to prosecute. You can use that sentiment to help defend your sister."

"I don't know if I can defend her, Jack. I've devoted my entire adult life to putting rapists and murderers in jail. Fighting for justice."

"If you do your job right, justice is on your side."

"How so?"

"In some countries, I, the Homicide chief, would just get to decide whether somebody's innocent or guilty. Maybe we'd have a trial, but it would be for show. Is that justice? Of course not. Our Founding Fathers didn't guarantee that every crime would be punished. But they guaranteed that every accused would get a defense attorney. Because it's not justice unless there's a fair trial, and in America we don't want a conviction unless it's a conviction beyond a reasonable doubt."

"But I always pictured myself fighting crime, not for criminals. I don't know if I can do it, Jack."

"Our justice system doesn't work unless there are great lawyers working hard on both sides of the V. I've made some mistakes in my life. Imagine if my career, and my family, and my whole life was on the line because of the worst mistake I'd ever made. I'd want someone great on my side. And there's no one I would want there more than you."

She loved the logic and calm he brought to every situation. She loved his deep, steady voice.

"I miss you," she whispered.

"I miss you more."

She wasn't sure who leaned forward first. Jack's lips were on hers, her arms were around his neck, and they were kissing with the intensity of two lovers reunited after a long absence. For a moment, she was only aware of the taste of his mouth, the scent of his skin, the warm, familiar curve of his chest. Then she remembered the red negligee upstairs. She slapped him, hard.

He pulled back. He met her eyes and looked simultaneously surprised, hurt, and like he understood completely.

She stood and stepped away from the couch. A horn honked from outside. She glanced out the window. Grace's white BMW idled in the driveway. Her hand stung.

"I'm sorry," she said. "If I didn't do that, I might've never stopped."

"No, I'm sorry," he said. "I'm so sorry to have hurt you. To keep hurting you."

"It's not your fault. But—I have to go."

Anna gave Raffles one final cheek scratch. Jack helped her carry and load the suitcases into Grace's car. They stood facing each other. She looked at his mouth, still tasting it, then looked away. She stuck out her hand. He smiled gently, and shook it. "Call me anytime. I'll do anything I can to help you."

She nodded, swallowed, and climbed in the car.

Grace gave her a sympathetic look. "You okay?"

"Mm hm," Anna managed, through the tightness of her throat. She watched Jack, watching her, as the car pulled away.

■ ■ ■

That night, Anna sat at Grace's elegant dining room table, sipping pinot grigio while Grace clicked through Apartments.com on her sleek silver Mac notebook.

"Ooh, look at this one-bedroom in Dupont Circle," Grace said. "Granite countertops, stainless-steel appliances, exposed brick walls."

"Mm," Anna said. It was beautiful, in a great neighborhood, and within her price range. She imagined living in it. Waking up in the spotless bedroom, showering in the luxurious bathroom. Her life would be much like the apartment: beautiful, sterile, and meaningless.

She thought of walking through Jack's house today, all the meaningful things inside it. And none of them were hers. Even the little girl she'd thought she would raise. None of that was permanent.

Anna remembered what Grace said about why sisters can be so cruel to each other: *Family is forever.* She looked at the computer, where Grace was clicking to another apartment, which was even more beautiful, sterile, and meaningless than the last.

Jody was the one thing Anna could count on—always had been. She was the one truly permanent thing in her life.

"Grace, I'm not sure I want a new apartment."

"You want to stay here at my place?"

Anna shook her head. She pulled out her phone and texted her sister.

Hi Jo. I'm sorry. I'd really like to come to your obygyn
appointment tomorrow. Would that be okay with
you? And then maybe we could talk afterward.

She'd be spending a small fortune on airfare, but she didn't
care. Better to do that than make the mistake of her life.

The screen flashed with little dots indicating Jody was reading
the text message. Anna waited for her response. It didn't come for
a long time.

32

When I woke up the morning after I made the report to Sergeant Gargaron, the pile of my clothes still lay on the floor in my bedroom. It had been two days since Owen Fowler raped me and sixteen hours since I'd reported it to the police. I stared at the pile. In it were my best going-out jeans, a pair of lavender Jockey underpants, my favorite padded bra, and a light blue shirt with a big silver snowflake on it. I loved that shirt.

Mom knocked on my open door and came in carrying a mug of cocoa. She sat on the edge of the bed and handed it to me. We both looked at the pile. It was like having a pile of dog poop in your room, and not being allowed to clean it up. She said, "I'll call again today."

"Okay." I nodded and took a sip of the hot chocolate. She'd even put tiny marshmallows on the top. She must've really felt sorry for me.

"I was thinking," she said. "Let's call Anna."

"No."

"She would come right home. Do not pass go, do not collect two hundred dollars."

"I don't want her to come home."

"She'd want to help you."

"I don't want her help. I don't want her to know."

"You know, your sister is your best friend. Sisters are always there for each other. Blood is thicker than—"

"Yeah, I know, Mom. You've told us that, like, a thousand times. But you don't have to tell your best friend everything. Don't tell her. Please. I don't want her to see me that way."

You were my hero, Annie. And I was ashamed. Worst-case scenario: you'd be disappointed in me. Best case: you'd feel sorry for me. Actually, maybe that was the worst case. You were "the smart one," but I was "the tough one." At least I was supposed to be tough. I couldn't stand the thought of you seeing me as a victim.

Mom said, "Sleep on it."

"I already did." I lay back down and pulled a pillow over my head.

"Good point." She tossed the pillow aside. "Time to get up."

I groaned. It was Monday. The idea of facing my classmates was unbearable. "I'm not going to school today."

"I would think not."

That made me perk up. "Can I just stay in bed?"

"No."

She made me get up, take a shower, and get dressed, which—I admit—did make me feel better. I tried to ignore the putrid pile of clothes as I stepped around it. We watched a marathon of *Law & Order* reruns and sat on the couch all day, eating Cherry Garcia out of the container. I love those crime dramas, how everything is tied up so neatly at the end. They always get some kind of closure and justice, unlike the real world.

Mom kept checking her cell phone. We didn't talk about it, but we both were waiting for the police to call and tell us what was going on with the case. The phone was silent.

Around noon, she ordered pizza. At some point, I realized she had taken another day off work. I gratefully laid my head on her lap during a commercial. She stroked my hair, which felt so good, I started crying again. She didn't say anything to try to comfort me— what could she say?—but she just kept running her fingers through my hair. Eventually, I dozed off.

I woke up to the sound of her phone ringing. I sat up into low evening light. Mom looked at the incoming number. "You ready?" she asked me.

"Yeah."

Mom answered, had a brief conversation, and handed the phone to me.

"Hello?" I asked.

"Hello." A deep male voice was on the line. It sounded more for-
mal than Sergeant Gargaron. "Is this Miss Jody Curtis?"

"Yes?"

"This is Lawrence Upperthwaite, Holly Grove's District Attorney."

My heartbeat picked up. I'd never spoken to a DA before. I said
something clever like, "Mm hm?"

"Sergeant Herb Gargaron briefed me on your case, and I'm calling to give you some information about it."

"Okay?"

"Unfortunately, there isn't enough evidence to go forward at this
point. But if that changes, we will let you know."

"Um. What if I don't agree? Can I get another lawyer? One who
believes in my case?"

"Ah, no. This isn't like a slip-and-fall, where you can hire any
lawyer you want. Criminal cases can only be brought by the DA's office. And we're declining to take this case. Which, I must tell you, is
probably the best thing for you in the long run. These things can get
quite ugly. Part of my consideration is protecting you from all that."

"Oh. Thanks."

"You're welcome. Feel free to call me if you have any questions."

He hung up. I handed Mom the phone.

"They're not bringing the case, are they?" she asked. "They
wouldn't tell me. Said they had to talk to the 'complaining witness.'"

I shook my head.

"Goddammit!" She paced the room. "Those bastards." She
launched into a string of curses, including some words I'd never heard
her say before or since. After a while, she seemed to notice me, still
sitting on the couch.

"Oh, honey." She wrapped me into her arms. "This is one messed-
up world. We women have always gotten the shit end of the stick.
It's just the way it is. I'm sorry you had to learn so young. I wanted to
protect you from it for a while longer."

We held each other tight. There was nothing else to hold on to.

After dinner, she picked up the clothes from my bedroom floor
and ran them through the washer and dryer in the basement of the

building. That night, we sat on the porch in our winter coats. She lit two cigarettes and handed me one. We smoked and watched the red and white lights speeding past each other on the highway.

For a long time, I believed what Mom said that day. Women are destined to inherit the scrap heap of the world. She had history at her back. Burkas. Child brides. Honor killings. The Salem witch trials. It's happened over and over, on every continent and in every era. Better to accept that, she thought, and get on with whatever life you can scrape together from the leftovers.

But you know what? Mom was wrong. She tried her best, and God bless her for everything she did, but she was wrong about a lot of things. Most of all, she was wrong about women being powerless. I know that now. If we band together, if we stand shoulder to shoulder, if we refuse to accept their shit anymore, we can do something about it.

You did, Anna. So did I. We just did it in different ways.

That night, though, I was still just a kid. I hadn't figured out my power or place in the world. After Mom went to sleep, I went to the basement and got my clothes from the dryer. I put them in a plastic grocery bag, walked out to the back of the building, and threw them into the Dumpster.

33

Anna walked into the doctor's office waiting room. The seats were filled with young couples poring over *Motherhood* magazines. Several of the women had round pregnant bellies. Some of them had brought their own ecstatic mothers, too. One young woman sat alone: her sister, Jody. Anna took a deep breath and walked over.

Anna had come here straight from the airport. Her bags sat in a rental car in the ob-gyn's parking lot. But she'd made it in time.

Anna sat next to her sister. Jody's pregnancy was not yet showing. She still wore her regular jeans and a T-shirt, although her breasts now strained against the fabric.

"You don't look pregnant," she said quietly. "You look like a porn star."

Jody looked up from her *People* magazine. "It's so cruel," she said. "I finally have some boobs, and I can't use 'em."

Anna smiled. "Thanks for letting me come today."

"Thanks for coming."

They were shown to a small examination room, where Jody changed into a paper tunic. A nurse took her blood and some other vitals, then left, saying, "The doctor will be right with you." As they waited, Jody sat shivering on the examination table. Anna took off her jacket and draped it around her sister's shoulders.

The obstetrician wore a white jacket, sensible pumps, and a salt-and-pepper ponytail. She had the kind, unflappable expression of someone who had seen every sort of crisis that could befall a woman. She glanced at Jody's bare ring finger and Anna in the guest chair, then smiled gently. "So," she said. "We tested your blood, and you are definitely pregnant."

Jody started to cry. "I'm such an idiot," she said. Anna stood and rubbed her back.

"It's okay," the doctor said, handing Jody a tissue. "Every week, I see intelligent, strong women in your situation. We live in a time when we control so much of our destiny. It can come as a big surprise when Mother Nature has an agenda of her own. Does the father know?"

Anna looked at Jody with interest.

Jody shook her head. "No."

"Do you plan to tell him?"

Jody let out a short, sharp laugh. "No. He's not the sort of person who's able to raise a child at this time."

The doctor asked about Jody's last period, then looked at the chart and did some calculations. "You got pregnant five weeks ago. Which means, technically, you're considered seven weeks pregnant. Your due date is March second or so."

Anna did some calculations of her own. That meant her sister had gotten pregnant about a week before the coach died.

The doctor turned off the lights and had Jody lie back on the examining table. The sonogram monitor looked like a small, fuzzy black-and-white TV. It lit the walls with a dim light and produced a static noise, making the room itself feel womblike. The doctor squirted a clear jelly onto Jody's abdomen and put a thick plastic wand onto her stomach.

The machine crackled then settled into a whooshing sound. There was a strong, slow heartbeat, which the doctor said was Jody's. She slid the wand around. At first, the screen was just a jumble of fuzzy gray splotches, with no discernible shape or meaning. The doctor angled the wand to the side and pressed into Jody's lower abdomen. A picture materialized on the screen: a round, black pool. Within the pool was a bright little bean that held a flickering white light inside it. The sound of a second heartbeat filled the room: faster and more urgent than Jody's, like a little bird falling out of a nest.

"That's the embryo." The doctor pointed to the white bean. "With a nice healthy heartbeat. You can see the heart there."

The tiny bright pinprick flickered in rhythm with the sound. The doctor pointed out the embryo's head—round and slightly bigger than the rest—and tail, tapering at the end. It lay curled in Jody's womb: just a bit of light in the darkness. Anna stared at the speck of a heart, its little white light pulsing hard and fast.

Jody stared at the screen like it was the most incredible thing she'd ever seen, which maybe it was. She might have felt conflicted about this baby before. Now, she was a woman in love. Anna reached out and held her sister's hand.

"Oh my God," Jody said. "It's beautiful."

"Yes."

"I can do this."

"It'll be hard. But you can do anything you set your mind to."

Jody turned to her. "Annie, I can't let my baby grow up without a mother. Please, will you help me?"

Looking at Jody's eyes, shining with tears, Anna knew two things. Jody was keeping this baby. And Anna would do anything in her power to keep her sister out of jail.

"Of course," she said.

"I'm sorry," Jody said. "For everything I said to you. You're not alone."

"You're not alone either. I'm here for you and this baby. And I'm sorry too."

■ ■ ■

That night, the sisters curled up on Jody's couch in front of the TV, a bowl of plain unbuttered popcorn between them.

"This tastes like wood," Jody said.

"It tastes healthy," Anna said. "Do you know what artificial butter is made of? Your baby eats everything you do."

Jody grimaced and took another handful. The show switched to a commercial for Ginsu knives. Jody put the volume to MUTE. "Did you see Jack while you were in D.C.?"

"Yeah."

"What was that like?"

"It hurt like hell." Anna watched the knives flashing on the TV screen. "Her presence was all over the house. She belongs there. I don't really."

"I'm sorry, Annie. But maybe seeing that was like having a bone reset. It hurt, but you needed to have that hurt in order to heal. You had to know that he's moved on to move on yourself."

"Maybe so." A paring knife sliced through a tomato, which bled juice onto a cutting board.

"You don't want to talk about it?"

"Neither of us wants to talk about our love lives, eh?" Anna turned to her sister and smiled, trying to keep it light.

"Fair enough." Jody met her eyes. "So I was watching an episode of *CSI.*"

"Uh-oh."

"This client was, like, confessing to her lawyer. And her lawyer was all, 'Don't tell me anything. If you tell me it happened one way, I won't be able to put you on the stand to say the opposite. I'm not allowed to suborn perjury. So don't tell me anything yet. We'll keep our options open.'"

"Yeah, I know that scene."

"What do you think of that strategy?"

"I don't agree with that strategy. I can defend you much better if I know what evidence I'm defending against."

"But—can we do it that way, Annie? You're the best lawyer I'll ever get, and definitely the one who cares the most. That public defender couldn't even remember my name. Represent me, defend me, kick some ass. But don't ask me any more questions. Can you work the case like that?"

Anna didn't like the idea of doing it that way. She wanted to learn as much as possible in advance, so she could get around the government's strengths and exploit its weaknesses. But she couldn't force her sister to tell the truth, and she didn't want to force any more lies out of her.

"Okay. I hope you'll reconsider. For now, I'll focus on getting everything I can from the government and other witnesses."

"Thanks, Annie." Jody leaned over and hugged her. "I love you."

Anna breathed in her sister's clean shampoo scent and let the relief wash over her. "Love you too, Jo."

■ ■ ■

The next morning, Anna unloaded groceries into Jody's refrigerator: everything BabyCenter.com said was good for an expectant mother. Organic milk, yogurt, and cheese sticks; kale, broccoli, and carrots; oatmeal, almonds, raspberries, and blueberries. She'd get cherries and apples from Cooper's farm. She pulled out a whole organic chicken, fresh pasta, and a loaf of seven-grain bread. No soft cheeses, no cold cuts, no alcohol or sushi, not that you could get sushi at Meijer.

As she set bottles of purified water on the counter, her phone buzzed with an incoming call. She glanced at the number. It was Jack.

She sank down at the kitchen table and stared at the screen. It was the first Saturday in July—the day that was their wedding in some alternate universe. Anna closed her eyes and allowed herself to imagine it. She was wearing a strapless white dress and walking down the aisle. Jack was waiting for her at the altar. Olivia was wearing the flower girl dress she'd chosen, the one with rose petals sewn into the tulle. There were heaping trays of cupcakes, a big band, an inn in the Shenandoah Valley, strings of white lights against a starry black sky. Fireflies floated up from the ground as Anna and the man she loved danced their first song as husband and wife.

She opened her eyes and returned to the hard Formica world of Jody's kitchen. Her phone flashed the words *Jack Bailey*. She let the call go to voice mail. She held the phone to her chest for a long time.

Jody came into the kitchen, still wearing her pajamas. "Morning, sis! Are you using that as a defibrillator?" She started rifling through the grocery bags. "Healthy, healthy, healthy. Where are the potato chips? Where are the Oreos?"

Anna looked up. "You don't want those. BabyCenter says that every bite you eat is a chance to send nutrients to your baby."

"My baby wants to get her nutrients from Cool Ranch Doritos. And a Blizzard."

"Your baby is going to be glad that Aunt Annie brought you some nice organic blueberries."

"My baby is going to be very glad for her aunt Annie, period." Jody sat next to her. "Seriously. You're all the family she'll have. If something happens to me, will you take care of the little bean?"

"Of course, Jo. But nothing's going to happen."

"If I go to jail—"

"You're not going to jail," Anna interrupted, too loudly to be convincing. She lowered her voice. "But if you do, I promise I'll look after the bean."

"Give her potato chips every once in a while."

"Whole-grain, free-range potato chips, of course."

"Of course."

"If I'm going to be this kid's guardian, can you please tell me who the father is?"

"If there's a father in the picture, would he have rights to the baby? To see her? To custody? Would his family have rights?"

Anna thought about it. "Yeah, probably."

"Then let's just say there's no father. No father means nobody to hurt the kid."

Jody got up, walked out, and returned a few seconds later holding a plate full of colorful cupcakes. "Me and the bean made these for you last night, while you were sleeping. We know what today is."

Anna's eyes misted. "Thanks, Jo."

"Now put on some hiking boots and pack a bikini. We're going to the Sleeping Bear Dunes. No work today. No moping. Only cupcakes, sand, and seashore. Got it?"

"Got it." Anna stood.

She chose a bright pink cupcake and took a bite. The buttery sweetness melted in her mouth, overwhelming all the bitterness. Jody gave her a hug. Anna's lungs expanded to take in more air than they had in days. Neither one of them might have the tools necessary to save the other. But they would both try their best. That counted for something.

34

Three weeks later, Anna sat at the defense table in Judge Upperthwaite's courtroom, waiting for the judge to take the bench. She glanced at Desiree Williams, who sat at the prosecutor's table, the one that by tradition was closer to the jury. That was where Anna belonged. Here, on the other side of the courtroom, Anna felt like she was living in a mirror.

Both she and Desiree wore black pantsuits. Both had wheeled in boxy litigation bags. Both nodded at each other as their eyes met, then went back to looking at their papers.

Jody came in and sat next to Anna. This was her third trip to the bathroom since they'd arrived at the courthouse forty minutes earlier. Anna wondered what life was going to be like when Jody reached her third trimester. For now, at ten weeks pregnant, Jody was still not showing. She wore a pair of black pants and a white blouse that wasn't meant to tuck in. Her clothes were tighter than usual, but not scandalously so. Anyone who knew Jody might think she'd put on a few pounds; anyone who didn't know her would just think she was naturally curvy.

At precisely 9:00 A.M., a side door opened and Judge Upperthwaite stepped through, followed by a stenographer, law clerk, and court security officer. "All rise!" called the clerk.

"Be seated," the judge intoned. "We're here today to hear arguments on the defendant's Motion to Unseal Five Sealed Cases."

Anna looked behind her. In the audience sat two people: an intern from the prosecutor's office and Cooper, who was allowed to come in as Anna's "investigator." The judge had closed the courtroom to the public because the mere existence of these police files was under seal.

"I've read the motions from both sides," the judge said. "Ms. Curtis, you may begin."

"Thank you, Your Honor." Anna stood. "The constitutional guarantee of due process requires that the prosecution turn over all sealed files involving Coach Owen Fowler. These documents are necessary for my sister to prepare her defense."

"In what way are these documents relevant to your theory of the case?" The judge's voice was slow but kindly, a smart but aging man trying to understand the argument.

"I don't know, exactly. That's our point. There is information that the coach was involved in some criminal activity. Contacts with the criminal justice system are often relevant. But we don't know if the coach was a crime victim, suspect, or witness. We don't know if the cases pertain to assault or identity fraud or a credit card scam. There might be all kind of leads to follow up."

"What are you currently planning as your defense?"

She shook her head. Jody didn't want to go with a blame-Wendy strategy. At this point, Anna wasn't sure *what* her strategy would be. "We are planning as the facts develop, Your Honor, and keeping our options open. Which makes this information all the more important."

"Mm. So you have no reason why they are relevant, and no theory of defense, but you're hoping if I give you these sealed files anyway, a theory will be found within them. Ms. Williams, do you have anything to add to the papers you've already filed?"

"No, sir," the prosecutor said. Desiree was apparently acquainted with the important courtroom rule *Shut up when things are going your way.*

"I have reviewed the files *in camera*," Judge Upperthwaite announced, "and determined that there is nothing that needs to be turned over to the defense at this time. The files have nothing to do with the incident charged in the indictment. There is no exculpatory material within them. The court will bear their facts in mind, however, and if at any point they do become relevant, I will alert the defense."

"Your Honor." Anna stood. "Can you give us any information about these cases at all? Was Coach Fowler the victim or suspect? Was it a crime of violence or dishonesty or something else? Might there be other people who had a motive to hurt him?"

"I appreciate your fervor, Ms. Curtis. But my decision is made." He smiled down at her. "Don't fret. If you did see these files, you would understand just how irrelevant they are to your sister's homicide case. Meanwhile, you're doing an excellent job of representing her. I have been very impressed with your writing, research, and mastery of the local rules."

Was he trying to distract her from the motion? Or just being a sweet old man? "Thank you, Your Honor. But I would ask—"

"Court is adjourned." The judge stood and walked out.

■ ■ ■

Jody declared herself hungry, again, so Anna, Jody, and Cooper went to the diner across the square. It looked like it had been built in the 1950s and not renovated since, with peeling linoleum, a flickering Bud Light sign, and a menu written with detachable letters on a wall board. They sat at the window, looking across the square at the courthouse, whose gold dome gleamed under the July sun. The rest of the diner was empty.

"I found some good information," Cooper said, after the waitress took their order.

Anna was surprised. She hadn't asked him to do anything recently. "What have you got?"

"Wendy put the lake house up for sale."

Jody looked shocked. She met Anna's eyes and said, "That was fast."

"How'd you find out?" Anna asked.

"There was a little ad in the *Holly Grove Observer*," Cooper said. "So I made an appointment to go see it."

"Why? We saw it at the memorial service."

"We saw what Wendy wanted us to see."

"True. So did you crack the case?"

He smiled. "No. But this Realtor was chatty. She said I could put in a lowball bid because the owner needs to sell it. Apparently, they owned the house free and clear at one point, but the coach borrowed almost a million dollars against its equity. Now, Wendy needs to get whatever she can out of it, to pay off a bunch more debts they racked up."

"A million dollars in debt," Anna said. "What'd they spend it on?"

"That, I couldn't tell you." Cooper said.

"I'll send out trial subpoenas to banks, credit cards, and the credit agencies," Anna said. "The problem with that is they won't have to give me anything until the day of trial."

They quieted as the waitress came back with their food. As they ate, Anna used her phone to log on to the Michigan courts' website and search for the articles of incorporation for Owen Fowler's companies. But they were too old. The website only had documents going back ten years.

After lunch, they went back to the courthouse, but instead of Judge Upperthwaite's beautiful courtroom, they descended to the basement, where the clerk's office was housed. Here, the building's magnificence gave way to grim function. Windowless halls were lit with fluorescent lights; old stone walls painted off-white led to a large room filled with mismatched filing cabinets. The room was separated from the hallway by a long Formica counter. The whole basement smelled dank, as if centuries of court records were slowly molding. A hauntingly pale man came over.

"Hi," Anna said. "I was hoping to see the articles of incorporation for any companies Owen Fowler owned."

"That might take a while," he said.

"I understand. We can wait. Thank you."

He turned and disappeared into the labyrinth of filing cabinets. An hour later, he came back and handed Anna a file full of papers. "It's ten cents a copy, so you owe me three dollars and seventy cents."

Anna fished out the money. "Thanks."

They walked up the stairs and back outside. The sunshine felt good after the gloom of the courthouse basement. The three of them sat on a bench in the square. Anna looked at the papers. The coach had created three corporations. The first was called Fowler Athletics. It had a number of prominent citizens on the board. According to the coach's website, this was the company through which he ran his summer camps. The second was Fowler Athletics Charity, the charitable, nonprofit arm of his camp, the part that served underprivileged kids. It, too, had a board of directors with titles like "mayor," "councilman," and "state senator." The final corporation was called FirstDown, LLC. It had been founded in 1996 and had only two people on the board: Owen Fowler and a woman named Lena Hoffmeister.

"FirstDown sounds like another football company. But who's Lena Hoffmeister?" Cooper said.

Anna and Jody shook their heads. Cooper pulled out his phone and tapped his Google icon. Ten minutes and fifteen dollars later, he had completed an online background check on Lena Hoffmeister. He held the screen so both sisters could see it.

The report listed basic biographical information. Lena was born in 1932 in Grand Rapids, Michigan. She graduated from Grand Blanc High School in 1950. And in 1954, she changed her name to Lena Upperthwaite, after marrying one Lawrence Upperthwaite.

Anna blinked. "This is Judge Upperthwaite's wife."

Jody looked up in surprise. "Judge Upperthwaite's wife was Coach Fowler's partner in this FirstDown company?"

Cooper nodded. "Looks like it."

35

Judge Upperthwaite shouldn't be sitting on Jody's case. His wife had been in business with the murder victim. Their families were financially intertwined. The judge should recuse himself.

But Anna was hesitant to file a recusal motion. It would suggest he was so tied up with the parties, personally, that he couldn't be a fair arbiter of the case. No judge—no person—wanted to think that way about himself. And Judge Upperthwaite would be the one to make the decision. He would be offended, and if he denied the motion, she'd still be stuck with him for the rest of the trial.

She considered going to talk to Lena Hoffmeister but dismissed the idea. It would infuriate the judge.

While she mulled the recusal issue, Anna moved for some advance-of-trial subpoenas, which would allow her to see the coach's financial information sooner than the first day of trial. The judge denied them all, without giving a reason.

After that, she decided to ask the judge to recuse himself. Jody deserved a judge whose family finances weren't intertwined with the dead man's. If Judge Upperthwaite denied the motion, at least Anna would have preserved the issue for an appeal. If—she hated to think about this, but she had to—Jody was convicted, Anna would need all the appellate arguments she could get.

She wrote a motion explaining that Lena Upperthwaite and Owen Fowler had been partners in FirstDown. She cited the leading cases on judicial conflict of interest, attached a copy of the articles of incorporation, and filed it.

Two days later, she got back a one-sentence order from the judge, summarily denying her motion. No reasons were given.

■ ■ ■

A week later, Anna found a large yellow envelope stuck in between the wooden door and the screen door of Jody's house. She picked it up. *Anna Curtis* was handwritten on the front. There was no stamp, address, or return label.

Anna took the envelope to the kitchen table. She grabbed a steak knife and sliced it open, cutting her finger in the process. "Ouch!" Blood dripped onto the yellow envelope.

Anna went to the bathroom and searched the medicine cabinet for a Band-Aid. It was so quiet and lonely in Jody's house. At the U.S. Attorney's Office, she already would've passed two detectives talking about swabbing her for DNA. After her finger was bandaged, she returned to the kitchen and opened the envelope more carefully this time. Five pieces of paper slid out: five police reports. There was no note saying who'd left the envelope or why. Whoever left it wanted to remain anonymous.

The first document was a police report from 1999, similar to the witness statement from Jody's report. Short, simple, and to the point:

> **CW: Deana Dominguez, DOB: 1/21/85**
> **S-1: Owen Fowler, DOB: 3/17/64**
> **Date of report: 7/5/99**
>
> **Witness Statement: CW reports that S-1 engaged in vaginal intercourse with her while in his car, in the 1500 block of Otis Place at approximately 23:00 on 7/1/99. CW does not wish to press charges.**

Anna looked up. Coach Fowler had sexually assaulted another girl, years before he assaulted Jody. Anna considered it a sexual assault, although she had no clue how it happened. He had been thirty-five; the girl had been fourteen. That was statutory rape, whether or not the child "consented."

She looked at the next piece of paper. It was a similar report from a thirteen-year-old girl, in 2006, who had sex with the coach in his car. The third file was a fifteen-year-old girl, in 2009, almost verbatim to the 2006 event. A fourteen-year-old girl reported in 2011; she had the distinction of sex in the coach's office in the school, as opposed to his car.

Coach Fowler was a serial rapist. And a pedophile.

And somebody, anonymously, wanted Anna to know it.

According to the reports, none of the girls wanted to press charges. Maybe the girls had all felt allegiance to him; they might've even thought he was their boyfriend. But it begged the question of why they had all gone to the police. It also made Anna wonder how many other "consenting" children might *not* have made a report.

Anna heard a soft squeaking noise and realized she was clenching her teeth. She forced her jaw to relax, then realized that her fists were clenched too. Her entire body was clenched. She saw exploitation and abuses of trust again and again as a sex-crimes prosecutor, and it always angered her. But this was a man she had known and trusted—and he was preying on girls like her own sister. It felt like a very personal betrayal.

Anna looked at the last page, a case from just a few months earlier, in March of 2014. She skimmed the witness statement, which had similar text to the others:

> **CW's mother claims that S-1 had sex with her in his car, on 3/7/14 at approximately 01:00. CW is uncooperative and refuses to give a statement.**

Anna looked at the girl's name and inhaled sharply. It was Hayley Mack—Kathy's daughter.

36

The MotorCity Casino was the most glamorous new building in Detroit. It featured musical acts, luxury restaurants, and hip nightclubs. With its attached parking garage and highly visible security guards, it was a glass-and-neon fortress, and thus one of the few places in Detroit to which suburbanites would venture. They could drive in, party, and drive out, without ever setting foot on an actual piece of city pavement.

When Anna and Cooper walked in, the casino was throbbing with a Friday night crowd. Colorful lights and chrome accents made the interior feel like a refurbished '57 Chevy on acid. Shiny motorcycles and pieces of classic cars were scattered about. The air thrummed with the clinking of slot machines and the calls of gamblers ordering free drinks.

Not everyone looked like they could afford the festivities. At the slot machines, old ladies pulled the handles down so regularly, they could have been working on an assembly line. A guy with gray skin clutched an oxygen tank as he played craps.

The blackjack area held an acre-long sprawl of bright green tabletops. The ten-dollar-minimum tables were filled with packs of giggling sorority girls, there to have fun and flirt. The hard-core players chain-smoked and focused on the action at the table. It was the only place Anna had seen in years where smoking was allowed indoors.

Kathy Mack was dealing cards at a table with a hundred-dollar minimum. Her uniform was a white button-down shirt and black bow tie, which helped camouflage how painfully thin she'd gotten.

Her long dark hair and full red lips helped offset the uniform's androgyny.

"Thank you," she said, smiling at players who tipped her.

Kathy fed the chips into a hole in the table and looked up. When she saw Anna and Cooper standing there, her smile became genuine. She turned to the center of the blackjack corral.

"Break!" she called.

A supervisor came over, checked her cards, and called in another dealer. The players moaned. "She's my good luck charm!" said a man who'd just tipped her.

Kathy nodded at them as she got up. "Good luck, gentlemen." She came around the table and gave Anna a hug. "Good to see you. Are you here to play?"

"I need to talk to you," Anna said softly. "About Hayley."

Kathy's smile faded, but she nodded. "Let's go somewhere else."

She led them to a restaurant called Iridescence. A live band played covers of Motown in front of a three-story wall of glass looking out over the city. In the darkness, the metropolis was a pretty cross-hatch of lights on a black background. You could sit here and feel cosmopolitan, at least in the nighttime, when you couldn't see the broken cement and burned-out buildings.

They sat at a tall table in the bar. Anna pushed Hayley's police report across the table. Kathy picked up the paper and read it. She shook her head with disgust.

"This is all that the police put in the report? Those assholes. How did you get this?"

"Someone left it on Jody's doorstep. Can you tell me what happened to Hayley?"

A waiter came over to take their order. Kathy said, "I can't drink while I'm working. But you should try their double martini, dirty, with extra olives."

"A double martini, dirty, with extra olives," Cooper told the waiter. Anna held up two fingers.

"How much do you know?" Kathy asked.

"I heard she was teased online," Anna said. "I have no idea how the coach came into the picture."

Kathy pulled out a pack of Camel Lights and tapped one from the pack. Cooper picked up a box of matches from the ashtray on the table and struck one to light the cigarette. She inhaled and nodded her thanks.

"Hayley was a volleyball player. Pretty good at it. I guess he 'mentored' her. He told her if she ever had a problem at a party or needed a ride, she should call him. One night, she went to that horrible party, drank too much, and passed out. When she came to, the kids were all laughing at her and she had writing all over her face. She didn't know exactly what had been done to her. She called Coach Fowler to rescue her. I wish she'd called me. But she was afraid she'd be in trouble if I found out she'd been drinking. Anyway, he picked her up. But he didn't drive her home. He drove her off to some secluded dirt road. He raped her."

The waiter returned and set down their drinks. Both Anna and Cooper pushed their martinis toward Kathy. She stubbed out her cigarette, picked up a drink, and took a long swallow. Her lipstick left a dark red stain on the rim.

"How did you find out?" Anna asked.

"She moped around the next day. At first, I thought it was typical teenage sullenness. Then she moped the next day. Then she came home 'sick' from school on Monday and refused to go on Tuesday. She still wouldn't tell me what was going on. I heard about it from a waitress here, whose son goes to the school. The kids at school were calling her—" Kathy's voice broke. She drained the first martini and reached for the second one. "Terrible names. I went home and talked to Hayley. It wasn't easy. But she finally came out with it.

"I marched her into the police station. God help me. The whole city's stacked in favor of Owen Fowler, the police most of all. I should have known better. Hayley wouldn't talk, so I told them her story. The police said they'd look into it. Couple days later, I get a call. They're declining the case. No evidence that the coach did anything to her.

"Those kids used her like she was a toy to be played with and thrown away. And then the coach came—and just took his own turn. The police helped him cover it up."

Kathy's face was hard as stone. She tipped back the second martini.

"Did she get a rape kit done?" Anna asked.

Kathy shook her head. "The police said too much time had passed. They made it sound like it was all Hayley's fault, for not reporting earlier. For drinking. For wearing a tight top. For not fighting the coach harder. She became depressed. She didn't want to go to school. I let her stay home for a week. Every day, she was sobbing. Then that stopped, and she was quiet. I thought that was a sign that things were getting better.

"I went back to work the next Saturday. I didn't hear from her that day. When I came home, it was quiet in the house. I went from room to room, calling her name, the dread growing with each step. I found her in the tub. The water was bright red. And my baby was lying in it."

Kathy stared straight ahead dry-eyed. She wore the expression of a woman who has already cried so many tears, she was out.

"Oh God, Kathy. I'm so sorry." Anna's words felt ridiculously insignificant.

"Hayley thought of the coach like a father. The football players were pricks and what they did hurt. But it was the coach who tore her heart out," Kathy said. "That was my fault. I was always working, and coming home exhausted. I wasn't there for her, not enough. If I'd been there more, she wouldn't have needed another parent."

"What choice did you have?" Cooper said. "You were working to support her. You were raising her on your own. You did everything for her. You were a great mother."

"No, I wasn't. I failed. There's no question about that. I failed and now she's gone." She looked at her watch. "I have to go. My break's only fifteen minutes."

"Kathy," Anna said. "Let me know if there's anything I can do."

What could she do? Take over a casserole?

"Here's what you can do," Kathy said, standing. "Get your sister off. That son of a bitch deserved worse than he got."

When a waiter came by, Anna ordered another dirty martini—for herself. It tasted like olive-flavored fire. Anna coughed and took another sip.

The alcohol burned a trail down to her stomach, sending up a sort of smoke that obscured the terrible images in her head. She began to understand why so many women in Holly Grove drank so much.

"So this is your life as a prosecutor," he said. "Listening to everyone's saddest story. And then you come home to Michigan and, just for a break, you do the same thing. Take a minute off. You need it. Dance with me."

Anna glanced down at his missing leg.

"I used to have two left feet," he said, "but now that I've only got one, I'm a great dancer."

She smiled and nodded. The band was playing a cover of "Tracks of My Tears." He took her hand and led her to the dance floor. His arms slipped easily around her. It felt good to lean against him.

"Who listens to *your* sad story?" he asked.

"Jody," she said.

Cooper really was a good dancer, holding her close enough that her body skimmed his, but gently enough that she didn't feel trapped. His movement was smooth; the prosthetic leg didn't matter. His arms were strong and steady. It was a relief to hold someone, sway together, and let the music wash over them. The wall of glass encircled the dance floor, providing a view of the lights flickering in the dark city. She leaned into him and let her nose almost graze his neck, inhaling the clean, woodsy scent of him. Anna became electrically aware of Cooper's hand on the small of her back. She could feel the warmth radiating from his skin.

The song changed to "Heard It Through the Grapevine." Anna shifted backward, getting ready to leave the dance floor. But Cooper kept his arm around her back and moved into the slightly faster rhythm. She relaxed and fell into step with him again.

He lifted her hand and looked at the bandage on her finger. "What happened here?"

"I cut myself opening a package."

He lifted her finger to his mouth and kissed it. A flush of heat spread through her hand, up her arm, and down to her belly. She inhaled and looked up at his face. His lips curved into a smile. She imagined how his mouth would feel on hers. She remembered how Jack's felt.

"Coop," she said. "Here's my sad story. I was engaged. We called it off. I'm . . . not over it. I'm no good for anybody right now."

"Then just dance with me."

Among all the flash and dazzle of the casino, his blue eyes shone steady and true. She nodded, fit her chin into the crook of his shoulder, and danced with him.

37

When you came home for Christmas break in 2004, you asked me why I was so quiet. I never could tell you. I never told anyone at school, either. I didn't want to. I just wanted things to be normal.

Of course, they weren't. I quit the track team, although *quit* is too active a verb for what I did. I just stopped showing up to practice. I withdrew from my friends too. Everyone talked about hooking up and parties. I couldn't stand that stuff anymore. I didn't want anyone to touch me. It was years before I allowed myself to be alone with a man again.

The football team won the Division I Championship that year. The whole town celebrated, it seemed, except me. They were still celebrating at Christmas break, and you wanted me to come to some parties with you. I wouldn't—and so you stayed home with me, eating Phish Food and watching *Law & Order* marathons. You were a good sister, so stop being so worried that I didn't tell you. There was nothing you could've done anyhow.

I know you're hurt that I never told you before. Please, Annie, know that it wasn't about you—it was about me. And I'm sorry. I should have told you. Sisters are each other's witnesses. You're the one person who's known me my entire life. You've seen me at my best and at my worst. You're the one person I know I'll still be telling my secrets to when I'm ninety—if I have any secrets worth telling at that point.

But that winter, I just wanted to forget it.

I tried to smile as much as I could when you were home but, I'm sorry to tell you this, it was a relief when you finally went back to college. I could just relax into my depression.

Things were never better for Coach Fowler, though! That was his third state championship; he was a mini Bo Schembechler. You remember that ad he did for Bronner's?

And his summer sports camp went big-time. Parents from Bloomfield Hills to Gross Pointe were lining up to get their little quarterbacks into his Holly Grove football camp. His rates went through the roof, and still he had a waiting list. He made a fortune.

Despite the long waiting list, he always kept the charity part of his sports camp, the piece that served "underprivileged" children. He got so many kudos for that. But you know why he did it, right? Not because he was some great humanitarian. No. Poor kids are easy prey. The more vulnerable the girl, the less likely she was to tell her parents, and the less likely the police were to believe her. Predators have a well-honed radar for vulnerability, don't they? Coach Fowler's radar must've been screeching when he first saw me: lonely, dreamy, scarred.

Over the next few years, he bought that big summer house on Lake Huron, a Cadillac Escalade, a Ford Bronco, and a Jag. Wendy got to use the Corvette more and more.

I started cutting classes and spending more time with the smokers by the south wall. My grades slipped, then fell. By the end of my sophomore year, I was close to failing out.

Coach Fowler changed my life forever. I had been on track to go to college—maybe not on scholarship like you, Annie, but to some other life outside of Holly Grove. But after he raped me, I lost all momentum. I never made it out of here. You thought I was content to stay with our friends and family, having a job I didn't take home with me every night, like yours. You assumed I wanted a simpler life than you. But that wasn't it. I just gave up on everything for a while.

The only thing that kept me from officially dropping out of school was seeing Kathy. Life without a high school degree was miserable. She was always losing her job or pleading with the landlord to give them more time to make rent. Three-year-old Hayley was the one bright spot in her life.

One day, Hayley decided she wanted a goldfish. Kathy said the last thing she needed was another mouth to feed, but Hayley begged so adorably, we eventually headed to Meijer. We picked out a fish bowl, purple marbles, and a fish with a big orange tail that made Hayley say, "Ooh!"

At the registers, I got in line behind a woman who was pushing her own baby. Unlike Hayley, this baby was an infant, buckled into a car seat attached to the cart.

The mother turned to coo at her baby, and I saw her profile. It was Wendy. I recognized the car seat as the one she was scanning when we saw her here, six months before. I peered over Wendy's shoulder and I saw her tiny pink baby, which was making those cute squeaky monkey sounds infants make. In my mind, I saw the Coach's other "baby," his blue Corvette. I saw the yellow pill the nurse gave me to prevent a baby from growing inside me. And I started to cry.

I lowered my head so no one could see my face. My tears splashed onto the gray linoleum floor. I tried to keep quiet, but I guess I didn't.

I felt a hand on my shoulder. At first, I thought it was Kathy, till I heard the voice. "Hey, hey, it's okay," Wendy said.

Wendy Fowler was the last person in the world I expected to offer comfort. I looked up to see if she was mocking me. She was wearing mirrored sunglasses, in which I saw a double reflection of my own crumpled face. The corner of her mouth went back a millimeter, into something between a smile and a grimace. She pushed the glasses up to the top of her head. She had a nasty black eye: deep purple fading to greenish yellow at the edges.

"Don't cry," Wendy said, handing me a tissue from her purse. "You got the better deal, in the end."

I stared at her, needing a moment to comprehend the meaning packed into that sentence. Kathy got it faster than I did. She looked from Wendy's brand-new baby to her brand-new black eye. And Kathy, who lived in a trailer, said to Wendy, who lived in a pink château: "You poor thing."

38

Desiree Williams's office in the Holly Grove County DA's office was eerily similar to Anna's in the U.S. Attorney's Office in D.C. Scuffed white walls, putty-colored filing cabinets, government-blue carpet. Anna wondered if a single carpet manufacturer supplied all the prosecutors' offices around America. Sitting in the guest chair, she again had the disconcerting sense of living on the other side of the looking glass.

"How can you go forward with the case against my sister when you know this?" Anna asked, tapping the police reports involving Coach Fowler. "This man was a serial pedophile. He should've been locked up years ago."

"First of all, these are unsupported allegations," Desiree said. "They were sealed for a reason. You never should've seen them. Second, whether or not they're true, your sister can't just go and kill the man."

"He was a monster."

"He was a person. His death leaves a grieving widow and a fatherless little girl."

"There were dozens of people who could have wanted him dead."

"Maybe. But there was only one person who slept with him the night he died, fought with him, and had his bloody clothes in her house."

"A jury will cheer for whoever killed him." Anna could hardly believe these words were coming from her mouth.

"No, it won't, because a jury will never hear about unsubstantiated allegations offered to dirty up the victim. Those cases are sealed, and the judge ordered them to stay sealed. Just because someone dropped them on your doorstep doesn't mean you can introduce them in court."

This was true.

"Why was this man never prosecuted?" Anna leaned forward, looking into the prosecutor's eyes. "I know these are hard cases. But six cases over fifteen years. Decline after decline after decline. What the hell was going on here?"

"Don't raise your voice at me." Desiree leaned forward at exactly the same angle. "How can you sit there and tell me I should have brought a statutory rape case with a recanting, uncooperative victim and no physical evidence—that means no evidence of any kind—but now I should *drop* a murder case with strong evidence because you find the victim unsavory? It's a crime to kill someone, whether they're a bad person or not."

"*Why* was there no evidence in the rape cases? Were sex kits done? If you had his semen and their birth certificates, you'd have a case."

Desiree looked down. "Sex kits were performed in some of the cases. They weren't processed."

"Weren't processed?" Anna stared at her. "You mean, they didn't test the swabs for whether there was semen? Or run a DNA profile? Why not?"

"Look, it's an ongoing problem. In Detroit alone, there are over ten thousand untested rape kits going back twenty-five years. Their prosecutor's office is as overworked and underpaid as we are. They're trying to go through the backlog, but nobody's got the spare $15 million it will take to do it. Detroit is talking about selling off the paintings at the Detroit Institute of Arts to pay its creditors. We have our share of untested kits in Holly Grove. Don't look at me like that."

"This is insane," Anna said.

"If you're upset, write an editorial in the *Free Press*. I applaud your concern. But it doesn't have a thing to do with your sister's case."

"Of course it does. Every one of his rape victims, their fathers, their brothers, are potential killers, who you didn't investigate." Anna handed Desiree a letter. "I'm requesting that you test the rape kits from those six sealed cases and turn over the results. I'm also requesting any information you have regarding these girls—especially their current whereabouts. I want to talk to them."

"Absolutely not. You aren't supposed to have these reports in the first place. These cases were sealed by court order. That's just as much to protect the complainant as the alleged wrongdoer. If you want anything more, ask the court." Desiree put the letter down and looked at Anna. "I don't want to tell you how to do your job, but the trial of your sister will focus on one simple question: Did she kill him or not? The coach's background is not relevant to that. The testing of old rape kits is not relevant to that."

"I understand your perspective," Anna said. "I hope you'll understand mine."

After their meeting, Anna walked to the steps of the courthouse next door. Three local news vans were parked at the curb. Earlier, she had e-mailed the stations, saying she was holding a press conference. She had even more to announce than she'd anticipated. She greeted the journalists and waited as they set up their cameras and microphones.

"Thank you for coming today," Anna said. "Some information about Coach Fowler has come to my attention. Over the past fifteen years, six underage girls reported to the police that he molested them. I'm asking anyone who made a report, or their family, to come forward and talk to me. I'm also asking anyone who was victimized by Owen Fowler, but who didn't make a report, to come forward now. Sexual assault is the most underreported crime in America. For every police report that exists, there are probably several girls who were assaulted but didn't tell anyone.

"I'm also calling on the Holly Grove Police Department and DA's office to perform DNA testing on the girls' rape kits. Apparently, these rape kits have been sitting, untested, for many years, along with thousands of other rape kits in Detroit and Holly Grove.

These kits are like gold, as an evidentiary matter. But not if they're sitting in a warehouse, untested and rotting."

"Why are you bringing this up now?" a reporter asked. "Owen Fowler is dead. Even if this is true, he can't hurt anyone else."

"This is a failure of the whole system, which is hurting the entire town. Coach Fowler used his position to victimize girls whose families trusted him. The failure to follow up on crucial evidence in this case enabled him. If this isn't fixed, it can happen again."

"You didn't call us here because you're a rape-crisis advocate," a reporter said. "You're defending your sister in a murder case. What does this have to do with the case?"

"Sex crimes thrive from secrecy. Talking about it is the first step in healing. The mothers and fathers of Holly Grove deserve to know." Anna looked at the cameras. "Ask your children. Talk to them about this. The truth is the first step to justice."

The reporters lobbed a few more questions—about her trial strategy and how Jody was doing—but Anna shook her head, thanked them, and walked from the steps.

Anna couldn't tell what the results of her news conference would be. Maybe nobody would listen or care. Maybe people wouldn't believe that the coach was a predator. But the only way to save her sister—and this town—was to get the truth out. Whatever bumps followed, she'd just have to ride out.

The first bump came sooner than she'd expected.

39

That night, the local TV stations played the clip of Anna's press conference. She and Jody sat on the couch and watched. A frowning reporter spoke to the camera. "The town of Holly Grove was rocked by scandal today, as the attorney for a woman charged with killing Coach Owen Fowler claims that he was a serial rapist. Is this a dark secret the championship football team has been hiding for two decades? Or a defendant's Hail Mary attempt to dirty up her murder victim's name before trial?"

Jody's landline rang. Anna picked it up. "Hello?"

"Burn in hell, you lying slut."

Click.

"Who was that?" Jody asked.

"Wrong number."

The house phone rang again. Anna looked at it, hesitated, then answered. "Hello?"

"I will kill you and your family and shit on your corpses."

She hung up and looked at Jody.

"I think you're going to need to get an unlisted number."

The phone rang again. Anna picked up, hung up, then left it off the hook.

She poured Jody a glass of milk and sat next to her on the couch.

"We're pissing a lot of people off," Jody said. "Some of them might be jurors."

"Anyone who would make threatening phone calls is not someone we wanted on the jury in the first place."

Jody nodded and sipped the milk. "Okay . . . but we're not gonna know who they are when we pick the jury, are we?"

A minute later, Anna's cell phone rang. "Oh, for Pete's sake." Anna went to turn it off but saw it was Cooper. She answered.

"Ballsy move," he said.

"Ballsy or stupid." Anna described the angry calls. "Jody's leaning toward stupid, I think."

Jody smiled at her.

"You want me to come stay over at Jody's house tonight?" Cooper asked.

Anna relayed the question to Jody, who shook her head.

"No thanks," Anna told Cooper. "We'll be fine."

Another call buzzed. She looked at the incoming number. It was Jack. She quickly said good-bye to Cooper and clicked over.

"Hi, Jack."

"Anna! Is everything okay?"

"Yeah, we're fine. How'd you hear? I thought it was just on the local news here."

"I have a Google alert out on you. I'm not stalking you, I'm just—worried about you."

She liked the idea that he was looking after her from afar.

"There's a lot of support for the football team here," Anna said. "It's the one thing everyone is proud of, especially with all the auto factories closing. People don't want to believe that their local hero could be so evil. They've seen so many other shining things turn to rust."

"Have you had any threats yet?"

"How did you know?"

"It's the way these things tend to go."

"Yeah, we've had a few phone calls. But Holly Grove folks are good people; they'll vent, but they won't hurt anyone."

"You're too trusting. Does Jody have an alarm system in her house?"

"No."

"I'm calling ADT and getting a guy to come out tomorrow."

"You don't need to do that," she said, although the idea made her happy. Twenty minutes after they hung up, she got an e-mail from him, forwarding an appointment with ADT for 4:00 P.M. the next day.

That night, lying in the dark, she wished they had a security system already. Every creak of the house sounded like footsteps of the bogeyman.

When she woke up the next morning, though, everything seemed fine. She went downstairs, groggily started the coffee, and logged on to the *Holly Grove Observer* website. The headline read: "Allegations of Sex Abuse Shake Community." The article made ample use of disclaiming words like *alleged*, *claimed*, and *if true*, laying out the facts but distancing the newspaper, making clear that it was just reporting the story, not believing it. The comments section was full of vitriol and misspellings.

> This is disgracefull. That girl killed this man, and is now draging his name thru the mud. Shame on her and her sister.

> I don't know what's worse, murdering this man, or defaming him now that he's dead and can't defend himself.

> Curtis sisters, you're the ones who diserve to be killed

> Coach Fowler was the best thing in Holly Grove. I hope this lying bitch rots in jail and gets gangraped every day.

Anna flagged the last two as "inappropriate" and hoped a moderator would take them down soon. She heard Jody emerging from her bedroom, and quickly clicked away from the comments. She would try to shield her sister from as much of this as she could. She heard Jody opening the front door to get the newspaper. A moment later came a scream.

"Anna!"

She ran to the front porch. Jody was standing in the yard in her pajamas, looking back at the front of the house. Anna came out and stood next to her. The words *SLUT*, *WHORE*, *BITCH*, *MURDERER*, and *LIAR* were spray-painted in black on the house's white siding. *YOU WILL BURN IN HELL* was in red over the door. The letters dripped downward, like they were oozing blood.

"I don't think the homeowners' association is going to approve this," Jody said.

"Oh God, Jo. I'm sorry."

Anna took pictures with her phone. Then they tried to scrub it off. They learned that spray paint does not come off with Fantastik, 409, steel wool, or bleach. Anna threw her own soiled clothes into the hamper and borrowed a pair of Jody's jeans and a T-shirt.

They went to Home Depot, where a grandmotherly salesperson recommended covering the graffiti with primer and paint. But, the salesperson said, aluminum siding didn't take well to being painted. The prettier but pricier option was replacing the siding. Anna and Jody went a few aisles over to look at samples. Jody ran her hands over different shades of beige siding. "I needed a home makeover anyhow." All things considered, she was calm.

Until she got a phone call from her neighbor. Anna could only hear Jody's side of the conversation.

"Hi, Tammy. Yeah, I'm at Home Depot. I'm fine. Anna's here, she's fine too. What's up? Oh my God. Oh shit. I'll be right there."

She grabbed Anna, and they ran out of the store, leaving their cart without buying anything.

40

Jody raced the Yukon home. They saw the column of smoke from a mile away: thick and black, snaking up against the pale autumn sky. Anna smelled it as Jody swerved the car into her subdivision. When they got to her street, fire trucks were parked at the curb, neighbors stood outside pointing, and firefighters sprayed hoses at the burning building. The flames crackled and danced as they consumed Jody's house.

"No!" Jody jumped out of the car and ran toward her house. "No! No!"

A firefighter grabbed her and held her back. She fought herself free and kept running. Another firefighter held out his arms and blocked her way. It took three men to restrain her. Finally, she collapsed on the lawn, sobbing. Anna crouched next to her and held her tight. The heat of the fire radiated from the house; the front of her body was hot, while her back was cold. A reporter ran over and held his microphone in front of Jody. She didn't seem to notice. She looked at Anna, tears streaking her face.

"It's everything I have," Jody wailed. "Everything. All my pictures of Mom, every card you wrote me, every corsage from every school dance I ever dried under a dictionary. My sonogram pictures. Everything I've worked for or ever cared about in my entire life."

Anna held her tight. "I know," Anna said. "But it's just things. It's only *things*. They didn't get you. They didn't get your memories of Mom. They didn't get your baby."

The flames roared, the house moaned, and the roof crashed down in a shower of sparks. A wave of heat flashed on her face, and Anna held up an arm to protect them both. The firefighters shouted and pushed everyone back, as the flames grew higher. Anna ended up standing with Jody on Tammy's lawn. Tammy held her baby on her hip and tried to comfort Jody too. The reporters crowded around them, asking questions, but Anna shook her head and asked them to please give her sister some space. The cameras moved a few steps back but kept rolling. Jody cried until her voice cracked, and then she cried until it was gone, and then she cried without making any noise.

■ ■ ■

Hours later, two blackened walls were left standing. The rest of the house had burned to the ground. The ruins were a charred, soggy mess. Anna stood with an arm around Jody's shoulders as they watched the firefighters spraying the final embers. The news vans loaded up and drove away. The air was thick with the scent of wet charcoal. All of Jody's possessions were ashes.

At 4:00, an ADT van drove up, and a serviceman hopped out. He stood looking between Jody's charred lot and his clipboard. Anna realized he was the guy Jack had hired to install a security system. A wave of hysteria bubbled up in her chest and she let out a sound that was close to a bray. She shook herself into some semblance of competence and sent the guy home.

She stood with Jody and patted her back. A firefighter came over to them. "Do you have a place to stay for the night? If not, we can put you up in a hotel."

Jody shook her head.

"We'd appreciate it," Anna said. "Thanks. Do you have any idea how the fire got started?"

"We'll need to sift through the scene. But, from the looks of it, I'd say it was an electrical fire."

"Electrical fire, my ass," Jody spoke in a hoarse whisper. "We all know this was straight-up retaliation."

"Ma'am, I understand how you feel. But no one saw anyone tampering with your house. There's no indication of arson. We'll let you know if we find anything to the contrary."

A blue Bulldogs football ribbon was pinned onto his uniform, right over his heart. Was there anyone in this town they could trust? Suddenly, she didn't want to be in a strange hotel where the Holly Grove authorities knew exactly what room number they were in.

"On second thought," Anna said. "We'll stay with a friend."

■ ■ ■

They went to Cooper's house. Sparky ran around the yard in circles, he was so excited to see them. Cooper embraced Anna, then Jody. "Thank God you're okay." He led them into his house and told them they should move their stuff back in his bedroom.

"We don't have any 'stuff,'" Jody's eyes were red and puffy. "I now own a car, a purse, and the clothes I'm wearing."

"Also the clothes I'm wearing," Anna said. "These are yours too."

They smelled of smoke and tears. Cooper insisted they rest while he made dinner. Jody went upstairs and took a shower. Anna grabbed a beer and went outside with Cooper into the cool fall evening. He prepared the grill to make burgers. The scent of charcoal made her queasy.

"What's wrong?" he asked, looking at her face.

"That's kind of what Jody's house smelled like."

He closed the grill and ordered two large pizzas from the one Little Caesars brave enough to operate nearby. Anna took her turn showering while he went to pick it up. Standing in the claw-foot tub with the water washing over her back, Anna smelled the smoke leaching from her skin and hair. She had to shampoo three times before it was gone.

They ate pepperoni pizza, slick and delicious with grease. Anna and Jody ate a large pie between the two of them. They hadn't eaten anything else the whole day and were ravenous. When the pizza was gone, Cooper took out Häagen-Dazs vanilla ice cream and served it with pitted black cherries on top. Anna felt her shoulders unclenching for the first time that day. Now that no one's life or home was in immediate danger, she became aware of the more mundane challenges facing them.

"Jody, we have to find you a place to rent," Anna said.

"You guys should stay here," Cooper said. "Through the trial. I love having you here. Sparky does too." The dog grinned at the mention of his name.

Anna was touched. She liked being here. She felt safe with Cooper in the same room. But an extended stay was too much to ask of him.

"Coop, that's so nice of you. But we can't impose on you like that."

"You're great houseguests. Totally brighten up the place."

"We leave long blond hairs in your shower drains," Jody said.

"Makes me look far cooler than I actually am."

"Seriously," Anna said. "It's too dangerous. Half of Michigan wants to lynch us."

"Which is exactly why you should stay here." His voice grew fierce. He patted his waist, where his gun was holstered. "I know my way around a battlefield, which seems to be what you've gotten yourself into. I know Michigan. I can protect you. Unlikely as this sounds, my house is one of the safest places for you to be right now."

Jody said, "You know things are really bad when Detroit is your safe haven."

Anna met his eyes. His offer was sincere. She was humbled by his generosity—and still uncertain she could accept it.

"Will insurance pay for you to live somewhere else while the house is rebuilt?" Anna asked.

"I have no idea. The thought of dealing with that is exhausting," Jody said. "But if they'll pay rent, let's just 'rent' from Cooper. Give the poor man some compensation for all his trouble. I want to stay here, Annie. It's far away from everyone who's trying to hurt me. And no one's getting past these two."

Jody gestured to Cooper and his dog. Anna took a deep breath. She felt so jittery. She realized she wanted to stay with Cooper but was scared to, at the same time. For a number of reasons.

She looked at her sister, who was scooping the last bit of ice cream from her bowl and looking calmer than she had all day. Anna would do what made Jody comfortable. She was already worried about the effect that stress might be having on the baby growing inside her sister's belly.

"Okay," she said. "Thank you, Coop."

"Attagirl."

After dinner, Anna asked Jody if she wanted to go over her insurance policy, but Jody shook her head. "Tomorrow. I need to think about anything but my own life right now." They moved to the living room and turned on the TV. Jody curled up in an easy chair, scrolled to HBO GO, and clicked on *True Detective*.

"Do you mind?" Cooper asked Anna, gesturing to his leg.

Anna shook her head, though she had no idea what he meant. He rolled up his jeans, unstrapped his metal prosthetic, and took it off his leg. He set the whole contraption to the side of the couch, then peeled a silicone cup from his limb and set it down too. For the first time, she saw where his own leg ended: just below his knee. The skin simply folded into a round nub with a seamlike scar at the end. He pulled the jeans down again quickly.

"It aches sometimes when I've been standing on it a long time," he said. "Sorry if that grossed you out."

"It didn't," Anna said. In fact, it made her want to put her arms around him.

They watched *True Detective* until a particularly gory murder scene made Jody blanch, and then Cooper picked up the remote and steered them through the cable channels. When they got to the news, Jody cried, "Stop! Go back."

He flipped back to CNN. The station was playing a video of Jody's house on fire. It cut to neighbors looking horrified, and then to Anna holding Jody while she sobbed on the ground. "It's everything I have," Jody sobbed on-screen. "Everything I've worked for." Seeing it from this angle, they looked very small and alone, huddled together on the lawn, just two young women with nothing else in the world. Anna bristled at first, thinking: *We are strong!* Then she accepted it. It was fine publicity, certainly sympathetic.

Jody was going to need all the sympathy she could use in the coming months.

"You've gone national," Cooper said.

Jody on the TV cried and keened. Jody on the couch said, "Oh, man. Have I really gotten that fat? I thought the camera was only supposed to add ten pounds."

Anna said, "You are three months pregnant. And you look as pretty as a woman can look while her house is burning behind her."

The picture went to Jake Tapper sitting at his glossy silver CNN desk. He spoke with an earnest gravitas that made the whole situation seem very dire. "What started as a murder trial in Holly Grove, Michigan, has turned into something much more complicated. The accused murderer is twenty-five-year-old Jody Curtis." They flashed a picture of Jody from the high school yearbook, looking younger, blonder, and far more innocent than she did today. "She is accused of killing her married lover, Owen Fowler, a high school football coach who led his team to several state championships. The coach was a local hero in his native Michigan. At least until yesterday.

"Yesterday, the victim's sister, who is also her lawyer, made a shocking accusation."

The video flashed to a clip of Anna on the Holly Grove courthouse steps, saying the coach was a serial pedophile and asking other victims to come forward. Just watching it sent a shot of adrenaline through her gut.

Tapper continued. "Sources within the Holly Grove Police Department, who wish to remain anonymous because they aren't authorized to speak about the matter, have confirmed that, between 1999 and 2014, six teenage girls reported that Coach Fowler sexually assaulted them. And, as the defense attorney alleged, the sex kits in those cases were never tested.

"The DA's office released a statement this afternoon saying the old rape kits will not be tested, as these cases became moot when Owen Fowler died.

"So far, no one has come forward as a victim. Instead, the town has rallied to the defense of its murdered hero."

The camera cut to an elderly woman standing in front of a 7-Eleven. "What that girl did was despicable. First, she kills her married lover, then she smears his name. I feel so bad for the family. A little girl lost her father and now she has to hear this garbage."

Tapper said, "For others, the reaction was even stronger." They showed Jody's house covered in graffiti, with Anna and Jody trying to scrub the words from the siding. A neighbor must have taken the photo this morning. Some of the words were too nasty for prime time and had been blurred out. "This morning, Curtis's house was covered in graffiti. And this afternoon, it burned down." The dancing orange flames made for dramatic TV footage. "The Holly Grove fire marshal says it was likely an electrical fire, but the string of incidents has raised eyebrows. And the vigilante group Anonymous has now gotten involved."

"They have?" Anna murmured.

Tapper continued, "Anonymous is the hacking collective known for, among other things, breaking into computer systems and publicizing their contents. They broke some key evidence in the Steubenville rape case and have protested during several of the most notorious rape cases over the past few years. The trial of Jody Curtis is scheduled for next February."

The screen showed a YouTube video dated this afternoon. Someone in a white plastic Guy Fawkes mask looked at the camera. The mask had arched black eyebrows, a soul patch on a pointy chin, and a sardonic grin. The wall behind him was black. When he spoke, his voice was deep and electronically twisted. He sounded like an evil robot.

"We are Anonymous. We are legion. We do not forgive. We do not forget. We expose hypocrisy and abuse. Holly Grove, Michigan: expect us."

41

That night, Anna couldn't sleep. Every random noise she heard could be someone coming to burn down Cooper's house. It could be an Anonymous protester coming to hack her computer and leave a white mask next to her pillow. It could be— She sat up in bed, forcing her imagination to stop before it really got on a roll. Jody lay next to her, snoring softly. Anna pulled the covers up to her sister's shoulder and kissed her forehead. She tiptoed down the steps, picturing a hot cup of tea and a good book to distract her. She kept a hand on the wall to make sure she didn't fall off the banister-less staircase in the dark. At the bottom, she fumbled around trying to find the light switch.

"Hey," a low voice whispered.

She jumped and let out a small shriek. Then she saw it was Cooper. He was sitting in the den, on a couch beneath a bay window that looked out onto his front yard. She put her hand to her chest, took a deep breath, and sat next to him. Sparky lay on the ground by his feet. The dog licked her ankle in greeting.

"Wow, I'm on edge," she said. "I don't usually shriek at scary stuff. And you're the least scary thing in Detroit."

"I'll have you know I'm extremely scary. Kids dress up like me for Halloween."

A breeze ruffled Cooper's dark hair. She saw that the window was open. There was no screen, but metal bars covered it. Something long and thin stood on the floor, propped against the sill. The window faced the empty street, where the single working streetlight provided the only illumination.

"What are you doing?" she asked.

"Sometimes Sparky and I just like to sit here and watch what's happening outside."

"You're keeping guard, aren't you?"

"Old habits die hard."

Anna heard a train passing, far away.

He said, "You had a tough day. You should get some sleep."

"I know. I can't."

"Yeah, I get that sometimes. The silver lining is you can get a lot done at one A.M. There's not much to interrupt you."

"Your glass is always half full. How are you so cheerful?" Anna said. She looked at his leg. "After—everything?"

He shrugged. "Happiness comes from inside you, not what happens to you. I read about this study: They looked at people who won the lottery and people who became paraplegic. For a while, the lottery winners were very happy, and the paraplegics were very depressed. But after a few months, they all returned to around whatever level of happiness they were at before. It's an internal thing. Being satisfied with how you're living your life. The connections you have to the people you care about."

"Still, I'd rather win the lottery."

He laughed. "I live in a mansion with two beautiful women sleeping in my bed. That's better than the lottery."

"You're a good sport, Coop."

From outside the window came the sound of whispering voices. Cooper turned and looked out. Sparky sat up and looked worriedly at him. Anna moved closer to Cooper and peered out the window with him.

Four figures in black ski masks and dark clothes came down the street. Their feet crunched on the gravel. They all held something small and metal in their hands. They turned up the driveway and silently advanced on the house.

Cooper lifted the long weapon from the sill and pointed it out the window, between the metal bars. As they came close to the porch, he closed one eye and aimed at the figures. He looked like an army sniper.

"You can't just shoot them," Anna whispered.

"This is Detroit," he said. "The rules are different."

His hands shifted and the weapon exploded. The first dark figure fell down with a shriek. The other three froze. Cooper aimed at them. Anna put a hand on his shoulder to pull him back but then saw that the instrument in his hands wasn't a rifle, but some sort of high-powered hose. A blast of water shot from it. He pointed it from one figure to the next, knocking them down with the force of the spray. All four fell to the ground. When the first one tried to get up, Cooper turned the hose and blasted him down again.

Then he strode to the front door and out to the lawn. Sparky ran next to him. Anna followed as far as the front porch. Cooper went up to the first intruder, grabbed the black ski mask, and pulled it off. Beneath was a mop of highlighted hair and pouty pink lips. He pulled off all four of the masks. Each person beneath was a pretty, soaking-wet teenage girl. They sat up and coughed up the water they'd inhaled. They held cans of spray paint. He took the cans.

Anna came down the steps. "Are you the ones who messed up Jody's house?"

The pink-lipped girl looked up at her with hate. "No. But you guys deserved it."

"This woman"—Cooper pointed at Anna—"is standing up for girls like you."

"She and her trashy sister are ruining our town."

"You need to spend more time finding the truth than trying to slut-shame the people who are brave enough to put it out there. But let me put it in simpler terms. You don't want to fuck with me."

De'Andre and Lamar stepped out from the backyard. De'Andre held a hoe, and Lamar held a shovel. De'Andre grinned, showing off his grille. "Yeah, the farmer's one crazy dude. War messed up his head. He could explode, any minute."

"Get out of here," Cooper said, "and tell your friends that the next person who steps foot on my property isn't going to step back off again."

The girls looked between Cooper, his giant dog, and his armed farmhands. They ran, tripping over themselves and the gravel, disappearing into the black.

Cooper turned to De'Andre and Lamar. "Thanks."

"This is, like, the best class I've ever taken. Do we get extra credit for this?"

"Definitely."

He told the interns to go home and get some rest. Back in the house, Cooper turned on the lights and went to the kitchen.

"How did you know?" Anna asked.

"I heard that a group of teenagers were coming. I didn't know it was going to be a bunch of girls. No offense."

"None taken."

"You have to hand it to them. They must really hate you. I mean, just driving into Detroit is a serious adventure for a gaggle of sixteen-year-old suburbanites." He poured cider into a cup and handed it to her. "You and Jody have seriously pissed off a lot of people."

"Yeah."

"Cheers to that."

They raised their glasses and drank the sweet cider.

He rinsed their cups, turned off the lights, and returned to the den, propping up the power sprayer on the windowsill again.

"You think anyone else will come?" Anna asked.

"Unlikely. But I'm gonna hang out here just in case."

"I'll keep you company." She sat down next to him. They talked about his time at MSU and her time at U of M, his brothers and her parents, whether ground buffalo was tastier than ground turkey. The night was quiet. After an hour, she rubbed her eyes.

"I'm completely exhausted but buzzing with adrenaline."

"Arson and marauding packs of teenyboppers can do that." He put his arm on the back of the couch. "Come here."

She looked at him. "Cooper, I'm sorry, I'm not—"

"I know," he interrupted. "Me neither. Not tonight, anyway. Just curl up. You need to sleep. This is my patented, no-fail, go-to-sleep method. You'll be sawing logs in no time."

His lopsided grin reminded her of the sunny farm boy who still lived inside this big Army Ranger's body. She fitted herself into the crook of his arm and laid her head on his chest. A cool breeze came in from the window, but she was warm and comfortable pressed against him. His arm wrapped around her.

"I'm going to tell you all about green farming," he said. "I think you'll find it riveting. There are certain goals everyone agrees on—economic, environmental, and social sustainability—but a lot of debate about the practical application. Recent environmental methods focus on crop rotations that mitigate weeds and disease, pest-control strategies that don't use toxic chemicals, and soil and water conservation practices that minimize adverse impacts to the immediate and off-farm environments."

"Oh my God." She yawned. "You're good."

"I didn't get a degree in agricultural, food, and resource economics for nothing. Wait till I get to irrigation technology." He continued talking. His voice was low and comforting, his words esoteric and dry. Anna's eyelids drifted down. She smelled cedar and cherries on his soft T-shirt and felt his thumb brushing her shoulder. She slept.

42

Owen Fowler deserved to die. I knew that for over a decade, from the day he raped me till the day he went up in flames. But I didn't kill him in that stupid muscle car . . . although, I have to admit, the poetic justice of that was pretty satisfying: in the car where he raped me, by way of the football stadium that allowed him to do so much evil over so many years. But that wasn't my plan. My plan was to drown him.

It was a warm night in May, and I was at Screecher's. He was sitting at the bar, sipping whiskey, straight up. That's what he did most nights after practice, if he didn't go to the casino. Other than in the stadium, he was most at home in Screecher's, that living shrine to him.

I wore jeans that hugged the curves of my ass, and a shiny black halter top that showed off all the cleavage I hadn't had back in high school. My long blond hair hung in fresh-washed splendor down my back. Several men watched me as I walked in ridiculously high heels over to Coach's side.

"What are you drinking?" I asked.

"Jim Beam." He smiled at me. "Hi . . ."

"Jody," I said. "Jody Curtis."

"Sure, sure. It's been a while."

In fact, it had been ten years. I occasionally saw him around town, and if our eyes met we would nod at each other, but we never stopped to chat.

Now, as we exchanged small talk, he didn't seem as wary as you might expect. I imagine it was because he'd targeted so many girls at that point. Some, like me, fought him. Some, like Wendy, liked it.

Many continued to crush on him for years afterward. It was probably hard to keep us straight.

The night he raped me changed the course of my life, but for him, it was just one in a series of the very similar events that played out on the seats of his expensive cars over decades. He might not even remember that I was one of the ones who fought.

The bartender came over. It was Grady Figler, in all his tattooed glory, and I almost fell off my bar stool. We'd hooked up the weekend before, after a friend's house party. He'd called once, but I hadn't gotten back to him. I was too busy plotting. Now, Grady greeted me with a big grin, like I was there to see him. I wasn't. I didn't even know he worked there, and seeing him there was awkward. I ordered a Jim Beam, straight up. When he brought it, I thanked him and turned to Owen. I saw Grady standing there—maybe confused, maybe a little hurt. I felt bad, but I had an important goal that night, and playing nice with Grady was not it. In my peripheral vision, I saw him eventually walk off and take someone else's order.

I lifted my glass to the coach. "Cheers to a great season."

He smiled and we clinked glasses. The whiskey burned going down.

"Who's going to be your first string this year?" I asked.

That was all it took to get Coach talking in earnest. He talked recruiting and practice. He talked scholarships and push-ups. He talked about the pressure of having the whole town's reputation on his back. I nodded sympathetically and interjected the appropriate exclamations. But mostly I was experiencing some major butterflies from being this close to him again.

I was riveted by his face—how much it had changed, and how much it hadn't over the last ten years. His blond hair had more silver in it now, especially around the temples. The lines around his blue eyes were deeper. But his figure was still slim and athletic; his polo shirt hugged him a bit tighter than it needed to, showing off that fact. His skin glowed with the perfectly even tan of someone who worked hard at it. He was fifty, but he was still very attractive, in a highly produced sort of way. It wasn't fair. But the world's not fair, and Coach Fowler's ability to stave off decrepitude was just a tiny sliver of that.

I was keenly aware of how a decade had changed our dynamic. We were still twenty-five years apart, but forty-to-fifteen feels very different from fifty-to-twenty-five. Ten years ago, he'd been a grown-up and I was a kid. I thought he knew everything. He was like a god, on a different dimension from me. Now, we were still far apart, but we inhabited the same universe. If necessary, I could hold my own as a fellow adult. The shift was subtle but powerful. He must have felt it too.

We had a friendly conversation, during which I made sure my bar stool crept closer to his. I started touching his arm when he made a funny point and tipping my head to expose the side of my neck. I flipped my hair back over my shoulder and licked my lips. When the moment was right, I put my hand lightly on his knee.

He smiled broadly, said how great it was to catch up, and left.

I felt like an idiot. The people watching me flirt now smirked at me sitting alone.

I could only come up with two explanations. First, he was suspicious because I accused him of rape ten years earlier. But I didn't get that vibe from him. Like I said, he didn't seem wary. And I wasn't sure he even knew I made a report to the police, much less remembered it now. Nothing had ever come of it.

I knew it wasn't loyalty to his wife.

That left one other explanation, and that's the one I thought more likely. He just wasn't interested. Now that I had my own grown-up power and control, the turn-on was gone. I had real breasts and hips and a mind of my own, all of which I enjoy, thankyouverymuch. But he liked girls who were young, awed, and easy to control. At twenty-five years old, I had aged out of his attraction.

Grady came over and poured another two fingers of Jim Beam into my glass. "Don't take it personally," he said. "That man's never gone home with anyone who's old enough to drink here."

43

"Good morning, sunshines!" Jody trilled. She stood in the doorway to the den, wearing pajamas and looking pleased. "Someone had a good night."

Anna lifted her head from Cooper's chest. Light streamed into the den through the open window, where the power sprayer was still propped. She looked around, trying to get her bearings. Cooper lay on his back with his arm around her; she was curled into him. They were both on the couch below the window. His eyes blinked open and met hers.

He said, "It *is* a good morning."

Anna sat up quickly. "Jody! Hi! Cooper and I were, uh, just talking last night, and I guess I fell asleep—"

"You don't need to explain to me," Jody said. "You two should've hooked up months ago. I'm going to have some cornflakes." She padded to the kitchen.

Cooper sat up. On his face was a day's worth of stubble and a grin.

"I'm sorry." Anna laughed self-consciously. "She can be so goofy."

"She's right, though."

Anna's laugh trailed off. "Coop." She looked down at her jeans. "My life is in D.C. now. I'm going back when the trial's over. I like you too much to hurt you."

"You think you can do worse than the Taliban?" A smile crinkled the corners of his eyes. He tucked a strand of her hair behind her ear. "Give it your best shot."

He stood, stretched, and trotted up the stairs. She watched him go.

■ ■ ■

Despite Anna's entreaties, Jody insisted on going to work. "They're not gonna scare me off," Jody announced. And then, less defiantly: "Plus I can't afford to lose my job."

"Call me when you get there," Anna finally conceded. "And then at your morning break, at your lunch break, and at your afternoon break. And then call me when you're on your way home."

The arson had scared *her*.

After Jody left, Cooper brought out a folding table and helped Anna set it up under the window in his living room. From there, she could do her work with a view of the apple trees, the goldfish pond below, and the Detroit skyline beyond. She thanked him, and he went off to work on his farm.

But what work could she do? She'd been working on Jody's computer, which had gone up in the blaze. She had lost all her work product for the case. Everything: her notes, her legal briefs, the five sealed police reports that had been anonymously left on Jody's doorstep. She wondered if that was the purpose of the fire. The thought made her stomach hurt. How far would the town go to stop her from defending her sister? How much danger were she and Jody still in?

She called her sister thirty minutes later and made sure she'd made it safely into the GM factory.

"I'm fine!" Jody answered.

"Thanks." Anna hung up and tried to be productive.

The first thing she needed was to buy a computer. The practice of law was fully computerized, and she couldn't use her DOJ equipment to work on Jody's case. She used her phone to do some research on laptops. After an hour, she ordered a Mac, which would be shipped to her.

A figure walked by outside, and she lowered her phone. It was Cooper, with Sparky trotting at his heels. He wore jeans and a flannel shirt and carried a bulky sack over his shoulder. She tried not to

stare at his rear—but failed. It was both a relief and a disappointment when he disappeared from view.

In quick sequence, Grace and Jack called, having seen the story
of the fire on the news. Anna was glad to hear familiar voices. She
heard the concern in theirs. She also heard, in the background of
Jack's call, a woman playing with Olivia. Anna thought of the red
negligee draped over the chair in Jack's bedroom. Her heart hurt.
She hung up as quickly as politely possible.

She turned back to Jody's case, trying to figure out how to rebuild all the work she'd lost. She could get another copy of everything the prosecutor had already turned over. She could get a copy
of all the documents she herself had filed with the court. But her
handwritten notes were irreplaceable, as were the sealed police reports that had landed on Jody's doorstep. She might never be able
to see those again. She did not have the information within them
memorized. It was a tremendous loss.

She used her phone's browser to skim through news websites,
looking for coverage of Jody. She found stories similar to the one
reported on CNN last night, but no new developments.

In the far distance, she caught a glimpse of Cooper pushing a
wheelbarrow toward the community garden. She watched until he
turned into a row of sunflowers and was out of her sight. She was
too easily distracted today. But, she realized, Cooper was one of
the few bright spots in her life right now. Was it really so bad to
think about something good for once? It was certainly better than
obsessing about that red negligee. Cooper was kind and smart. He
had her back. She let herself linger on the memory of how warm
and comfortable she felt this morning waking up with him on the
couch. The moment when she looked up and met his eyes—she
wanted to kiss him. That was crazy, of course. She shouldn't risk
the single good thing in her life by adding the wild card of romance.
But . . . was that really a healthy way to think? If something was
good, you should want more of it, not less.

Anna shook her head and vowed to get something—anything—
done workwise. She logged on to the Westlaw app on her phone

and searched for cases where the government had been forced to turn over sealed materials.

After a while, she gave up and admitted that she couldn't concentrate. She set her phone down again. She stood and looked out the window, trying to see where Cooper had gone. She sat and chewed her thumbnail.

Then she was on her feet, striding out the door, through the orchard, and across the street to the community garden.

It was a perfect Indian summer day. In a bright blue sky, the sun smiled down, just strong enough to warm her skin. The air smelled of soil, grass, and apples. At the edge of the garden, she found a row of butterfly bushes, which hadn't been there earlier this summer. Dozens of butterflies danced around the cone-shaped purple flowers. A few blossoms had fallen to the ground; she picked one up and inhaled its sweetness.

She found Cooper in a field of sunflowers, shoveling loam from the wheelbarrow onto the ground. The yellow flowers were taller than him, with thick green stalks.

"These really grew," she said. "When I was here in June, they were only waist high."

He pitched the blade into the earth and straightened with a smile. "Every living thing reaches for the sun."

"Not everything."

He nodded and took the purple flower from her hand. He held it still in his palm. After a moment, a pair of butterflies, one orange, one yellow, flitted around each other and floated down to his hand. They landed on the flower and drank from it. Their velvety black antennae brushed against each other.

"I'm glad you found the butterfly bushes," he said. "I planted them after the memorial service. You liked the flock of monarchs. And it seemed like an interesting experiment to see if I could get butterflies in Detroit."

She looked from his hands to his face. His eyes were strikingly beautiful—lightest blue irises encircled by deep indigo—but what she liked most was how much kindness they held.

"It can only be a fling," she said. Her voice was hoarse, and she cleared her throat. "Just two friends having fun. Until I go back to D.C."

He stepped forward and tossed the purple flower to the side. The butterflies flew off into the sunflowers. He cupped her face in his hands and smiled down at her.

"For once," he said, "try to enjoy the moment and stop making rules."

He kissed her, lightly at first and then more deeply. She put her arms around his neck and pulled her body flush against his. His hands slid down to the small of her back and pressed her closer, as his thumbs traced her hip bones. He tasted like Honeycrisp apples. Then his lips were on her neck, exploring the soft skin between her ear and the hollow of her throat. She heard something that sounded like a purr and realized it was coming from her.

"Come on," he said. He took her hand, and they walked back to the house. Sparky followed them. In the foyer, Cooper said, "Stay." The dog sat on the tarp and watched as they went up the stairs.

He led her to a bedroom that had a polished dark wood floor, a white marble fireplace, and a new bed with a bright white comforter. The room was flooded with sunlight, which seemed to glow on the white walls. It was one of the few rooms in the house that had been fully rehabilitated. He shut the door.

She pushed off his flannel shirt and tugged his T-shirt off his head, then inhaled sharply. His chest was carved with muscles like the statue of David, but at his waist was a smattering of scars radiating upward. They made a pattern like fireworks—from the IED, she realized. She ran her hands over the scars, feeling their raised ridges beneath her fingertips. His breath came fast as his eyes met hers.

"You'd better see the merchandise," he said softly. "And make an educated decision about whether you're in the market for it."

He pushed down his jeans and boxers and stepped out of them. He stood naked before her. He looked like an Olympic athlete who was missing a fraction of himself. His chest was broad, his waist narrow, his legs muscled and athletic, except below his left knee, which ended in the prosthetic. The scars from the explosion were thickest around his knee and went upward, tapering completely at his stomach.

"You are beautiful," she said. She put a hand on his erection and stroked it lightly up and down. "And the essential parts seem to be in excellent working order."

"But wait," he said. "There's more."

He sat on the edge of the bed, unfastened his prosthetic leg, and set it on the floor. She could see where his leg ended, below his knee, and the seam that closed off the skin. He met her eyes, a question in his.

She pulled off her own clothes and stood naked before him. The sunlight through the windows warmed her skin. She pointed to a small circular scar near her belly button.

"I had the chicken pox once."

"Well, shoot. That's a deal breaker."

She laughed. He put his hands on her hips and brought his mouth to her stomach. His lips left an electric trail on the hollow of her belly.

She ran her hands over his shoulders, then pushed him back on the bed. She was dizzy with the excitement of meeting a new lover. She hadn't done that many times in her life, and doing it with an old friend felt like a new adventure. They explored each other until she was out of breath and aching for him. He pulled her on top of him, and she looked into his clear blue eyes. What a luxury, to do something just because it felt good.

"No one will get hurt," she said. "This is just two friends having fun."

"This is totally fun."

She slipped him inside her, groaned, and, for few minutes at least, stopped making rules.

44

When Jody came home from work, Anna was in the kitchen, washing fresh vegetables for a salad and humming "Girl on Fire." Through the window, Anna could see Cooper out in the backyard, grilling. Sparky sat on his foot. The sight made her smile.

Jody walked into the kitchen, set her bag on the table, and looked at her sister. "You guys finally did it, didn't you?"

Anna laughed. "What makes you think that?"

"You're humming. Your cheeks are pink. And you look happier than you have since you got to Michigan."

Anna set an heirloom tomato on the cutting board and turned to her sister. She couldn't help the smile that spread across her face. "We did it."

"Eee!" Jody ran over and grabbed Anna's hands and they did the same little dance they used to do when they were excited about something in elementary school. "I take it it was pretty good?"

"Amazing."

"Hee hee."

"I'm just, you know, worried I'm going to break his heart when I leave."

"Oh, stop. He wants the same chance to have his heart broken as a guy with two legs. Besides, look on the bright side, maybe he'll break yours." Jody lowered her voice. "How is he . . . down there?"

"Impressive."

"Good. I wondered if that was affected by the bomb."

"But listen." Anna glanced outside and saw Cooper transferring the meat from the grill to a plate. He threw a piece to Sparky, who jumped up and caught it in his mouth. "I don't know where I should sleep tonight. First off, I don't want to abandon you."

"No offense, sis, but if I had as much chemistry with a man as you have with Cooper, there's no way I'd be in bed with you."

"Thanks," Anna said. "But, I don't know, there's a broader issue. Like, we're living in his house already. I don't know how this works. There isn't room for the traditional let's-see-each-other-a-couple-nights-a-week dating sort of thing."

"Nope," Jody grabbed a slice of cucumber and popped it in her mouth. "This is definitely not textbook. But here's how I see it. This trial has taken you away from your life, your job, and your friends. You're isolated out here in the middle of postindustrial nowhere, trying to clear your dumb-ass sister from a murder charge."

"Hey, you're not a dumb-ass."

"Whatever. Take your pleasure where you can find it, Annie. You're here. He enjoys you. You enjoy him. Until one of those things changes, just go with it. Right?"

Anna shook her head. "How do you make everything so simple?"

"Everyone has their talent."

Cooper walked in carrying a plate of barbecued chicken. He looked at the sisters, huddled together by the veggies. "Uh-oh. What are you two conspiring about?"

"Just discussing what a ridiculously lucky guy you are." Jody nodded approvingly at him. "Well done, Coop."

"I am lucky." He kissed Anna softly on the lips, making her cheeks flush with heat. "Let's eat."

That night, Anna went to sleep in Cooper's new bed, spooned in his arms. He intertwined his fingers with hers and held her hand to her heart. His lips brushed her ear as he described the agricultural efficacy of ladybugs. She slept better than she had in months.

■ ■ ■

Jody's approval of Anna's romantic development didn't translate into agreement on legal strategy, however. She still refused to let

Anna blame Wendy at the trial. Anna said, "Without that, I don't know what our defense will be."

They brainstormed, without coming up with any viable options. Jody asked if an alibi would be helpful. Anna reminded her that court rules prohibited attorneys from putting on any evidence they knew was false. "Besides, you already told the police you were with the coach that night. An alibi would just mean you lied to them," she said. *And me*, she thought.

Over the next week, a few women contacted Anna and spoke to her about being sexually assaulted by the coach. Their stories were similar to Jody's. Many were prepared to testify at trial, if the judge allowed it. Anna warned them that their testimony would likely be excluded. In the meantime, she helped them find counselors.

Kathy came over for dinner one night. Over spaghetti with meatballs they talked about the upcoming trial. "You know, I saw the coach at the casino a lot," Kathy said. "He was a big gambler. Always at the high roller's table."

Anna made a mental note to follow up with a subpoena to the casino. "Thanks. Anything that shows that he was in debt is helpful."

Kathy said, "There was a guy who threatened him once."

Anna stopped, a forkful of spaghetti midway to her mouth.

"What do you mean?"

"I was on a bathroom break, and I passed Coach Fowler in the hallway. I knew who he was, but the coach didn't know me. This man came over and jacked Coach Fowler up against a wall. He said, 'If you don't pay up, you're dead. You'll be an example to everyone else.' Then he punched him in the stomach and walked away. The coach looked like he'd shit his pants. I asked him if he wanted me to get help but he said no."

Anna glanced at Cooper, then Jody. They looked as surprised as she felt.

"Did anyone else see this?" Anna asked.

"No, just me. I'm sorry, I should've told you before."

"What did the guy look like?"

"He had black hair that was in a widow's peak, and a scar through one eyebrow. He wore a black leather jacket."

"An extra from *Get Shorty* threatened the coach." Cooper met Anna's eyes, and she saw her own reaction reflected in his face. She appreciated that she wasn't alone in her skepticism.

She thanked Kathy and told her she'd get back to her. But Anna wouldn't call her as a witness if she could help it. She didn't know who she would call. Five months until the trial, and she still didn't know what her defense would be.

■ ■ ■

Over the following months, Jody continued going to work. When her belly started getting in the way, GM let her move from the assembly line to a desk job. She bought maternity clothes and a body pillow to drape her legs over at night, trying to stay comfortable as she got bigger.

Anna did her USAO work at the table in Cooper's living room and occasionally helped him on the farm. She got to know De'Andre, Lamar, and the neighbors who had plots in his garden. She used to think Cooper might feel isolated out here, but she realized he was at the center of a community of people who were trying to make the city better.

With every person who told her how smart or creative Cooper was, she felt a little burst of pride. It was not the feeling a woman got with a friend she was "just having fun with." It was the pride of ownership. She tried to shake herself out of it. He wasn't hers, and she wasn't his. This was just a fling until she went back to D.C. But she found that talking to Cooper over coffee in the morning was her favorite part of the day. Each time she looked up from her computer and saw him working outside with Sparky, it made her smile. She admired what he was doing with his life, and she appreciated that his presence made hers richer. If she didn't know better, she would think she was falling for him. Obviously, she wasn't. It was just a fling.

Every afternoon, after her prosecutorial work for the USAO

was done, she transitioned into defense attorney mode and worked on Jody's case. Cooper occasionally came with her, when she needed a witness present for conversations. On lunch breaks, he would take her to see unexpected parts of the city: Eastern Market, a vibrant district filled with fresh food, flowers, and antiques; the Heidelberg project, a house covered in stuffed animals.

Anna went with Jody to her seemingly endless round of ob-gyn appointments. They learned that the baby was going to be a girl, and Jody hooted with glee. She soon went from looking voluptuous, to looking pudgy, to looking unmistakably pregnant. She and Anna took a prenatal class together. Anna wanted to throw her a baby shower, but Jody didn't want one—yet. "You can throw me a shower once I'm allowed to attend without an ankle bracelet." Anna hoped that wouldn't mean when Jody was in prison.

When the nights grew colder, Cooper started building fires in the fireplaces to help heat the big old house. At night, he and Anna lay beneath a big white feather blanket and found increasingly enjoyable ways to keep each other warm. The embers glowed orange in the fireplace.

■ ■ ■

In early December, Anna got a letter from Detective Rob Gargaron, setting a time when she could go to the police storage facility and view the items from Jody's search warrant. She arrived at the appointed time with Cooper. It was a warehouse in the commercial district. Inside, Rob was waiting for them.

"Hey, Coop. You're a criminal investigator now?"

"Yep. Not sure if it's a promotion or demotion from urban farmer."

Rob glanced at Anna. "Seems to have some nice benefits."

He led them past metal shelves covered with boxes and paper bags. In an open space in the middle of the warehouse sat a table covered in items that the police had taken from Jody's house. Ironically, these were the only items that survived the fire.

Cooper took pictures, as Anna walked around, looking at

everything. A baseball bat. Some pots and pans. The pillowcases and blankets that had been on Jody's bed. The washing machine, kitchen sink, pipes, and toilets sat on the concrete floor. The remnants of a life that had gone up in flames.

"Was the coach's blood found in or on any of these?" she asked Rob.

"You'll get a full report," he said. "But the short answer is: no. Not a trace."

Thank God.

"I did get a report on the bedsheets," Anna said, "and no semen or hair from the coach was found on the those, right?"

"Yup."

She got to a part of the table that held Jody's sports trophies. Twenty-three in total. For a short time, Jody had been a promising runner and one of the best high jumpers in the state. This accomplishment had been important enough to Jody that she'd kept these awards from ten years ago, lugged them with her from apartment to apartment till she settled in her house. The golden girls were frozen atop faux wooden or marble stands.

"Any blood on these? Hair or fibers of note?"

"Nope."

Anna remembered when Jody won some of these. There was third place in the hundred-meter dash in Northville, and a big silvery cup for the remarkable time that Jody, as a freshman, had placed sixth in the state at the high jump. But Anna didn't see the trophy Jody treasured most, from the time in 2004 when she'd broken Anna's school record for high jump, during a track meet in Flint. Anna looked once, then twice, and a third time just to be certain. It was not there.

"Is this everything?" Anna asked Rob.

"Yup. You looking for something else?"

"Nope." She turned to Cooper. "I think we're done here."

He nodded and put the camera back in his pocket.

Rob walked them out. "You'll see another report, too, in a couple days. They tested the old rape kits in the six sealed cases. Leapfrogged them right in front of older ones in the backlog. Amazing what a little publicity can do. Anyway, Coach Fowler's semen was found in three of those kits. It wasn't present in one. And in two, including Jody's, the kit itself was so badly degraded, the swabs were unusable."

"Unusable how?"

"You should see where they were stored. Water dripping from the roof, mold growing on the boxes. Plus the natural degradation of DNA over time. It's a wonder they got a profile on three."

Anna shook her head. "That is appalling."

"It is. And let me tell you something," Rob said. They reached the small, empty waiting area. "From here on out, it'll only get harder for you. You poked a hornet's nest. Look for when they come flying at you."

"Is that a threat?" Cooper said, putting his hands on his hips.

"Furthest thing from it." Rob brushed his thumb across his mustache. "Just some words of advice from someone who's been in this little corner of the world longer than either of you. Watch your back, Anna."

She searched Rob's face and found no malevolence there. But Cooper took a step forward, fists clenched at his side. She put a hand on his arm and felt his muscles coiled with tension. She hoped Cooper wouldn't have a PTSD episode here. She patted his arm gently, recalling the poking that Sparky did. Cooper looked at her, took a deep breath, and seemed to shake himself. His voice was low and controlled as he said, "I'll be watching her back, too."

Rob nodded. "Glad to hear it."

45

When I went to Screecher's the second time, I tried a different tack. Instead of a push-up bra, I wore a minimizing one. I braided my hair into two long Heidi-like braids. I wore a tiny checkered skirt, a tight Holly Grove High School tank, and white Keds. My getup basically screamed "jailbait."

This time, Coach's eyes got a little rounder when I approached. His voice got a little huskier as we talked. His knee inched closer to mine, all on its own. Grady watched in disapproving silence. He wasn't the only one. The other people at the bar were very interested. I felt them watching but ignored them. Coach did too, and he loved it.

At the end of the night, though, when I tried to close the deal, Coach dissed me again. Politely and all, in a way that let me know he enjoyed the attention. But he left me there at the bar. Just shook his head with a rueful smile when I whispered that I'd like to meet up with him a bit later, when everyone wasn't watching. I watched him drive away in his Corvette.

It was definitely the power thing. No matter how I dressed, no matter how flat I smushed my boobs against my chest, I was twenty-five years old. I looked it. Most of all, I felt it—and the coach felt it too. I wasn't awed by him, or scared. And so he wasn't turned on.

I realized he was never inviting me into his Corvette again.

The next time I went to Screecher's, a couple days later, I brought a Visine bottle full of GHB with me. I chose GHB because there were multiple reasons for it to be in his blood. Everyone knew that Coach Fowler was obsessed with keeping in shape as he got older. And, in addition to being the date-rape drug of choice for high school boys,

GHB is used by bodybuilders to grow muscle. As you saw, it was plausible that the coach was using it himself.

Cooking the GHB was the easy part. You can get the recipe on the Internet. The ingredients are legal industrial solvents, available for purchase from specialty stores. The hard part was getting it into Coach Fowler.

By that third night in Screecher's, he greeted me like an old friend. I sat on the stool next to him, talked football, and waited for my chance. It wasn't easy. He liked to hold his tumbler of whiskey as he spoke, his fingers tracing the rim. He liked to take the final sip from each glass before he went to the bathroom.

When the coach's fourth whiskey came, I asked if he would show me his trophies. His eyes shone; he said he would love to. As he got up and turned his back to me, I leaned over the bar, like I was going to get a napkin, and I squirted the GHB into his tumbler. My heart pounded, but I was pretty sure no one saw. I grabbed a napkin for cover, then followed Coach to the case, where I provided the proper *oohs* and *aahs* to each of the trophies.

When we sat back down, he took a nice long swig of his drink. Then he held up the glass to the light and studied the golden liquid. I almost panicked, worrying that he noticed the taste. But he was several drinks in at that point. If he did notice anything, he ignored it. He just kept going.

Ten minutes later, he was slurring his words. Ten minutes after that, his eyes were fluttering shut, and his head was drooping onto the bar.

"Coach," Grady said. "Coach, you okay?"

Coach mumbled something about wanting to go home. Grady said he'd call a car.

"No, that's okay," I said, helpfully. "I'll take him home. I'm fine to drive."

Grady scowled—I'm pretty sure *he* wanted to be the one I took home—but helped me take Coach to the car. It's a good thing he did, because Coach was heavy, and his own legs weren't doing much in the way of holding him up. We fished the keys out of his pocket and got him buckled into the passenger seat. Then I went around to the other side. I slid into the car and took a deep breath as I got behind the wheel.

The purr of the motor took me back ten years. I shut the door and sat there for a moment. I looked over at Coach, whose head was bobbing forward. It was the same car where he raped me, ten years earlier. But I was finally the one in the driver's seat.

Grady was still standing on the sidewalk as I pulled the Corvette out of the parking lot. I rolled down the window and waved into the warm night. "Bye! Thanks!"

Then we were out on the road, just me and the coach, driving into the darkness. Coach's head knocked quietly against the side window with each bump in the road. He was fully passed out. We approached the high school, empty and dark, then passed it. I kept driving: through the remnants of downtown, then through the burbs, and finally onto the empty stretch of highway. Soon, the road was surrounded by trees.

I drove to Lake Huron. The coach's summer "cottage" was lit up like a stone and log palace on the edge of the water. He'd been living there ever since he and Wendy split up. She was living with their daughter in their house in town.

"Here we are, Coach Fowler," I said, pulling the car into the long driveway, past the thick stand of trees that hid the house from view. His right cheek was pressed flat against the window, which puckered his lips and made drool run down the side of his chin. I no longer had to hide the hate in my voice.

"Welcome home, asshole."

46

The first day of Jody's trial dawned on a freezing February morning. The cold of Michigan in winter was inescapable. Anna drove the Yukon over icy roads to the courthouse, shivering although the heat was on full blast. The problem was that the windows were all open, and the icy air sliced through the interior of the truck. She glanced at Cooper, who sat in the passenger seat. His hand gripped the door handle so tightly it looked like he was trying to strangle it. "You okay?" Anna asked.

He nodded. "I can do this."

It was too cold for him to ride his motorcycle, but he insisted on coming to Jody's trial. With the windows open, the doors unlocked, and some deep breathing exercises, he might just make it through the car ride. Sweat beaded his forehead. He was ready to jump out at any moment. She understood the massive effort this cost him. She put a hand on his leg and hoped he would make it.

The woman who faced life in prison sat in the backseat, cradling her round stomach and looking placidly out the window.

The world was buried beneath a skein of white. Icicles hung from every building, reflecting the stark winter sun like rows of knives. Bare branches clawed against the pale gray sky. The world was silent except for the crunch of tires on salt.

When they approached Holly Grove's downtown, Anna could hear a low roar, like an ocean from far away. As they got closer, the noise resolved into the sound of a crowd: hundreds of voices shouting. And when they turned into the courthouse square, she had to brake.

"Holy crap," Jody said.

The square was full of people. Shoulder to shoulder, packing the park in front of the courthouse and streaming in from the streets surrounding it. A smattering of protesters had come for the hearings and legal miscellanea that preceded the trial. But today, for opening statements, they were fully a mob. It was astounding, in this cold weather, that anyone had come out, much less a crowd that filled several city blocks. They were bundled in winter jackets, hats, snow boots, and scarves covering their mouths. Some huddled around barrels lit with fires. Half the people wore white Guy Fawkes masks over their faces. Clouds of breath rose from the mouth holes. They looked like a field of grinning, malevolent puppets.

Many people spilled onto the icy streets, and Anna had to slow to avoid hitting them. Someone in the crowd recognized them and yelled, "Jody!"

Soon, several people were chanting. "Jody! Jody! Jody!" They crowded near the car, not to obstruct, but to show their support. They held up their fists and signs in the air.

Anna loved her sister. *She* would stand in the cold for her. That a crowd of strangers would do so was awing.

Press vans were parked throughout the square. There were national outlets, not just the local stations. They wanted to talk to Jody. Luckily, Anna had been given permission to park in the structure beneath the courthouse during the trial. They took the elevator straight up into the courthouse.

Inside the courtroom, they took their positions. They had discussed the setup beforehand. Anna and Jody sat at the table by themselves. The more alone and helpless Jody appeared to the jurors, the better. Cooper sat in the front row, behind them. Anna could consult with him or have him make phone calls if necessary. He was also there for the sisters' safety. The courthouse had security, but Anna knew there were chinks in every system. Both she and Jody had gotten death threats.

Jody wore minimal makeup: just enough to cover blemishes and bring out the pink in her cheeks. Anna wanted her looking fresh-faced and innocent. Jody's hair was cut into a chin-length bob, which she wore neat and straight. It was attractive but not sexy. Female jurors did not like sexy. Plus, Jody was eight months pregnant. They decided to play up that fact instead of trying to hide it under shapeless clothes. Jody wore a dove-gray maternity dress with a pink ribbon tied in a bow over her belly, accentuating its roundness. She looked angelic, glowing with maternal energy, which was perfect.

Anna and Desiree wore similar black pantsuits. Anna wore a pink blouse under hers, while Desiree wore blue. The women nodded at each other and unpacked their files. They moved in synchronicity, except that Anna's hands shook as she straightened her papers. She'd handled plenty of trials, but never one with such personal stakes.

Her phone buzzed with an incoming text:

Good luck, sweetheart.

It was from Jack. Her heart hiccuped. She lowered her phone and hoped Cooper hadn't seen. She hadn't heard from Jack in a few weeks. While she appreciated his good wishes, his use of the word *sweetheart* rankled. She wasn't his sweetheart anymore. She texted back:

Thanks.

She powered off her phone. She looked at Cooper, surprised to realize how important he had become to her.

At precisely nine o'clock, Judge Upperthwaite took the bench. His clerk, the stenographer, and a CSO took their places. The audience quieted before the judge said a word. He just had that effect. Anna guessed it had something to do with his flowing silver hair.

"Are both parties ready to begin?" the judge asked. His voice was deep and grandfatherly. Anna and Desiree both stood and said, "Yes, Your Honor," in stereo.

The jury was led in. They sat down looking fresh, interested, and eager to hear the story. It was the first day of trial; they hadn't yet experienced the interminable waits, the annoying objections, the long sidebars with the husher on. For the moment, they basked in the perceived honor of being selected to decide the biggest criminal trial Holly Grove had ever seen.

They were six women and eight men, including two alternates. During jury selection, Anna had tried to avoid people who were fervent about Bulldog football. In this town, that was like trying to avoid people who enjoyed eating, drinking, and breathing. Months ago, she'd moved to transfer the trial to another venue, where jurors would be less personally tied to the team, but Judge Upperthwaite had greeted that motion with the same enthusiasm with which he'd greeted the one to recuse himself. So here they were.

Juror number 3, a retired autoworker, was wearing a Bulldogs T-shirt. Anna swallowed back a bubble of nausea and made a mental note to find a way to get him stricken off the jury. Hopefully, he would admit to some prohibited conduct like googling the case.

"The government may make its opening statement," Judge Upperthwaite said.

Anna rose a few inches from the chair before she remembered that she wasn't "the government" in this case. She sat down quickly. As far as she could tell, only her sister noticed. Jody gave her a small smile.

Desiree stood up and walked in front of the jury.

"This is a case about jealousy," the prosecutor said. "It's about a woman who was in love with a man for most of her adult life. But he was married to someone else. And when he refused to leave his wife, this woman flew into a rage and bludgeoned him to death."

Here Desiree looked in Jody's eyes and pointed right at her, demonstrating to the jury that she held the same conviction she would ask them to have. Ever since *Presumed Innocent*, any prosecutor with the slightest literary bent pointed at the defendant.

Jody reacted as Anna had instructed her for this moment. She met Desiree's eyes and shook her head. Jody wore an expression of perfect sadness and disbelief, as if she were still grieving the tragedy of the coach's death and shocked to learn that anyone would think her responsible for it. In another life, Anna thought, Jody would've made a great actress.

"The defendant killed Owen Fowler." Desiree kept her finger pointed a couple sentences more, to prove that she was not convinced by Jody's show. "She staged a car accident to cover it up. She hoped that she could fool the authorities, and fool you, into believing this was an accident. But it's hard to commit the perfect crime, and this defendant is no criminal mastermind. She made mistakes. She left a trail of crumbs, if you will, from the site of the car crash all the way back to her own house. Let's follow them."

First, Desiree talked about the coach: what a great guy he was. Anna listened carefully. If Desiree opened the door, talking too much about his good character, Anna might be able to rebut it with evidence of his serial pedophilia. As things stood now, the judge had prohibited such evidence from coming in. They were to stick to the facts relevant to the night of June 3, 2014, the night of the coach's death. Desiree was smart. She described his job as a coach, his charity camp, and the fact that he was married for ten years with a daughter. Connecting the dots, the coach sounded like a good citizen and a reliable man, although the prosecutor never used the words *good* or *reliable*—and thus Anna would not be allowed to introduce evidence to rebut these concepts.

"In the summer of 2004, the defendant attended Coach Fowler's summer camp."

Desiree nodded to a paralegal who sat at her table. He tapped on the computer and a picture flashed up onto a large screen that hung on the wall across from the jury. It was a picture of Coach Fowler's summer camp of 2004. All the kids stood smiling from the bleachers, with the coach and his assistants standing to the side of them. The paralegal enlarged the section where the coach stood. The jurors looked at the picture of him projected on the screen. He was handsome and clean-cut with a confident, friendly smile. He looked like an L.L.Bean model of what a coach should look like.

The paralegal cut away from the coach and now highlighted

Jody. She stood in the middle of a middle row, her blond hair tied in a ponytail, her fifteen-year-old face in profile. She was gazing at the coach, a dreamy look on her face. If a picture could tell a whole story, this picture told the story of a girl with her first flush of puppy love.

"The defendant had a crush on Coach Fowler."

Anna considered objecting, but let it go. Objecting annoyed the jury. Plus, there was going to be plenty of evidence to show that Jody had an attachment to the coach.

"You will hear that the defendant spent a lot of time talking to Coach Fowler at the sports camp. You will hear that she spent a good part of school dances not with her friends and peers, but standing with the coach, who was there in his role as a chaperone. You will hear that, during the 2004 Homecoming football game, the defendant got into a physical fight with the coach's fiancée, Wendy Weiscowicz Fowler, during an argument the two women had about the coach. This was in full view of ten thousand people." The juror in the Bulldogs T-shirt nodded. He had probably been there. "Imagine what she could do when no was watching."

"Objection."

"Sustained. Just the facts, Ms. Williams. Jurors, disregard the prosecutor's last comment."

Juror number 3 folded his arms across his chest. He was definitely *not* disregarding the prosecutor's last comment.

"You will also hear that the defendant, in 2004, accused the coach of having sex with her in his car. You will see the police report she made. And you will see that she did not want to press charges. It is our position that she made this report to try to create friction between the coach and his wife shortly after they married, in order to break up the marriage."

"And you will hear," Desiree continued, "that the defendant continued to be infatuated with Coach Fowler, long after he married his wife, Wendy."

Desiree called Jody "the defendant" deliberately. During the course of the trial, she would never purposely call her "Jody" or

"Ms. Curtis." This was Prosecutor 101. It was far easier for the jury to send "the defendant" to jail. The defendant was faceless and not really human. "Jody" was a woman who could be your friend or neighbor.

"The defendant herself never married. And in the spring of 2014, the defendant began frequenting a bar that Coach Fowler was known to patronize. Several people saw her flirting aggressively with him on several occasions.

"You will hear from the defendant herself, by way of a videotaped statement she made to Detective Rob Gargaron on June 4, 2014, the day after the coach was killed. She admitted that she had been seeing the coach romantically. She admitted that she took the coach to her home the night before. She admitted that she had sexual relations with him. Then she claimed that he drove away, happy and unhurt. She would like you to believe that the coach died in a car accident on the way home.

"But you'll hear that that was not true. The defendant's next-door neighbor will tell you that she heard the sound of fighting coming from the defendant's home sometime between two and four that morning. The police conducted a search warrant on her home later that day. Among other things, they found this."

Desiree held up the clear plastic evidence bag with the sock from behind Jody's washing machine.

"DNA tests confirm that the spots on this sock are blood, and that the blood is Coach Fowler's.

"You will hear from the coroner. He will testify that the car crash did not kill the coach. Coach Fowler had died hours before his car hit the stadium. He died of several blunt force injuries to his head—injuries that were inflicted with a sharp, square object, creating a pattern in his skull that could not have been caused merely by hitting the windshield.

"Finally, you will hear from an automotive expert who will testify that cars generally do not explode upon impact. He will tell you that the burn pattern on the coach's body is more consistent with being set on fire with gasoline than being burned in a car accident.

"You will be here for many weeks. By the end of this case, you will know the evidence like the back of your hand. And then I will have a chance talk to you again, and I will ask you to return the only verdict consistent with that evidence, the only just verdict: that the defendant is guilty of murder in the first degree. Thank you."

Several of the jurors nodded at Desiree as she took her seat. When they turned to Anna, they narrowed their eyes. They had already decided they didn't like her or what she represented. Her sister was in trouble.

47

Anna was shaking as she stood up. This happened, to some extent, before every opening statement. She knew if she could just power through the first few paragraphs, her adrenaline would dissipate, her heart rate would normalize, and she could speak to the jurors like they were just people. But she'd never been this shaky before.

"Good morning," Anna said. She paused and waited with a smile, until the jurors chorused back: "Good morning."

This was one of the few opportunities for interaction with the jury. The rest of the trial, Anna would be talking and presenting evidence. The jury would sit and listen. Only during this brief moment, at the beginning of the day, could there be an actual *exchange* of words. And this was the time they would be paying the most attention, so she spoke the most important words now.

"Jody Curtis did not kill Coach Fowler. She loved him; whether or not that love was wise, you can decide. But she never hurt him. Jody Curtis sits before you an innocent woman."

Anna stood behind Jody and put her hands on her sister's shoulders. This was the opposite of pointing and saying "the defendant." Anna was telling the jury: *I love this woman, and you should too. She is a good person. She means a lot to me. I am not scared of her. No one needs to be scared of her.* Jody gazed up at her with a warm, sisterly smile. They'd practiced the move repeatedly, like actors preparing for a Broadway play, until it looked natural and unrehearsed.

She gave Jody's shoulder a pat and walked into the well of the court. "My name is Anna Curtis. As you've heard, I have the honor and pleasure of being Jody's lawyer as well as her older sister.

"The prosecutor talked about knowing the evidence 'like the back of your hand.'" Anna held hers up. "And we know what she means. You know your knuckles, the path your veins take very well. Similarly, the prosecutor thinks she knows this story quite well. But there's always another side to a story, just as there is another side to your hand."

Anna flipped her hand over so the jury now saw her palm. "The fingerprints, the life lines, the parts studied by forensic analysts and fortune-tellers. You have to look at both sides of a hand to really know it, just as you have to learn both sides of a story before you can make a decision. And so I'm going to ask you, first and foremost, to keep an open mind. The prosecution gets to present their case first. You'll hear all their evidence before I'm allowed to put on a word of mine. So listen, evaluate, but please: reserve judgment. As you listen to the government's case, understand that you're only seeing one side.

"When we get to my sister's turn, you'll hear a very different story. You'll hear that Owen Fowler was a man who was deep in debt. He had a gambling problem and was falling further and further behind in his losses. He took out hundreds of thousands of dollars in a home equity line of credit. And despite these loans, he owed money to many people."

Desiree raised an eyebrow. She had not heard this before. Defense obligations to turn over evidence were far less stringent than the prosecution's.

"In fact, you will hear that there were many people who had a reason to dislike or to hurt Coach Fowler. To want him dead." Anna wanted to tell the jury about the other girls he had raped. But the judge had ruled that inadmissible unless the prosecution opened the door. She didn't want to promise in her opening statement something that she couldn't show them later on. And so she kept it vague.

"But one thing you *won't* hear is that Jody Curtis had any dislike for him. In fact, every witness will tell you that their interactions seemed friendly, cordial, and warm. Just because Jody had a tense relationship with the coach's wife, doesn't mean she had any problem with *him*."

Here, Anna wanted to talk about Wendy's relationship with the coach. The beatings, the separation, the financial motive Wendy had to kill her husband. But Jody had prohibited that. So she bit her lip and moved on.

"Jody Curtis is a sweet, innocent girl who has never been in trouble before. She has no criminal record. She graduated from Holly Grove High School in 2006 and has held the same job on the line at the GM auto assembly plant for the last eight years. She saved enough money to buy her own house, solely through her own elbow grease and determination. She is well liked by her neighbors and is known as a truthful and peaceful member of the community. There is no reason why this hardworking homeowner would suddenly fly into a homicidal rage.

"The fact is, the prosecutor's theories don't make sense. First, Jody had no motive to hurt the coach. As the prosecutor said, she loved him. Second, as a physical matter, she couldn't have killed him. You'll hear that she is five foot six, weighing one hundred thirty pounds at the time of his death. He was six foot one and two hundred thirty pounds. She could not have overpowered this highly trained athlete, who was seven inches taller and a hundred pounds heavier. Third, she couldn't have covered it up. Two hundred thirty pounds of dead weight is nearly impossible for a woman her size to carry. You'll hear that from an expert on the subject, and you'll get a chance to try it out yourself on a firefighter's training mannequin. Fourth, Jody couldn't make the car crash into the stadium. This was not a remote control car. The police's own investigative team will tell you there was no evidence of any tampering with the steering wheel, the accelerator, or any part of the car.

"As you listen to the prosecutor's case, you'll find yourself asking many questions. For every question, look to one place."

Now, Anna did the pointing. She pointed at Desiree Williams. "You look to the prosecutor. It is *her burden* to tell you what happened. It is always the government's burden to prove the defendant guilty, beyond a reasonable doubt. Under the American system, the defendant comes into this courtroom cloaked in the presumption of innocence. It is the same privilege you would enjoy if, God forbid, anyone ever accused you of a crime.

"Presume Jody innocent as she sits here today. Presume her innocent as each witness comes up to talk. And any questions you have, put them at the desk of the prosecutor. It is her burden to tell the full story and to prove beyond a reasonable doubt what happened on the night of June third. If you have any questions about what happened, if there are any holes or parts of the story that don't make sense, the government has not met its burden, and there is not enough evidence to send this woman to jail."

Anna had been on the receiving end of this argument enough times to understand its full weight.

"Ladies and gentleman, after this trial is finished, you will have far more questions than answers. But one thing will be clear: Jody Curtis did not harm Owen Fowler. I will ask you to send her back home, where she belongs. Thank you."

Anna sat down and put a hand on Jody's arm. "You okay?" she said.

Jody nodded, smiled solemnly at Anna, and cradled her belly. Anna hoped the jurors were watching.

48

Wendy made a pretty little widow. Her strawberry-blond hair shone against her black dress. Her eyes welled with delicate tears. She dabbed her rosy cheeks. The jurors watched her performance in the witness chair with rapt attention.

The government always wanted to start a case with an emotional punch: often, that meant a grieving family member describing what a great person the victim was. Hence, the prosecutor called Wendy Fowler as her first witness. Wendy gave the same sort of testimonial she had at the memorial service: he was a devoted father, a loving husband, a coach who cared about his players. She wiped away another tear.

Juror number 8, a gray-haired lady in a blue sweater, dabbed her own tears.

"Tell us about the evening of June 3, 2014," Desiree said. "Where were you?"

"I was at the Cedar Point amusement park with my daughter, Isabel, and my cousin, Brynn."

"And that's located in Sandusky, Ohio? About two hours away from your home?"

The prosecutor wasn't supposed to ask leading questions, but Anna let it go. She didn't want to appear obstructionist for petty reasons. She and probably every juror had been to Cedar Point; the "roller coaster capital of the world" was a pilgrimage for every midwesterner.

"Yes. We stayed at the Hilton. Isabel had been asking to go for ages. We left early that morning and came back later the next afternoon. I have the hotel receipt if you need it."

"Thank you, that won't be necessary."

Wendy wasn't on trial. She didn't need to provide an alibi.

"Did you hear from your husband?" Desiree said.

"Yes. He called at around ten that evening to wish us good night. He spoke to Isabel and told her to have a fun trip. We expected to see him the next day."

"Did you see him the next day?"

"No. Around six the next morning, I got a phone call from Detective Rob Gargaron, informing me that my husband had died in a car accident earlier that morning." Wendy dabbed her eyes. "We drove home immediately. There was talk of identifying his body, but there was really nothing for me to identify. He was," she choked, "burned to the point where he was not recognizable. They identified him through dental records."

Anna could have objected, but didn't. Wendy had no personal knowledge on which to testify about dental records and identification—that was for the coroner to say. But there was no point in alienating the jury by interrupting the teary-eyed widow's testimony. No one disputed that it was the coach who died in the car that night.

Anna knew Wendy was telling the truth. Anna had obtained the hotel receipt. Wendy had checked into the Hilton at 3:06 P.M. on June 3, and checked out at 7:13 A.M. the next morning, exactly as she'd testified. Anna had even obtained Wendy's cell-phone records, which showed that Wendy's phone had been in Sandusky, Ohio, the whole time. The woman had been in Cedar Point. Anna couldn't have blamed the coach's death on Wendy even if Jody had approved of that strategy.

But that didn't mean Wendy was useless to the defense. When the prosecutor finished, Anna went to the podium to cross-examine her. She had to be very careful with this witness. This would be a "soft cross." Anna had to make her points as gently as possible. The jury liked the pretty young widow. They felt sorry for her. They would hate Anna if she was in any way perceived as mean or callous to Wendy.

"I'm so sorry for your husband's death, Ms. Fowler," Anna said quietly.

"Thank you." Wendy folded her tissue and set it on her lap.

"I need to ask you some questions, but I understand this is difficult for you. So please let me know if you need to take a break at any point."

"I will. Thank you."

Anna glanced at her notes, as if she needed reminding. "You were married to Owen Fowler for ten years, is that correct?"

"Yes."

"You two shared finances?"

"That's correct."

"You had a joint bank account?"

"Yes."

"And you had two mortgages, which you held jointly?"

"Yes."

On cross-examination, a lawyer could ask leading questions. Structured properly, the lawyer was essentially the one testifying. Wendy was just confirming the points Anna wanted to make. Or denying them, if that was more dramatic.

"So you were aware that he had taken over a million dollars out of your lake house in a series of home equity lines of credit?"

Wendy shook her head. "I was not aware of that until after he died."

Anna looked up from her notes, as if shocked. "He took out a million dollars and never told you?"

"No."

"So then . . . you don't know where that money went?"

"I don't, strictly speaking. I had to sell the lake house. I'm struggling to hold on to the house in Holly Grove. It was also heavily mortgaged."

Anna glanced at the jurors. Anna had told them this in her opening statement; the fact that Wendy confirmed it gave Anna instant credibility. Plus it tore down the idea of the coach as a perfect husband. Anna wanted the jurors to mull that over. She turned to the judge.

"Would now be a good time for the midmorning break?"

"Certainly," Judge Upperthwaite said. "We will break for fifteen minutes and resume at ten forty-five."

Anna and Cooper hustled Jody to the bathroom two floors up, where they were less likely to run into anyone. Jody walked with an adorable waddle, although she didn't appreciate hearing her gait described that way. This hallway was empty and quiet. Through the windows, Anna could see the crowd of Anonymous protesters filling the square, waving their signs and waiting in the cold.

"You hanging in there?" Anna asked her sister.

"You're the one doing the work. All I have to do is sit there and look pretty."

"You're great at that."

Jody patted her enormous stomach. "Liar. It feels like there's a bowling ball between my legs."

"Tell that baby to stay in there until this trial is over."

"Stay in there, baby." Jody smiled at Anna. "Are you going to ask Wendy about the loan shark?"

Anna shook her head. "An old trial-lawyer rule is: Never ask a question for which you don't know the answer. A trial is a place to present evidence, not fish for it. For the rest of Wendy's cross, I have 'control documents' to prove my point if Wendy lies. I've got no control document for the mysterious loan shark."

Jody put a hand on Anna's arm and looked her square in the eyes. "Ask. She's not going to hurt us."

Anna met Jody's eyes and found certainty there. It made her extremely nervous.

Back in the courtroom, the trial reassembled. Wendy returned to the witness stand, and Anna continued her cross-examination.

"Your husband spent about four or five nights a week at Screecher's bar or in the MotorCity Casino, is that correct?"

Charges from the casino were listed in black and white on the credit card receipts.

"Yes. He needed time to unwind after his very stressful job."

"He was not home until very late hours, roughly four to five nights a week, true?"

"True."

Anna paused, considering whether to go on. Everything she'd ever learned in law school said she shouldn't ask the next question. She took a deep breath and went for it anyway.

"Were you aware of anyone ever threatening your husband?"

"Yes," Wendy said. "A few weeks before his death, a man came to my house. A stranger. He asked for my husband. I said he wasn't home. The man told me to pass a message on to him. He said I should tell Owen that he'd break his kneecaps if Owen didn't pay up."

Juror number 8 gasped.

"Objection!" Desiree stood up. "Hearsay."

"Not offered for the truth of the matter," Anna said. Out-of-court statements were only considered hearsay if they were offered to prove the truth of the matter asserted in the statement. "The fact that a threat was made is critically important, but we're not offering this to prove that the stranger was actually going to break the decedent's kneecaps."

"I'll allow it," the judge said. "Just for that purpose."

"Can you describe this man?" Anna asked.

Wendy nodded and spoke earnestly to the jurors. "He was in his fifties, a white man, with black hair—very black—and a widow's peak. I remember thinking maybe he used hair dye, because a man his age should have more gray. He had a scar in one eyebrow."

Juror number 11 *tsk*, *tsked*, apparently unhappy that this did not come out during the government's direct examination.

"What did he wear?" Anna said.

"Dark pants and a black leather jacket, as I recall."

Anna took a sip of water as she absorbed that information. Wendy's description exactly matched the description Kathy had given of the thug who roughed up Owen Fowler at the casino.

There were only two possible explanations for this, and Anna didn't want to think about one of them.

She should sit down. She couldn't possibly hope for the testimony to get better than this. But something in Wendy's face made her press on.

"Did you pass the message along to your husband?"

"Yes, I told Owen later that night. He admitted that he'd borrowed money from a—what do you call it?—a loan shark. And he was having trouble paying it back. He was scared the man might kill him."

Too late, the prosecutor shot out of her seat. "Hearsay!"

"Indeed," Judge Upperthwaite said. "I'll strike that. The jurors will disregard that testimony."

Anna sat down, knowing there was no way the jurors could disregard that. "No further questions."

49

After the loan shark testimony, Anna politely asked Desiree to dismiss the charges. The prosecutor politely declined. And so the trial went on.

In fact, two trials went on: one in the courtroom, and one outside. Outside, the trial was about the failure of the system: the rape kits untested, the child sex-abuse charges unbrought, and how one man had managed to victimize so many girls for so long. Regardless of whether Jody killed him, the protesters didn't think she should go to jail.

Inside the courtroom, Anna was prohibited from introducing evidence of the coach's prior sex assaults. She couldn't go with the killer-as-hero theory. Plus, the people of Holly Grove—including her jurors—loved Coach Fowler. In the courtroom, she stuck with the theory of a good but flawed man being chased by shady creditors.

Outside, Anonymous protesters called for the trial to stop, because Jody had killed the right man. Inside, Anna tried to convince the jurors that Jody had killed no one.

Outside, journalists interviewed women who came forward to talk about being sexually assaulted by the coach when they were teenagers. They ranged in age, appearance, and socioeconomic status but had one thing in common: they all adored him for a time. Some "consented" to having sex with him, to the extent that a thirteen-year-old can be said to consent, and they continued to adore him afterward, at least for a while. Some of them fought him and he overpowered them, and they hated him consistently afterward. All of them now felt that what he'd done was wrong. Some remained private, but many came forward to talk to Oprah, Katie Couric, Jezebel, and *USA Today*.

Outside, the question was: Why was the coach never held accountable? Inside, the question was: Who was the loan shark who'd threatened to break the coach's knees?

The jurors had been instructed not to watch any television or read any news stories about the case. *Good luck enforcing that*, Anna thought. She didn't mind if the jurors saw the news. That would only give them one more reason to acquit her sister.

Desiree continued to put on her case. An auto expert talked about how cars don't generally explode on impact. A coroner talked about how the side of the coach's skull was bashed in before ever hitting the windshield. For cross-examination Anna simply asked them whether they saw Jody doing anything to the coach. They all had to answer no.

On the third day of trial, Desiree said, "The government calls Grady Figler to the stand."

Jody sat up straighter as the door swung open. A couple of women in the audience made approving clucks as the bartender strode in. He cleaned up nicely, Anna thought. He wore dark pants and a white button-down shirt, which showed off his muscular chest but hid the tattoos that covered his arms. His oft-broken nose looked tamer with combed hair and a fresh shave. He gave Anna a friendly nod, but his eyes got big when he saw Jody. He slowed and stared at her big belly. She held it with both hands and looked away from him.

Grady sat in the witness chair and answered the prosecutor's questions in a slow, deep drawl. His testimony was exactly what he'd told Anna when she visited him at Screecher's eight months earlier. It was his body language that was interesting. He couldn't take his eyes off of Jody, although she refused to meet his gaze.

After his testimony, the court took a break. Jody bolted for the bathroom two stories up. Anna beckoned Cooper and they followed her up there. Anna went in and found her sister bent over the sink, splashing water on her face. She checked the stalls. They were alone.

"What's going on, Jo?"

She didn't answer. But Anna had a pretty good idea. She handed Jody some paper towels, which Jody used to wipe her face. Jody looked at herself in the mirror, took a deep breath, and walked out into the hallway. Both Grady and Cooper were standing there.

"Jody," Grady said. He stepped forward and met her eyes. They stood several feet apart, staring straight at each other. Anna could feel the electricity passing between them. Grady reached his hand toward her belly, but stopped a few inches away from it. He whispered, "Is it mine?"

Jody shook her head. "I'm not supposed to talk to witnesses until the trial is over."

"You won't call me back. Fine. You won't reply to my texts. Fine. But sooner or later you're gonna have to answer this question."

"Later," Jody said.

She turned to walk away. Grady put his hand on her arm—and in an instant he was hurled up against the wall. Cooper pinned him there. Anna stared. She hadn't realized that Cooper could move so fast. That anyone could move so fast.

"Leave her alone, man." Cooper said. "She'll talk to you after the trial."

"It's okay," Jody said. "He wasn't hurting me."

Grady held his hands up in a gesture of peace. Cooper let him go. Grady straightened his shirt and looked at Jody for a long moment. Then he walked away, pushing the door below an Exit sign so forcefully, it banged against the wall. Jody flinched.

When he was gone, Anna turned to her sister. "Why don't you want to talk to him?" she asked softly. She knew it wasn't because of courtroom rules.

"I might be in jail when this baby is born," Jody said. "I had a one-night stand with Grady. I don't know him. The one thing I know about men is they can't be trusted. If I go to jail, this baby goes to *you*, Anna. No one else."

■ ■ ■

The most damning evidence was the bloody sock the police found behind Jody's washing machine. Anna could see the jurors' eyes narrow as the DNA analyst explained that the blood on the sock was the coach's, to a mathematical certainty. The police had done their evidence collection well. The scientists had done their analysis well. There was no getting around the blood. There was just minimizing it.

"Were you there when those specks of blood landed on that sock?" Anna asked the DNA analyst.

"No, of course not."

"So you can't say whether or not the coach just nicked himself cutting an apple?"

"Right."

"The largest bloodstain on that sock was about a centimeter in diameter, right?"

"Right?"

"About the size of a pea?"

"Yes."

"Coach Fowler could've been sitting next to Jody on the couch, and he picked a hangnail and a little blood dripped down, right?"

"I couldn't say. I wasn't there. All I know is that it's his blood, on her sock, which was found in her house."

At the close of the government's case, Anna made a motion for judgment of acquittal. She asked the judge to declare that the government had not met its burden of proof—that no reasonable jury could find Jody guilty based on the evidence that had been elicited so far. The judge denied the motion. It was not a surprise—such motions were rarely granted—but it was a disappointment. The case was going to the jury. And juries were unpredictable.

For her first witness, Anna called a firefighter from a neighboring county. She had deliberately chosen someone who did not have roots in Holly Grove. The firefighter was a giant man named

Tyrone Murphy. She got him qualified as an expert in the area of moving bodies, based on his years of training and experience. Then she asked him, "In your experience, sir, can a one-hundred-thirty-pound woman carry a two-hundred-thirty-pound man?"

"No, ma'am. People don't realize how heavy that is. I'm six foot six, two hundred and eighty pounds. I could carry that body, but only because I spend a lot of time at the gym, and as a trained firefighter I know some techniques for lifting bodies. I don't expect a little woman who's had no training could do that."

As a demonstrative aid, the firefighter had brought a life-size training mannequin. Four police officers carried it in and laid it on the courtroom floor. It was the size and shape of an adult man.

"How big is this mannequin?" Anna asked.

"Five ten, one hundred eighty pounds."

"So the coach would be fifty pounds heavier, at two hundred thirty pounds?"

"Right."

"Can you show us how you'd carry this mannequin?"

Tyrone got up from the stand, came down to the floor, and made a show of rolling the body to the side, getting his arms under it, putting it over his shoulder, and lifting with his knees. But he had to grunt and groan, and beads of sweat popped out on his forehead.

"Ideally, I'd have help if I had to carry a person this big."

"Thank you," Anna said. He put it down with a thump.

"Now, Your Honor, I'd like each juror to have a try." She'd cleared this with the judge before.

He nodded. "I'll allow it."

One by one, the jurors were called out of the box and allowed to try to move the mannequin. Anna herself had tried moving it. She'd only been able to scoot it a couple inches. The female jurors had the same experience. A couple of the bigger men got it to move a few feet, but with a lot of grunts and groans. There was some laughing, which was good. She wanted them to think the idea of Jody moving the coach's body was laughable.

When the mannequin exhibit was finished, it was 4:00 P.M. The judge asked if the parties wanted to adjourn for the night.

"I have one more witness for today," Anna said. "She'll be brief, I think."

"Then go ahead and call her."

"The defense calls Kathy Mack."

Desiree was on her feet. "Objection!"

"Sidebar," the judge said. He called them up to the bench and put the husher on, creating a staticy white noise so the jurors couldn't hear what was being said at the bench.

Jody waddled up to the judge's bench. She could have remained at the table and listened to the sidebar on an earpiece, but Anna liked any opportunity for Jody to stand or walk in front of the jurors. It allowed them to see how very pregnant she was.

At the bench, the women stood on their tiptoes to talk to the judge. You never felt more like a supplicant than when you were standing at someone's feet while he sat looking down at you. But his voice was kindly.

"What's your objection, Ms. Williams?" the judge asked.

"This is the mother of a girl who reported that Coach Fowler sexually assaulted her," the prosecutor said. "You explicitly ruled that this sort of testimony would be inadmissible."

"Ms. Curtis?"

"I'm not going to ask about her daughter. The witness will only talk about an event she saw in the casino where she works. The event involved Coach Fowler."

"I need to review this." The judge flipped off the husher and turned to the jury. "The lawyers and I need to resolve a legal matter. The jurors are excused for the night. We will reconvene tomorrow morning at precisely nine o'clock, as usual. As always, I instruct you to talk to no one about this case, including one another, and to refrain from watching or reading any coverage of this case in the press."

The jurors nodded and filed out of the courtroom. Judge Upperthwaite stood and spoke to the lawyers. "We'll hold this hearing in my chambers." There was groaning. The rest of the audience—the press, spectators, and Anonymous protesters—would not hear it.

The judge's office was an enormous, beautiful space. Ten-foot ceilings had gold-painted panels; the polished parquet floor was covered in oriental rugs. The judge's giant oak desk looked like an expensive antique, as did the rest of his polished wood furniture. A large window overlooked the courthouse square. When she was standing, Anna could see that the protesters were still there, five stories below. When she sat down, she could only see the white winter sky.

Anna chose a chair between Jody and the prosecutor. The judge's clerk, Donald, sat on a couch to the side, near the court reporter, who rested her fingers on her portable stenographic machine. As the judge came into chambers, Donald popped out of his seat. The judge unzipped his robe with trembling hands. Donald helped him slip out of it, then hung it in a closet. The judge sank slowly into his chair, holding on to his desk for balance. Judge Upperthwaite wore a button-down shirt, wool pants, and brown sweater vest. On the bench, he looked like a Wise Man. Here, he looked like a frail old grandfather.

Behind him was a picture of a sweet-looking silver-haired lady. Anna guessed this was his wife, Lena Hoffmeister Upperthwaite.

"Ms. Curtis, I'd like a proffer from you," the judge said. "What will your witness testify to, if I do allow this testimony?"

The stenographer's fingers danced over the keys of her machine.

"Kathy Mack is a blackjack dealer at the MotorCity Casino," Anna said. "In that capacity, she has two things to add to this trial. First, she will testify that she saw Coach Fowler at the casino, gambling a lot. This will support our theory that he was a man deeply in debt."

"You can establish that with financial records." The judge waved a knotty hand. "What else can Ms. Mack shed light on?"

"A few weeks before the coach's death, Kathy Mack saw a man threaten Coach Fowler and then punch him in the stomach. The man she saw matches the description of the loan shark who Wendy Fowler described coming to her house."

"I see. Ms. Williams, what is your position on this?"

"I don't believe this story for a minute, Your Honor. I've interviewed all of these women, and I never heard about this mystery man before trial started. Moreover, Kathy Mack is the woman whose daughter, Hayley, accused the coach of sexually abusing her and then committed suicide shortly thereafter. Ms. Mack is highly biased against Coach Fowler. But I can't effectively cross-examine her about this bias without introducing the inadmissible and prejudicial sex-abuse allegations that the defense has been trying to get in."

"I agree with the government. This testimony is more prejudicial than it is probative. I am excluding it. Ms. Mack will not be allowed to testify." The judge stood with effort. "This hearing is adjourned. I will see all the parties back in court tomorrow at nine A.M. sharp. Have a pleasant evening."

50

Jody was furious. She paced the empty hallway two floors up, passing Cooper and Anna, turning, and passing them again. She held her belly in her hands. Her heels resounded like gunfire against the marble floor. "This is total bullshit!" she said. "He can't do this."

"He can and he did," Anna said drily. She leaned back against the window ledge. "It gives us something to take up on appeal."

"I have a right to put on my defense. He is deliberately fucking with me. It's just the same as it's ever been in Holly Grove."

"What do you mean?" Anna said.

"He's the one who declined my case when Coach Fowler raped me."

Anna stared at her. "You said you *wanted* to have sex with the coach. You said that case was declined because you didn't want to press charges."

"Annie." Jody stopped walking. She looked down at her swollen ankles. "I haven't been totally honest with you. But I don't think now is the time to start."

Anna took a deep breath. "Start with this. The coach *forced* you to have sex with him when you were fifteen?"

"Yes."

"You wanted charges brought against him then?"

"Yeah."

"And Judge Upperthwaite refused to bring them?"

"He was the DA then, not a judge. But—yeah."

"Christ, Jody." Now Anna started pacing. "This is not the best time for me to discover this! I've made our opening statement. There are no take backs."

"I'm sorry, Annie."

She stared at her sister, as several things suddenly became clear. "You never took the coach back to your house, did you? That's why the police didn't find any of his semen or blood on your sheets?"

Cooper stepped forward and put a hand on her arm. "Let's not talk about this here."

Anna looked around the empty courthouse hallway. "Right. Thanks." She put up a hand. "Just give me a minute to get my bearings." She turned and stared out the window. In the square below, the protesters were gathering up to leave for the day.

Anna had come here believing in the system, its structure as a whole and its players generally. Not that it was perfect—far from it—but it aimed for justice, with well-meaning participants. She wouldn't have spent her career working in it if she believed otherwise.

She'd been blind. Jody had done what she'd done because the system had failed her entirely. And it was still broken. With sudden clarity, Anna understood why.

"I have to go to see Rob."

■ ■ ■

Fifteen minutes later, Anna strode into Detective Rob Gargaron's office. He glanced over from his computer, saw her expression, and stood. He closed the door and they faced each other.

Anna said, "You're the one who left the sealed cases at Jody's house, aren't you?"

He nodded.

"Did you know that Coach Fowler was a serial pedophile the whole time?"

"Not until he died. After you asked the prosecutor for the old cases, I pulled them. What I saw in there made me sick. I couldn't do anything about it, not if I wanted to keep my job. But I knew you'd be able to do something with them. So I left them on your doorstep."

"Thank you," she said. "For being the one good cop in Holly Grove."

"There are plenty of good cops here. Don't let a few bad apples ruin your impression of the whole force."

"I still need your help."

"What can I do?"

She handed him a trial subpoena.

"I sent this to the clerk's office months ago. They said they couldn't find an answer, that the cases were too old. But I'll bet you could find out. Who nolle'd all those sealed cases? Who decided not to prosecute Owen Fowler, time and again?"

"Are you prepared for what will happen if you do this?" Rob said.

"No. But I'm doing it anyway."

"If you shoot at the king, you'd better kill the king. Because if you don't, he'll come after you."

"I understand."

"My father took the reports before he retired. I honestly think he didn't believe the girls. Or if he did, he thought they wanted the coach, and he didn't think the coach should be punished."

"But your father didn't decline the cases," Anna said. "Not by himself."

"No. A prosecutor had to do that—or a judge could refuse to sign a warrant."

"Who?"

"Judge Upperthwaite. And before that, District Attorney Upperthwaite."

pressed the clicker, and the garage door slid up, revealing the coach's gleaming four-car garage. I pulled in, closed the garage door, and turned off the car. The garage was cavernous, brightly lit, and empty. In days past, Coach would have parked many of his automotive toys here. Now, with all his creditors closing in, the Corvette had all four spots to itself.

I got out, went around, and opened the passenger door. Coach crashed into me; I yelped and leaped back. But he was still unconscious. His legs were strapped in, but his arms dangled onto the concrete floor.

I took a deep breath, tucked my hands under his armpits, and pushed his torso back into the seat. It wasn't easy. You don't realize how heavy a body is, or how difficult it is to move if the body itself isn't providing momentum. There was no way I could move his whole body by myself.

But that was okay; I didn't have to. The door to the house opened and Wendy and Kathy came out. They moved with the efficient calm of competent women who know exactly what they're doing. Wendy unfolded a wheelchair that was tucked into a corner of the garage. She pushed it to the passenger side of the Corvette and lifted the arm so the seat of the wheelchair was level with the seat of the car. Between the three of us, and with a lot of grunting, we were able to slide his body from the car to the wheelchair.

Kathy brought over a gym bag that held three thick sweatshirts, three pairs of sweatpants, and two rolls of duct tape. We put all the clothes on him, over what he already wore. The sweatshirts were easy enough, but for the pants, two of us had to lift his bottom off the chair while the third slid the waistband over his hips. It took some doing.

When he was more padded than the kid from the Cottonelle ad, we duct-taped his arms to the armrests of the wheelchair, starting with his wrists and wrapping round and round till we got to his armpits. We did the same with his legs, from ankle to thigh, and then his torso, securing him to the back of the chair from hips to chest. When we were done, he looked like a giant silver mummy reigning in a small wheeled throne.

By padding his skin and spreading out the restraints, we minimized pressure points and avoided making indents in his skin. We wanted his body to be perfect when we were done with it.

Wendy went to a side wall and flicked a panel of switches, turning off the outdoor lights. She opened the garage's side door, and Kathy pushed the unconscious coach out into the backyard. The night was warm, lovely, and black. As my eyes adjusted to the dark, I saw that the yard was landscaped beautifully. There was a flagstone patio, with a path leading to the edge of the sandy cliff side. Lake Huron was black and quiet beyond. A wooden ramp led down to the dock.

Wendy wheeled him down to the lake. The wheelchair thumpety-thumped on the wooden slats of the ramp. The bottom of the cove was perfectly secluded. The sandy cliff and the trees shielded us from any neighbor's eyes. When Wendy stopped the wheelchair, the night was silent except for chirping frogs and water lapping softly on the shore. It was dark except for the stars above. There was no human sound except our breathing.

A pontoon boat was tied to the dock. Wendy said he'd had to sell off his other boats. But this one would work for us. Kathy and I pulled the boat flush with the dock and Wendy pushed the chair on.

The pontoon was a big flat square, surrounded by a long cushioned bench seat. The floor was covered in green AstroTurf. In one corner sat a white plastic bucket. In the middle was a captain's wheel, which Wendy helmed. She expertly untied the boat, turned on the ignition, and steered us away from the shore. Kathy held on to the wheelchair and put on the brakes so it wouldn't roll around with the motion.

Lake Huron is big, more than twenty thousand square miles. But I'd say we only went a mile or so from shore. Far enough so that no one was around, and no one on land could hear anything. When the lights from land were just pinpricks, Wendy turned off the motor. The stars seemed closer than the houses. They blazed bright, with no city lights to compete with. Long ago, the Incas living in the Andes made constellations not from the stars but from the dark spaces between them. That's what the sky looked like over Lake Huron on that June night.

There was nothing to do until the coach woke up. The three of us sat next to each other on the bench seats.

"You okay?" Wendy asked me.

I nodded. "You?"

"Absolutely."

We looked to Kathy, who shook her head. She looked like she was going to vomit. She pulled out a flask and took a sip, then held it out to me. I smelled pure vodka and shook my head. She'd been drinking a lot ever since her daughter died. I probably should've taken the flask away from her, but at the time, I thought anything that would steady her nerves was good. I held her hand.

It took close to an hour for the coach to come to. He started mumbling, then moving his head. He might've tried to move other body parts as well but couldn't because of the duct tape. Eventually, his eyes blinked open. He looked at the three of us. He looked down at his silver-cocooned body, which must've felt like a full-body cast. He looked at the blackness of the lake surrounding him. And he started to scream.

52

You're wondering how the three of us agreed to abduct a man, aren't you? We're not mobsters. None of us had ever been part of a murderous conspiracy before. We were just three regular women, trying to find a little justice in a man's world.

You know that Kathy and I were friends forever. But Wendy and I kept in touch, too, over the years. We weren't social friends. She wouldn't be comfortable at the dive bars I hung out at, or Kathy's trailer park. I certainly wouldn't be comfortable in Wendy's Junior League meetings or her big pink house, where I might run into the coach. But after that day in Meijer when I saw Wendy's black eye, we had a bond. We talked on the phone every couple months, just checking up on each other, keeping each other sane. Every so often, she'd come have coffee at my place. I always sent a present for Isabel's birthday. She sent flowers when I bought my house.

The first time we talked about killing the coach was last spring. The three of us didn't get together to plot a murder. We got together to garden.

See, Cooper had bought the lots across the street from his farm, to make that community garden. But farming in Detroit is a funny thing. Before you plant a single seed, you need to clear away everything that came before. It was a mess, and he needed hundreds of man-hours. He asked for help, sending out an e-mail to a few friends. They e-mailed a few more friends, and soon it went viral. Someone set up a Facebook page. Everyone in Holly Grove wanted to pitch in. When Cooper came home from the army minus a leg, everyone tried to lend a hand. This was the first time he actually accepted help.

It was a beautiful Saturday in April, a few weeks after Hayley died.

I made Kathy come with. She'd been drinking a lot. I thought the fresh air and sunshine would do her good.

When we got to Cooper's house, he had put up a sign that said: THE DETROIT CITY GARDEN CLUB. Ha. The lots were overgrown with weeds and full of garbage. Our job was gathering all the crap and hauling it into two piles: flammable and nonflammable. There was a lot of it: bricks, pipes, old sinks and TVs, charred wood from the old houses that used to stand there, tree stumps, random trash, you name it.

Wendy came too. She brought her own pair of pink gardening gloves, but she got down in the dirt with everyone else. She has a lot more substance than people give her credit for.

Tons of people showed up that day. It was like a Holly Grove High School reunion. Cooper made us a huge lunch, which we ate on paper plates. Then we hauled more trash and tilled the ground. We got sweaty, dirty, and sore—but in a good way, the kind of exhausted you get from a real workout instead of insomnia.

At the end of the day, there were two massive piles of trash on a few acres of cleared land, all nice brown soil ready for planting. It was a satisfying sight. As the sun was setting, Cooper gave out tins of granola like goody bags to thank people. Folks headed home.

"Will the city come pick this all up?" I asked, gesturing at the two enormous piles.

"Ha," Cooper said. "I can't even get the city to come pick up one bag of garbage. I've been trying for months."

"So what will you do with this?"

He gestured to the first pile, the one with bricks, sinks, and non-flammable stuff. "I'll haul that stuff to the dump."

"And this one?" I pointed to the second pile, heaped with wood, tree stumps, and paper products.

Cooper smiled. "You don't want to know."

"Yes, we do," Wendy trilled.

"It's not technically legal."

I said, "Cool."

We were the only three volunteers left. Turns out, we three women had a lot in common, though we didn't know the full extent of it. At that point, we had nowhere better to go, and holes in our lives we were trying to fill. We were happy to be somewhere with other people. I think we all sensed that loneliness in each other.

Cooper doused the pile of flammable debris with lighter fluid. We each dropped a match onto a section. A massive bonfire whooshed up, the flames reaching high above our heads. It felt like a pagan festival.

It must've violated all sorts of city rules, but no authorities showed up. It's hard to get officials to come to house arsons in Detroit, much less burning trash. Cooper said if he was going to live here, he had to find a way to deal with the trash himself. This was what his family did on the farm; they burned their own garbage.

"I have to do some chores around the orchard," Cooper said, as the sky grew dark. "Can you guys keep an eye on this?"

"Happy to," I said.

Kathy got a round of beers out of the cooler and passed them around. The three of us stood watching the fire.

That night had a magical quality. We felt like we were the only people for miles. Maybe it was the fire, or the fact that we spent the day working together, or the beer, but our talk veered toward the sort of truthfulness you don't usually get in after-dinner conversations.

"Where's Isabel tonight?" Kathy asked. "With her father?"

"I try to keep her away from her father as much as possible," Wendy said. "She's sleeping over at a friend's house tonight."

Kathy and I glanced at each other. I asked, "Why do you keep Isabel away from her father?"

Wendy took a sip of beer and looked at me. Her face glowed yellow in the firelight. "Because he's a pedophile. I expect you know that."

I felt my eyes get big. Of course I knew it. But I didn't expect his wife to say it. In all our conversations, she'd never said it before.

I nodded. "But he's her father. So how can you keep him away from her?"

"That's a problem. If I file for divorce, he'll get at least partial custody. And then he'll have Isabel half the time. Alone." Wendy looked into the flames. "I don't know how to protect my daughter from her own father."

Kathy started sobbing. I had no idea why. I put my arm around her and tried to comfort her. My first thought was that the coach had raped her, too, when she was a kid. In between her sobs, she told us what had happened to Hayley. Before then, I thought Hayley killed herself because of the teasing by other kids. Now Kathy told us that the coach had raped Hayley, and that was what pushed the girl over the brink. Wendy came over and put her arm around Kathy too.

I felt like someone had punched me in the chest. "This is my fault," I said. Coach Fowler had done exactly the same thing to me when I was Hayley's age, but I was too ashamed to warn Kathy—or any of the other moms in Holly Grove. Their daughters were vulnerable because I hid what happened to me. Sure, I went to the police, ten years ago, but I folded way too easy when they declined the case.

I should've made a fuss. I should've gone to the press. I should have done *something*. If I had, Hayley would still be alive. Instead, the coach had been free to keep doing the same thing, again and again, to God knows how many girls over the next decade.

I told them what the coach did to me. I told them why it was my fault. Wendy shook her head. She said, "I'm so sorry. It's *my* fault more than anybody's. I had the most to gain from him not being caught. I didn't know for sure, but I suspected this. The first time we had sex, he was forty and I was a twiggy seventeen. After I had Isabel—after I had a woman's body—he lost all interest in sex, at least with me. But I didn't really *want* to know. I wanted to be living the life everyone thought I was living."

"We could go forward now," I said.

Wendy shook her head. "He has the town in his pocket. Police, judges, parents—everyone's on his side. It's why I'd never be able to win full custody."

I looked at the pile of burning trash, orange flames against a black sky. I said, "Sometimes you have to deal with garbage yourself. If the city won't come and take it, you have to get rid of it your own way."

Wendy met my gaze and nodded slowly. Her eyes reflected the bonfire. She said, "You have to clear out the ugliness and waste in order to let the beautiful new things grow."

Kathy said nothing, she just looked at me fearfully. And then she nodded, too.

We made a decision that night. I know it's not what you believe in, Annie. You believe in working within the system, changing things from the inside. And . . . you're right. We live in America, not one of those countries where girls are sold as brides, where women are treated as property and have no voice. We could have gone about things differently. And, probably, we should have.

The world needs order. If it doesn't have that, if people take matters into their own hands, you end up with your house and everything in it being burned to the ground.

And you end up with some horrible memories. You can never get them out of your head.

I still have nightmares about what we did. I deserve them.

But that night, watching the bonfire of trash, the answer seemed so obvious. Kathy, Wendy, and I had tried the system, each one of us. It hadn't worked. So we decided to get rid of the garbage ourselves. We'd take care of our own.

Once it was clear that we all agreed on the outcome, the rest was just planning the logistics. We put aside the beer, sat on a rock, and talked details. We're very organized women. We covered everything. Or so we thought.

53

The glassy black water of Lake Huron seemed to amplify Coach Fowler's screams. Kathy and I each grabbed one of the handles of the wheelchair and tipped it backward until the chair was reclining fully on its back and Coach's head was on the AstroTurf floor of the boat. Wendy picked up the white plastic bucket, which was full of lake water. She poured it over his face. The screaming was replaced with gurgling.

When the bucket was empty, Wendy dipped it into the lake and refilled it. She set it down near the wheelchair and knelt by her husband's head. He was choking and snuffling on the water in his lungs. She stroked his hair, pushing his soaked bangs out of his eyes. "Shh," she said. "Shh, Owen." When he quieted enough to take a breath, she said, "Scream again, and I'll do that again. Keep quiet and we can talk like grown-ups. Deal?"

He coughed, then nodded as vigorously as his position would allow. Kathy and I righted the chair. He choked up more water, then dry heaved. He was fully awake now, his eyes wide, his wet blond hair plastered back. His head was the only part of his body he could move and he kept turning it back and forth, desperately trying to take in the situation. But now he was quiet.

Wendy opened one of the bench seats, which held a large storage area beneath the cushion. She pulled out a red milk crate full of odds and ends. Kathy angled the wheelchair until the coach was facing a bench. The three of us sat down together.

The most powerful man in Holly Grove stared at three regular women wearing T-shirts and jeans. A jury of his peers? Not exactly. But it was the closest we'd ever get.

We didn't put a piece of tape on his mouth. That might have left a mark. And we wouldn't be able to hear what he had to say.

I stood up and said, "Owen Fowler, you are charged with three counts of being an evil, perverted asshole. How do you plead?"

"What?"

"This is your trial. The one you deserve. The one that was never going to happen in Holly Grove."

"This is crazy. Let me go, and we'll pretend this was one big joke."

"I'll take that as a 'not guilty' plea. Fine. For my first witness, I call Wendy Fowler."

You're looking at me like I'm insane, Annie. I understand. Why not just kill the man? We considered it. We could've just shot him as he came out of Screecher's one night and made it look like a mugging. That certainty would've been simpler. But it would've been too easy for him. Our goal was protecting future girls, yes, but it was also justice. And for justice, he had to know that he was being punished for what he'd done. He had to understand what was happening to him, who was doing it, and why.

Wendy reached into the crate and pulled out a small pink Cinderella sleeping bag. She stood up and put it on his lap. "Do you remember this? From the night of Isabel's last sleepover?"

He nodded, his eyes growing big.

"I always suspected you were touching the girls from the high school. I saw them come to your summer camp, all smiles and hope, and then drop out, all haunted and hollow. I knew what you did to me, on the seat of your Corvette, when I was seventeen. But I couldn't prove you were doing it to other girls. And I didn't want to.

"It wasn't easy putting up that front. I felt like a fraud. All the concealer and sunglasses I wore to cover my bruises. The willful blindness to your after-school activities."

"Wendy, I don't know what you're talking about," he said. "I always loved you. I—"

"Shut up," she said. "You'll have your chance. And don't tell me you loved me. You were a good provider, that's all. I had a roof over my head—two, actually. I didn't have to scrape by for everything, like my family had. I thought that would be enough. Even if my husband didn't love me. At least you loved Isabel. And for Isabel's sake, you'd restrain yourself. Our home was an out-of-bounds zone. I believed that; I had to believe it. Until the night of the sleepover."

She picked up the sleeping bag.

"You just couldn't keep your hands off those girls, could you? Not even in our own house? I came down that night to get a glass of milk. And there you were, with Zoë Malone—Isabel's best friend!—on your lap, showing her the Holly Grove yearbook. Telling her she was a good girl. Your hand was pushing up Zoë's nightgown—it was up past her thighs. She was ten! What would have happened if I hadn't come down then?"

He pursed his lips and looked away. She grabbed his face and turned it to hers, like he was her disobedient child.

"Answer me!" she said. "I was your wife for ten years. I cooked your meals, washed your underwear, made you respectable. I deserve an answer."

"Baby doll." His voice was soft and pleading. "I was just showing a little girl a book. I would never do what you're suggesting. Not when I had you upstairs. The most beautiful woman in Holly Grove in my bed, and I'm going to mess around with a ten-year-old? That's crazy."

"You had an *erection*." She whispered the last word. Nice churchgoing mom didn't like potty language, not even in the middle of Lake Huron. She let go of his face and took a step back. "You were rubbing that little girl against your *erection*."

"No, no, no. You were tired, baby doll. You thought you saw something that you didn't actually—"

"Don't insult my intelligence, Owen. I *know* what I saw. Do you think I'd have you here—like this—if I weren't sure? I *know* who you are. I know you better than anyone else in this world does. You might be able to fool the town, but not me." She stared at him. "You're a child molester."

He looked down at his silver-wrapped knees. He nodded.

It was an acknowledgment. And that made me pause. There's something about a bad man admitting his sins that has power.

But it was my turn, and I wasn't giving it up, not after all this.

I reached into the milk crate and pulled out the big trophy I got when I set the record for the high jump in 2004. It was a standard track-and-field trophy: a large brass woman frozen midstride, standing atop a heavy wood and marble base.

"I trusted you," I said. "I thought you cared about me. I fell in love with you. And then you raped me. After that, I never trusted another man. For ten years. I barely graduated from high school. And here I am. A dead-end life. Because of you."

"I thought—" He glanced at his wife. "I thought you wanted me as much as I wanted you. I thought it was, you know, consensual."

"I said 'no.' And I was a kid."

"But you got me all riled up! You can't tease a man like that and just expect him to pull back. You were the one who—"

He noticed us glaring at him. He stopped and cleared his throat. "I'm sorry," he said. "You're right. I'm very, very sorry."

There's not much to say after someone apologizes. It makes me wonder why people don't do it more often. I sat down.

Kathy's hands were shaking as she reached into the milk crate. She pulled out a tiny lavender ski jacket. It was the one Hayley used to wear when she was a little girl. It was the one she'd worn in Meijer that day that Kathy put on the big fruity hat and Hayley tried to eat the "gapes."

"She was my little girl," Kathy whispered. "My baby. She was all I had. And you killed her."

Kathy might have had more to say, but she couldn't. She sat down and cried. Wendy sat and put her arm around her.

I looked at Coach Fowler. "Do you have anything you want to say in your defense?"

"God, I'm so sorry, Kathy." His voice cracked. He looked at each of us, one by one. "I can't tell you how sorry I am. Wendy, I'm not a good husband. I know that. You deserve better. Jody, I'm sorry for what I did to you, and what it did to your life. You deserved better too."

"Then why didn't you *do* better?" Wendy said.

"I wanted to." He started to cry. "I just couldn't. I'm sick. I know what I did was wrong. I tried to change. I couldn't."

"You're always telling your athletes about self-discipline. Was that just BS? Or does it not apply to you?"

"I wanted it to be true. I tried." He was sobbing. "I know exactly what those girls went through. I went through it too."

"What are you talking about?" Wendy asked angrily.

With his face scrunched in pain and his hair slick as a wet rat, he was barely recognizable as the golden god who reigned over the football field. He choked out the words between sobs. "My stepfather . . . used to . . . to touch me . . . when I was a boy."

We stared at him, at each other, then back at him.

What makes someone evil? The devil? I don't believe in that. Biology? Maybe some people are predisposed to that sort of thing. But mostly, I think it's evil happening to them. Kids who are victims are more likely to grow up to become predators. That doesn't mean it's their destiny; a lot of survivors never hurt anyone else. But for those who don't escape, who stay in the line of succession like unlucky crown princes, evil is passed down like a monstrous heirloom. We're all victims of the victims who came before us.

"I don't . . . know why . . . that made me . . . do it . . . it's not the person . . . I wanted to be . . ." He could barely get the words out. "I'm so sorry . . . I need help . . . please . . . I'm sick . . . help me."

Tears mixed with the lake water on his cheeks. Snot dangled from his nose in long shuddering strings before landing in slimy loops on the duct tape. He shivered beneath his silver body cast. If I've ever seen a more pathetic sight, I can't think of what it was.

I reached in my pocket for a tissue at the same time that Wendy reached under the steering wheel for a rag. She cleaned him with it, briskly wiping the tears and snot off his face. As she did, she looked over and saw that I was holding out a crumpled Kleenex. In unison, we said: "Oh shit."

We realized it at the same time. The urge to clean off his face was a tipping point. You can't murder in cold blood an unarmed person you still have the instinct to nurture.

We couldn't kill Owen Fowler. But we had no clue what to do with him now.

54

Anna didn't want to fight with Cooper in the car. He was having a hard enough time simply sitting in it while she drove toward the courthouse through the morning rush-hour traffic. But he wouldn't let the issue go.

"Don't do it this way," he said, again.

"I have to. It's the only way to get justice."

"The judge has all the power in this town. He'll send *both* you and Jody to jail."

"He has power because no one's ever challenged him. He'll lose that power once this comes out."

"He won't go down without a fight. He has contacts, in and out of jail. He might have you killed first."

"Oh, come on. He's corrupt. He's not Scarface."

"He may wear a robe, but a man acts like any other animal when he's cornered." Cooper was sweating, although winter blew in from the open windows. He wiped his brow on his shirt and turned around to look at Jody. "Can you talk some sense into her?"

"I think this is the most sensible thing she's planned since she got here." Jody grinned at Anna in the rearview mirror. Anna grinned back.

Cooper slapped the dashboard so hard, Anna jumped. "Dammit, Anna!"

"Coop," she said. "Let's not fight in the car."

"Where else are we going to fight? This is it! You're about to throw yourself on a funeral pyre."

"Look," she said. "I went all the way to D.C. to help people.

I didn't realize how much Holly Grove needed help. This is my chance. This could change everything."

Anna turned onto Main Street and approached the courthouse square. There were more protesters than ever. She slowed to avoid hitting them. People in Guy Fawkes masks raised their fists and chanted Jody's name when they saw the SUV.

"You don't have to get yourself killed trying to fix the world," Cooper said.

"Isn't that what you signed up for in Afghanistan?"

"I was serving my country. It was my duty."

"This is *me* serving my country," Anna said. "This is *my* duty."

"What about us? What am I supposed to do when my girlfriend gets killed?"

Anna was silent.

"Right," Cooper said. "There is no 'us.' We're just 'friends having fun' while you're on a break from your real life."

"Coop." She brought the car to a halt at a stop sign and turned to him. "That's not—"

"I can't watch you drive into an ambush. And I can't be in this car." He swung the door open, got out, and slammed it shut behind him. He strode into the square, where he was quickly swallowed up by the crowd of protesters.

Anna was so startled, she just sat there looking into the place where he'd disappeared. A car behind her honked, and she turned forward, blinked, and put her foot on the accelerator again.

"Don't mind him," Jody said from the backseat. "That was just his claustrophobia speaking."

Anna nodded and gripped the steering wheel tightly, so Jody wouldn't see that her hands were trembling.

Twenty minutes later, the sisters sat next to each other in court, waiting for the judge to take the bench. Anna's heart pounded painfully against her ribs.

She glanced back behind her. A dozen reporters sat in the row behind them. She wished she had copies of her motion to give them.

But it was already 9:00 A.M. The side door opened and Judge Upperthwaite walked out, followed by his legal entourage.

"All rise and come to order," the clerk called. "This court is now in session."

Anna and Desiree came to their feet in sync. Jody was slower; she groaned softly as she rose. Her stomach had gotten so large, it looked like it was going to pop right out of her striped poplin shirt.

"When last we adjourned," the judge said, "we dealt with an issue concerning a witness. Now that that issue has been resolved, does the defense intend to call any more witnesses, or does it rest?"

"Neither," Anna said, rising to her feet. "I am moving for you to recuse yourself from this case, declare a mistrial, and dismiss all charges against Jody Curtis."

The audience murmured.

"Ms. Curtis, we have been through this, months ago. I have already ruled on your recusal motion, quite clearly. You have your record, and when—if—Ms. Curtis is convicted, you may appeal. I'm certainly not declaring a mistrial. If you have another witness, I will call in the jury. If you do not have one, I will consider the defense to have rested."

"The defense does not rest," Anna said. "I want that clear for the record."

The stenographer nodded at Anna as her fingers flew over the machine.

"I am filing my Motion for Dismissal and my second Motion for the Honorable Lawrence Upperthwaite to Recuse Himself." Anna walked up to the law clerk and handed him four copies of the papers to time-stamp and file. She set one on the prosecutor's table.

"Ms. Curtis, your conduct is close to contumacious." Judge Upperthwaite's voice dropped to a low growl that would have scared Anna back when she was a rookie lawyer. "I have made my ruling and told you to move on. Now *move on*."

She heard movement in the audience and turned to see what it was. Cooper sat in the front row, passing out copies of her motion to the press. It was exactly what she needed done. Technically, the journalists had a right to the motion, but she wasn't confident that Judge Upperthwaite would allow them access to it. Cooper smiled at her, and she smiled back.

Her motion described the FirstDown company and the relationship between the judge's wife and the coach. It also listed the criminal cases Upperthwaite had dismissed as DA and judge. She'd attached the paperwork Rob gave her yesterday and sent a copy to the Fraud and Public Corruption Unit at the Department of Justice. And, God bless him, Cooper was making sure the press had it.

She turned back to the court, feeling stronger now that she knew Cooper was behind her. "My first Motion for Recusal was based on the fact that your wife was a business partner with Coach Fowler in a company called FirstDown. Further research has shown that you are the person who declined to bring all the cases against the coach. You did this in your capacity as a DA, and when you were elected to the bench, you continued to do it by declining arrest warrants. You were also the person who placed all these cases under seal."

"Ms. Curtis, I'm warning you."

"The coach needed someone to cover up all his abuse over the years. He might have paid some families directly. Some girls might not have made complaints. But the ones who went to the police— now, that was a problem for him. But you were the Holly Grove DA for fifteen years. And judge for the last five."

"Ms. Curtis! You are in contempt!"

"Was FirstDown a front? Is that how Coach Fowler paid you?" Anna's questions were not for the judge. They were for the reporters.

"Guards!" The judge's voice shook with fury. "Step her back."

A CSO pulled her arms behind her back and handcuffed them. She didn't resist.

"Sorry, Ms. Curtis," the guard mumbled.

Anna met Cooper's eyes. He looked extremely unhappy. This was exactly what he feared.

She looked back at the courtroom as she was being led out.

The last thing she saw was journalists looking through the papers Cooper had handed out. Someone took a cell-phone picture of her being led away. And then the door swung shut. She was in a foul-smelling back room. The guard put her in a cinder block holding cell, shut the door, and locked her in.

55

etter bring your toothbrush" was a joke that Anna and her prosecutor friends made when a lawyer really messed up. The idea was that a judge would hold them in contempt and lock them up for the night. Of course, that rarely happened in real life; before this, Anna had only ever seen one lawyer "stepped back." But now, Anna really wished she had a toothbrush. It was going to be a long night.

The holding cell behind the courtroom was bare except for a bench and a small seatless toilet. It stank of urine and bleach. Still, when the CSO came to get her a few hours later, Anna didn't want to leave. Because she knew the place they would take her next would be worse.

She was taken to the garage and loaded into a cold van with a bunch of other inmates. A guard chained her handcuffs to the van wall. The back of the van was freezing cold, and Anna shivered for the whole ride. At the central cell block, she was fingerprinted and photographed, then put in a holding pen.

It was a larger, smellier version of the courtroom holding cell, only with company. There were nine other women, ranging from homeless meth heads to carjacking bank robbers. Anna was the only one wearing a suit. She sat on the bench in a corner and tried to make herself invisible. The wall radiated coldness and sucked all the warmth from her body. She shivered and hugged her knees.

A big woman came over and stood in front of Anna. She wore a hooded sweatshirt over a Bud Light T-shirt. She had huge calloused hands and pockmarked cheeks. "Hey," she said. "You that lawyer says Coach Fowler was a rapist?"

"That's me." Anna stood. She had to tilt her head up to meet the woman's eyes. The inmate had at least five inches and sixty pounds on her. Anna tried to remember some moves from her self-defense course. Most of them involved kicking the assailant in the groin, which wouldn't be so effective here in the female holding cell.

"Good on ya," the woman said. "He did it to my cousin too. She was never the same after. Hope that man rots in hell. Hey, you're shivering. You cold?"

The woman pulled off her sweatshirt and held it out. Anna took it with wonder.

"Thank you. I hope your cousin is okay."

"Eh. We all got scars. Some's just harder to see."

Anna pulled on the sweatshirt and curled up on the bench. She lay awake, wishing she knew more about Michigan contempt rules. She only knew that contempt of court had no statutory limit. In theory, a person could be held in jail on a contempt charge forever. But the press had seen the whole thing. DOJ had received her motion. At the very least, Jack would raise a ruckus. She hoped she would be free when her niece was born. Jody, too.

She lay on the bench, wishing sleep would come.

At 4:00 A.M., Anna was handcuffed and led to an underheated transport van. The guards wouldn't tell her where she was going or why. There were no windows in the back of the van. She had no idea where she was.

When the van stopped, the back doors swung open. Anna was led out into a dimly lit parking garage. After a moment of discombobulation, she recognized the place. It was the subterranean garage of the courthouse. She was led into a service elevator and to the holding cell behind Judge Upperthwaite's courtroom. The CSO locked her in, and the van driver left.

"Why am I here?" she asked the CSO.

"Your sister refused the new lawyer the judge appointed her. Said she already had a lawyer, and it was you. Guess the judge had to let you come back, because of her right to counsel. If he didn't, it'd be a mistrial, or something. The judge wants her to be convicted fair and square. So you get to make your closing argument now."

At 8:55 A.M., Anna was uncuffed and taken back into the courtroom. The contrast between the cold cinder block cell and the warm rococo courtroom was startling. Desiree sat at the prosecutor's table; Jody sat at the defense. The audience section was packed, with Cooper sitting in the front row directly behind Jody. Anna became aware that she was still wearing the stained old sweatshirt. She took it off. Underneath was the same smelly suit she'd worn in court the night before, but at least she looked like a lawyer, albeit a wrinkled one.

Jody jumped up and hugged her. Her belly got in the way, but her arms squeezed her tight. "You okay?"

"Yeah, you?"

Jody nodded, held her stomach, and grimaced.

"Don't go having that baby while I'm locked up, okay?"

"I'll try. This kid already has a mind of her own."

Cooper leaned over the rail and wrapped his arms around her. "Thank God," he said. He felt so warm after the cold holding cells.

"Did you hear the news?" he asked.

She shook her head. "I've been on a bit of an Internet vacation." He took out his phone and pulled up the *Detroit News* website. The first headline said: "Anonymous Hacks Judge, Claims to Find Evidence of Bribery."

"After your little speech yesterday," Cooper said, "Anonymous hacked into FirstDown's bank records. It turns out, only the coach paid in. Only the judge's wife took money out. And the deposits were made on dates that correspond to cases the judge nolle'd for the coach. To the tune of almost a million dollars."

Anna's eyes were drawn to a chart that the *News* had compiled, in which they compared the evidence in her motion to the financial information that Anonymous hacked. It showed a pattern of the coach depositing, and the judge's wife withdrawing, six-figure sums in the weeks after each case against the coach that the judge dismissed. The coach had been bribing the judge for years, to cover up his abuse.

At precisely 9:00 A.M., the side door opened and Judge Upperthwaite walked out. The look on his face reminded Anna of a cornered animal.

56

Plan all you want, it is a very different thing to actually kill a person than to fantasize about it. In your fantasy, you have superhuman strength. Or your action takes no strength at all. You just do it, your arms gliding effortlessly through the weightlessness of your dream world. In reality, you have to plunge a knife or pull a trigger. You have to look into the eyes of an actual person. You see their humanity. You have to push past the respect for life that has been drilled into you since before you could talk.

I'm not saying it's impossible. It happens every day. But for normal people who have lived their whole lives as law-abiding citizens, trying to be polite and well-mannered, respectful of their elders and kind to animals, good listeners and good employees; for people who use their turn signals, and hurry to get to work on time, leave tips for their letter carrier, and put dollars in the Salvation Army's red bucket, hoping to make the world a little better—killing another human being is not an easy thing.

We had a good plan. The problem was in the execution.

We sat, three women stumped, on the bench seat. Owen Fowler faced us in the wheelchair, his teeth chattering despite the warm summer night. He was soaked from Wendy's earlier waterboarding. Maybe he was cold, despite the layers of sweatshirts, or maybe he was terrified.

Our plan had been to drown him. Let him know why we were doing it, let him feel the full weight of our justice, then waterboard him to death, cut off the duct tape, and throw him into the lake. His body would be unscathed except for lake water in his lungs. It would look like a boating accident. He'd gone drunk-boating often enough—and had been *seen* drunk-boating often enough—to make this plausible.

But the idea of pouring water on his face, as his eyes bulged in terror, until he died—it was impossible. He was a monster, but he didn't want to be a monster. And even if he was monstrous, he was a person, made by God, in all his flaws.

"I can't do it," I said. It sounded like I was admitting I couldn't read, or drive.

Wendy nodded in agreement. She couldn't either. "Kathy?"

Kathy shook her head. She took out her flask of vodka and took another swig.

We stared at him. He shivered back at us.

"We can't let him go," I said.

"We can't hold him in that wheelchair forever. Eventually, he'll have to pee."

"He probably already has."

"I promise, ladies, I won't tell anyone. Please. Let me go. We'll pretend this never happened."

"That's doubtful," his wife said.

"I swear." He spoke through chattering teeth. "I didn't realize how much I'd hurt everyone. I thought no one would be affected, that this was something that would happen in private. You forced me to realize how many people I've hurt. If you let me go, I swear, I'll do everything I can to make things right."

"There's nothing you can do."

"I could pay the families of the girls. I could get counseling, and then help others like me. I could start a charity."

"Like the charity arm of your sports camp?"

"No, no, no." His eyes leaked tears. "This is a real wake-up call for me. I swear, it'll be different now. Please, let me prove it to you."

"Or you could just go get your rifle and kill us."

"I wouldn't do that. I swear. No harm, no foul. Wendy, you're the mother of my daughter. She needs both of us. Kathy, I've taken so much from you, I wouldn't take any more. Jody—I—I care about you. I always have. I wouldn't hurt you. Please, ladies. Give me a chance. You won't be sorry."

He met our eyes with his. He was completely at our mercy, and that is a powerful and humbling feeling.

I doubted that he had "always cared" about me, which threw doubt on everything else he said. He would obviously say anything at that point. But, despite logic, the urge to believe him was strong. I *wanted* to believe he had been concerned about me all those years, despite his complete radio silence. I wanted to believe that he could change, that *people* could change, and that I could be an instrument of that change. And I had an instinct to try to help him now that he'd asked for my help. What is in female DNA that makes us want to fulfill others' requests? It's amazing how much you can get from us just by asking.

"He deserves justice," Wendy said. Her voice was so cold it was like ice water on my face, startling me awake from my Kumbaya daydreams. "And we'll never get justice in Holly Grove."

We sat there, thinking. What do you do with the pedophile you've drugged and kidnapped but do not have the will to murder?

"We could cut off his balls?" I suggested.

"Uh-huh. We can't kill him, but we slice off his testicles?" Wendy grimaced. "Who's volunteering for that one?"

"Hey, I'm just trying to be creative. How about tattooing his chest, like *Girl with the Dragon Tattoo?*"

"Do you own tattooing equipment?"

"No."

"Should we go to Meijer now and buy some?"

"Yeah, I could use some Doritos, too."

The sound of semi-hysterical female laughter, shrill as loons, rolled out over the glassy black lake.

"Besides," Kathy said, as the echoes of our laughter died down. "How does that help? The girls he rapes don't see his chest anyhow. Or if they do, it's too late."

I nodded.

Kathy turned to the coach. "Did my daughter see your chest when you raped her?"

"Um." His eyes flitted around, as if he could find the right answer in the sky, or on the lake, or by my shoes. "Um. I don't think so."

"You don't *think* so? What does that mean? You don't remember? Hayley was so unimportant that you can't recall the details?"

"No, she was very important. I cared about her. A lot."

Wendy crossed her arms and raised her eyebrows at him. He looked anxiously at her. I almost laughed at his dilemma. How do you convince the mother of your underage rape victim that you cared about her—in front of your wife? Coach's eyes went back and forth between Wendy and Kathy. He finally settled on Wendy, apparently deciding she was his likelier ally—or more dangerous threat.

"Baby," he said, "not more than I cared about you."

"Did you look into her eyes?" Wendy's voice was slow and dangerous. "The way you looked in mine, the first time we made love? Did she stare back at you in wide-eyed wonder, like I did?"

"No, honey, no. It wasn't like that. *You were special.* I did her from behind. Doggy style."

Kathy let out a shriek, grabbed my golden running woman off the floor, and swung the trophy at him. The base hit the side of his skull, making a sharp cracking sound. He yelped as the wheelchair tipped onto its side and landed on the floor. "She was a little girl!" Kathy wailed. "Not a dog! Not a toy for you to use and throw away!" She brought the trophy down on his head again. The sound was juicier this time. Coach grunted and twitched within his duct-tape encasing. "You killed my baby!"

"Kathy!" I shouted. "Stop!"

"No!" Wendy yelled. "Not like that!"

Kathy didn't seem to hear. She hit his head again and again. The sound became slushier with each impact. Wendy and I ran over and grabbed her arms. Kathy fought us. "I'll kill him!" she screamed. "I will kill him!"

"Kathy, no, no, no, Kathy!"

We stopped her with the trophy midswing. After a moment, she seemed to come back to herself. She lowered the trophy. "I'm sorry," she said. "Oh my God, I'm sorry."

We looked down. The coach's head was crumpled like a Jag that's been hit by a semi. Bits of flesh and blood covered the boat. Guess that's where the blood on my sock came from.

"Jesus." I crouched down and tried to find a pulse in his throat. There was none.

I looked up at my friends and shook my head. When I took my hand from his neck, I saw that my fingers were stained red.

I stared at his body. He deserved to die. I wanted him dead, even if I couldn't kill him with my own hands. So now I waited to feel . . . joy? Terror? Vengeance-is-mine? *Something.* But all I felt was the urgent academic need to solve a difficult logic question, like the kind I blew off in school ten years ago. Because we could no longer package this as a drunk-boating accident.

57

Blood pooled on the AstroTurf under Coach Fowler's head, like a dark amoeba creeping outward, exploring the floor of the boat. The duct tape kept him strapped in a fetal position in the overturned wheelchair.

"Oh my God. I killed him." Kathy dropped the trophy and looked down at her blood-flecked shirt. "What do we do now?"

I pulled the Kleenex out of my pocket and wiped my bloody fingers.

"We improvise."

I listed all the things we'd need. Bleach, rags, mop, hose. Bicycle helmet, leather jacket, ski mask, gloves, pillows. Wendy said the lake house had all of them. She steered the pontoon boat back across the lake. Kathy was shaking in her seat. I put my arm around her shoulders and tried to say comforting things. "I hope Hayley saw that from heaven."

Kathy half laughed and half sobbed. "No. She was innocent. Hayley, I'm sorry." She pulled out her flask and took another drink.

We didn't bother to right Coach Fowler in his wheelchair. He lay on his side during the whole ride back to shore. Because: fuck him.

Turns out, that attitude is not helpful when you're conspiring to murder someone and cover it up. When the boat was tied to the dock, I finally righted the chair to push him to land—and saw that the entire left side of his body, the side that had been pressed to the floor, was now dark purple. I guess once his heart stopped beating, gravity took over and his blood pooled on that side. I should have thought of that, but, heck, it was the first time I'd ever been part of killing someone. Next time, I'll be more careful. Kidding.

His neck was cocked at a stiff, unnatural angle. Blood soaked his hair. Between the bashed-in right side of his face, and the puffy purple streak going down his left, he finally appeared on the outside like the monster he was within.

He also looked like someone who'd lain on his side for half an hour after dying. He didn't look like someone who'd died sitting up in a car. I could see that with my own civilian eyes. What could a coroner tell from the corpse?

"Gasoline," I said. "We're gonna need a lot of gasoline. And some of those big gallon-size Ziploc bags."

Wendy nodded. "We have gasoline for the boat."

We wheeled him to the garage, where we cut him out of the duct tape and loaded his body into the passenger seat of the Corvette. He seemed to have gotten heavier since dying. Even with the three of us, he was very difficult to move. Touching him was horrible. His body was stiff and cool and sticky with blood.

There were two main jobs remaining. Kathy was too drunk and freaked out for either of them. It made sense for Wendy to clean the boat since she knew the grounds. I did not envy her, scrubbing down her husband's flesh and blood. But she did a good job, as you saw. That boat had never been so clean, before or after. When Wendy does a job, she does it right. And now you know why Wendy held the memorial service there. Dozens, maybe hundreds of people walked all over that property that day, especially to visit the open bar on the boat. As you might say: the crime scene was thoroughly contaminated.

I volunteered to drive the car. That made sense, too. If anyone was going to get caught, it should be me. Wendy had Isabel to raise. Plus, as his long-suffering wife, she'd be the first suspect the police looked at. Kathy had her mother to look after, in the nursing home. And she would also be a prime target, with her daughter having just made a report against the coach. This started with me, and I would end it.

My heart raced the whole drive back to Holly Grove. The coach's corpse tipped over onto me at some point, and I yelped and shoved it away. But I stayed precisely within the speed limit and obeyed every traffic law. If a cop had pulled me over at that point, not even your legal skills could have saved my ass.

My idea was admittedly low-tech. There were more interesting things I could have done if we'd had more time to plan and prepare. On the fly, this was the best I could come up with.

I drove toward the high school. When I got to the bend in the road before the stadium, I pulled the car to the shoulder and put it in park. I got out, opened the door to the passenger side, and pushed the coach over to the driver's seat. It was hard; I had to use my legs.

I put on the leather jacket, ski mask, gloves, and bicycle helmet. It was hot and claustrophobic, but I hoped this would protect me from the impact. I've seen enough crash-test videos at GM to know what a head-on collision can do to a body. I got into the passenger side and buckled my seat belt. Obviously, I didn't buckle up the coach. I stuffed two pillows on the dashboard in front of me. I tucked another pillow between my chest and the seat belt.

"Hang on tight, Coach."

I put the car into drive, reached my left leg across the bench seat, and pressed the accelerator to the floor. The Corvette leaped forward. It had plenty of horses under its hood—but no power steering. I had to pull hard on the steering wheel to keep it pointed straight at the stadium.

The car went down the road, over the shoulder, and across the grass. It rushed toward the thick concrete wall. It was like flying. For a moment, I felt like I used to at the high jump, suspended above the world, apart from all the pain and complications. Then the wall was a few feet away.

I thought about the cinder block Wendy had suggested we put on the accelerator. Wouldn't that have been a better option than my own fragile self? But a cinder block couldn't have kept the car steering straight. And, it would have left concrete chunks all over the car, and the police would've known it was a staged crash. It had to be me, to make it look like a drunk-driving accident. I was trying to save my friends.

People talk about their life flashing before their eyes. That didn't happen to me. Instead, I saw a bunch of other girls' lives. A streaming reel of their faces. Some, I knew well: Hayley Mack, Isabel Fowler, Zoë Malone, Wendy Weiscowicz. Some of the girls looked vaguely familiar, and some, I'd never seen before. One after another, the girls looked at me, steady and serious. Blondes, redheads, brunettes, African American, Hispanic, white.

I think, in that moment, I saw all Coach Fowler's past victims. Maybe his future ones too. Girls who wouldn't have to go through what we had, because we killed him. They were the reason for what I was doing. They were worth it.

The car met the wall. The cry of collapsing metal and shattering glass filled the world. In my periphery, Coach's body launched into the windshield. My own body heaved forward, and, despite the pillow, my ribs felt the full battle between the car's momentum and the tensile strength of a fifty-year-old seat belt. The last thing I remember is putting out my hands to try to stop the dashboard, which was flying toward my face. Then everything went black.

58

When I came to, the stadium's thick concrete wall was inches from my face. The car's hood was smashed into a triangle. Coach slumped in his seat, now *extremely* mangled, although there was no new blood on him. Guess you only bleed when you have a beating heart.

My wrist hurt like crazy, probably from hitting the dashboard. I was dizzy and nauseous from the pain but knew I didn't have much time. I got out of the car, staggering to stay on my feet. The wreckage was smoking and creaking, but there was no fire. Yet.

I could hear sirens in the distance.

I took off the jacket, ski mask, gloves, and bike helmet and threw them into the car, where they would burn. I reached behind the passenger seat and pulled out the twelve gallon-size Ziploc bags filled with gasoline. I poured eleven bags of gasoline on the car, soaking every inch I could.

I took one last look at Coach Fowler. His body was mangled and frozen into a weird angle. His skin was gray and his face was mashed. His hair was matted stiff with dark blood.

I poured the last bag of gasoline on him. I hoped he would burn down to ashes, like a cremation. Now I know that ashes take more heat and time than I had that night.

The sirens were getting louder. I threw the empty Ziploc bags into the car, where they would melt away. I wiped my hands on my jeans, hoping I wouldn't catch myself on fire. Then I pulled out the matches, struck a flame, and threw it onto the car.

The fire whooshed up instantly. The car looked like a marshmallow in a campfire: for a moment it was just a car surrounded by flames, like a hologram. And then the flames started to eat the car, turning it black. The seats started to melt. Coach himself seemed to burn faster than anything else.

I could see the flashing lights coming up the road as I limped off through the woods. Behind me, the car exploded. The force knocked me to the ground and knocked the breath out of me for a minute. I got up and walked away, the flames warming my back as the sirens got closer.

I walked all the way home, trekking though woods, yards, and back roads. It was three miles away.

At home, I used my burner phone to call Wendy's burner phone. She'd made it back to Cedar Point, establishing her alibi. Then I called Kathy's burner phone. She'd gone to her own house, which wasn't the plan. She was supposed to be spending the night at her mother's nursing home—that was her alibi. She'd snuck out of there earlier that night. I guess she was too rattled, or too drunk, to remember to go back there. I told her she had to go, now. She said she didn't want to get caught driving drunk. That seemed like the least of our potential problems. I yelled at her: "Kathy, you have to go. Get in your car! Now!" Stuff like that. Eventually, she went, and she had her alibi.

That must've been the screaming that Tammy heard coming from my house that night. Luckily, she didn't see me throwing my burner phone into her bushes.

I stripped off my clothes and threw them into the washing machine with a lot of soap and Borax. I took the second-longest shower of my life. I ran the clothes through the washing machine again. I didn't realize the one sock had fallen behind the machine. Damn that sock.

Then I climbed into my bed and fell into a dead sleep for the next twelve hours. I woke up to the sound of the police pounding on my door. Your old boyfriend Rob was standing on my porch, asking if I wouldn't mind swinging by the police station for a quick chat. You know what happened after that.

59

Judge Upperthwaite took his seat at the bench and looked around at his little kingdom. "We are ready to begin closing arguments," he said. "Donald, please bring in the jury."

The law clerk stared at him but didn't move. Anna stood. "Your Honor, I renew my motion for you to recuse yourself, especially in light of the financial information disclosed by Anonymous last night."

"That is preposterous. I will not be defamed or intimidated by these hooligans. This is my courtroom, and I call the shots. This case will go on. Now call the jury in, Donald."

"No," Desiree spoke up. "Don't call the jury in, Donald."

"Excuse me?" the judge said.

"The government is dismissing, with prejudice, the charges against the defendant."

The prosecutor walked up to the clerk and handed him some papers, which he time-stamped. She dropped a copy on Anna's desk before returning to her own. Anna looked at the paper, which was captioned: "Motion to Dismiss All Charges Against Defendant Jody Curtis." Her eyes got big. She handed the paper to Jody.

"You cannot do that," the judge boomed. "You can't let a murderer get off just because I had a business relationship with the victim."

"Your Honor, with all due respect," Desiree said. "You're not a prosecutor anymore. I am. And I'm declining to go forward with these charges."

"This is ridiculous. This is a small town. Of course I'm going to have business with some of the citizens. There's nothing improper about that."

"Yes, sir. There may be a perfectly good explanation for everything. If you'd like, you can talk about it to FBI Agents Steve Quisenberry and Samantha Randazzo, who have flown in from Washington, D.C., for exactly that purpose."

Desiree motioned behind her. Anna glanced into the audience and saw her two favorite FBI agents standing in the aisle. More tears came to her eyes, she was so relieved to see their familiar, reliable faces.

The judge adjusted his glasses with trembling hands. He looked at the agents in dark suits, standing by the doors. "Certainly," he said. "Certainly. Certainly. I look forward to the chance to straighten this all out. I just need to change out of my robe. Agents, please come to my chambers in ten minutes."

The judge stepped off the bench so abruptly he tripped on his robe. His clerk caught him, and the judge straightened up. "Thank you, son." He hurried out of the courtroom. The young law clerk looked around at the packed, silent courtroom.

"Um," the clerk said. "This case is adjourned?"

The courtroom erupted in noise.

"Oh my God," Jody stood. "We won?"

"We won," Anna said. "They dismissed with prejudice, which means you can never be charged with this murder again. It's over."

Jody started crying. Anna put her arm around her. A slew of reporters came up to Anna with questions. She didn't want to comment on the facts, not if the FBI was investigating the judge. She said, "We're happy and relieved that justice was done. My sister is innocent. We are so gratified that the prosecution had the honor to dismiss the charges when all the information was available."

Anna went over to the prosecutor. "Thank you, Desiree. For everything."

Desiree didn't have to dismiss the charges with prejudice. The prosecutor could have requested a mistrial, and tried to convict Jody in a new trial. Maybe Desiree had made a strategic decision about the continuing viability of her case. Maybe her office had made a political decision about the atmospherics. Or maybe Desiree had simply decided to use the tools at her disposal to achieve some justice in a situation where the justice system had failed for so many years. Whatever the case, Anna was humbled and grateful.

Desiree shook her hand. "Good luck, Anna. Hope to see you back on the other side of the courtroom soon."

Anna smiled. "Thanks."

She wended her way to the back row, but her FBI friends were no longer there. She heard a screeching noise from outside. She and several other people looked out the courtroom window. A blue Cadillac careened out of the courthouse garage and onto the road that encircled the town square. Several protesters had to jump out of the way to avoid being hit.

"That's Judge Upperthwaite's car!" said the stenographer.

The Cadillac sped away, disappearing onto a side street. A minute later, a dark sedan with government plates followed. The FBI sedan screeched around the same turn that the judge had taken. Anna smiled. A chase was exactly the sort of thing Randazzo loved. Quisenberry would be holding tight to the armrest and shouting for her to watch out for pedestrians. From above, Anna heard the *thwump-thwump-thwump* of a helicopter.

Her heartbeat picked up with the thrill of the chase, the instinct to go after the bad guy. Her adrenaline surged. She shook her head, smiled, and walked away from the window. She had only one task here.

She went to Jody with a smile. "Let's get you home."

"No." Jody shook her head.

"Why not?"

Jody held her stomach and smiled through a grimace. "This baby isn't gong to wait any more."

60

Anna waved good-bye to Cooper, hustled Jody down to the garage, and rushed her to the hospital. By the time they filled out the hospital paperwork, Jody's contractions were coming once every five minutes. She was quickly admitted and given a bed.

The ob-gyn examined her, and looked up, surprised. "You're dilated to seven," the doctor said. "And this is your first baby. You've probably been in labor for a day or two. Did you feel the contractions?"

"Yep." Jody smiled at Anna. "I felt 'em. But I couldn't have this baby until I was sure that my sister was okay."

It was too late for an epidural. Anna held Jody's hand, recited encouraging platitudes, and told Jody to breathe, just like she'd learned in the prenatal class. Jody panted, pushed, and told Anna to fuck off. The doctor said it was a textbook delivery.

At 3:13 P.M. on March 3, the baby girl came into the world with a loud, healthy cry. The nurses wrapped her up and placed her on Jody's chest. The infant quieted and looked up into her mother's eyes. Jody gazed adoringly down at her newborn.

"Oh my God. She's so beautiful. She's *so* beautiful."

Anna looked at her sister and niece and thanked God that this happened here rather than in a prison infirmary. Anna held the baby, who looked back at her with surprised blue eyes. Anna felt her heart expanding to fill with more love than she'd ever thought possible.

"Thanks for hanging in until your mama was ready, little bean," Anna whispered.

"I'm going to call her Leigh Anna," Jody said. "After you."

Anna blinked back happy tears. "That's the greatest honor I've ever had."

She rocked Leigh until the baby started making squeaky little cries. Jody held out her arms. "Let me give this a try." Anna set the infant in Jody's arms. Jody pulled the baby to her breast. The child rooted around, the new mama shifted things about, and then Leigh latched on and began suckling. "There you go, little one," Jody said. "Good job."

"Wow." Anna watched with amazement. "You're going to be a great mother."

"Thank you, Annie," Jody said. "For everything you did to make that happen."

"I had to keep you out of jail. I wasn't ready to take a kid myself."

The next day, Anna sent e-mails to everyone she knew. Cooper visited the hospital with flowers. Two days later, Jody checked out.

"Taking your baby home is such a special time," said an orderly, as Anna loaded the baby and car seat into the Yukon.

Anna shot a sympathetic glance to her sister. Jody still didn't have a home. She had an empty lot, some charred bricks, and a lot of paperwork from the insurance company. There were many things for Jody to figure out about her life postbaby and posttrial. For now, Anna drove them to Detroit.

With the sisters' help, Cooper's house had undergone a transformation over the winter. The foyer floor was no longer covered with a tarp, and the wood floors were polished to their former glory. A new iron handrail laced the stairs. Peeling wallpaper had been torn down and the walls were painted in deep, warm colors. Rotten wood had been replaced, old wood had been polished, and everything shone with a new coat of lacquer. Anna had done much of the work herself. She felt a sense of ownership, not the kind you get with money, but the kind you get from building a home. A bouquet of ivory roses sat on the kitchen table, with a note of congratulations from Grace.

That night, Anna woke up at 3:00 A.M. to help Jody with a

feeding, then climbed back into bed with Cooper. The moonlight streamed in through the bedroom windows and lit up the white walls. They faced each other, looking at each other's eyes, stroking each other. The pleasure of his skin against hers was particularly powerful tonight.

"Coop," she whispered.

"Hm?"

"I'm not sure I can go back to D.C."

"Why?"

"Jody. The baby." She met his eyes. "You."

"Well, that makes it easy." He grinned. "Stay."

Amazing, the power that single word had. *Stay.* She hadn't thought about it before, hadn't allowed her mind to peek past the point where her sister might go to jail. But here she was. She grinned back.

"Maybe I will."

■ ■ ■

The next morning, as Anna and Cooper were sitting at the kitchen table, drinking coffee and trading sections of the newspaper, there was a knock at the door. Anna got up and opened it. She found a large, handsome man holding a giant bouquet of pink roses. His cheeks were freshly shaven and he wore a spotless yellow polo shirt, from which a few tattoos peeked.

"Grady," she said. "Hi."

"Hi, Anna. Can I come in?"

Cooper walked over and stood with his hand on her back. She liked how that felt.

"Sure. Wait here with Coop."

She went upstairs to the bedroom. Jody sat in bed, holding Leigh over her shoulder and patting her back to burp her.

"You have a visitor," Anna said. "A very tall, very cute one. Carrying a florist's worth of pink roses. What do you think?"

Jody kept patting the baby's back. Leigh let out a resounding belch.

Jody smiled. "I think the kid wants me to go for it."

They laughed. Anna took the baby so Jody could take a shower. Twenty minutes later, Jody came out of the bathroom, gussied up and looking as pretty as Anna had ever seen her. She gathered Leigh from Anna's arms and changed the baby from her MSU onesie into a pretty pink dress.

"Let's go see your daddy, little one," she whispered.

Jody went down the stairs. Anna followed.

Grady stood from the couch in the den. He looked at Jody, and then at the child in her arms. A smile spread across his face, and his eyes shone like this was the most beautiful sight he'd ever seen, which maybe it was.

Anna and Cooper went to the kitchen so the new parents could have some space to get to know each other.

When Grady left two hours later, Jody was beaming. She stood on the front porch holding the baby and waving as he drove off. Anna stood next to her sister.

"How'd it go?" she asked, although she could tell by the dreamy look on her sister's face.

"He's coming back tomorrow," Jody said. "And he's bringing his mom."

. . .

Later that afternoon, Jody got her second set of visitors. Kathy, Wendy, and Isabel came carrying balloons and colorful bags of baby presents. Anna, who by now guessed that they shared some secrets, was glad they hadn't visited in the hospital. It wouldn't do to be seen in public together. Not for a while. Anna led them back to the living room.

"Oh my God! Let me get a look at the baby," Wendy said, sitting next to Jody. "She's gorgeous! She has your eyes."

Kathy sat next to Wendy and reached out to touch Leigh's tiny hand. The infant grasped her finger, and Kathy smiled. The woman looked healthier. She had some color in her cheeks and her figure no longer looked so emaciated. Jody had mentioned that Kathy was going to AA. Anna hoped she'd be able to find some measure of peace.

Isabel frowned at the baby. "She looks like an old man," said the girl. "A wrinkly, pickled, pink old man."

"That's what all babies look like," Wendy said. "It's what you looked like when you were a newborn."

"It's what Hayley looked like," Kathy said softly. Wendy put her arm around her shoulders.

Anna's phone rang. It was Jack. She excused herself and went out to the foyer.

"Jack! Hi! Guess what? Jody had her baby. A little girl."

"Congratulations! Tell me all about it."

She told him about the baby's birth and the judge's arrest.

"Well done," he said. "I'm proud of you. And maybe the timing was meant to be."

"What do you mean?"

"Anna, I called to ask you to come back to me and Olivia. There's no question, nothing left to be sorted. I love you. You're the person I want to spend the rest of my life with. You're everything I ever wanted. There's a beautiful white dress hanging in the closet. There's a diamond ring sitting here in a box, just waiting for your finger. Come home, and let's put it to good use."

"Oh, Jack. I . . ." She stared out the window, at the community garden. She looked inside, at the floors she'd helped polish. Had her time in Michigan just been a brief interruption in the already-scheduled program of marrying Jack? Or had her life shifted so inexorably that it was now on an entirely different course? She heard her niece mewling, her sister and the other women laughing. She saw Cooper walking outside, Sparky trotting at his heels.

"I don't know."

■ ■ ■

After the women left, Anna sat on the couch and handed Jody today's *Detroit News*, which featured a story about Judge Upperthwaite. The Department of Justice had opened an investigation into his conduct. He had resigned his seat on the bench, and the courthouse was being renamed. Below the headline was a picture of workers prying the words *LAWRENCE P. UPPERTHWAITE* from the entrance.

"So," Anna said. "It's done."

"It's done. Thank you." Jody said, putting down the newspaper. "What you did was amazing. As a lawyer and a sister. I never thought you'd be happy for a group like Anonymous to get involved in one of your cases."

"I never realized how much I was willing to bend the rules until they were all stacked against you."

"Maybe a little of me rubbed off on you, and a little of you rubbed off on me."

"I have been swearing more."

Jody laughed. "Do you want to hear the whole story now?"

"Of course I do."

"What about your lawyerly obligations? Will you have to report the stuff I tell you if, hypothetically, it involved some criminal activity?"

"Not as long as it's done. If you're planning to go kill someone tonight, I might have an obligation to tell somebody. But past crimes are the opposite. As your lawyer, it's my duty *not* to disclose any confidences you share with me."

"Okay," Jody said. "I wanted to tell you. But it wasn't just my secret. It belonged to two other women, who were in equal danger. The three of us had a pact. We swore we'd never tell anyone. And I was going to do whatever I could to protect them. I didn't want you to throw them under the bus to save me. But just now, while Isabel was outside playing, Wendy and Kathy told me I should tell you. So now it's a pact of four."

"Okay."

"Where should I start?"

"Start at the beginning."

Anna would close her mouth and try to refrain from questions and commentary. This was Jody's story, and Anna had waited and worked a very long time to hear it. All she had to do now was listen.

Leigh let out a hungry cry. Jody shifted the baby, pulled up her shirt, and unclasped her nursing bra. Leigh latched on, making happy cooing clucks between swallows.

"Well, let's see. I guess it all started with the high jump." Jody stroked the soft hair on Leigh's head. "When I was fifteen, my favorite place in the world was the high-jump setup at the school track. The bar provided a simple obstacle with a certain solution. You either cleared it or you didn't. In a world of tangled problems with knotty answers, that was bliss . . ."

AUTHOR'S NOTE

The rape-kit backlog referenced in this novel is a real and scandalous problem in America. Most jurisdictions don't even keep track of how many rape kits are processed. While no one knows the precise numbers, it's estimated that hundreds of thousands of rape kits are sitting in warehouses, untested. Some have been rotting there for years—even decades—the forensic value of their DNA samples degrading with each passing month. As a tool for solving crime and getting predators off the streets, rape kits are worth their weight in gold. For example, when Detroit started testing its more than eleven thousand untested rape kits, the city found over one hundred serial rapists in the first sixteen hundred tests. But these kits only work if they're tested. Apathy and lack of funding still contribute to the national backlog. To learn more about the problem and how to end it, visit www.endthebacklog.com.

ACKNOWLEDGMENTS

One of my favorite steps in crafting a novel is the research that happens before a single word is written. I owe thanks to many generous people who shared their time, knowledge, and experience, and provided so many rich details for this story. Any mistakes are my own.

I am very grateful to my friend, Gemma D'eustachio, and her boyfriend, Johnathon Mullen, an Army veteran who lost both legs in an IED blast in Afghanistan. Their candor in speaking to me about their experiences—as a military amputee dealing with his return to America, and as the strong young woman who fell in love with him—helped me envision Cooper's life and the relationship between Anna and Cooper. Johnathon's sacrifice to this country is awe-inspiring, as were his kindness and humor when my young sons asked about his "robot legs." I was also inspired by Johnathon's determination to reinvent himself stateside as a photographer. He took my author photo; if you flip this book over, you'll see his talented work.

Thank you to Detective Jeff Folts of MPD's Major Crash Unit for sharing his expertise on car accidents and automobile deaths; Dr. Joseph Scott Morgan, a death investigator and acclaimed author, for his keen and startling forensics insights; and defense attorney Steven Levin, for his sage advice on how *not* to bribe public officials (because, of course, none of his clients would do such a thing). Thanks to Toni Kalem, from whom I stole the line, "Sisters are each other's witnesses."

I am grateful to the wonderful authors in my critique group: Alma Katsu, Kathleen McCleary, and Rebecca Coleman. They helped me fashion this story as I wrote it, and their wise advice improved it remarkably.

Many thanks go to the usual suspects, the good friends on whom I rely for storytelling advice, real-life crime tales, and the occasional stiff drink: Lynn Haaland, Jessica Mikuliak, Jenny McIntyre, Jeff Cook, M.R., Moira Campion McConaghy, Jen Wofford, Ed, Steve Quisenberry, and Glenn Kirschner, who gave me the inspiration for this book's title.

I am fortunate to work with two incredible women: my agent, Amy Berkower, and my editor, Lauren Spiegel. Their instincts and guidance are invaluable. I am also grateful to Amy's associate, Genevieve Gagne-Hawes, who helped develop this concept from the first inkling to the final rewrite. I am very grateful to the entire team at Simon & Schuster and Touchstone for all their work in making this book and this series come to life.

And of course, an infinity of thanks to Mike and my boys. I love you.

A GOOD
KILLING

This reading group guide for *A Good Killing* includes an introduction, discussion questions, and a Q&A with author Allison Leotta, and ideas for enhancing your book club. The suggested questions are intended to help your reading group find new and interesting angles and topics for your discussion. We hope that these ideas will enrich your conversation and increase your enjoyment of the book.

FOR DISCUSSION

1. The book opens with Jody addressing Anna directly, explaining events from her point of view. Why do you think the author chose this kind of opening?

2. Jody loved being on the track-and-field team in high school, and she calls the high-jump setup "my favorite place in the world." Do you have a similarly positive place, activity, or memory? What made it significant for you? Discuss with your group.

3. Early in the story Jody says, "Nothing fuels hate like love gone wrong." Do you agree with this idea? How does it apply to Jody's relationship with Coach Fowler? How does it apply to Anna's broken engagement?

4. Anna had been "relieved when she'd left [Holly Grove], and she never liked coming back." Why did she feel this way? Contrast her behavior with that of Jody, who stayed in Holly Grove her entire life. What do you think caused each sister to make the decision to move away or stay?

5. With their mother deceased and their father absent since their childhood, Anna and Jody grew up essentially without parents. How does this affect their relationship with each other?

6. In telling her story about Coach Fowler Jody says, "There's something about being fifteen that makes everything that happens stay clear and bright." How does this phenomenon affect her life? Discuss any memories, positive or negative if you are comfortable doing so, from your teenage years that are still particularly vivid for you.

7. In the courtroom Anna has "the disconcerting sense of living on the other side of the looking glass." What does she mean? Before coming to help her sister, how had Anna been sheltered in her own convictions of right and wrong? What factors helped open her eyes?

8. While Anna is being held in jail a fellow inmate tells her, "We all got scars. Some's just harder to see." What is the significance of scars in the story? Compare characters in the story who have visible scars to those whose scars are emotional.

9. While pondering Coach Fowler's behavior, Jody wonders, "What makes someone evil?" She concludes that "we're all victims of the victims who came before us." Do you agree with her opinion? Why or why not?

10. When Coach Fowler pleads to her for mercy, Jody wonders, "What is in female DNA that makes us want to fulfill others' requests? It's amazing how much you can get from us just by asking." Do you think Jody is correct? Is the idea of fulfilling requests an intrinsic part of being a woman, or do culture or environment play a part? Is it necessarily a bad thing?

11. Reflect back on the Italian proverb used in the epigraph, "Since the house is on fire, let us warm ourselves." How does that sentiment apply to Jody's actions toward coach Fowler? What does fire represent in the story?

12. Were Jody, Wendy, and Kathy justified in what they did to Coach Fowler? Do the ends justify the means?

13. After the book's conclusion, do you think Anna will decide to stay with Cooper, leaving her life in D.C. behind? If so, how do you think she will adjust?

A CONVERSATION
WITH ALLISON LEOTTA

Your character Cooper lives in Detroit, and he is active in helping to revitalize the city. That idea seems to be gaining momentum: the television show *Rehab Addict* features a woman dedicated to renovating dilapidated houses in Detroit and improving the community. As Cooper says, "Today we've got musicians and artists, hipsters and farmers, city planners and community activists, all sorts of creative thinkers figuring out how to find beauty and meaning in the ruins." Because you feature this aspect of Detroit, do you feel a part of this community? Do you think your book will have a positive impact on the city?

I grew up near Detroit and was fascinated by the city: its beauty and its problems, both of which are world-class. Detroit has been the symbol of the best and the worst that America can be. And right now, it's at a historic brink, poised between utter ruin and creative people who see an exciting, unprecedented opportunity to try new things. Cooper embodies that optimism, and I love him for that. I hope my book will have a positive impact on the city and get people thinking about the possibilities and creative solutions.

If you're interested in reading more about Detroit, I'd recommend two terrific nonfiction books: *Detroit: An American Autopsy* by Charlie LeDuff, which chronicles the city's decline in wry, devastating prose, and *Detroit City Is the Place to Be* by Mark Binelli, which explores the radical sense of possibility that comes when a city hits rock bottom.

This is your fourth novel. Has the writing process changed for you in any way? Has it gotten easier or more challenging?

The process is definitely not easier! In part, that's because I'm trying to challenge myself, get better, and push my abilities further with each story.

I feel very lucky that I can concentrate on writing full-time now. When I wrote my first two books, I was still working at the U.S. Attorney's Office, and could only write from 5:00 till 7:00 A.M., before heading in to my day job. Now that I'm a full-time writer, I can sleep a little later! But I also have to be extremely disciplined with how I use my time.

Being a published author is like running a small business out of your house. I generally write in the morning, and use the afternoon for the business side of things. Blogging, social media, public speaking, opining, networking, and generally "building [my] platform." That's one of any modern author's biggest challenges—balancing the writing of the books with the promotion of them.

Your experience as a federal prosecutor certainly affects your subject matter. How closely do your stories reflect your own experiences with actual cases?

I try to take the most interesting parts of my real cases and make them elements of my stories. Some of the most implausible plot twists are things that actually happened in D.C. Superior Court! I am also pulled by the emotions that come with these incredibly personal cases. There's terrible heartbreak and tragedy, but also moments of real courage, love, and healing. I was inspired by the people—victims who had the courage to come forward, police officers devoted to helping their community, prosecutors working late into the night to try to make a difference. It's very satisfying when I write a scene and feel like I've captured that.

In the bio section of your website you say, "I wanted to create stories that would both entertain and teach about the way the criminal justice system works—and doesn't work." While your career as a prosecutor must have caused you to experience frustrating or dark moments, are there aspects about it that you miss?

I loved being a sex-crimes prosecutor. I think it's one of the most rewarding legal careers in America. There's nothing like waking up every day knowing that your job is to put predators in jail, figure out the truth, help make your community safer, and, most of all, do the right thing (a luxury most lawyers don't have).

Being a writer now is a dream come true—but it's very solitary. I miss my friends and colleagues at the U.S. Attorney's Office. They're an amazing group of talented and devoted public servants. The bonding that goes on there is a bit like boot camp—many of my best friends are the people with whom I worked there, and I expect they will be for the rest of my life.

Being a lawyer and a writer seem to be vastly different careers. In what ways has your life changed since you chose the latter?

My commute is fantastic! I can work in my pajamas if I want. And, it turns out, I don't want to work in my pajamas. You feel really gross by 2:00 P.M. I treat writing as if it were a nine-to-five job. I get up, get dressed, and keep my butt in my chair, regardless of whether the muse is with me that day.

Being home all day also meant I could finally get a dog (I'd been debating my husband on this for years). We adopted a half-beagle puppy named Maggie. She's sitting at my feet as I write this.

What books have you found to be particularly inspiring or significant?

As a lawyer: *To Kill a Mockingbird*, of course, and *Presumed Innocent* by Scott Turow. In nonfiction, *Guns, Germs, and Steel* by Jared Diamond fundamentally changed the way I look at the world.

In upcoming novels, do you plan to keep writing the Anna Curtis series or will you possibly introduce a new protagonist?

The interest in Anna has been wonderful and unexpected. I never intended to write a series. But as long as readers want to hear more of her story, I'm thrilled to keep writing it. At the same time, I have some ideas for stand-alone books, and I hope to have the chance to make those happen, too.

Describe your writing room.

Funny you should ask. I wrote my first three books at my kitchen table. After I turned in *Speak of the Devil*, I decided I was a "real" writer who should have her own office. I converted a bedroom into an office: getting new furniture, painting the walls blue because I heard that color inspires creativity, and splurging on a standing desk and ergonomic chair. After all that, it turns out I can only write at . . . my kitchen table.

The topic of sex crimes is an especially somber one. What do you do to balance that—to relax or have fun?

I started writing because it was cheaper than therapy. Seriously, writing about the job did help me process the things I saw as a prosecutor.

I used to have more hobbies—running, playing guitar,

and I was a docent at the National Zoo. These days, I'm a mom, and keeping up with my two crazy, terrific little boys is the most fun, wonderful part of my life. But between mommying and writing a book a year, I don't have time for much else. After the boys are in bed, I read. I've always loved getting lost in a good story. Reading is the one thing I always find time for.

ENHANCE YOUR BOOK CLUB

1. Find out more about Allison online. On her website, AllisonLeotta.com, you can read about her other books, read her bio, and find out where she'll be appearing at upcoming events. Fans of television crime dramas will appreciate her blog, Prime-Time Crime Review, where Allison takes programs such as *Law & Order: SVU* to task, revealing what aspects of the shows are realistic, and what are completely made up. In addition to her blog, you can also connect with Allison on Facebook and follow her on Twitter.

2. Cooper is a staunch supporter of local and grassroots businesses in economically challenged Detroit. As a group, research locally owned businesses in your area. You can select a local cafe or restaurant as your group's meeting place, choose regionally sourced foods to serve, or visit a farmers' market as a group.

3. The book focuses on a sexual crime committed on a young girl. Research crisis support centers in your area. If possible, consider volunteering time or other resources, or find out if you can help get the word out about the centers to local schools and youth groups.

Turn the page for a preview
of Allison Leotta's next book in the Anna Curtis series,

THE LAST
GOOD GIRL

Available from Touchstone

FRIDAY

1

The guy had beautiful white teeth and a dimple that appeared when she made him laugh, but all Emily could think was, *College is where romance goes to die.*

They stood on prime real estate, belly-up to the bar at Lucky's, pressed together by the swell of bodies around them. The air was thick with sweated perfume, cheap beer, and the recycled breath of hundreds of young adults in their sexual prime. The boy drained his Bud, set the bottle on the bar, and issued a mating call.

"Wanna do shots?"

Translation: *Wanna get wasted, get laid, get out of my bed, and never to talk to me again?* There were no boyfriends in college. There were only hookups.

Emily smiled at the boy, tilting her head cutely to the side. To the world, she probably looked like any other carefree girl basking in a Friday night. It made her wonder how many of these girls were just like her. Pretending. Maybe all of them, in one way or another.

"Sure," she said.

The dimple reappeared. The boy turned to wave over a bartender.

Over the hum of conversation and Pitbull, Emily heard the bells of the clock tower outside, striking midnight. Twelve solemn bongs marking the start of March 24, 2015. She'd heard those bells chiming on the hour, every hour, her entire life. As a girl, she'd lain in her pretty pink bedroom listening to their bass chimes, wondering what it'd be like when she was a college student herself, the adventures and grown-up secrets that would finally be revealed to her like beautiful presents to be unwrapped, one by one. That seemed like a very long time ago.

Tonight, the chimes meant Dylan and his friends would walk into the bar soon. She had to get out of here.

The bartender delivered two shot glasses filled with shimmery blue potion.

"I'm sorry," she told the boy. "You're totally nailing the horny-but-caring-frat-boy thing. Maybe put your hand gently on my shoulder when you look in my eyes? Try it on one of them." She gestured to all the shiny, uncomplicated girls who thought their prince was behind the next $1 pitcher of beer. Emily missed being one of them. "I gotta go."

She picked up the first shot glass and downed the blue drink, then shotgunned the second one too. She tossed a twenty on the bar, grabbed her white North Face jacket, and threaded her way through the crowd. Preya and the other girls were somewhere in here, but Emily couldn't see them.

Wrapping her silvery scarf around her neck, she pushed out the front door and into the quiet night. She coughed on the cold air. March was Michigan's ugliest month. Dirty snow huddled at the curb, trapped in the purgatory between white powder and the warm April sun. Across the street, the bell tower shone like a warning as its twelfth chime echoed over shivering trees. The night seeped through Emily's sweater, pulling goose bumps from her skin. She shuddered, zipped her jacket, and looked down the street—right at what she feared most.

A raucous bunch of Beta Psi boys rounded the corner. Dylan was in front, of course. He was the alpha dog in any pack of males. Tall and swaggering, dressed in clothes that were both effortlessly casual and painfully expensive, he could be a poster boy for fratty privilege. The other guys clustered around him, vying for position.

Emily froze a few feet from the entrance to Lucky's. Its cone of light still surrounded her.

Dylan's eyes locked on hers. He smiled, walked over, and stood in her space. Too close. The other boys formed a semicircle around her. She felt unsteady.

"I don't want any trouble," she said.

"Doesn't seem that way," Dylan drawled. "Seems like you're doing everything you can to stir the pot."

"Whore," said one of Dylan's minions. The kid snorted, cocked back his head, and spat. His phlegm arced through the air, reflecting the light from the bar's neon signs, glittering and ugly. Everyone watched the loogie as it hung suspended for a moment at the top of its arc. Then it headed back down and splatted on her boot. The boys' laughter was loud and vicious. Anger pulsed through her gut, more acidic than any shot at Lucky's.

"You're disgusting," she told Dylan. "And you can't even fight your own fights."

Dylan frowned at his friends, and they stilled. Their silence was more ominous than their laughter. Emily was keenly aware that she could not control this situation.

"Head in," Dylan told the other guys. "I'll be right there."

"You sure, dude?"

"Yeah."

The boys did what they were told. Music pulsed then quieted as the bar's door swung open and shut. Emily tried to move away, too, but Dylan's hand clamped onto her arm. They faced each other, a boy and a girl alone on an empty stretch of sidewalk, breathing fog into the night.

"Have you thought about what you're doing?" he said. "Like, really thought about it? Because, it's kinda crazy that this is how you want to play it."

"I'm not playing."

His fingers squeezed her arm through the puffy coat. "You know what this means for you? You are *done*."

"Oh, Dylan." She smiled. "I'm just beginning. I'm writing an editorial too. It'll be in next week's *Tower Times*."

"Bitch," he said slowly. "My family will end you."

"I know who your family is. And pretty soon they'll know who you are too."

Emily yanked her arm away and strode off, warmed with the satisfaction that her words had cut him. For a moment, she heard nothing but the sound of her footsteps clacking triumphantly on the pavement. The whisper of wind through trees. A car passing, its tires slicing through salty slush.

Then footsteps, sharp and angry, behind her. She glanced back. Dylan was following her.

"Leave me alone!" she yelled.

He strode faster. His hands were fists.

On her left were shops, closed for the night—dark. On her right was North Campus Street, then campus itself—darker. Trees, dorms, the library. A little farther in was the president's house and the pretty pink bedroom of her childhood. None of these places offered safety.

Ahead, the lights from the shops ended in a yawning stretch of black. It was a block-long hole dug out for construction, surrounded by a chain-link fence. Students called it the Pit.

She hugged her purse and tried to walk faster, but her ankle-high boots had disastrously high heels. Dylan wore rubber-soled boat shoes. The slap of his footsteps grew louder, closer.

She broke into a run.

So did he.

She looked over her shoulder—he was right behind her. Wind whipped her long brown hair into her eyes. She shoved it back, stumbled, and pushed herself harder. She was running as fast as she could when she felt his breath on her neck.

SATURDAY

2

The fire crackled and sighed, saturating the room with golden light. Anna balanced a laptop on her knees as she edited an appellate brief. Jody sat next to her, flipping through TV channels while holding her infant to her breast. The baby finished feeding and unlatched, and Jody wiped her daughter's mouth with a cloth. The infant met Anna's eyes with a milk-drunk smile. Anna felt the surge of love she did every time she looked at her little niece. She set her laptop on the coffee table and reached over. "Let me burp her."

"Thanks." Jody handed Leigh to her sister and refastened her nursing bra. She stood and stretched, then padded to the kitchen. "God, I can't stop eating."

"You're burning like a thousand calories a day just producing milk. Go crazy." Anna spread the cloth on her shoulder and shifted the baby onto it. Three weeks ago, she had no idea how to hold an infant. Then Leigh was born. After helping with dozens, maybe hundreds, of feedings over the past three weeks, Anna was starting to feel like a pro. She stood and walked around the room, stroking Leigh's back and humming "Hush Little Baby."

She stopped as an image flashed on the TV: grainy surveillance video, the type that only became relevant when something terrible happened. It showed a pretty young woman in a white jacket talking to a handsome young man on a sidewalk. The young woman's long dark hair was elaborately curled, her mouth stained with lipstick. She'd clearly prepared for a big night out, maybe primping for some boy—maybe this boy. The young man held her arm and leaned into her space. Anna couldn't tell if they were sharing a secret or having a fight. The girl pulled her arm back, turned, and walked away from him. The boy strode offscreen after her. The news anchor, Carmen Harlan, looked grave as she said, "Emily Shapiro has not been seen since around midnight last night. Anyone who has information about her whereabouts is asked to call the police at the number below."

Anna murmured a few words of prayer then turned away from the screen. She felt an instinct to jump in, but this was not her jurisdiction. It was not her case.

"Poor baby," she murmured, her lips brushing Leigh's soft hair. "So much scariness in the world. You'll stay with me and your mama till you're thirty, right?"

Anna inhaled the sweet baby scent and wondered if there was anything more satisfying than the feel of a warm, contented baby on your shoulder. The thought surprised her. She'd never longed for a baby before.

Now wasn't the time to start.

She walked to the back window and looked out at the backyard. A few chickens pecked through the pale winter grass. Beyond them were rows of apple trees, bare for the winter, then an abandoned warehouse, its windows shattered and black. A mile farther, the Renaissance Center lit up the night sky. The linked skyscrapers were Detroit's iconic, ironic skyline, an attempt at renewal that had been a blip in the city's steady decline. But it did make a striking backdrop to the orchard. Not many farmers had a view of skyscrapers. Cooper's urban farm was the ugliest, most beautiful place Anna had ever lived.

She caught a glimpse of Cooper walking through a row of apple trees. He wore well-loved jeans, work boots, and a flannel shirt that stretched across his chest. His big white shepherd, Sparky, trotted at his heels. Cooper saw Anna in the window, smiled, and lifted a jug of cider in greeting. Anna waved back. The mere sight of him made her smile; it was an involuntary reaction, like her mouth watering for fresh-baked cookies.

It was too bad, really. Because, like a batch of cookies, Cooper was something to be savored briefly. His very deliciousness was his danger.

Anna had carefully built a life for herself in Washington, D.C. Everything she'd ever worked for—and she'd worked hard—was in D.C. Nine months ago, she'd come home to Michigan to defend Jody in a criminal case. Cooper had protected them when the whole world was against them. They'd been living in Cooper's house ever since Jody's home burned down. Cooper was a good friend and they shared a strong attraction, so Anna supposed it was natural that she'd ended up in his bed. But she'd been clear with him from the start. She was still reeling from her broken engagement. What she and Cooper had was a fling, just two friends having fun. They both knew she was going back to D.C.

And yet . . .

The back door opened and the click of the dog's paws preceded Cooper's asymmetrical footsteps. He walked up to Anna, bringing the scent of fresh air and pine trees with him. He kissed her lightly, then bent down to kiss the baby in her arms. She leaned her head up to meet his eyes.

"You look gorgeous," he said. She was dressed up for a night out with him.

"Thanks. You don't look so shabby yourself."

"I look like a man who needs a shower and a shave. But who am I kidding? With you on my arm, no one'll be looking at me."

In fact, Cooper got more than his share of double takes. He was tall, with a shock of black hair and cornflower blue eyes. His body was honed from farmwork rather than a gym. Anna had known him since he was a skinny, bookish boy in her elementary school. Back then, his lopsided grin looked too big for his face; now it fit him perfectly. She was still surprised every time she glanced at her old friend and saw how gracefully he'd grown into his skin.

Anna's phone buzzed in her pocket. Cooper took the baby so she could pull her phone from her jeans. The picture of the incoming caller showed a chiseled African American man with shining green eyes, holding a laughing six-year-old girl on his shoulders. Jack and his daughter, Olivia. Anna had taken the photo a year ago, back when she and Jack were still engaged to be married. Back when she thought she'd be Olivia's mother. Before everything fell apart.

She looked at Cooper apologetically as her thumb hovered over the send button. Cooper saw the picture and sighed.

"I'll be upstairs taking a shower," he said.

Anna watched him walk to the living room to give Leigh to Jody. His gait had a little hitch that strangers might interpret as a swagger but which was the result of an IED explosion. Cooper had served as an Army Ranger in Afghanistan, where he lost the lower part of his left leg. After coming home, he'd chosen urban farming because he loved Detroit and wanted to help rebuild it. And maybe he had to prove that he could do anything. He was optimistic, determined, and resilient. He'd be fine, Anna assured herself.

She pressed send. "Hello."

"Hi, sweetheart," Jack said.

She broke into a smile. "Hi, Jack. How are things in D.C.?"

"Actually, I'm in Michigan. Staying at a hotel in Ann Arbor. A few miles from you."

She pulled the phone away as if it had burned her ear. In her life, there were two worlds: D.C., home to her job, Jack, and her friends; and Michigan, home to her sister, Jody, and their rusting hometown, where Anna had nursed her broken heart and found comfort in Cooper's arms. These two worlds were separate and did not overlap. Hearing that Jack was in Michigan was like watching Han Solo walk into a *Hunger Games* movie.

"Wow. That's a surprise." Anna's mind and heart raced. "Why are you here?"

"You've heard that the Department of Justice assembled a task force to investigate sex assaults on college campuses?"

"Sure."

"The head of the task force was named Acting Deputy Attorney General last week. The AG asked me to fill her shoes. I said yes, of course. Now I'm visiting colleges, and I'm here on the midwestern leg of the tour."

Anna's emotions cycled through relief and disappointment. Jack wasn't in Michigan to see her. He was just here for work. Jack was the Homicide chief at the U.S. Attorney's Office in D.C., the country's largest USAO. His reputation for integrity, hard work, and effectiveness made him one of the most respected federal prosecutors in America. When the Justice Department had a high-profile investigation, it often called on Jack for leadership.

"That's an important task force," Anna said. "Good to know you're on it."

"I'm actually calling to ask for your help."

She paused. They'd broken up for complicated reasons last year. Three weeks ago, Jack had called, resolved every complication, and asked her to come back to him. She hadn't given him an answer yet. She still didn't know it herself.

She wondered if this phone call was his way of tipping the scales—asking her to work with him because that was where they'd always bonded. As teammates, joined together to fight crime and keep communities safe. He knew the task force was exactly the sort of job she'd love.

"I appreciate you thinking of me," she said. "But I have to say no. It would be too messy for us to work on the task force together."

"I agree," he said. "I'm not asking you to join the task force."

"Oh."

"I just need your help brainstorming. Have you seen the video of the missing girl from Tower U?"

"Yeah, on the news. Her poor parents."

"I need to figure out a way we can investigate."

"Mm, that's tough," Anna said. "Kidnapping, assault, homicide—it's all local crime. The DA's office has jurisdiction."

"I know. That's what makes it so frustrating. The boy in the video—his father, Robert Highsmith, is Michigan's lieutenant governor. Before that, Robert served as a DA himself. He has all kinds of ties to state law enforcement. A lot of people around here owe him favors. I'm not confident the locals will conduct a fair investigation."

"I see." Anna looked into the living room, at the baby sleeping in Jody's arms. One day, Leigh would grow up and, with any luck, go to college. Anna thought of Olivia, whom she loved like a daughter, and who would head to college in about ten years. Both girls would face all the wonderful and terrible things that could happen to young women on their own for the first time. "Did the kid call her any names?"

"He called her a bitch. It's clear on the video."

"We could investigate it as a federal hate crime."

"I like your aggressiveness," Jack said, "but you know what a high bar that is. Assaulting a woman isn't enough to make it federal. It has to have been *because* of her gender."

"'Bitch' is based on her gender."

"If that was the test, half the DV assaults in America would be hate crimes."

"Look," Anna said, "it's enough to open a grand jury and see if there's any *further* evidence of gender-based animus. The grand jury's powers are wide and broad. It gets us in. Now, today. When it's crucial. You know how important the first forty-eight hours are. Maybe this girl wandered, drunk, into a ditch and is freezing in the cold. Or maybe she was abducted. The best chance to find her alive is now—and getting smaller every minute."

"True. Okay. Is there a federal prosecutor around here you'd recommend? Someone who knows Michigan but doesn't have ties to the Highsmith family? Someone we can trust."

"Jack. I see what you're doing."

"Of course you do."

"I'm in."

"Thank you." He sounded genuinely relieved. "You'll run the investigation into her disappearance with a couple good FBI agents. You'll report to me and coordinate with the task force."

"Got it." Anna transitioned into full work mode. "Is there any criminal history on either the boy or the girl?"

"Nothing as adults. But they're both young—she's eighteen and he's twenty-one. Anything they did as juveniles, any campus disciplinary charges, wouldn't show up in NCIC."

"Has a grand jury been convened?"

"Here in Detroit. I introduced the case to them, and we have full subpoena power."

"To investigate a federal hate crime?"

He paused just a second before saying, "Yes."

Right. Jack didn't need her to advise him on the federal hook. Anna didn't care. If she could help this girl, she had to.

"What's the case number?" she asked.

She found a notebook and jotted down the information. Names, dates, DOBs, addresses. Still on the line with Jack, she jogged up the stairs to change into work clothes and apologize to Cooper for postponing their date.

"Anna, one more thing," Jack said. "This is a sensitive case. Emily's father is the president of Tower University. Dylan belongs to Beta Psi, a college fraternity in the Skull-and-Bones tradition. Four U.S. presidents were alumni, along with countless senators and CEOs. People are already making calls. These are the big boys. Handle them with care, and watch your back."

"Got it."

She'd prosecuted congressmen, street gangs, serial rapists. She could handle a bunch of frat boys.

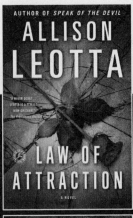
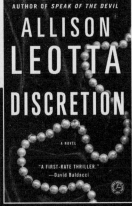
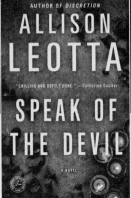
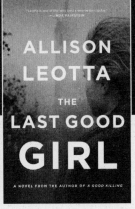